FIRST KING

O F

SHANNARA

TERRY BROOKS

A Del Rey® Book

BALLANTINE BOOKS • NEW YORK

A Del Rey® Book
Published by Ballantine Books

Copyright © 1996 by Terry Brooks

Endpapers map copyright © 1996 by Laura Hartman Maestro

All rights reserved under International and Pan-American Copyright
Conventions. Published in the United States by Ballantine Books, a division
of Random House, Inc., New York, and simultaneously in Canada by
Random House of Canada Limited, Toronto.

Library of Congress Cataloging-in-Publication Data
Brooks, Terry.
First king of Shannara / by Terry Brooks. — 1st ed.
p. cm.
ISBN 0-345-39652-9
1. Shannara (Imaginary place)—Fiction. I. Title.
PS3552.R6596F57   1996
813'.54—dc20   95-52321
                                                         CIP

Manufactured in the United States of America

First Edition: March 1996

10 9 8 7 6 5 4 3 2 1

For Melody, Kate, Lloyd, Abby, and Russell
Booksellers Extraordinaire

THE

 ALL

OF

CHAPTER

1

THE OLD MAN JUST APPEARED, seemingly out of nowhere. The Borderman was watching for him, sitting well back within the concealing shadows of a spreading hardwood high on a hillside overlooking the whole of the Streleheim and the trails leading out of it, everything clearly visible in the light of a full moon for at least ten miles, and he still didn't see him. It was unnerving and vaguely embarrassing, and the fact that it happened this way every time didn't make it any more palatable. How did the old man do it? The Borderman had spent almost the whole of his life in this country, kept alive by his wits and experience. He saw things that others did not even know were there. He could read the movements of animals from their passage through tall grass. He could tell you how far ahead of him they were and how fast they were traveling. But he could not spy out the old man on the clearest night and the broadest plain, even when he knew to look for him.

It did not help matters that the old man easily found him. Moving quite deliberately off the trail, he came toward the Borderman with slow, measured strides, head lowered slightly, eyes tilted up out of the shadow of his cowl. He wore black, like all the Druids, cloaked and hooded, wrapped darker than the shadows he passed through. He was not a big man, neither tall nor well muscled, but he gave the impression of being hard and fixed of purpose. His eyes, when visible, were vaguely green. But at times they seemed as white as bone, too—now, especially, when night stole away colors and reduced all things to shades of gray. They gleamed like an animal's caught in a fragment of light—feral, piercing, hypnotic. Light illuminated the old man's face as well, carving out the deep lines that creased it from forehead to chin, playing across the ridges and valleys of the ancient skin. The old man's hair and beard were gray going fast toward white, the strands wispy and thin like tangled spiderwebs.

The Borderman gave it up and climbed slowly to his feet. He was tall, rangy, and broad-shouldered, his dark hair worn long and tied back, his brown eyes sharp and steady, his lean face all planes and angles, but handsome in a rough sort of way.

A smile crossed the old man's face as he came up. "How are you, Kinson?" he greeted.

The familiar sound of his voice swept away Kinson Ravenlock's irritation as if it were dust on the wind. "I am well, Bremen," he answered, and held out his hand in response.

The old man took it and clasped it firmly in his own. The skin was dry and rough with age, but the hand beneath was strong. "How long have you been waiting?"

"Three weeks. Not as long as I had expected. I am surprised. But then I am always surprised by you."

Bremen laughed. He had left the Borderman six months earlier with instructions to meet him again on the first full moon of the quarter season directly north of Paranor where the forests gave way to the Plains of Streleheim. The time and place of the meeting were set, but hardly written in stone. Both appreciated the uncertainties the old man faced. Bremen had gone north into forbidden country. The time and place of his return would be dictated by events not yet known to either of them. It was nothing to Kinson that he had been forced to wait three weeks. It could just as easily have been three months.

The Druid looked at him with those piercing eyes, white now in the moonlight, drained of any other color. "Have you learned much in my absence? Have you put your time to good use?"

The Borderman shrugged. "Some of it. Sit down with me and rest. Have you eaten?"

He gave the old man some bread and ale, and they sat

4

hunched close together in the dark, staring out across the broad sweep of the plains. It was silent out there, empty and depthless and vast beneath the night's moonlit dome. The old man chewed absently, taking his time. The Borderman had built no fire that night or on any other since he had begun his vigil. A fire was too dangerous to chance.

"The Trolls move east," Kinson offered after a moment. "Thousands of them, more than I could count accurately, though I went down into their camp on the new moon several weeks back when they were closer to where we sit. Their numbers grow as others are sent to serve. They control everything from the Streleheim north as far as I can determine." He paused. "Have you discovered otherwise?"

The Druid shook his head. He had pushed back his cowl, and his gray head was etched in moonlight. "No, all of it belongs now to him."

Kinson gave him a sharp look. "Then . . ."

"What else have you seen?" the old man urged, ignoring him.

The Borderman took the aleskin and drank from it. "The leaders of the army stay closed away in their tents. No one sees them. The Trolls are afraid even to speak their names. This should not be. Nothing frightens Rock Trolls. Except this, it seems."

He looked at the other. "But at night, sometimes, at watch for you, I see strange shadows flit across the sky in the light of moon and stars. Winged black things sweep across the void, hunting or scouting or simply surveying what they have taken—I can't tell and don't want to know. I feel them, though. Even now. They are out there, circling. I feel their presence like an itch. No, not like an itch—like a shiver, the sort that comes to you when you feel eyes watching and the owner of those eyes has bad intentions. My skin crawls. They do not see me; I know if they did I would be dead."

Bremen nodded. "Skull Bearers, bound in service to him."

"So he is alive?" Kinson could not help himself. "You know it to be so? You have made certain?"

The Druid put aside the ale and bread and faced him squarely. The eyes were distant and filled with dark memories.

"He is alive, Kinson. As alive as you and I. I tracked him to his lair, deep in the shadow of the Knife Edge, where the Skull Kingdom puts down its roots. I was not sure at first, as you know. I suspected it, believed it to be so, but lacked evidence that could stand as proof. So I traveled north as we had planned, across the plains and into the mountains. I saw the winged hunters as I went, emerging only at night, great birds of prey that patrolled and kept watch for living things. I made myself as invisible as the air through which they flew. They saw me and saw nothing. I kept myself shrouded in magic, but not of such significance that they would notice it in the presence of their own. I passed west of the Trolls, but found the whole of their land subdued. All who resisted have been put to death. All who could manage to do so have fled. The rest now serve him."

Kinson nodded. It had been six months since the Troll marauders had swept down out of the Charnals east and begun a systematic subjugation of their people. Their army was vast and swift, and in less than three months all resistance was crushed. The Northland was placed under rule of the conquering army's mysterious and still unknown leader. There were rumors concerning his identity, but they remained unconfirmed. In truth, few even knew he existed. No word of this army and its leader had penetrated farther south than the border settlements of Varfleet and Tyrsis, fledgling outposts for the Race of Man, though it had spread east and west to the Dwarves and Elves. But the Dwarves and Elves were tied more closely to the Trolls. Man was the outcast race, the more recent enemy of the others. Memories of the First War of the Races still lingered, three hundred and fifty years later. Man lived apart in his distant Southland cities, the rabbit sent scurrying to earth, timid and toothless and of no consequence in the greater scheme of things, food for predators and little more.

But not me, Kinson thought darkly. Never me. I am no rabbit. I have escaped that fate. I have become one of the hunters.

Bremen stirred, shifting his weight to make himself more comfortable. "I went deep into the mountains, searching," he continued, lost again in his tale. "The farther I went, the more convinced I became. The Skull Bearers were everywhere. There were other beings as well, creatures summoned out of the spirit world, dead things brought to life, evil given form. I kept clear of them all, watchful and cautious. I knew that if I was discovered my magic would probably not be enough to save me. The darkness of this region was overwhelming. It was oppressive and tainted with the smell and taste of death. I went into Skull Mountain finally—one brief visit, for that was all I could chance. I slipped into the passageways and found what I had been searching for."

He paused, his brow wrinkling. "And more, Kinson. Much more, and none of it good."

"But he was there?" Kinson pressed anxiously, his hunter's face intense, his eyes glittering.

"He was there," affirmed the Druid quietly. "Shrouded by his magic, kept alive by his use of the Druid Sleep. He does not use it wisely, Kinson. He thinks himself beyond the laws of nature. He does not see that for all, however strong, there is a price to be paid for what is usurped and enslaved. Or perhaps he simply doesn't care. He has fallen under the sway of the Ildatch and cannot free himself in any case."

"The book of magic he stole out of Paranor?"

"Four hundred years ago. When he was simply Brona, a Druid, one of us, and not yet the Warlock Lord."

Kinson Ravenlock knew the story. Bremen himself had told it to him, though the history was familiar enough among the Races that he had already heard it a hundred times. Galaphile, an Elf, had called together the First Council of Druids five hundred years earlier, a thousand years following the devastation of the Great Wars. The Council had met at Paranor, a gathering of the wisest men and women of all the Races, those who had memories of the old world, those who retained a few tattered, crumbling books, those whose learning had survived the barbarism of a thousand years. The Council had gathered in a last, desperate effort to bring the Races out of the savagery that had consumed them and into a new and better civilization. Working together, the Druids had begun the laborious task of assembling their combined knowledge, of piecing together all that remained so that it might be employed for a common good. The goal of the Druids was to work for the betterment of all people, regardless of anything that had gone before. They were Men,

Gnomes, Dwarves, Elves, Trolls, and a smattering of others, the best and wisest of the new Races risen from the ashes of the old. If some small wisdom could be gleaned from the knowledge they carried, there was a chance for everyone.

But the task proved a long and difficult one, and some among the Druids grew restless. One was called Brona. Brilliant, ambitious, but careless of his own safety, he began to experiment with magic. There had been little in the old world, almost none since the decline of faerie and the rise of Man. But Brona believed that it must be recovered and brought back. The old sciences had failed, the destruction of the old world was the direct result of that failure, and the Great Wars were a lesson that the Druids seemed determined to ignore. Magic offered a new approach, and the books that taught it were older and more tried than those of science. Chief among those books was the Ildatch, a monstrous, deadly tome that had survived every cataclysm since the dawn of civilization, protected by dark spells, driven by secret needs. Brona saw within its ancient pages the answers he had been seeking, the solutions to the problems the Druids sought to solve. He resolved to have them. His course of action was set.

Others among the Druids warned him of the dangers, others not so impetuous, not so heedless of the lessons history had taught. For there had never been a form of power that did not evoke multiple consequences. There had never been a sword that did not cut more than one way. Be careful, they warned. Do not be reckless. But Brona and those few followers who had attached themselves to him would not be dissuaded, and in the end they broke with the Council. They disappeared, taking with them the Ildatch, their map of the new world, their key to the doors they would unlock.

In the end, it led only to their subversion. They fell sway to its power and became forever changed. They came to desire power for its own sake and for their personal use. All else was forgotten, all other goals abandoned. The First War of the Races was the direct result. The Race of Man was the tool they employed, made submissive to their will by the magic, shaped to become their weapon of attack. But their effort failed in the face of the Druid Council and the combined might of the other

Races. The aggressors were defeated, and the Race of Man was driven south into exile and isolation. Brona and his followers disappeared. It was said they had been destroyed by the magic.

"Such a fool," Bremen said suddenly. "The Druid Sleep kept him alive, but it stole away his heart and soul and left him a shell. All those years, we believed him dead. And dead he was, in a sense. But the part that survived was the evil over which the magic had gained dominance. It was the part that sought still to claim the whole of the world and the things that lived within it. It was the part that craved power over all. What matter the price that reckless use of the Sleep demanded? What difference the changes exacted for the extension of a life already wasted? Brona had evolved into the Warlock Lord, and the Warlock Lord would survive at all costs."

Kinson said nothing. It bothered him that Bremen could condemn so easily Brona's use of the Druid Sleep without questioning at the same time his own. For Bremen used the Sleep as well. He would argue that he used it in a more balanced, controlled way, that he was cautious of its demands on his body. He would argue that it was necessary to employ the Sleep, that he did it so that he would be there for the Warlock Lord's inevitable return. But for all that he might try to draw distinctions, the fact remained that the ultimate consequences of the use were the same, whether you were Warlock Lord or Druid.

One day, it would catch up with him.

"Did you see him, then?" the Borderman asked, anxious to move on. "Did you see his face?"

The old man smiled. "He has no face or body left, Kinson. He is a presence wrapped in a hooded cloak. Like myself, I sometimes think, for I am little more these days."

"That isn't so," Kinson said at once.

"No," the other quickly agreed, "it isn't. I keep some sense of right and wrong about me, and I am not yet a slave to the magic. Though that is what you fear I will become, isn't it?"

Kinson did not answer. "Tell me how you managed to get so close. How was it that you were not discovered?"

Bremen's eyes looked away, focusing on some distant place and time. "It was not easy," he replied softly. "The cost was high."

He reached again for the aleskin and drank deeply, the weariness mirrored in his face so heavy it might have been formed of iron links dragging against his skin. "I was forced to make myself appear one of them," he said after a moment. "I was required to shroud myself in their thoughts and impulses, in the evil rooted within their souls. I was cloaked in invisibility, so that my physical presence did not register, and I was left only with my spirit self. That I cloaked in the darkness that marks their own spirits, reaching deep within myself for the blackest part of who I am. Oh, I see you question that this was possible. Believe me, Kinson, the potential for evil lodges deep in every man, myself included. We restrain it better, keep it buried deeper, but it lives within us. I was forced to bring it out of concealment in order to protect myself. The feel of it, the rub of it against me, so close, so eager, was terrible. But it served its purpose. It kept the Warlock Lord and his minions from discovering me."

Kinson frowned. "But you were damaged."

"For a time. The walk back gave me a chance to heal." The old man smiled anew, a brief twist of his thin lips. "The trouble is that once brought so far out of its cage, a man's evil is reluctant thereafter to be contained. It presses against the bars. It is more anxious to escape. More prepared. And having lived in such close proximity to it, I am more vulnerable to the possibility of that escape."

He shook his head. "We are always being tested in life, aren't we? This is just one more instance."

There was a long moment of silence as the two men stared at one another. The moon had moved across the sky to the southern edge of the horizon and was sinking from view. The stars were brightening with its passing, the sky clear of clouds, a brilliant black velvet in the vast, unbroken silence.

Kinson cleared his throat. "As you said, you did what was required of you. It was necessary that you get close enough to determine if your suspicions were correct. Now we know." He paused. "Tell me. Did you see the book as well? The Ildatch?"

"There, in his hands, out of my reach, or I would surely have taken it and destroyed it, even at the cost of my own life."

The Warlock Lord and the Ildatch, there in the Skull King-

10

dom, as real as life, not rumor, not legend. Kinson Ravenlock rocked back slightly and shook his head. Everything true, just as Bremen had feared. As they had both feared. And now this army of Trolls come down out of the Northland to subdue the Races. It was history repeating itself. It was the First War of the Races beginning all over again. Only this time there might not be anyone to bring it to an end.

"Well, well," he said sadly.

"There is more," the Druid observed, lifting his eyes to the Borderman. "You must hear it all. There is an Elfstone they search for, the winged ones. A Black Elfstone. The Warlock Lord learned of it from the Ildatch. Somewhere within the pages of that wretched book, there is mention of this stone. It is not an ordinary Elfstone like the others we have heard about. It is not one of three, one each for the heart, mind, and body of the user, their magic to be joined when summoned. This stone's magic is capable of great evil. There is some mystery about the reason for its creation, about the use it was intended to serve. All that has been lost in the passing of time. But the Ildatch makes deliberate and purposeful reference to its capabilities, it seems. I was fortunate to learn of it. While I clung to the shadows of the wall in the great chamber where the winged ones gather and their Master directs, I heard mention of it."

He leaned close to the Borderman. "It is hidden somewhere in the Westland, Kinson—deep within an ancient stronghold, protected in ways that you or I could not begin to imagine. It has lain concealed since the time of faerie, lost to history, as forgotten as the magic and the people who once wielded it. Now it waits to be discovered and brought back into use."

"And what is that use?" Kinson pressed.

"It has the power to subvert other magic, whatever its form, and convert it to the holder's use. No matter how powerful or intricate another's magic might be, if you hold the Black Elfstone, you can master your adversary. His magic will be leached from him and made yours. He will be helpless against you."

Kinson shook his head despairingly. "How can anyone stand against such a thing?"

The old man laughed softly. "Now, now, Kinson, it isn't really that simple, is it? You remember our lessons, don't you? Every use of magic exacts a price. There are always consequences, and the more powerful the magic, the greater that consequence will be. But let's leave that argument for another time. The point is that the Warlock Lord must not be allowed to possess the Black Elfstone because consequences matter not at all to him. He is beyond the point where reason will hold sway. So we must find the Elfstone before he does, and we must find it quickly."

"And how are we to do that?"

The Druid yawned and stretched wearily, black robes rising and falling in a soft rustle of cloth. "I haven't the answer to that question, Kinson. Besides, we have other business to attend to first."

"You will go to Paranor and the Druid Council?"

"I must."

"But why bother? They won't listen to you. They mistrust you. Some even fear you."

The old man nodded. "Some, but not all. There are a few who will listen. In any case, I must try. They are in great danger. The Warlock Lord remembers all too well how they brought about his downfall in the First War of the Races. He will not chance their intervention a second time—even if they no longer seem a real threat to him."

Kinson looked off into the distance. "They are foolish to ignore you, but ignore you they will, Bremen. They have lost all touch with reality behind their sheltering walls. They have not ventured out into the world for so long that they no longer are able to take a true measure of things. They have lost their identity. They have forgotten their purpose."

"Hush, now." Bremen placed a firm hand on the tall man's shoulder. "There is no point in repeating to ourselves what we already know. We will do what we can and then be on our way." He squeezed gently. "I am very tired. Would you keep watch for a few hours while I sleep? We can leave after that."

The Borderman nodded. "I'll keep watch."

The old man rose and moved deeper into the shadows beneath the wide-boughed tree, where he settled down comfortably within his robes on a soft patch of grass. Within minutes he was asleep, his breathing deep and regular. Kinson stared down at him. Even then, his eyes were not quite closed. From behind narrow slits, there was a glimmer of light.

Like a cat, thought Kinson, looking away quickly. Like a dangerous cat.

TIME PASSED, and the night lengthened. Midnight came and went. The moon dropped below the horizon, and the stars spun in vast, kaleidoscopic patterns across the black. Silence lay heavy and absolute over the Streleheim, and on the emptiness of the plains nothing moved. Even within the trees where Kinson Ravenlock kept watch, there was only the sound of the old man's breathing.

The Borderman glanced down at his companion. Bremen, as much an outcast as himself, alone in his beliefs, exiled for truths that only he could accept.

They were alike in that regard, he thought. He was reminded of their first meeting. The old man had come to him at an inn in Varfleet, seeking his services. Kinson Ravenlock had been a scout, Tracker, explorer, and adventurer for the better part of twenty years, since the time he was fifteen. He had been raised in Callahorn, a part of its frontier life, a member of one of a handful of families who had remained in the Borderlands when everyone else had gone much farther south, distancing themselves from their past. After the conclusion of the First War of the Races, when the Druids had partitioned the Four Lands and left Paranor at the crux, Man had determined to leave a buffer between itself and the other Races. So while the Southland reached as far north as the Dragon's Teeth, Man had abandoned almost everything above the Rainbow Lake. Only a few Southland families had stayed on, believing that this was their home, finding themselves unwilling to move to the more populated areas of their assigned land. The Ravenlocks had been one of these.

So Kinson had grown up as a Borderman, living on the edge of civilization, but as comfortable with Elves, Dwarves, Gnomes, and Trolls as with Men. He had traveled their lands and learned their customs. He had mastered their tongues. He was a student of history, and he had heard it told from enough different points of view that he thought he had gleaned the most important of the truths that it had to offer. Bremen was a student of history as well, and right from the beginning they had shared some common beliefs. One of these was that the Races could succeed in their efforts to maintain peace only by strengthening their ties to one another, not by distancing themselves. A second was that the greatest obstacle to their success in doing so was the Warlock Lord.

Even then, even five years earlier, the rumors were already being passed around. There was something evil living in the Skull Kingdom, a collection of beasts and creatures like nothing ever seen before. There were reports of flying things, winged monsters scouring the land by night in search of mortal victims. There were stories of men going north and never being seen again. The Trolls stayed away from the Knife Edge and the Malg. They did not attempt to cross the Kierlak. When they traveled in proximity to the Skull Kingdom, they banded together in large, heavily armed groups. Nothing would grow in this part of the Northland. Nothing would take root. As time passed, the whole of that devastated region became shrouded in clouds and mist. It became arid and barren. It turned to dust and rock. Nothing could live there, it was said. Nothing that was really alive.

Most dismissed the stories. Many ignored the matter entirely. This was a remote and unfriendly part of the world in any case. What difference did it make what lived or didn't live there? But Kinson had gone into the Northland to see for himself. He had barely escaped with his life. The winged things had tracked him for five days after they had caught him prowling at the edge of their domain. Only his great skill and more than a little luck had saved him.

So when Bremen approached him, he had already made up his mind that what the Druid was saying was true. The Warlock Lord was real. Brona and his followers lived north in the Skull Kingdom. The threat to the Four Lands was not imagined. Something unpleasant was slowly taking shape.

He had agreed to accompany the old man on his journeys,

to serve as a second pair of eyes when needed, to act as courier and scout, and to watch the other's back when danger threatened. Kinson had done so for a number of reasons, but none so compelling as the fact that for the first time in his life it gave him a sense of purpose. He was tired of drifting, of living for no better reason than to see again what he had already seen before and to be paid for the privilege. He was bored and directionless. He wanted a challenge.

Bremen had certainly given him that.

He shook his head wonderingly. It surprised him how far they had come together and how close they had grown. It surprised him how much both of those things mattered to him.

A flicker of movement far out on the empty stretches of the Streleheim caught his eye. He blinked and stared fixedly into the dark, seeing nothing. Then the movement came again, a small flutter of blackness in the shadow of a long ravine. It was so distant that he could not be certain what he was seeing, but already he suspected. A cold knot tightened in his stomach. He had seen movement like this before, always at night, always in the emptiness of some desolate place along the borders of the Northland.

He remained motionless, watching, hoping he was wrong. The movement came again, closer this time. Something lifted from the earth, hung suspended against the dark patchwork of the night plains, then dipped downward once more. It might have been a great winged bird in search of food, but it wasn't.

It was one of the Skull Bearers.

Still Kinson waited, determined to make certain of the creature's path. Again the shadow lifted away from the earth and soared into the starlight, angling along the ravine for a distance before moving away, coming steadily closer to where the Borderman and the Druid were concealed. Again it dipped downward and disappeared into the blackness of the earth.

Kinson realized with a sinking feeling what the Skull Bearer was doing. It was tracking someone.

Bremen.

He turned quickly now, but the old man was already beside him, staring past him into the night. "I was just about to . . ."

"Wake me," the other finished. "Yes, I know."

Kinson looked back across the plains. Nothing moved. "Did you see?" he asked softly.

"Yes." Bremen's voice was alert, but calm. "One of them tracks me."

"You are certain? It follows your trail, not another's?"

"Somehow I was careless in my passage out." Bremen's eyes glittered. "It knows I have passed this way and seeks to find where I have gone. I wasn't seen within the Skull Kingdom, so this is a chance discovery. I should have used more caution crossing the plains, but I thought myself safe."

They watched as the Skull Bearer reappeared, lifting skyward momentarily, gliding soundlessly across the landscape, then lowering into shadow once more.

"There is time yet before it reaches us," Bremen whispered. "I think we should be on our way. We will disguise our tracks to confuse it should it choose to follow us further. Paranor and the Druids await. Come, Kinson."

Together they rose and slipped back through the shadows and down the far side of the hill into the trees. They went soundlessly, their movements smooth and practiced, their dark forms seeming to glide across the earth.

In seconds they had disappeared from view.

CHAPTER

2

THEY WALKED the remainder of the night through the sheltering forest, Kinson leading, Bremen a shadow following in his footsteps. Neither spoke, comfortable with the silence and each other. They did not see the Skull Bearer again. Bremen used magic to hide their tracks, just enough to conceal their passing without calling attention to it. But it seemed the winged hunter had chosen not to go below the Streleheim in its search, for had it done so they would have sensed its presence. As it was, they sensed only the creatures who lived there and no others. For the moment at least, they were safe.

Kinson Ravenlock's stride was tireless, its fluid movement honed and shaped from dozens of years of travel afoot through the Four Lands. The Borderman was big and strong, a man in the prime of his life, still able to rely on reflex and speed when the need arose. Bremen watched him admiringly, remembering his own youth, thinking how far down the path of his life he had traveled. The Druid Sleep had given him a longer life than most—a longer one than he was entitled to by nature's law—but still it was not enough. He could feel his strength leaking from his body almost daily. He could still keep up with the Borderman when they traveled, but it was no longer possible to do so without the aid of his magic. He supplemented himself at almost every turn these days, and he knew that the time left to him in this world was growing short.

Still, he was confident in himself. He had always been so,

and that more than anything had kept him strong and alive. He had come to the Druids as a young man, his training and skills in the fields of history and ancient tongues. Times had been much different then, the Druids still active in the evolution and development of the Races, still working to bring the Races together in the pursuit of common goals. It was only later, less than seventy years ago, that they had begun to withdraw from their involvement in favor of private study. Bremen had come to Paranor to learn, and he had never stopped wanting and needing to do so. But learning required more than closeted study and meditation. It required travel and interaction with others, discussions on subjects of mutual interest, an awareness of the tide of change in life that could only come from observance, and a willingness to accept that the old ways might not offer all the answers.

So it was that early on he accepted that magic might prove a more manageable and durable form of power than the sciences of the world before the Great Wars. All the knowledge gleaned from memories and books from the time of Galaphile forward had failed to produce what was needed of science. It was too fragmented, too removed in time from the civilization it was needed to serve, too obscure in its purpose to provide the keys to unlock the doors of understanding. But magic was another matter. Magic was older than science and more readily accessible. The Elves, who had come from that time, had knowledge of it. Though they had lived in hiding and isolation for many years, they possessed books and writings far more decipherable in their purpose than those of the old-world sciences. True, much was still missing, and the great magics of faerie were gone and would not be easily recovered. But there was better hope for these than for the sciences over which the Druid Council continued to struggle.

But the Council remembered what evocation of magic had cost them in the First War of the Races, what had befallen Brona and his followers, and they were not about to unlock that door again. Study of magic was permissible, but discouraged. It was treated as a curiosity with few usable tools, the practice in general not to be embraced as a doorway to the future under any circumstances. Bremen had argued the point endlessly and without success. The majority of the Druids at Paranor were hidebound and not open to the possibility of change. Learn from your mistakes, they intoned. Do not forget how dangerous the practice of magic can be. Best to forget your momentary interests in place of serious study. Bremen would not, of course—could not, in fact. It went counter to his nature to discard a possibility simply because it had failed once. Failed because of blatant misuse, he would remind them—something that did not necessarily have to happen a second time. A few agreed with him. But in the end, when his persistence grew intolerable and he was banished from the Council, he departed alone.

He traveled then to the Westland and lived with the Elves for many years, studying their lore, poring over their writings, trying to recover some of what they had lost when the creatures of faerie gave way to mortal men. A few things he brought with him. The secret of the Druid Sleep was already his, though still in its rudimentary form. Mastery of its intricacies and acceptance of its consequences took time, and it did not serve as a useful tool until he was already quite old. The Elves embraced Bremen as a kindred spirit and gave him access to their store of small magics and all but forgotten writings. In time, he discovered treasures amid the discards. He went out into the other lands, discovering bits of magic there as well, though not so highly developed and in many instances foreign even to the people whom they served.

All the while he worked steadily to confirm his growing conviction that the rumors of the Warlock Lord and his Skull Bearers were true, that these were the rebel Druids who had fled Paranor all those years ago, that these were the creatures who had been defeated in the First War of the Races. But the proof had been like the scent of flowers carried on the wind, there one moment and gone the next. He had tracked it relentlessly, across borders and kingdoms, through villages near and far, from one tale to the next. In the end, he had tracked it to the Skull Kingdom itself, to the heart of the Warlock Lord's domain, there in the catacombs where he had concealed himself with the dark one's minions, waiting out events that would allow him to escape with his truth. Had he been stronger, he might have gotten to that truth sooner. But it had taken him years to develop the skills necessary to survive a journey north. It had taken years of study and exploration. It might have taken less time had the Council supported him, had they put aside their superstitions and fears and embraced the possibilities as he had, but that had never happened.

He sighed, remembering it now. Thinking of it made him sad. So much time wasted. So many opportunities missed. Perhaps it was already too late for those at Paranor. What could he say now to convince them of the danger they faced? Would they even believe him when he told them what he had discovered? It had been more than two years since he had visited the Keep. Some probably thought him dead. Some might even wish him so. It would not be easy to convince them that they had been wrong in their assumptions about the Warlock Lord, that they must rethink their commitment to the Races, and, most important, that they must reconsider their refusal to use magic.

They passed out of the deep forest as dawn broke, the light brightening from silver to gold as the sun crept over the rim of the Dragon's Teeth and poured down through breaks in the trees to warm the damp earth. The trees thinned before them, reduced to small groves and solitary sentinels. Ahead, Paranor rose out of the misty light. The fortress of the Druids was a massive stone citadel seated on a foundation of rock that jutted from the earth like a fist. The walls of the fortress rose skyward hundreds of feet to form towers and battlements bleached vivid white. Pennants flew at every turn, some honoring the separate insignia of the High Druids who had served, some marking the houses of the rulers of the Four Lands. Mist clung to the high reaches and swathed the darker shadows at the castle base where the sun had not yet burned away the night. It was an impressive sight, Bremen thought. Even now, even to him who was outcast.

Kinson glanced inquiringly over his shoulder, but Bremen nodded for him to go on. There was nothing to be gained by delay. Still, the very size of the fortress gave him pause. The weight of its stone seemed to settle down across his shoulders, a burden he could not overcome. Such a massive, implacable force, he thought, mirroring in some sense the stubborn resolve of those who dwelled within. He wished it might be otherwise. He knew he must try to make it so.

They passed out of the trees, where the sunlight was still an intruder amid the shadows, and walked clear of the fading night down the roadway to approach the main gates. Already there were a handful of armed men emerging to meet them, part of the multinational force that served the Council as the Druid Guard. All were dressed in gray uniforms with a torch emblem embroidered in red on their left breast. Bremen looked for a recognizable face and found none. Well, he had been gone two years, after all. At least these were Elves set at watch, and Elves might hear him out.

Kinson moved aside deferentially and let him step to the fore. He straightened himself, calling on the magic to give him added presence, to disguise the weariness he felt, to hide any weakness or doubt. He moved up to the gates determinedly, black robes billowing out behind him, Kinson a dark presence on his right. The guards waited, flat-faced and expressionless.

When he reached them, feeling them wilt just a bit with his approach, he said simply, "Good morning to all."

"Good morning to you, Bremen," replied one, stepping forward, offering a short bow.

"You know me then?"

The other nodded. "I know of you. I am sorry, but you are not allowed to enter."

His eyes shifted to include Kinson. He was polite, but firm. No outcast Druids allowed. No members of the race of Man either. Discussion not advised.

Bremen glanced upward to the parapets as if considering the matter. "Who is Captain of the Guard?" he asked.

"Caerid Lock," the other answered.

"Will you ask him to come down and speak with me?"

The Elf hesitated, pondering the request. Finally, he nodded. "Please wait here."

He disappeared through a side door into the Keep. Bremen and Kinson stood facing the remaining guards in the shadow of the fortress wall. It would have been an easy matter to go by them, to leave them standing there looking at nothing more than empty images, but Bremen had determined not to use magic to gain entry. His mission was too important to risk incurring the anger of the Council by circumventing their security and making them look foolish. They would not appreciate tricks. They might respect directness. It was a gamble he was willing to take.

Bremen turned and looked back at the forest. Sunlight probed its deep recesses now, chasing back the shadows, brightening the fragile stands of wildflowers. It was spring, he realized with a start. He had lost track of time on his journey north and back again, consumed with his search. He breathed the air, taking in a hint of the fragrance it bore from the woods. It had been a long time since he had thought about flowers.

There was movement in the doorway behind him, and he turned. The guard who had left reappeared and with him was Caerid Lock.

"Bremen," the Elf greeted solemnly, and came up to offer his hand.

Caerid Lock was a slight, dark-complected man with intense eyes and a careworn face. His Elven features marked him distinctly, his brows slanted upward, his ears pointed, his face so narrow he seemed gaunt. He wore gray like the others, but the torch on his breast was gripped in a fist and there were crimson bars on both shoulders. His hair and beard were cut short and both were shot through with gray. He was one of a few who had remained friends with Bremen when the Druid was dismissed from the Council. He had been Captain of the Druid Guard for more than fifteen years, and there was not a better man anywhere for the job. An Elven Hunter with a lifetime of service, Caerid Lock was a thorough professional. The Druids had chosen well in determining who would protect them. More to the point, for Bremen's purpose, he was a man they might listen to if a request was proffered.

"Caerid, well met," the Druid replied, accepting the other's hand. "Are you well?"

"As well as some I know. You've aged a few years since leaving us. The lines are in your face."

"You see the mirror of your own, I'd guess."

"Perhaps. Still traveling the world, are you?"

"In the good company of my friend, Kinson Ravenlock," he introduced the other.

The Elf took the Borderman's hand and measure by equal turns, but said nothing. Kinson was equally remote.

"I need your help, Caerid," Bremen advised, turning solemn. "I must speak with Athabasca and the Council."

Athabasca was High Druid, an imposing man of firm belief and unyielding opinion who had never much cared for Bremen. He was a member of the Council when the old man was dismissed, though he was not yet High Druid. That had come later, and then only through the complex workings of internal politics that Bremen so hated. Still, Athabasca was leader, for better or worse, and any chance of success in breaching these walls would necessarily hinge on him.

Caerid Lock smiled ruefully. "Why not ask me for something difficult? You know that Paranor and the Council both are forbidden to you. You cannot even enter these walls, let alone speak with the High Druid."

"I can if he orders it," Bremen said simply.

The other nodded. Sharp eyes narrowed. "I see. You want me to speak to him on your behalf."

Bremen nodded. Caerid's tight smile disappeared. "He doesn't like you," he pointed out quietly. "That hasn't changed in your absence."

"He doesn't have to like me to talk with me. What I have to tell him is more important than personal feelings. I will be brief. Once he has heard me out, I will be on my way again." He paused. "I don't think I am asking too much, do you?"

Caerid Lock shook his head. "No." He glanced at Kinson. "I will do what I can."

He went back inside, leaving the old man and the Borderman to contemplate the walls and gates of the Keep. Their warders stood firmly in place, barring all entry. Bremen regarded them solemnly for a moment, then glanced toward the sun. The day was beginning to grow warm already. He looked at Kinson, then walked over to where the shadows provided a greater measure of shade and sat down on a stone outcropping. Kinson followed, but refused to sit. There was an impatient look in his dark eyes. He wanted this matter to be finished. He was ready to move on. Bremen smiled inwardly. How like his friend. Kinson's solution to everything was to move on. He had lived his whole life that way. It was only now, since they had met, that he had begun to see that nothing is ever solved if it isn't faced. It wasn't that Kinson wasn't capable of standing up to life. He simply dealt with unpleasantness by leaving it behind, by outdistancing it, and it was true that things could be handled that way. It was just that there was never any permanent resolution.

Yes, Kinson had grown since those early days. He was a stronger man in ways that could not be readily measured. But Bremen knew that old habits died hard, and for Kinson Raven-lock the urge to walk away from the unpleasant and the difficult was always there.

"This is a waste of our time," the Borderman muttered, as if to give credence to his thoughts.

"Patience, Kinson," Bremen counseled softly.

"Patience? Why? They won't let you in. And if they do, they won't listen to you. They don't want to hear what you have to say. These are not the Druids of old, Bremen."

Bremen nodded. Kinson was right in that. But there was no help for it. The Druids of today were the only Druids there were, and some of them were not so bad. Some would still make worthy allies. Kinson would prefer they deal with matters on their own, but the enemy they faced was too formidable to be overcome without help. The Druids were needed. While they had abandoned their practice of direct involvement in the affairs of the Races, they were still regarded with a certain def-erence and respect. That would prove useful in uniting the Four Lands against their common enemy.

The morning wore on toward midday. Caerid Lock did not reappear. Kinson paced for a time, then finally sat down next to Bremen, frustration mirrored on his lean face. He sat wrapped in silence, wearing his darkest look.

Bremen sighed inwardly. Kinson had been with him a long time. Bremen had handpicked him from among a number of candidates for the task of ferreting out the truth about the War-lock Lord. Kinson had been the right choice. He was the best Tracker the old man had ever known. He was smart and brave

24

and clever. He was never reckless, always reasoned. They had grown so close that Kinson was like a son to him. He was certainly his closest friend.

But he could not be the one thing Bremen needed him to be. He could not be the Druid's successor. Bremen was old and failing, though he hid it well enough from those who might suspect. When he was gone, there would be no one left to continue his work. There would be no one to advance the study of magic so necessary to the evolution of the Races, no one to prod the recalcitrant Druids of Paranor into reconsidering their involvement with the Four Lands, and no one to stand against the Warlock Lord. Once, he had hoped that Kinson Ravenlock might be that man. The Borderman might still be, he supposed, but it did not seem likely. Kinson lacked the necessary patience. He disdained any pretense of diplomacy. He had no time for those who could not grasp truths he felt were obvious. Experience was the only teacher he had ever respected. He was an iconoclast and a persistent loner. None of these characteristics would serve him well as a Druid, but it seemed impossible that he could ever be any different from the way he was.

Bremen glanced over at his friend, suddenly unhappy with his analysis. It was not fair to judge Kinson so. It was enough that the Borderman was as devoted as he was, enough that he would stand with him to the death if it was required. Kinson was the best of friends and allies, and it was wrong to expect more of him.

It was just that his need for a successor was so desperate! He was old, and time was slipping away too quickly.

He took his eyes from Kinson and looked off into the distant trees as if to measure what little remained.

It was past midday when Caerid Lock finally reappeared. He stalked out of the shadows of the doorway with barely a glance at the guards or Kinson and came directly to Bremen. The Druid climbed to his feet to greet him, his joints and his muscles cramped.

"Athabasca will speak with you," the Captain of the Druid Guard advised, grim-faced.

Bremen nodded. "You must have worked hard to persuade him. I am in your debt, Caerid."

The Elf grunted noncommittally. "I would not be so sure. Athabasca has his own reasons for agreeing to this meeting, I think." He turned to Kinson. "I am sorry, but I could not gain entrance for you."

Kinson straightened and shrugged. "I will be happier waiting here, I expect."

"I expect," agreed the other. "I will send you out some food and fresh water. Bremen, are you ready?"

The Druid looked at Kinson and smiled faintly. "I will be back as soon as I can."

"Good luck to you," his friend offered quietly.

Then Bremen was following Caerid Lock through the entry of the Keep and into the shadows beyond.

THEY WALKED DOWN cavernous hallways and winding, narrow corridors in cool, dark silence, their footsteps echoing off the heavy stone. They encountered no one. It was as if Paranor were deserted, and Bremen knew that was not so. Several times, he thought he caught a whisper of conversation or a hint of movement somewhere distant from where they walked, but he could never be certain. Caerid was taking him down the back passageways, the ones seldom used, the ones kept solely for private comings and goings. It seemed understandable. Athabasca did not want the other Druids to know he was permitting this meeting until after he had decided if it was worth having. Bremen would be given a private audience and a brief opportunity to state his case, and then he would be either summarily dismissed or summoned to address the Council. Either way, the decision would be made quickly.

They began to climb a series of stairs toward the upper chambers of the Keep. Athabasca's offices were well up in the tower, and it was likely that he intended to see Bremen there. The old man pondered Caerid Lock's words as they proceeded. Athabasca would have his reasons for agreeing to this meeting, and they would not necessarily be immediately apparent. The High Druid was a politician first, an administrator second, and a functionary above all. This was not to demean him; it was simply to categorize the nature of his thinking. His primary focus would be one of cause and effect—that is, if one thing happened, how would it impact on another. That was the way his mind worked. He was able and organized, but he was calculating as well. Bremen would have to be careful in choosing his words.

They were almost to the end of a connecting corridor when a black-robed figure suddenly stepped out of the shadows to confront them. Caerid Lock instinctively reached for his short sword, but the other's hands were already gripping the Elf's arms and pinning them to his sides. With so little effort that it seemed to be an afterthought, the robed figure lifted Caerid from the floor and set him to one side like a minor impediment.

"There, there, Captain," a rough voice soothed. "No need for weapons among friends. I'm after a quick word with your charge, and then I'll be out of your way."

"Risca!" Bremen greeted in surprise. "Well met, old friend!"

"I'll thank you to remove your hands, Risca," snapped Caerid Lock irritably. "I wouldn't be reaching for my weapons if you didn't jump at me without announcing yourself!"

"Apologies, Captain," the other purred. He took his hands away and held them up defensively. Then he looked at Bremen. "Welcome home, Bremen of Paranor."

Risca came forward then into the light and embraced the old man. He was a bearded, bluff-faced Dwarf with tremendous shoulders, his compact body stocky and broad and heavily muscled. Arms like tree trunks crushed briefly and released, replaced by hands that were gnarled and callused. Risca was like a deeply rooted tree stump that nothing could dislodge, weathered by time and the seasons, impervious to age. He was a warrior Druid, the last who remained of that breed, skilled in the use of weapons and warfare, steeped in the lore of the great battles fought since the new Races had emerged. Bremen had trained him personally until his banishment from the Keep more than ten years ago. Through all that had happened, Risca had stayed his friend.

"Not of Paranor any longer, Risca," Bremen demurred. "But it feels like home still. How have you been?"

"Well. But bored. There is little use for my talents behind these walls. Few of the new Druids have any interest in battle arts. I stay sharp practicing with the Guard. Caerid tests me daily."

The Elf snorted. "You have me for breakfast daily, you mean. What are you doing here? How did you know to find us?"

Risca released Bremen and looked about mysteriously. "These walls have ears, for those who know how to listen."

Caerid Lock laughed in spite of himself. "Spying—another finely honed art in the arsenal of warrior skills!"

Bremen smiled at the Dwarf. "You know why I've come?"

"I know you are to speak with Athabasca. But I wanted to speak with you first. No, Caerid. You may remain for this. I have no secrets I cannot reveal to you." The Dwarf's countenance turned serious. "There can be only one reason for your return, Bremen. And no news that can be welcome. So be it. But you will need allies in this, and I am one. Count on me to be your voice when it matters. I have seniority in the Council that few others who support you can offer. You need to know how matters stand, and they do not favor your return."

"I hope to persuade Athabasca that our common need requires us to set aside our differences." Bremen furrowed his brow thoughtfully. "It cannot be so difficult to accept this."

Risca shook his head. "It can and it will. Be strong, Bremen. Do not defer to him. He dislikes what you represent—a challenge to his authority. Nothing you say or do will transcend that. Fear is a weapon that will serve you better than reason. Let him understand the danger." He looked suddenly at Caerid. "Would you advise differently?"

The Elf hesitated, then shook his head. "No."

Risca reached forward to grip Bremen's hands once more. "I will speak with you later."

He wheeled down the corridor and disappeared back into the shadows. Bremen smiled in spite of himself. Strong in body and mind, unyielding in all things. That was Risca. He would never change.

They continued on once more, the Elf Captain and the old man, navigating the dimly lit corridors and stairways, winding deeper into the Keep, until finally they came to a landing at the top of a flight of stairs that fronted a small, narrow, ironbound door. Bremen had seen this door more than a few times in his years at the castle. It was the back entry to the offices of the High Druid. Athabasca would be waiting within to receive him. He took a deep breath.

Caerid Lock tapped on the door three times, paused, then tapped once more. From within, a familiar voice rumbled, "Enter."

The Captain of the Druid Guard pushed the narrow door open, then stepped aside. "I have been asked to wait here," he advised softly.

Bremen nodded, amused by the solemnity he found in the other's face. "I understand," he said. "Thank you again, Caerid."

Then he stooped to clear the low entry and moved inside.

The room was a familiar one. It was the exclusive chamber of the High Druid, a private retreat and meeting place for the Council's leader. It was a large room with a high ceiling, tall windows of leaded glass, bookcases filled with papers, artifacts, diaries, files, and a scattering of books. Massive, ironbound double doors were centered on the front wall, across from where he stood. A huge desk rested at the chamber's center, swept clean for the moment of everything, the wood surface burnished and shining in the candlelight.

Athabasca stood behind the desk, waiting. He was a big, heavyset, imperious man with a shock of flowing white hair and cold blue eyes set deep in a florid face. He wore the dark blue robes of the High Druid, which were belted at the waist and free of any insignia. Instead, he wore about his neck the Eilt Druin, the medallion of office of High Druids since the time of Galaphile. The Eilt Druin was forged of gold and a small mix of strengthening metals and laced with silver trappings. It was molded in the shape of a hand holding forth a burning torch. The hand and the torch had been the symbol of the Druids since the time of their inception. The medallion was said to be magic, though no one had ever seen the magic used. The words "Eilt Druin" were Elven and meant literally "Through Knowledge, Power."

Once, that motto had meant something for the Druids. Another of life's small ironies, Bremen thought wearily.

"Well met, Bremen," Athabasca greeted in his deep, sonorous voice. The greeting was traditional, but Athabasca's rendering of it sounded hollow and forced.

"Well met, Athabasca," Bremen replied. "I am grateful that you agreed to see me."

"Caerid Lock was quite persuasive. Besides, we do not turn from our walls those who were once brethren."

Once, but no more, he was saying. Bremen moved forward into the room to stand on the near side of the great desk, feeling himself separated from Athabasca by more than the broad expanse of its polished top. He wondered anew at how small the big man could make another feel in his presence, how like a little boy. For while Bremen was older by some years than Athabasca, he could not escape the sense that he stood in the presence of an elder.

"What would you tell me, Bremen?" Athabasca asked him.

"That the Four Lands stand in peril," Bremen answered. "That the Trolls have been subjugated by a power that transcends physical life and mortal strength. That the other Races will fall as well if we do not intervene to protect them. That even the Druids are in great danger."

Athabasca fingered the Eilt Druin absently. "What form does this threat take? Is it one of magic?"

Bremen nodded. "The rumors are true, Athabasca. The Warlock Lord is a real creature. But more, he is the reincarnation of the rebel Druid Brona, who was thought vanquished and destroyed more than three hundred years ago. He has survived, kept alive by malicious, reckless use of the Druid Sleep and by the destruction of his soul. He no longer has form, only spirit. Yet the fact remains that he lives and is the source of the danger that threatens."

"You have seen him? You have searched him out in your travels?"

"I have."

"How did you accomplish this? Did he permit you entry? Surely you must have entered in disguise."

"I cloaked myself with a magic of invisibility for some of the journey. Then I cloaked myself in the dark trappings of the Warlock Lord's own evil, a disguise that even he could not penetrate."

"You made yourself one with him?" Athabasca had clasped his hands behind him. His eyes were steady and watchful.

"For a time, I became as he was. It was necessary to get close enough to make certain of my suspicions."

"And what if by becoming one with him, you were in some way subverted, Bremen? What if by use of the magic you lost your perspective and your balance? How can you be certain that what you saw was not imagined? How can you know that the discovery you carry back to us is real?"

Bremen forced himself to stay calm. "I would know if the magic had subverted me, Athabasca. I have given years of my life to its study. I know it better than anyone."

Athabasca smiled, chilly and doubting. "But that is exactly the point. How well can any of us appreciate the magic's power? You broke from the Council to undertake on your own a study that you were warned against. You pursued the very same course that another once pursued—the creature you claim to hunt. It subverted him, Bremen. How can you be so certain that it has not subverted you as well? Oh, I am confident you believe you are impervious to its sway. But that was true of Brona and his followers, too. Magic is an insidious force, a power that transcends our understanding and cannot be relied upon. We have looked to its use before and been deceived. We look to its use still, but we are more cautious than we once were—cautious, because we have learned through the misfortune of Brona and the others what can happen. Yet how cautious have you been, Bremen? The magic subverts; that much we know. It subverts all who use it, one way or another, and in the end it destroys its user."

Bremen kept his voice steady as he replied, "There are no absolutes to the results of its application, Athabasca. Subversion can come by degrees and in different forms, depending on the ways in which the magic is applied. But this was true with the old sciences as well. All applications of power subvert. That does not mean they cannot be utilized for a higher good. I know you do not approve of my work, but there is value to it. I do not regard the power of magic lightly. But neither do I disdain the limits of its possibilities."

Athabasca shook his leonine head. "I think you are too close to your subject matter to judge it objectively. It was your failing when you left us."

"Perhaps," Bremen acknowledged quietly. "But none of this matters now. What matters is that we are threatened. The Druids, Athabasca. Brona surely remembers what led to his downfall in the First War of the Races. If he intends to try to conquer the Four Lands once more, as now seems probable, he will seek first to destroy what threatens him most. The Druids. The Council. Paranor."

Athabasca regarded him solemnly for a moment, then turned and walked to one of the windows and stood looking out at the sunlight. Bremen waited a moment, then said, "I have come to ask that you allow me to address the Council. Allow me the chance to tell the others what I have seen. Let them weigh for themselves the merits of my argument."

The High Druid turned back, chin lifted slightly so that he seemed to be looking down on Bremen. "We are a community within these walls, Bremen. We are a family. We live with one another as we would with brothers and sisters, engaged in a single course of action—to gain knowledge of our world and its workings. We do not favor one member of the community over another; we treat all as equals. This is something you have never been able to accept."

Bremen started to protest, but Athabasca held up his hand for silence. "You left us on your own terms. You chose to abandon your family and your work for private pursuits. Your studies could not be shared with us, for they transgressed the lines of authority that we had established. The good of the one can never be allowed to displace the good of the whole. Families must have order. Each member of the family must have respect for the others. When you left us, you showed disrespect for the Council's wishes in the matter of your studies. You felt you knew better than we did. You gave up your place in our society."

He gave Bremen a cold look. "Now you would come back to us and be our leader. Oh, don't bother with denials, Bremen! What else would you be but exactly that? You arrive with knowledge you claim is peculiar to yourself, with studies of power known only to you, and with a plan for the salvation of the Races that only you can implement. The Warlock Lord is real. The Warlock Lord is Brona. The rebel Druid has subverted the magic to his own use and tamed the Trolls. All will march against the Four Lands. You are our only hope. You must advise us on what we are to do and then command us in our duties as we set out to stop this travesty. You, who abandoned us for so long, must now lead."

Bremen shook his head slowly. Already he knew how this must end, but he forged ahead anyway. "I would lead no one. I would advise on the danger I have discovered and nothing more. What happens after must be determined by you, as High Druid, and by the Council. I do not seek to return as a member of the Council. Simply hear me out, then send me on my way."

Athabasca smiled. "You still believe so strongly in yourself. I am impressed. I admire you for your resolve, Bremen, but I think you misguided and deceived. Still, I am but one voice and not of a mind to make a decision on this by myself. Wait here with Captain Lock. I will call the Council together and ask it to consider your request. Will it choose to hear you or not? I shall leave it to them."

He rapped sharply on the desk and the narrow back door to the chamber opened. Caerid Lock came through and saluted. "Stay with our guest," Athabasca ordered, "until I return."

Then he went out through the wide double doors at the front of the chamber without looking back.

ATHABASCA WAS GONE for almost four hours. Bremen sat on a bench by one of the tall windows and stared out into the hazy light of the late afternoon. He waited patiently, knowing he could do little else. He talked with Caerid Lock for a time, catching up on the news of the Council's work, discovering that it progressed in much the same way as it had for years, that little changed, that almost nothing was accomplished. It was depressing to hear, and Bremen soon gave up on pursuing his inquiries. He thought of what he would say to the Council and how its members might respond, but he knew in his heart it was an exercise in futility. He realized now why Athabasca had agreed to see him. The High Druid believed it better to admit him and hear him out than to dismiss him out of hand, better to give some semblance of consideration than to give none at all. But the decision was already made. He would not be listened to. He was outcast, and he would not be allowed back in. Not for any reason, no matter how persuasive, how compelling. He was a dangerous man, in Athabasca's mind—in the minds of others, too, he supposed. He used magic with disdain. He played with fire. There could be no listening to such a man. Not ever.

It was sad. He had come to warn them, but they were beyond his reach. He could feel it. He waited now only to have it confirmed.

Confirmation arrived swiftly on the heels of the four hours' close. Athabasca came through the doors with the brusque attitude of a man with better things to get on to. "Bremen," he greeted and dismissed him at the same time. He paid no attention to Caerid Lock at all, did not ask him to stay or go. "The Council has considered your request and rejected it. If you would like to submit it again in writing, it will be given to a committee to consider." He sat down at his desk with a sheaf of papers and began studying them. The Eilt Druin glimmered brightly as it swung against his chest. "We are committed to a course of noninvolvement with the Races, Bremen. What you seek would violate that rule. We must stay out of politics and interracial conflicts. Your speculations are too broad and entirely unsubstantiated. We cannot give them credence."

He looked up. "You may supply yourself with whatever you need to continue your journey. Good luck to you. Captain Lock, please escort our guest back to the front gates."

He looked down again. Bremen stared wordlessly, stunned in spite of himself at the abruptness of his dismissal. When Athabasca continued to ignore him, he said quietly, "You are a fool."

Then he turned and followed Caerid back through the narrow door into the passageway that had brought them. Behind him, he heard the door close and lock.

CHAPTER

3

CAERID LOCK AND BREMEN DESCENDED the back stairs in silence, their footsteps echoing in lonely cadence through the twisting passageway. Behind them, the light from the landing and the door leading to the High Druid Athabasca's chambers receded into blackness. Bremen fought to contain the bitterness that welled up within him. He had called Athabasca a fool, but maybe he was the real fool. Kinson had been right. Coming to Paranor had been a waste of time. The Druids were not prepared to listen to their outcast brother. They were not interested in his wild imaginings, in his attempts to insinuate himself back into their midst. He could see them turning to one another with amused, sarcastic glances as the High Druid informed them of his request. He could see them shaking their heads in resentment. His arrogance had blinded him to the size of the obstacle that he was required to surmount in order to gain their belief. If he could just speak to them, they would listen, he had thought. But he had not gotten the chance to do even that much. His confidence had undone him. His pride had tricked him. He had miscalculated badly.

Still, he countered, trying to salvage something from his failed effort, he had been right to try. At least he did not have to live with the guilt and pain he might feel later for having done nothing. Nor could he be certain of the result of his effort. Some good might yet come of his appearance, a small change in events and attitudes that he would not be able to discern until much later. It was wrong to dismiss his effort out of hand. Kinson might have been right about the end result, but neither of them could know that nothing would come of this visit.

"I am sorry you were not allowed to speak, Bremen," Caerid said quietly, glancing over his shoulder.

Bremen looked up, aware how depressed he must seem. This was no time for self-indulgence. He had lost his chance to speak directly to the Council, but there were other tasks to be completed before he was dismissed from the Keep forever, and he must see to them.

"Caerid, would there be time for me to visit Kahle Rese before leaving?" he asked. "I need only a few moments."

They stopped on the stairs and regarded each other, the frail-looking old man and the weathered Elf. "You were told to gather what you needed for your journey," Caerid Lock observed. "There was nothing said about what those needs might be. I think a short visit would be in order."

Bremen smiled. "I will never forget your efforts on my behalf, Caerid. Never."

The other man gave a short wave of dismissal. "They were nothing, Bremen. Come."

They continued along the stairs to a back passageway that took them through several doors and down another flight of stairs. All the time, Bremen was thinking. He had given his warning, for better or worse. It would be ignored by most, but those who would harken to it must be given what chance there was to survive the foolishness of the others. In addition, some effort must be made to protect the Keep. There was not a great deal he could do in the face of the Warlock Lord's power, but he must do what little he could. He would begin with Kahle Rese, his oldest and most trusted friend—even though he knew that once again he faced almost certain disappointment in his intended effort.

When they reached the doorway that led into the main hall, just a short distance from the libraries where Kahle spent his days, Bremen turned again to Caerid.

"Will you do me one more favor?" he asked the Elf. "Will you summon Risca and Tay Trefenwyd to speak with me? Have them wait in the passageway until I finish my visit with Kahle.

I will meet them there. I give you my word I will go nowhere else and do nothing to violate the terms of my visit."

Caerid looked away. "Your word is not necessary, Bremen. It never has been. Have your visit with Kahle. I'll bring the other two and meet you here."

He turned and went back up the stairs into the gloom. Bremen thought how lucky he was to be able to count Caerid among his friends. He remembered Caerid as a young man, still learning his craft, but intense and steady even then. Caerid had come from Arborlon and stayed on past his initial appointment, committed to the Druid cause. It was rare for a non-Druid to take such an interest. He wondered if Caerid would do so again, if given the chance to live his life over.

He stepped through the door into the corridor beyond and turned right. The hall was arched and framed with great wooden beams that gleamed with polish and wax. Tapestries and paintings hung from the castle walls. Pieces of ancient furniture and old armor occupied protected space in small alcoves, lit by slow-burning candles. Age and time were captured within these walls where nothing changed but the hours of the day and the passing of the seasons. There was a sense of permanence to Paranor, the oldest and strongest fortress in the Four Lands, the guardian of its givers of knowledge, the keeper of its most precious artifacts and tomes. What few advancements had been made coming out of the wilderness of the Great Wars had originated here. Now it was all in danger of ending, of being forever lost, and only he seemed aware of it.

He reached the library doors, opened them quietly, and stepped inside. The room was small for a library, but it was crammed with books. There were few books to be found since the destruction of the old world, and most of those had been compiled by the Druids in the last two hundred years, painstakingly recorded by hand from the memories and observations of the handful of men and women who still remembered. Almost all were stored here, in this room and the next, and Kahle Rese was the Druid responsible for their safekeeping. All had value, but none more so than the Druid Histories, the books that chronicled the results of the Council's efforts to recover the lost knowledge of science and magic from the centuries before the

Great Wars, of its attempts at uncovering the secrets of power that had given the old world the greatest of its advancements, and of its detailing of all possibilities however remote concerning devices and formulas, talismans and conjuring, reasoning and deductions that might one day find understanding.

The Druid Histories. These were the books that mattered most to Bremen. These were the books that he intended to save.

Kahle Rese was standing on a ladder arranging a worn and shabby collection of leather-bound tomes when Bremen entered. He turned and started when he saw who was standing there. He was a small, wiry man, hunched slightly with age, but nimble enough to climb still. There was dust on his hands, and the sleeves of his robe were rolled up and tied. His blue eyes blinked and crinkled as a smile lit his face. Quickly he scurried down the ladder and came over. He held out his hands and gripped Bremen's own tightly.

"Old friend," he greeted. His narrow face was like a bird's— eyes sharp and bright, nose a hooked beak, mouth a tight line, and beard a small, wispy tuft on his pointed chin.

"It is good to see you, Kahle," Bremen told him. "I have missed you. Our conversations, our puzzling through of the world's mysteries, our assessments of life. Even our poor attempt at jokes. You must remember."

"I do, Bremen, I do." The other laughed. "Well, here you are."

"For a moment only, I'm afraid. Have you heard?"

Kahle nodded. The smile slipped from his face. "You came to give warning of the Warlock Lord. Athabasca gave it for you. You asked to speak to the Council. Athabasca spoke for you. Took rather a lot on himself, didn't he? But he has his reasons, as we both know. In any case, the Council voted against you. A few argued quite vigorously on your behalf. Risca, for one. Tay Trefenwyd. One or two more." He shook his head. "I am afraid I remained silent."

"Because it did no good for you to speak," Bremen said helpfully.

But Kahle shook his head. "No, Bremen. Because I am too old and tired for causes. I am comfortable here among my books and seek only to be left alone." He blinked and looked Bremen over carefully. "Do you believe what you say about the Warlock Lord? Is he real? Is he the rebel Druid, Brona?"

Bremen nodded. "He is what I have told Athabasca and a great threat to Paranor and the Council. He will come here eventually, Kahle. When he does, he will destroy everything."

"Perhaps," Kahle acknowledged with a shrug. "Perhaps not. Things do not always happen as we expect. You and I were always agreed on that, Bremen."

"But this time, I'm afraid, there is little chance they will happen any other way than I have forecast. The Druids spend too much time within their walls. They cannot see with objectivity what is happening without. It limits their vision."

Kahle smiled. "We have our eyes and ears, and we learn more than you suspect. Our problem is not one of ignorance; it is one of complacency. We are too quick to accept the life we know and not quick enough to embrace the life we only imagine. We think that events must proceed as we dictate, and that no other voice will ever have meaning but ours."

Bremen put his hand on the small man's narrow shoulder. "You were always the best reasoned of us all. Would you consider making a short journey with me?"

"You seek to rescue me from what you perceive to be my fate, do you?" The other man laughed. "Too late for that, Bremen. My fate is tied irrevocably to these walls and the writings of these few books I manage. I am too old and too set in my ways to give up a lifetime's work. This is all I know. I am one of those Druids I described, old friend—hidebound and moribund to the last. What happens to Paranor happens also to me."

Bremen nodded. He had thought Kahle Rese would say as much, but he had needed to ask. "I wish you would reconsider. There are other walls to live within and other libraries to tend."

"Are there?" Kahle asked, arching one eyebrow. "Well, they wait for other hands, I suspect. I belong here."

Bremen sighed. "Then help me in another way, Kahle. I pray I am wrong in my assessment of the danger. I pray I am mistaken in what I think will occur. But if I am not, and if the Warlock Lord comes to Paranor, and if the gates should not hold against him, then someone must act to save the Druid Histories." He paused. "Are they still kept separate within the adjoining room—behind the bookcase door?"

"Still and always," Kahle advised.

Bremen reached into his robes and withdrew a small leather pouch. "Within is a special dust," he told his friend. "If the Warlock Lord should come within these walls, throw it across the Druid Histories, and they will be sealed away. The dust will hide them. The dust will keep them safe."

He handed the pouch to Kahle, who accepted it reluctantly. The wizened Druid held the pouch out in the cup of his hand as if to measure its worth. "Elf magic?" he asked, and Bremen nodded. "Some form of faerie dust, I suppose. Some form of old-world sorcery." He grinned mischievously. "Do you know what would happen to me if Athabasca found this in my possession?"

"I do," Bremen replied solemnly. "But he won't find it, will he?"

Kahle regarded the pouch thoughtfully for a moment, then tucked it into his robes. "No," he agreed, "he won't." His brow furrowed. "But I am not sure I can promise I will use it, no matter what the cause. I am like Athabasca in this one matter, Bremen. I am opposed to involvement of the magic in the carrying out of my duties. I deplore magic as a means to any end. You know that. I have made it plain enough before, haven't I?"

"You have."

"And still you ask me to do this?"

"I must. Who else can I turn to? Who else can I trust? I leave it to your good judgment, Kahle. Use the dust only if circumstances are so dire that the lives of all are threatened and no one will be left to care for the books. Do not let them fall into the hands of those who will misuse the knowledge. That would be worse than any imagined result of employing magic."

Kahle regarded him solemnly, then nodded. "It would, indeed. Very well. I will keep the dust with me and use it should the worst come to pass. But only then."

They faced each other in the ensuing silence, all the words spoken, nothing left to say.

"You should reconsider your decision to come with me," Bremen tried a final time.

Kahle smiled, a brittle twist of his thin mouth. "You asked

me to come with you once before, when you chose to leave Paranor and pursue your studies of the magic elsewhere. I told you then I would never leave, that this is where I belong. Nothing has changed."

Bremen felt a bitter helplessness creep through him, and he smiled quickly to keep it from showing. "Then goodbye, Kahle Rese, my oldest and greatest friend. Keep well."

The small man embraced him, hands gripping the old man's slender frame and holding fast. "Goodbye, Bremen." His voice was a whisper. "This one time, I hope you are wrong."

Bremen nodded wordlessly. Then he turned and went out the library door without looking back. He found himself wishing that things could be different, knowing they could not. He moved swiftly down the hallway to the door that opened into the back stairs passageway that had brought him. He found himself looking at the tapestries and artifacts as if he had never seen them—or perhaps as if he would never see them again. He felt some part of himself slipping away, just as it had when he left Paranor the first time. He did not like to admit it, but this was still more home to him than any other place, and as it was with all homes, it laid claim to him in ways that could not be judged or measured.

He went through the door into the near darkness of the landing beyond and found himself face-to-face with Risca and Tay Trefenwyd.

Tay came forward immediately and embraced him. "Welcome home, Druid," he said, clapping the old man on the back.

Tay was an Elf of unusual height and size, lanky and rather awkward-looking, as if he were constantly in danger of tripping over his own feet. His face was decidedly Elven, but his head seemed to have been grafted onto his body by mistake. He was young still, even with fifteen years of service at Paranor, his face smooth and clean-shaven. He had blond hair and blue eyes, and always bore a ready smile for everyone.

"You look well, Tay," the old man replied, giving the other a quick smile in return. "Life at Paranor agrees with you."

"Seeing you again agrees with me more," the other declared. "When are we leaving?"

"Leaving?"

"Bremen, don't be coy. Leaving for wherever it is you are going. Risca and I are decided. Even if you hadn't called us to meet with you, we would have caught up with you on your way out. We have had enough of Athabasca and the Council."

"You were not there to witness their performance," Risca sneered, shouldering into the light. "A travesty. They gave your request the same consideration they would an invitation to become a victim of the plague! There was no debate allowed or reasoning undertaken! Athabasca presented your request in such a manner that there was no doubt where he stood. Others backed him up, sycophants all. Tay and I did our best to condemn his machinations, but we were shouted down. I have had enough of their politics, enough of their shortsightedness. If you say the Warlock Lord exists, then he exists. If you say he is coming to Paranor, then come he will. But I will not be here to greet him. Let those others stand in my place. Shades, how can they be such fools?"

Risca was all brawn and heat, and Bremen smiled in spite of himself. "So you gave a good account of yourselves on my behalf?"

"We were small whispers in a windstorm," Tay laughed. His arms lifted and fell helplessly within his dark robes. "Risca is right. Politics rule at Paranor. They have since Athabasca became First Druid. You should have held that position, Bremen, not him."

"You could have been First Druid, if you had wanted to be," Risca pointed out irritably. "You should have insisted."

"No," said Bremen, "I would not have done the job well, my friends. I was never one for administration and management. I was meant to seek out and recover what was lost, and I could not do that from the high tower. Athabasca was a better choice than I."

"Hogwash!" snapped Risca. "He has never been a good choice for anything. He resents you even now. He knows that his office was yours for the asking, and he has never forgiven you for that. Nor that you could walk away from it. Your freedom threatens his reliance on order and obedience. He would have us all placed carefully on a shelf and taken down when it suits his purpose. He would dictate our lives as if we were children. You escaped his reach by leaving Paranor, and he will not forgive you that."

Bremen shrugged. "Ancient history. I regret only that he would not pay greater heed to my warning. I think the Keep in real danger. The Warlock Lord comes this way, Risca. He will not step around Paranor and the Druids. He will grind them beneath his army's boots."

"What are we to do?" Tay pressed, glancing about as if afraid someone might be listening. "We have continued practicing our magic, Bremen. Each of us, Risca and I, in our own way, employing our own disciplines. We knew you would come back for us someday. We knew the magic would be needed."

Bremen nodded, pleased. He had relied on these two above all the others to pursue their conjuring skills. They were not as learned or practiced as he, but they were able enough. Risca was the weapons master, skilled in the war arts, in the study of arms. Tay Trefenwyd was a student of the elements, of the forces that created and destroyed, of the balance of earth, air, fire, and water in the evolution of life. Each was an adept, just as he, capable of summoning magic when called upon to protect and defend. The practice of magic was forbidden within the walls of Paranor, except under strict supervision. Conjuring was undertaken almost exclusively on a basis of need. Experimentation was discouraged and often punished if discovered. The Druids lived in the shadow of their own history and the dark memory of Brona and his followers. They had been rendered moribund by guilt and indecision. They could not seem to understand that their ill-conceived course of action threatened to swallow them whole.

"You were right in your assumptions," he told them. "I relied on you not to abandon the magic. And I do want you to come with me. I will need your skills and your strength in the days ahead. Tell me, are there any others we can call upon? Others, who have accepted the need for magic's use?"

Tay and Risca exchanged a brief glance. "None," said the latter. "You must make do with us."

"You shall do fine," Bremen advised, his aged face crinkling with the smile he forced upon himself. Only these two to join Kinson and himself! Only these two against so many! He sighed. Well, he should have expected as much, he supposed. "I am sorry I must ask this of you," he said, and genuinely meant it.

Risca snorted. "I should feel slighted if you did not. I am bored to tears of Paranor and her old men. No one cares for the practice of my craft. No one follows in my footsteps. I am an anachronism to all. Tay feels as I do. We would have left long ago if we had not agreed to wait for you."

Tay nodded. "It is no cause for sadness to find you in need of traveling companions, Bremen. We are quite ready."

Bremen took each by the hand and thanked him. "Gather what you would carry with you and meet me by the front gates tomorrow morning. I will tell you of our journey then. Tonight, I will sleep without in the forest with my companion, Kinson Ravenlock. He has accompanied me these two years past and proven invaluable. He is a Tracker and a scout, a Borderman of great courage and resolve."

"If he travels with you, he needs no other recommendation," said Tay. "We will leave now. Caerid Lock waits for you some-where on the stairs below. He asks that you descend until you come upon him." Tay paused meaningfully. "Caerid would be a good man to have with us, Bremen."

The old man nodded. "I know. I will ask him to come. Rest well. I will see you both at sunrise."

The Dwarf and the Elf slipped through the passageway door and closed it softly behind them, leaving Bremen alone on the landing. He stood there for a moment, thinking of what he must do next. Silence surrounded him, deep and pervasive within the fortress walls. Time slipped away. He did not require much of it, but he would have to be quick in any case.

And he would need Caerid Lock's cooperation.

He hurried down the stairway, intent on his plan, mulling over the details in his mind. The musty smell of the close passage assailed his nostrils, causing his nose to wrinkle. Elsewhere, in the main corridors and stairways of the Keep, the air would be clean and warm, carried up from the fire pit that heated the castle throughout the year. Dampers and vents controlled the airflow, but none of these were present in hidden passages like this one.

He found the Captain of the Druid Guard two landings farther down, standing alone in the shadows. He came forward at Bremen's approach, his worn face impassive.

"I thought you might visit more comfortably with your friends alone," he said.

"Thank you," Bremen replied, touched at the other's consideration. "But we would have you be one of us, Caerid. We leave at sunrise. Will you come?"

Caerid smiled faintly. "I thought that might be your plan. Risca and Tay are eager enough to depart Paranor—that's no secret." He shook his head slowly. "But as for me, Bremen, my duty lies here. Especially if what you believe is true. Someone must protect the Druids of Paranor, even from themselves. I am best suited. The Guard is mine, all handpicked, all trained under my command. It would not do for me to abandon them now."

Bremen nodded. "I suppose not. Still, it would be good to have you with us."

Caerid almost smiled. "It would be good to come. But the choice is made."

"Then keep careful watch within these walls, Caerid Lock." Bremen fixed him with his gaze. "Be certain of the men you lead. Are there Trolls among them? Are there any who might betray you?"

The Captain of the Druid Guard shook his head firmly. "None. All will stand with me to the death. Even the Trolls. I would bet my life on it, Bremen."

Bremen smiled gently. "And so you do." He glanced about momentarily as if seeking someone. "He will come, Caerid—the Warlock Lord with his winged minions and mortal followers and perhaps creatures summoned out of some dark pit. He will descend on Paranor and attempt to crush you. You must watch your back, my friend."

The seasoned veteran nodded. "He'll find us ready." He held the other's gaze. "It's time to take you back down to the gates. Would you like to take some food with you?"

Bremen nodded. "I would." Then he hesitated. "I almost forgot. Would it be possible for me to have one final word with Kahle Rese? I am afraid we left each other under rather strained circumstances, and I would like to correct that before I go away.

Could you give me just a few minutes more, Caerid? I will come right back."

The Elf considered the request silently for a moment, then nodded. "Very well. But hurry, please. I have already stretched Athabasca's instructions to their limit."

Bremen smiled disarmingly and went back up the stairs once more. He hated lying to Caerid Lock, but there was no reasonable alternative open to him. The Captain of the Druid Guard would never have been able to sanction what he was about to do under any circumstances, friend or no. Bremen ascended two levels, passed through a doorway into a secondary passage, quickly followed it to its end, then went through yet another door to a second set of stairs, this one more narrow and steep than the first. He went quietly and with great care. He could not afford to be discovered now. What he was about to do was forbidden. If he was observed, Athabasca might well cast him into the deepest dungeon and leave him there for all time.

At the head of the narrow stairs he stopped before a massive wooden door secured by locks made fast with chains as thick as his aged wrists. He touched the locks carefully, one after the other, and with small snicks they fell open. He released the chains from their securing rings, pushed at the door, and watched with a mix of relief and trepidation as it swung slowly away.

He stepped through then and found himself on a platform high up within the Druid's Keep. Below, the walls fell away into a black pit that was said to core all the way to the center of the earth. No one had ever descended to its bottom and returned. No one had ever been able to cast a light deep enough to see what was down there. The Druid Well, it was called. It was a place into which the discards of time and fate had been cast—of magic and science, of the living and the dead, of mortal and immortal. It had been there since the time of faerie. Like the Hadeshorn in the Valley of Shale, it was one of the few doorways that connected the worlds of life and afterlife. There were tales of how it had been used over the years and of the terrible things it had swallowed. Bremen had no interest in the tales. What mattered was that he had determined long ago that the pit was a shaft that channeled magic from realms no living soul had ever visited, and within the blackness that cloaked its secrets lay power that no creature would dare to challenge.

Standing at its edge, he lifted his arms and began to chant. His voice was soft and steady, his conjuring studied and deliberate. He did not look down, even when he heard the stirrings and the sighs from within the depths. He moved his hands slightly, weaving out the symbols that commanded obedience. He spoke the words without hesitation, for even the slightest waver could bring the spell to an end and doom his effort.

When he was finished, he reached into his robes and withdrew a pinch of greenish powder, which he cast into the void. The powder sparkled with wicked intent as it fluttered on the air currents, seeming to grow in size, to multiply until the few grains had turned to thousands. Momentarily, they hung suspended, shining in the near black, and then they winked out and were gone.

Bremen stepped back quickly, breathing hard, feeling his courage fail as he leaned against the cold stone of the tower wall. He had not the strength that he once had. He had not the resolve. He closed his eyes and waited for the stirrings and the sighs to fade back into silence. Use of the magic required such effort! He wished he were young again. He wished he had a young man's body and determination. But he was old and failing, and it was pointless to wish for the impossible. He must make do with the body and determination he had.

Something scraped on the stone walls below him—a rasp of claws perhaps, or of scales.

Climbing to see if the spell caster was still there!

Collecting himself, Bremen stumbled back through the door and pushed it closed tightly behind him. His heart still beat wildly, and his face was coated in a sheen of sweat. *Leave this place*, a harsh voice whispered from somewhere beyond the door, from far down in the pit. *Leave it now!*

Hands shaking, Bremen resecured the locks and chains. Then he scurried back down the narrow stairs and through the empty passageways of the Keep to rejoin Caerid Lock.

4

REMEN AND KINSON RAVENLOCK SPENT the night in the forest some distance back from Paranor and the Druids. They found a grove of spruce that provided reasonable concealment, wary even here of the winged hunters that prowled the night skies. They ate their dinner cold, a little bread, cheese, and spring apples washed down with ale, and talked over the day's events. Bremen revealed the results of his attempts to address the Druid Council and reported his conversations with those he had spoken to within the Keep. Kinson confined himself to sober nods and muttered grunts of disappointment and had the presence of mind and good manners not to tell the older man, when advised of his failure to convince Athabasca, that he had told him so.

They slept then, worn from the long trek down out of the Streleheim and the many nights spent sleepless before. They took turns keeping watch, not trusting even the close presence of the Druids to keep them safe. Neither really believed he would be safe anywhere for some time to come. The Warlock Lord moved where he wished these days, and his hunters were his eyes in every corner of the Four Lands. Bremen, standing watch first, thought he sensed something at one point, a presence that nudged at his warning instincts from somewhere close at hand. It was midnight, he was nearing the end of his duty and beginning to think of sleep, and he almost missed it. But nothing showed itself, and the prickly feeling that ran the length of his spine faded almost as quickly as it had come.

Bremen's sleep was deep and dreamless, but he was awake before sunrise and thinking of what he must do next in his efforts to combat the threat of the Warlock Lord when Kinson appeared out of the shadows on cat's feet and knelt next to him.

"There is a girl here to see you," he said.

Bremen nodded wordlessly and rose to a sitting position. The night was fading into paler shades of gray, and the sky east was faintly silver along the edge of the horizon. The forest about them felt empty and abandoned, a vast dark labyrinth of shaggy boughs and canopied limbs that enclosed and sealed like a tomb.

"Who is she?" the old man asked.

Kinson shook his head. "She didn't give her name. She appears to be one of the Druids. She wears their robe and insignia."

"Well, well," Bremen mused, rising now to his feet. His muscles ached and his joints felt stiff and unwieldy.

"She offered to wait, but I knew you would be awake already."

Bremen yawned. "I grow too predictable for my own good. A girl, you say? Not many women, let alone girls, serve with the Druids."

"I didn't think they did either. In any case, she seems to offer no threat, and she is quite intent on speaking with you."

Kinson sounded indifferent to the outcome of the matter, meaning that he thought it was probably a waste of time. Bremen straightened his rumpled robes. They could do with a washing. For that matter, so could he. "Did you see anything of the winged hunters on your watch?"

Kinson shook his head. "But I felt their presence. They prowl these forests, make no mistake. Will you speak with her?"

Bremen looked at him. "The girl? Of course. Where is she?"

Kinson led him from the shelter of the spruce to a small clearing less than fifty feet away. The girl stood there, a dark and silent presence. She wasn't very big, rather short and slightly built, wrapped in her robes, the hood pulled up to conceal her face. She didn't move as he came into view, but stood there waiting for him to approach first.

Bremen slowed. It interested him that she had found them

so easily. They had deliberately camped well back in the trees to make it difficult for anyone to discover them while they slept. Yet this girl had done so—at night and without the benefit of any light but that of stars and moon where it penetrated the heavy canopy of limbs. She was either a very good Tracker or she had the use of magic.

"Let me speak with her alone," he told Kinson.

He crossed the clearing to where she stood, limping slightly as his joints attempted to unlimber. She lowered the hood now so that he could see her. She was very young, but not a girl as Kinson had thought. She had close-cut black hair and enormous dark eyes. Her features were delicate and her face smooth and guileless. She was indeed dressed in Druid robes, and she wore the raised hand and burning torch of the Eilt Druin sewn on her breast.

"My name is Mareth," she told him as he came up to her, and she held out her hand.

Bremen took it in his own. Her hand was small, but her grip was strong and the skin of her palm hardened by work. "Mareth," he greeted.

She took back her hand. Her gaze was steady and held his own, her voice low and compelling. "I am a Druid apprentice, not yet accepted into the order, but allowed to study in the Keep. I came here ten months ago as a Healer. I came from several years of study in the Silver River country, then two years in Storlock. I began my study of healing when I was thirteen. My family lives in the Southland, below Leah."

Bremen nodded. If she had been allowed to study healing at Storlock, she must have talent. "What do you wish of me, Mareth?" he asked her gently.

The dark eyes blinked. "I want to come with you."

He smiled faintly. "You don't even know where I'm going."

She nodded. "It doesn't matter. I know what cause you serve. I know that you take the Druids Risca and Tay Trefenwyd with you. I want to be part of your company. Wait. Before you say anything, hear me out. I will leave Paranor whether you take me with you or not. I am in disfavor here, with Athabasca in particular. The reason I am in disfavor is that I choose to pursue the study of magic when it has been forbidden me. I am to be a Healer only, it has been decided. I am to use the skills and learning the Council feels appropriate."

For a woman, Bremen thought she might add, the phrase hidden in the words she spoke.

"I have learned all that they have to teach me," she continued. "They will not admit this, but it is so. I need a new teacher. I need you. You know more about the magic than anyone. You understand its nuances and demands, the complications of employing it, the difficulties of assimilating it into your life. No one else has your experience. I would like to study with you."

He shook his head slowly. "Mareth, where I go, no one who is not experienced should venture."

"It will be dangerous?" she asked.

"Even for me. Certainly for Risca and Tay, who at least know something of the magic's use. But especially for you."

"No," she said quietly, clearly ready for this argument. "It will not be as dangerous for me as you think. There is something about me that I haven't told you yet. Something that no one knows here at Paranor, although I think Athabasca suspects. I am not entirely unskilled. I have use of magic beyond that which I would master from study. I have magic born to me."

Bremen stared. "Innate magic?"

"You do not believe me," she said at once.

In truth, he did not. Innate magic was unheard of. Magic was acquired through study and practice, not inherited. At least, not in these times. It had been different in the time of faerie, of course, when magic was as much a part of a creature's inherited character as the makeup of his blood and tissue. But no one in the Four Lands for as long as anyone could remember had been born with magic.

No one human.

He continued to stare at her.

"The difficulty with my magic, you see," she continued, "is that I cannot always control it. It comes and goes in spurts of emotion, in the rise and fall of my temperature, in the fits and starts of my thinking, and with a dozen other vicissitudes I cannot entirely manage. I can command it to me, but then sometimes it does what it will."

She hesitated, and for the first time her gaze fell momentarily before lifting again to meet his own. When she spoke, he thought he detected a hint of desperation in her low voice. "I must be wary of everything I do. I am constantly hiding bits and pieces of myself, keeping careful watch over my behavior, my reactions, even my most innocent habits." She compressed her lips. "I cannot continue to live like this. I came to Paranor for help. I have not found it. Now I am turning to you."

She paused and then added, "Please."

There was a poignancy in that single word that surprised him. For just a moment she lost her composure, the iron-willed, hardened appearance she had perfected in order to protect herself. He didn't know yet if he believed her; he thought that maybe he did. But he was certain that her need, whatever its nature, was very real.

"I will bring something useful to your company if you take me with you," she said quietly. "I will be a faithful ally. I will do what is required of me. If you should be forced to stand against the Warlock Lord or his minions, I will stand with you." She leaned forward in a barely perceptible motion, little more than an inclining of her dark head. "My magic," she confided in a small voice, "is very powerful."

He reached for her hand and held it between his own. "If you will agree to wait until after sunrise, I will give this matter some thought," he told her. "I will have to confer with the others, with Tay and Risca when they arrive."

She nodded and looked past him. "And your big friend?"

"Yes, with Kinson also."

"But he has no skill with magic, does he? Like the rest of you?"

"No, but he is skilled in other ways. You can sense that about him, can you? That he is without the use of magic?"

"Yes."

"Tell me. Did you use magic to find us here in this concealment?"

She shook her head. "No. It was instinct. I could sense you. I have always been able to do that." She stared at him, catching the look in his eye. "Is that a form of magic, Bremen?"

"It is. Not a magic you can identify as easily as some, but

magic nonetheless. Innate magic, I might add—absent acquired skill."

"I have no acquired skill," she said quietly, folding her arms into her robes as if she were suddenly cold.

He studied her for a moment, thinking. "Sit there, Mareth," he said finally, pointing to a spot behind her. "Wait with me for the others."

She did as she was asked. Moving to a patch of grass that had grown up where the trees did not shut out the sun, she folded her legs beneath her and seated herself in the huddle of her robes, a small dark statue. Bremen watched her for a moment, then moved back across the clearing to where Kinson waited.

"What did she want?" the Borderman asked, turning away with him to walk to the edge of the trees.

"She has asked to come with us," Bremen answered.

Kinson arched one eyebrow speculatively. "Why would she want to do that?"

Bremen stopped and faced him. "She hasn't told me yet." He glanced over to where she was seated. "She gave me reasons enough to consider her request, but she is keeping something from me still."

"So you will refuse her?"

Bremen smiled. "We will wait for the others and talk it over."

The wait was a short one. The sun rose out of the hills and crested the forest rim minutes later, spilling light down into the shadowed recesses, chasing back the last of the gloom. Color returned to the land, shades of green, brown, and gold amid the fading dark, and birds came awake to sing their welcome to a new day. Mist clung tenaciously to the darker alcoves of the brightening woods, and through a low curtain that yet masked the walls of Paranor walked Risca and Tay Trefenwyd. Both had abandoned their Druid robes in favor of traveling clothes. Both wore backpacks slung loosely across their broad shoulders. The Elf was armed with a longbow and a slender hunting knife. The Dwarf carried a short, two-handed broadsword, had a battle-axe cinched at his waist, and bore a cudgel as thick as his forearm.

They came directly to Bremen and Kinson without seeing Mareth. As they reached him, she rose once more and stood waiting.

Tay saw her first, glancing back at the unexpected movement caught from the corner of one eye. "Mareth," he said quietly.

Risca looked with him and grunted.

"She asks to travel with us," Bremen announced, forgoing any preliminaries. "She claims she might be useful to us."

Risca grunted again, shifting his bulk away from the girl. "She is a child," he muttered.

"She is out of favor with Athabasca for trying to study magic," Tay said, turning to look at her. The smile on his Elven face broadened. "She shows promise. I like her determination. Athabasca doesn't frighten her one bit."

Bremen looked at him. "Can she be trusted?"

Tay laughed. "What a strange question. Trusted with what? Trusted to do what? There's some who say no one's to be trusted but you and me, and I can only speak for me." He paused and cocked his head toward Kinson. "Good morning, Borderman. I am Tay Trefenwyd."

The Elf shook hands with Kinson; then Risca made his greeting as well. Bremen apologized for forgetting introductions. The Borderman said he was used to it and shrugged meaningfully.

"Well, then, the girl." Tay brought the conversation back around to where it had started. "I like her, but Risca is right. She is very young. I don't know if I want to spend my time looking after her."

Bremen pursed his thin lips. "She doesn't seem to think you will have to. She claims to have use of magic."

Risca snorted this time. "She is an apprentice. She has been at Paranor for less than three seasons. How could she know anything?"

Bremen glanced at Kinson and saw that the Borderman had figured it out. "Not likely, is it?" he said to Risca. "Well, give me your vote. Does she come with us or not?"

"No," said Risca at once.

Kinson shrugged and shook his head in agreement.

"Tay?" Bremen asked the Elf.

Tay Trefenwyd sighed reluctantly. "No."

Bremen took a long moment to consider their response, then nodded. "Well, even though you vote against her, I think she should come." They stared at him. His weathered face creased with a sudden smile. "You should see yourselves! All right then, let me explain. For one thing, there is something intriguing about her request that I failed to mention. She wishes to study with me, to learn about the magic. She is willing to accept almost any conditions in order to do so. She is quite desperate about it. She did not beg or plead, but the desperation is mirrored in her eyes."

"Bremen . . ." Risca began.

"For another," the Druid continued, motioning the Dwarf into silence, "she claims to have innate magic. I think that perhaps she is telling the truth. If so, we might do well to discover its nature and put it to good use. After all, there are only the four of us otherwise."

"We are not so desperate that . . ." Risca began again.

"Oh, yes, we are, Risca," Bremen cut him short. "We most certainly are. Four against the Warlock Lord, his winged hunters, his netherworld minions, and the entire Troll nation—how much more desperate could we be? No one else at Paranor has offered to help us. Only Mareth. I am not inclined to turn down anyone out of hand at this point."

"You said earlier that she keeps secrets from you," Kinson pointed out. "That hardly inspires the trust you seek."

"We all keep secrets, Kinson," Bremen chided gently. "There is nothing strange in that. Mareth barely knows me. Why should she confide everything in our first conversation? She is being careful, nothing more."

"I don't like it," Risca declared sullenly. He leaned the heavy cudgel against his massive thigh. "She may have magic at her disposal and she may even have the talent to use it. But that doesn't change the fact that we know almost nothing about her. In particular, we don't know if we can depend on her. I don't like taking that kind of chance with my life, Bremen."

"Well, I think we should give her the benefit of the doubt," Tay countered cheerfully. "We will have time to make up our minds about her before there is need to test her courage. There are things to be said in her favor already. We know she was chosen to apprentice with the Druids—that alone speaks highly of her. And she is a Healer, Risca. We might have need of her skills."

"Let her come," Kinson agreed grudgingly. "Bremen has already made his mind up anyway."

Risca frowned darkly. His big shoulders squared. "Well, he may have made up his mind, but he hasn't necessarily made up mine." He rounded on Bremen and stared wordlessly at the old man for a moment. Tay and Kinson waited expectantly. Bremen did not offer anything further. He simply stood there.

In the end, it was Risca who backed down. He simply shook his head, shrugged, and turned away. "You are the leader, Bremen. Bring her along if you like. But don't expect me to wipe her nose."

"I will be sure to tell her that," Bremen advised with a wink to Kinson, and beckoned the young woman over to join them.

THEY SET OUT SHORTLY AFTERWARD, a company of five, with Bremen leading, Risca and Tay Trefenwyd at either shoulder, Kinson a step behind, and Mareth trailing. The sun was up now, cresting the Dragon's Teeth east to light the heavily forested valley, and the skies were bright and blue and cloudless. The company traveled south, winding along little-used trails and footpaths, across broad, calm streams, and into the scrub-covered foothills that lifted out of the woodlands to the Kennon Pass. By midday they were climbing out of the valley into the pass, and the air had turned sharp and cool. Looking back, they could see the massive walls of Paranor where the Druid's Keep rested high on its rocky promontory amid the old growth. The sun's intense light gave the stone a flat, implacable cast amid the wash of trees, a hub at the center of a vast wheel. They glanced back on it, one after the other, lost in their separate thoughts, remembering events past and years gone. Only Mareth showed no interest, her gaze turned deliberately forward, her small face an expressionless mask.

Then they entered the Kennon, its rugged walls rising about them, great slabs of stone split by the slow swing of time's axe, and Paranor was lost from view.

Only Bremen knew where they were going, and he kept the information to himself until they camped that night above the Mermidon, safely down out of the pass and back within the sheltering forests below. Kinson had asked once when he was alone with the old man and Risca had asked in front of everyone, but Bremen had chosen not to respond. His reasons were his own, and he kept them that way, offering no explanation to his followers. No one chose to contest his decision.

But that night, after they had built their fire and cooked their food (Kinson's first hot meal in weeks), Bremen revealed at last their destination.

"I will tell you now where we are going," he advised quietly. "We are traveling to the Hadeshorn."

They were seated about the small fire, their dinner finished, their hands busy with other tasks. Risca worked to sharpen the blade of his broadsword. Tay sipped from an aleskin and sketched pictures in the dust. Kinson worked a fresh length of leather stitching through one boot where the sole was loosening. Mareth sat apart and watched them all with her strange, level gaze that took in everything and gave nothing back.

There was a silence when Bremen finished, four heads lifting as one to stare at him. "I intend to speak with the spirits of the dead in an effort to discover what it is that we must do to protect the Races. I will try to learn something of how we should proceed. I will try to discover our fates."

Tay Trefenwyd cleared his throat softly. "The Hadeshorn is forbidden to mortals. Even Druids. Its waters are poisonous. One taste and you are dead." He looked at Bremen thoughtfully, then looked away again. "But you already knew that, didn't you?"

Bremen nodded. "There is danger in visiting the Hadeshorn. There is greater danger still in calling up the dead. But I have studied the magic that wards the netherworld and its portals into our own, and I have traveled such roads as exist between

the two and returned alive." He smiled at the Elf. "I have journeyed far since last we were together, Tay."

Risca grunted. "I'm not sure I want to know my fate."

"Nor I," Kinson echoed.

"I will ask for whatever they will give me," Bremen advised.
"They will decide what we should know."

"You believe that the spirits will speak words that you can
understand?" Risca shook his head. "I didn't think it worked
that way."

"It doesn't," Bremen acknowledged. He eased himself closer
to the fire and held out his hands to capture its warmth. The
night was cool, even below the mountains. "The dead, if they
appear, offer visions, and the visions speak for them. The dead
have no voices. Not from the netherworld. Not unless . . ."

He seemed to think better of what he was about to say
and brushed the matter aside with an impatient wave. "The
fact remains that the visions will give voice to what the spirits would tell us—if they choose to speak at all. Sometimes,
they do not even appear. But we must go to them and ask
their help."

"You have done this before," said Mareth suddenly, making
it a statement of fact.

"Yes," the old man admitted.

Yes, thought Kinson Ravenlock, remembering. For he had
been there on the last occasion, a terrifying night of thunder
and lightning, of rolling black clouds and torrents of rain, of
steam hissing off the surface of the lake and of voices calling
out from the subterranean chambers of death's mansion. He had
stood there at the rim of the Valley of Shale and watched as
Bremen had gone down to the water's edge and called forth the
spirits of the dead into weather that seemed made for their eerie
purpose. What visions there were had not been his to see. But
Bremen had seen them, and they had not been good. His eyes
alone had revealed that much when finally he had climbed back
out of the valley at dawn.

"It will be all right," Bremen assured them, his smile faint
and worn within the creases of his shadowed face.

As they prepared for sleep, Kinson went to Mareth and bent

down next to her on one knee. "Take this," he offered, handing her his travel cloak. "It will help ward off the night's chill."

She looked at him with those large, disturbing eyes and shook her head. "You need it as much as I do, Borderman. I ask no special consideration from you."

Kinson held her gaze without speaking for a moment. "My name is Kinson Ravenlock," he said quietly.

She nodded. "I know your name."

"I stand the first watch and do not need the weight or warmth of the cloak while I keep it. No special consideration is being offered."

She seemed put off. "I must stand watch, too," she insisted.

"You will. Tomorrow. Two of us each night." He kept his temper firmly in check. "Now, will you take the cloak?"

She gave him a cool look, then accepted it. "Thank you," she said, her voice neutral.

He nodded, rose, and walked away, thinking to himself that it would be a while before he offered her anything again.

The night was deeply still and breathtakingly beautiful, the strangely purple heavens dotted thick with stars and a silvered quarter-moon. Vast and depthless, free from clouds and empty of conflicting light, the sky looked to have been swept by a great broom, the stars spread like diamond chips across its velvet surface. Thousands were visible, so many in some places that they seemed to run together like spilled milk. Kinson looked up at them and marveled. Time eased away with the smoothness of glass. Kinson listened for the familiar sounds of forest life, but it was as if all who dwelled within these woods were as awestruck as he and had no time for ordinary pursuits.

He thought back to when he was a boy living in the borderland wilderness east and north of Varfleet in the shadow of the Dragon's Teeth. It was not so different for him even then. At night, when his parents and his brothers and sisters were asleep, he would lie awake looking out at the sky, wondering at its size, thinking of all the places it looked down upon that he had never been. Sometimes he would stand before the bedroom window, as if by moving closer he might see more of what waited out there. He had always known he would go away, even while the others had begun the process of settling into more sedentary lives. They grew, married, had children, and moved into their own homes. They hunted, trapped, traded, and farmed in the country in which they had been born. But he only drifted, always with one eye on that distant sky, always with a promise to himself that one day he would see all of what lay beneath it.

He was still looking, even now, with more than thirty years of his life behind him. He was still searching for what he hadn't seen and didn't know. He thought that would never change. He thought that if one day it did, he would become a different man than he had ever imagined being.

Midnight arrived, and with it Mareth. She appeared unexpectedly from out of the shadows, wrapped in Kinson's cloak, so light-footed that anyone else might have missed her approach entirely. Kinson turned to greet her, surprised because he was expecting Bremen.

"I asked Bremen to give me his turn at watch," she explained when she reached him. "I did not want to be treated differently."

He nodded, saying nothing.

She took off the cloak and handed it to him. She seemed small and frail without it. "I thought you should have this back for when you sleep. It's gotten cold. The fire has died away to nothing, and it might be best to leave it that way."

He accepted the cloak. "Thank you."

"Have you seen anything?"

"No."

"The Skull Bearers will track us, won't they?"

How much did she know? he wondered. How much, of what they faced? "Perhaps. Did you sleep at all?"

She shook her head. "I could not stop thinking." Her huge eyes stared off into the dark. "I have been waiting for this for a long time."

"To come with us on this journey?"

"No." She looked at him, surprised. "To meet Bremen. To learn from him, if he will teach me." She turned away quickly, as if she had said too much. "You had better sleep while you can. I will keep watch until morning. Good night."

He hesitated, but there was nothing left to say. He rose and walked back to where the others were rolled into their cloaks about the ashes of the fire. He lay down with them and closed his eyes, trying hard to make something of Mareth, then trying not to think of her at all.

But he did, and it was a long time before he slept.

CHAPTER

5

THEY ROSE BEFORE SUNRISE and walked east through the day until sunset. They passed along the base of the Dragon's Teeth above the Mermidon, keeping back within the shadow of the mountains. Bremen warned them that they were at risk even there. The Skull Bearers felt sure enough of themselves to come down out of the Northland. The Warlock Lord marched his armies east toward the Jannisson Pass, which meant they probably intended to descend upon the Eastland. If they were bold enough to invade the country of the Dwarves, they certainly would not hesitate to venture into the Borderlands.

So they kept close watch of the skies and the darker valleys and rifts of the mountains where the shadows left the rock cloaked in perpetual night, and they did not take anything for granted as they journeyed on. But the winged hunters did not show themselves this day, and aside from a few travelers glimpsed at a distance in the forests and plains south, they saw no one. They stopped to rest and to eat, but did not pause otherwise, keeping a steady pace through the daylight hours.

By sunset they had reached the foothills leading up into the Valley of Shale and the Hadeshorn. They camped in a draw that faced back toward the plains south and the winding blue ribbon of the Mermidon where it branched east into the Rabb, the river gradually diminishing until it died away into streams and ponds on the barren flats. They cooked vegetables and a rabbit that Tay had killed, and ate their dinner while it was still light, the sun bleeding red and gold into the western horizon. Bremen told them they would go up into the mountains after midnight and wait for the slow hours before sunrise when the spirits of the dead could be summoned.

They kicked out the fire as night descended and rolled into their cloaks to get what sleep they could.

"Do not worry so, Kinson," Bremen whispered to the Borderman once in passing on seeing his face.

But the advice was wasted. Kinson Ravenlock had been to the Hadeshorn before and knew what to expect.

SOMETIME AFTER MIDNIGHT, Bremen took them up into the foothills fronting the Dragon's Teeth where the Valley of Shale was nestled. They climbed through the rocks on a night so black that they could barely make out the person immediately ahead. Clouds had moved in after sunset, thick and low and threatening, and all signs of moon and stars had disappeared hours ago. Bremen led the way cautiously, concerned for their well-being even though the terrain they passed through was as familiar to him as the back of his hand. He did not speak to the others as they proceeded, keeping his attention focused on the task at hand and the one that lay ahead, intent on avoiding any missteps either now or later. For a meeting with the dead required foresight and caution, a screwing up of courage and a hardening of determination that would permit neither hesitation nor doubt. Once contact was made, even the smallest distraction could be life-threatening.

It was still several hours before dawn when they reached their destination. They paused on the rim of the valley and stared down into its broad, shallow bowl. Crushed rock littered its sides, black and glistening even in the deep gloom, reflecting back the strange light of the lake. The Hadeshorn sat at the center of the bowl, broad and opaque, its still, flat surface glimmering with some inner radiance, as if the lake's soul pulsed within its depths. It was still and lifeless within the Valley of Shale, empty of movement, devoid of sound. It had the look and feel of a black hole, an eye looking down into the world of the dead.

"We will wait here," Bremen advised, seating himself on the flat surface of a low boulder, his cloak wrapped about his thin frame like a shroud.

The others nodded, but stood staring down into the valley for a time, unwilling to turn away just yet. Bremen let them be. They were feeling the weight of the valley's oppressive silence. Only Kinson had been here before, and even he could not prepare himself for what he must be feeling now. Bremen understood. The Hadeshorn was the promise of what awaited them all. It was a glimpse into the future they could not escape, a frightening dark look into life's end. It spoke in no recognizable words, but only in whispers and small mutterings. It revealed too little to give insight and just enough to give pause.

The old man had been here twice now, and each time he had come away forever changed. There were truths to be learned and there was wisdom to be gained from a meeting with the dead, but there was a price to be paid as well. You could not brush up against the future and escape unscathed. You could not see into the forbidden and avoid damage to your sight. Bremen remembered the feeling of those previous meetings. He remembered the cold that had worked its way down into his bones and would not leave for weeks afterward. He remembered his pervasive longing for what he had missed in the years gone past that could never be recaptured. He was frightened even now of the possibility that somehow he would stray from the narrow path permitted him in making this forbidden contact and be swallowed up in the void, a creature consigned to a limbo existence between life and death, neither all of one or the other.

But the need to discover what he could of how the Warlock Lord might be destroyed, of the choices and opportunities open to him in his effort to save the Races, and of the secrets of the past and future hidden to the living but revealed to the dead, far outweighed fear and doubt. He was compelled so fiercely by his need that he was forced to act on it even at the risk of his own well-being. Yes, there were dangers in making this contact. Yes, he would not emerge from it unharmed. But it did not matter in the scheme of things, for even giving up his life was an acceptable price if it meant putting an end to his implacable enemy.

The others had forced themselves away from the valley's rim and drifted over to sit with him. He made himself smile reassuringly at them, one by one, beckoning even the recalcitrant Kinson to come close.

"In the hour before dawn, I will go down into the valley," he told them quietly. "Once there, I will summon the spirits of the dead and ask them to show me something of the future. I will ask them to reveal the secrets that would help us in our efforts to destroy the Warlock Lord. I will ask them to give up any magic that might aid us. I must do this quickly and all within that short span of time before the sun rises. You will wait here for me. You will not come down into the valley, whatever happens. You will not act on what you see, even though it might seem as if you must. Do nothing but wait."

"Perhaps one of us should go with you," Risca offered bluntly. "There is safety in numbers, even with the dead. If you can speak with their spirits, so can we. We are Druids all, save the Borderman."

"That you are Druids does not matter," Bremen said at once. "It is too dangerous for you. This is something I must do alone. You will wait here. I want your promise, Risca."

The Dwarf gave him a long, hard look and then nodded. Bremen turned to the others. Each nodded reluctantly in turn. Mareth's eyes met his own and held them with secret understanding.

"You are convinced this is necessary?" Kinson pressed softly.

The lines of Bremen's aged face crinkled slightly deeper with the furrowing of his brow. "If I could think of something else to do, something that would aid us, I would leave this place. I am no fool, Kinson. Nor hero. I know what coming here means. I know it damages me."

"Then perhaps . . ."

"But the dead speak to me as the living cannot," Bremen continued, cutting him short. "We need their wisdom and insight. We need their visions, flawed and bereft of understanding as they sometimes are." He took a deep breath. "We need to see through their eyes. If I must give up something of myself to gain that insight, then so be it."

They were silent then, lost in their separate thoughts, mulling over his words and the misgivings they generated. But there was no help for it. He had told them what was necessary, and there was nothing else to say. They would understand better, perhaps, when this matter was done.

So they sat in the darkness and glanced surreptitiously at the shimmering surface of the lake, their faces bathed in the weak light as they listened to the silence and waited for the dawn to draw closer.

And when at last it did, when it was time to go, Bremen rose and faced his companions with a small smile, then went past them wordlessly and down into the Valley of Shale.

Once more, his progress was slow. He had come this way before, but familiarity did not aid where the terrain was so treacherous. The rock underneath was slippery and loose at every point, and the edges were sharp enough to cut. He picked his way carefully, testing each step on the uncertain surface. His boots crunched and ground on the rock, the sound echoing in the deep silence. From west where the clouds massed thickest, thunder rumbled ominously, signaling the approach of a storm. Within the valley, there was no wind, but the smell of rain permeated the dead air. Bremen glanced up as a flicker of lightning splintered the black skies, then repeated its pattern farther north against the backdrop of the mountains. Dawn would bring more than the sunrise this day.

He reached the bottom of the valley and slogged forward at a more rapid pace, his footing steadier on the level ground. Ahead, the Hadeshorn glimmered with silvery incandescence, the light reflecting from somewhere below its flat, still surface. He could smell death here, an unmistakable mustiness, an arid and fetid decay. He was tempted to look back to where the others waited, but knew he must not distract himself even in that small way. He was already running through the ritual he must follow when he reached the lakeshore—the words, the signs, the conjuring acts that would bring the dead to speak with him. He was already hardening himself against their debilitating presence.

All too soon he stood upon the edge of the lake, a frail, small figure in a vast arena of rock and sky, all withered skin and old bones, the strongest part of him his determination, his stubborn will. Behind him, he could hear again the rumble of thunder from the approaching storm. Overhead, the clouds began to roil, stirred to movement by the winds that bore on their back the coming rain. Below, he could feel the earth shiver as the spirits sensed his presence.

He spoke to them softly, calling out his name, his history, his reason for coming to speak with them. He made the signs with his arms and hands, made the gestures that would summon them from the world of the dead to the world of the living. He saw the waters begin to stir in response, and he quickened his pace. He was confident and steady; he knew what would follow. First came the whispers, soft and distant, rising like invisible bubbles from the waters. Then came the cries, long and deep. The cries increased in volume, growing from a few to many, rising in tenor and impatience. The waters of the Hadeshorn hissed with dissatisfaction and need, and began to roil as rapidly as the clouds overhead, stirred by their own coming storm. Bremen gestured to them, bade them respond. The learning he had mastered in his studies with the Elves buttressed and enabled him, a bedrock on which to build the summoning magic. *Answer me*, he called to them. *Open to me.*

Spray flew out of the center of the now violent waters, rising in a fountain, collapsing back, rising again. A rumble sounded deep within the earth, a groan of dissatisfaction. Bremen felt the first trace of doubt steal into his heart, and it was with an effort that he forced himself to ignore it. He could feel a vacuum forming around him, spreading out from the lake to encompass the whole of the valley. Only the dead would be allowed within its perimeter—the dead, and the one who had summoned them.

Then the spirits began to rise from the lake: small, white filaments of light given vaguely human form, bodies bathed in a firefly radiance that glimmered against the blackness of the clouded night. The spirits spiraled out of the mist and spray snakelike, lifting from the dark, dead air of their afterlife home to visit briefly the world they had once inhabited. Bremen kept his arms raised in a warding gesture, feeling vulnerable and bereft of power, though he had done the summoning, though he had brought the spirits to life. Cold ran down his brittle limbs in a rush, ice water through his veins. He held himself firm against the fear that raced through him, against the whispers that asked accusingly: *Who calls us? Who dares?*

Then something huge broke the water's surface at its exact center, a black-cloaked figure that dwarfed the smaller glowing forms, scattering them with its coming, soaking up their fragile light and leaving them whirling and twisting like leaves in the wind. The cloaked figure rose to stand upon the dark, churning waves of the Hadeshorn, only vaguely substantial, a wraith without flesh or bones, yet of firmer stuff than the smaller creatures it dominated.

Bremen held himself steady as the dark figure advanced. This was whom he had come to see; this was the one he had summoned. Yet he was no longer certain he had done the right thing. The cloaked form slowed, so close now that it blotted out the sky above and the valley behind. Its hood lifted, and there was no face, no sign of anything within the dark robes.

It spoke, and its voice was a rumble of discontent.

—Do you know me—

Flat, dispassionate, and empty, a question without a question's inflection, the words hung upon the silence in a lingering echo.

Bremen nodded slowly in response. "I do," he whispered.

AT THE RIM OF THE VALLEY, the four he had left behind watched the drama unfold. They saw the old man stand upon the shores of the Hadeshorn and summon the spirits of the dead. They saw the spirits rise amid the roiling of the waters, saw their glowing forms, the movement of their arms and legs, the twisting of their bodies in a macabre dance of momentary freedom. They watched as the huge, black-robed form lifted from their midst, enveloping them in its wake, absorbing their light. They watched the figure advance to stand before Bremen.

But they could hear nothing of what they saw. Within the

valley, all was silent. The sounds of the lake and the spirits were closed away. The voices of the Druid and the cloaked figure, if they spoke, were inaudible. They could hear only the wind that rushed past their ears and the beginning patter of raindrops on the crushed stone. The expected storm was breaking, rolling out of the west in a mass of dark clouds, descending on them with sheets of rain. It reached them at the same moment the cloaked figure reached Bremen, and it swallowed everything in an instant's time. The lake, the spirits, the cloaked figure, Bremen, the whole of the valley—all were gone in the blink of an eye.

Risca growled in dismay and glanced quickly at the others. They were cloaked now against the storm, hunched down within their coverings like crones bent with age. "Can you see?" he demanded anxiously.

"Nothing," Tay Trefenwyd answered at once. "They're gone."

For a moment, no one moved, uncertain what they should do. Kinson peered through the downpour's haze, trying to distinguish something of the shapes he thought he could just make out. But everything was shadowy and surreal, and there was no chance of making sure from where they stood.

"He may be in trouble," Risca snapped accusingly.

"He told us to wait," Kinson forced himself to say, not wanting to be reminded of the old man's instructions when he feared so for him, but not willing to ignore his promise either.

Rain blew into their faces in sudden gusts, choking them.

"He is all right!" Mareth cried out suddenly, her hand brushing the air before her face.

They stared at her. "You can see them?" Risca demanded.

She nodded, her face lowered into shadow. "Yes."

But she could not. Kinson was closest to her and saw what the others missed. If she was seeing Bremen, it was not through her eyes. Her eyes, he realized in shock, had turned white.

WITHIN THE VALLEY OF SHALE, no rain fell, no wind blew, nothing of the storm penetrated. There was for Bremen no sense of anything beyond the lake and the dark figure that stood upon it before him.

—Speak my name—

Bremen took a deep breath, trying to still the trembling of his limbs and the rush of cold that filled his chest. "You are Galaphile that was."

It was an expected part of the ritual. A spirit summoned could not remain unless its name was spoken by the summoner. Now it could stay long enough to give answers to the questions Bremen would ask—if it chose to answer at all.

The shade stirred, suddenly restless.

—What would you know of me—

Bremen did not hesitate. "I would know whatever you would tell me of the rebel Druid Brona, of he who has become the Warlock Lord." His voice was shaking as badly as his hands. "I would know how to destroy him. I would know what is to come." His voice died away in a dry rattle.

The Hadeshorn hissed and spit as if in response to his words, and the moans and cries of the dead rose out of the night in a strident cacophony. Bremen felt the cold stir anew in his chest, a snake coiling as it prepared to strike. He felt the whole of his years press down upon him. He felt the weakness of his body betray the strength of his determination.

—You would destroy him at any cost—

"Yes."

—You would pay any price to do so—

Bremen felt the snake within spring deep into his heart. "Yes," he whispered in despair.

The spirit of Galaphile spread its arms as if to enfold the old man, as if to shelter and protect him.

—Watch—

Visions began to appear against the black spread of its cloaked form, taking shape within the shroud of its body. One by one, they materialized out of the darkness, vague and insubstantial, shimmering like the waters of the Hadeshorn with the coming of the spirits. Bremen watched the images parade before him, and he was drawn to them as to light in darkness.

There were four.

In the first, he stood within the ancient fortress of Paranor.

All around him there was death. No one lived within the Keep, all slain by treachery, all destroyed by wicked stealth. Blackness cloaked the castle of the Druids, and blackness stirred within its shadows in the form of assassins waiting, a deadly force. But beyond that blackness shone with gleaming certainty the bright, shimmering medallion of the High Druids, awaiting his coming, needful of his touch, an image of a hand raised aloft with a burning torch—the cherished Eilt Druin.

The vision vanished, and he soared now across the vast expanse of the Westland. He looked down, amazed, unable to account for his flight. At first he could not determine where he was. Then he recognized the lush valley of the Sarandanon and beyond, the blue expanse of the Innisbore. Clouds obscured his vision momentarily, changing everything. Then he saw mountains—the Kensrowe or the Breakline? Within their mass were twin peaks, fingers of a hand split outward from each other in a **V** shape. Between them a pass led to a vast cluster of fingers, all jammed together, crushed into a single mass. Within the fingers was a fortress, hidden away, ancient beyond imagining, a place come out of the time of faerie. Bremen swooped down into its blackness and found death waiting, though he could not spy out its face. And there, within its coils, lay the Black Elfstone.

This vision vanished, too, and now he stood upon a battlefield. The dead and wounded lay all about, men from all the Races and things from no race known to man. Blood streaked the earth, and the cries of the combatants and the clash of their weapons rang out in the fading gray light of a late afternoon sky. Before him stood a man, his face turned away. He was tall and blond. He was an Elf. He carried in his right hand a gleaming sword. Several yards farther away was the Warlock Lord, black-robed and terrible, an indomitable presence that challenged all. He seemed to wait on the tall man, unhurried, confident, defiant. The tall man advanced, raising high the sword, and beneath the gloved hand on the weapon's handle was the insignia of the Eilt Druin.

One last vision appeared. It was dark and clouded and filled with sounds of sorrow and despair. Bremen stood once more in the Valley of Shale before the waters of the Hadeshorn. He faced anew the shade of Galaphile, watching as the smaller, brighter spirits swirled about it like smoke. At his side was a boy, tall and lean and dark, barely fifteen, so solemn he might have been in mourning. The boy turned to Bremen, and the Druid looked into his eyes . . . his eyes . . .

The visions faded and were gone. The shade of Galaphile drew itself into a tighter coalescence, masking away the images, stealing away the brief light they had given. Bremen stared, blinking, wondering at what he had witnessed.

"Will these happen?" he whispered to the shade. "Will they come to pass?"

—Some have come to pass already—

"The Druids, Paranor . . . ?"

—Do not ask more—

"But what can I . . . ?"

The shade gestured, dismissing out of hand the old man's questions. Bremen caught his breath as bands of iron tightened around his chest. The bands released, and he swallowed down his fear. Spray flew from the Hadeshorn in a bright geyser, diamonds against the black velvet night.

The shade began to recede.

—Do not forget—

Bremen lifted his hand in a futile effort to slow the other's departure. "Wait!"

—A price for each—

The old man shook his head in confusion. A price for each? Each what? For whom?

—Remember—

Then the Hadeshorn boiled anew, and the ghost sank slowly back into the churning waters, drawing down with it all of the brighter, smaller spirits that had accompanied it. Down they went in a rush of spray and mist, amid cries and whimpers from the dead, back to the netherworld from which they had come. Water exploded in a massive column as they disappeared, breaking apart the silence and dead air in a frightening explosion.

Then the storm came flooding in, with wind and rain, with

thunder and lightning, hammering into the old man. Bremen went down with the blow, felled in an instant.

Eyes open and staring, he lay senseless at the water's edge.

MARETH REACHED HIM FIRST. The men were larger and stronger, but her footing was surer on the damp, slippery rock, and she fairly flew across its polished surface. She knelt immediately and cradled the old man in her arms. Rain poured down relentlessly, pocking the now smooth, quiet surface of the Hadeshorn, washing down the black, glistening carpet of the valley, turning the dawn light hazy and vague. It soaked through Mareth's cloak to her skin, chilling her, but she ignored it, her small features twisting in concentration. Her face lifted to the darkened skies and her eyes closed. The other three slowed as they reached her, uncertain what was happening. Her arms tightened about Bremen. Then she shuddered violently and slumped forward, and the men rushed ahead to catch her. Kinson lifted her away from Bremen, while Tay picked up the old man, and in a knot they fought their way back through the downpour and out of the Valley of Shale.

Once clear, they found shelter in a grotto they had passed on their way in. There they laid the girl and the old man on the stone floor and wrapped them in their cloaks. There was no wood for a fire, so they were forced to remain sodden and chilled, waiting out the rain. Kinson checked for heartbeat and pulse and found both strong. After a time, the old man came awake, then almost immediately after, the girl. The three watchers crowded around Bremen to ask what had happened, but the old man shook his head and told them he did not wish to speak just yet. They left him reluctantly and moved away again.

Kinson paused beside Mareth, thinking to ask what she had done to Bremen—for it seemed clear that she had done something—but she glanced up at him and turned away immediately, so he abandoned the attempt.

The day brightened marginally, and the rains moved on. Kinson shared the food he carried with the others. Only Bremen would not eat. The old man seemed to have retreated somewhere deep inside himself—or perhaps he was still somewhere back within that valley—staring at nothing, his seamed, weathered face an expressionless mask. Kinson watched him for a time, searching for some sign of what he was thinking, failing in his effort to do so.

Finally the old man looked up as if just discovering they were there and wondering why, then beckoned them to sit close to him. When they were settled, he told them of his meeting with the shade of Galaphile and of the four visions he had been shown.

"I could not decide what the visions meant," he concluded, his voice weary and rough-edged in the silence. "Were they simply prophecies of what is to come, a future already decided? Were they the promise of what might be if certain things were done? Why were these particular visions selected by the shade? What response is expected of me? All these questions, left unanswered."

"What price are you being asked to pay for your involvement in all of this?" Kinson muttered darkly. "Don't forget that one."

Bremen smiled. "I have asked to be involved, Kinson. I have put myself in the position of being protector of the Races and destroyer of the Warlock Lord, and I do not have the right to ask what it will cost me if my efforts succeed.

"Still," he sighed, "I believe I understand something now of what is required of me. But I will need help from all of you." He looked at them in turn. "I must ask you to put yourselves in great danger, I'm afraid."

Risca snorted. "Thank goodness. I was beginning to think nothing at all would come of this adventure. Tell us what we must do."

"Yes, best to get started with this journey," Tay agreed, leaning forward eagerly.

Bremen nodded, gratitude reflected in his eyes. "We are agreed that the Warlock Lord must be stopped before he subjugates all of the Races. We know that he has tried and failed once already, but that this time he is stronger and more dangerous. I told you that because of this I believe he will attempt to destroy the Druids at Paranor. The first vision suggests that I was right." He paused. "I am afraid perhaps that it has already come to pass."

There was a long silence as the others exchanged wary glances. "You think the Druids are all dead?" Tay asked softly.

Bremen nodded. "I think it is a possibility. I hope I am wrong. In any event, whether they are dead or not, I must retrieve the Eilt Druin in accordance with the first vision. The visions taken together make it clear that the medallion is the key to forging a weapon that will destroy Brona. A sword, a blade of special power, of magic that the Warlock Lord cannot withstand."

"What magic?" Kinson asked at once.

"I don't know yet." Bremen smiled anew, shaking his head. "I know hardly anything beyond the fact that a weapon is needed and if the vision is to be believed, the weapon must be a sword."

"And that you must find the man who will wield it," Tay added. "A man whose face you were not shown."

"But the last vision, that dark image of the Hadeshorn and the boy with the strange eyes . . ." Mareth began worriedly.

"Must wait until its time." Bremen cut her short, though not harshly. His gaze settled on her face, searching. "Things reveal themselves as they will, Mareth. We cannot rush them. And we cannot allow ourselves to be constrained by our concern for them."

"So what are you asking us to do?" Tay pressed.

Bremen faced him. "We must separate, Tay. I want you to return to the Elves and ask Courtann Ballindarroch to mount an expedition to search out the Black Elfstone. In some way the Stone is critical to our efforts to destroy Brona. The visions suggest as much. The winged hunters already search for it. They must not be allowed to find it. The Elf King must be persuaded to support us in this. We have the particulars of the vision to help us. Use what it has shown us and recover the Stone before the Warlock Lord."

He turned to Risca. "I need you to travel to Raybur and the Dwarves at Culhaven. The armies of the Warlock Lord march east, and I believe they will strike there next. The Dwarves must make themselves ready to defend against an attack and must hold until help can be sent. You must use your special skills to see that they do so. Tay will speak with Ballindarroch to ask the Elves to join forces with the Dwarves. If they do so, they will be a match for the Troll army that Brona relies upon."

He paused. "But mostly we must gain time to forge the weapon that will destroy Brona. Kinson, Mareth, and I will return to Paranor and discover whether the vision of its fall is true. I will seek to gain possession of the Eilt Druin."

"If he still lives, Athabasca will not give it up," Risca declared. "You know that."

"Perhaps," Bremen replied mildly. "In any case, I must determine how this sword that I was shown is to be forged, what magic it shall possess, what power it needs to be imbued with. I must discover how to make it indestructible. Then I must find its wielder."

"You must perform miracles, it seems to me," Tay Trefenwyd mused ironically.

"All of us must do so," Bremen answered softly.

They looked at each other in the gloomy light, an unspoken understanding taking shape between them. Beyond their shelter, rainwater dripped in steady cadence from the rocky outcroppings. It was midmorning, and the light had turned silvery as the sun sought to fight its way through the lingering stormclouds.

"If the Druids at Paranor are dead, then we are all that is left," Tay said. "Just the five of us."

Bremen nodded. "Then five must be enough." He rose, looking out into the gloom. "We had better get started."

CHAPTER

6

THAT SAME NIGHT, west and north of where Bremen confronted the shade of Galaphile, deep within the stone ring of the Dragon's Teeth, Caerid Lock made his rounds of the watch at Paranor. It was nearing midnight when he crossed an open court on the parapets facing south and was momentarily distracted by a wicked flash of lightning in the distant skies. He paused, watching and listening to the silence. Clouds banked from horizon to horizon, shutting out moon and stars, cloaking the world in blackness. Lightning flashed a second time, momentarily splintering the night like shattered glass, then vanishing as if it had never been. Thunder rolled in its wake, a long, deep peal that echoed off the mountain peaks. The storm was staying south of Paranor, but the air smelled of rain and the silence was deep and oppressive.

The Captain of the Druid Guard lingered a moment longer, contemplative, then moved on through a tower door and into the Keep. He made these same rounds every night, disdaining sleep, a compulsive man whose work habits never varied. The times of greatest danger, he believed, were just before midnight and just before dawn. These were the times when weariness and sleep dulled the senses and made you careless. If an attack was planned, it would come then. Because he believed that Bremen would not give warning without reason, and because he was cautious by nature, he had determined to keep an especially sharp eye these next few weeks. He had already increased the number of guards on any given watch and begun the laborious process of strengthening the gate locks. He had considered sending night patrols into the surrounding woods as an added precaution, but was worried that they would be too vulnerable beyond the protection of the walls. His guard was large, but it was not an army. He could provide security within, but he could not give battle without.

He descended the tower stairs to the front courtyard and crossed. Half a dozen guards were stationed at the entry, responsible for the gates, portcullis, and watchtowers that fronted the main approach to the castle. They snapped to attention at his approach. He spoke with the officer in charge, confirmed that all was well, and continued on. He recrossed the open court, listening to a new roll of thunder break the deep night silence, glancing south to search for the flash of lightning that had preceded it, realizing as he did that it would already be gone. He was uneasy, but no more so this night than any other, as wary as he was compulsive about his responsibilities. Sometimes he thought he had stayed too long at Paranor. He did his job well; he knew he was still good at it. He was proud of his command; all of the guards presently in service had been selected and trained by him. They were a solid, dependable bunch, and he knew he could take credit for that. But he was not getting any younger, and age brought a dulling of the senses that encouraged complacency. He could hardly afford that. The fall of the Northland and the rumors of the Warlock Lord made these dangerous times. He sensed change in the wind. Something bad was coming to the Four Lands, and it would most certainly sweep up the Druids in its wake. Something bad was coming, and Caerid Lock was worried that he would not recognize its face until it was too late.

He passed through a doorway at the end of the court and walked down a hall that ran to the north wall and the gate that opened there. There were four gates to the Keep, one for each approach. There were a number of smaller doors as well, but these were constructed of stone and sealed with iron. Most were cleverly hidden. You could find them if you looked hard enough, but to do that you had to stand right up against the wall where the light was good and the guards on the battlements would see you. Nevertheless, Caerid kept a man at each during the hours between sunset and sunrise, taking nothing for granted. He passed two on his way to the west gate, fifty yards apart along the winding corridor. The guard at each acknowledged him with a sharp salute. Alert and ready, they were saying. Caerid gave a nod of approval both times and passed on.

He frowned though, when out of sight, troubled by their deployment. The man at the first door, a Troll from the Kershalt, was a veteran, but the man at the second, a young Elf, was new. He did not like stationing new men by themselves. He made a mental note to correct that before the next watch.

He was concentrating on the matter as he passed a back stairway leading down from the Druid sleeping quarters and so missed the furtive movement of the three men hiding there.

THE THREE PRESSED THEMSELVES TIGHTLY against the stone wall as the Captain of the Druid Guard passed unseeing below them. They remained very still until he was gone, then detached themselves once more and continued down. They were Druids, all of them, each with more than ten years of service to the Council, each with a zealot's burning conviction that he was destined for greatness. For they had lived within the Druid order and chafed at its dictates and rules and found them foolish and purposeless and unfulfilling. Power was necessary if life was to have meaning. A man's accomplishments meant nothing if they did not result in personal gain. What purpose did private study serve if it could not be put to practical use? What sense did it make to brush up against all those secrets of science and magic if they could not ever be tested? So they had asked themselves, these three, separately at first, then all together as they came to realize that they shared a common belief. They were not alone in their dissatisfaction, of course. Others believed as they did. But none so fervently—none so that, like these three, they would allow themselves to become subverted.

There was no hope for them. The Warlock Lord had been looking for them for a long time, planning his revenge on the Druids. He found them out eventually and made them his own. It had taken time, but bit by bit he had won them over, just as he had won over those who had followed him from the Keep three hundred and fifty years earlier. Such men were always there, waiting to be claimed, waiting to be used. Brona had been sly in his approach, not revealing himself to them in the beginning, letting them hear his voice as if it were their own, exposing them to the possibilities, to the scent of power, to the lure of magic. He let them chain themselves to him with their own hands, let them forge locks of expectation and greed, let them make themselves slaves by growing addicted to false dreams and cravings. In the end, they would have begged him to take them, even after they had discovered who he was and what price they must pay.

Now they crept through Paranor's corridors with dark intent, committed to a course of action that would doom them forever. They stole in silence from the stairwell and along the corridor to the doorway at which the young Elf stood watch. They clung to the shadows where the torchlight did not reach, using small conjurings of magic given them by the Master— sweet taste of power—to cloak themselves from the young guard's eyes.

Then they were upon him, one of them striking a sharp blow to his head to knock him senseless. The other two worked quickly and furiously at the locks that secured the stone door, releasing them one by one, hauling back on the heavy iron grate, lifting off the massive bar from its fittings, and finally, irrevocably, pulling open the door itself so that Paranor lay open to the night and the things that waited without.

The Druids stepped back as the first of those things slouched into the light. It was a Skull Bearer, hunched and massive within its black cloak, claws extended before it. All sharp edges and flat planes, all hardness and bulk, it filled the corridor and seemed to suck away the very air. Red eyes burned into the three who cowered before it, and it shoved its way past them disdainfully. Leathery wings beat softly. With a hiss of satisfaction, it seized the young Elven guard, ripped out his throat, and cast him aside. The Druids flinched as the rending sprayed them with the victim's blood.

The Skull Bearer beckoned to the darkness without, and other creatures poured through the doorway, things of tooth and nail, twisted and gnarled and bristling with dark tufts of hair, armed and ready, quick-eyed and furtive in the silence. Some were vaguely recognizable; perhaps they had once been Trolls. Some were beasts of the netherworld and looked in no way human. All had been waiting since just after sunset in a dark alcove in the shelter of the outer walls where they could not be seen from the parapets. There they had hidden, knowing these three pitiful beings who cowered before them had been claimed by the Master and would gain them access to the Keep.

Now they were inside and eager to begin the bloodletting that had been promised them.

The Skull Bearer sent one back out into the night to summon those still within the forest. There were several hundred, waiting for the signal to advance. They would be seen from the walls as they emerged from the trees, but the alarm would come too late. By the time Paranor's defenders could reach them, they would be inside the Keep.

The Skull Bearer turned and started down the hall. It did not acknowledge the three Druids. They were less than nothing to it. It left them behind, discards, leavings. It was up to the Master to decide what would become of them. All that mattered to the winged hunter was the killing that lay ahead.

The attackers divided into small groups as they went. Some crept up the stairway to the Druid sleeping chambers. Some turned down a secondary corridor that led deep into the Keep. Most continued with the Skull Bearer along the passageway that led to the main gates.

Soon, the screams began.

CAERID LOCK CAME RACING back across the courtyard from the north gate when the alarm was finally given. The screams came first, then the sound of a battle horn. The Captain of the Druid Guard knew everything in an instant. Bremen's prophecy had come true. The Warlock Lord was inside the gates of Paranor. The certainty of it chilled him to the bone. He called his men to him as he ran, thinking there might still be time. They charged into the Keep and down the corridor that led to the door the traitor Druids had breached. As they rounded a turn, they found the passageway ahead packed with black, hunched forms that squirmed through the opening out of the night. Too many to engage, Caerid realized at once. He took his men back quickly, and the beasts were quick to pursue. The guards abandoned the lower level and went up the stairs to the next, closing doors and dropping gates behind them, trying to seal their attackers off. It was a desperate gamble, but it was all that Caerid Lock could think to do.

On the next floor, they were able to close off the lesser entrances and move to the main stairs. By then, they were fifty strong—but still not enough. Caerid sent men to wake the Druids, to beg their assistance. Some among the elders knew magic, and they would need whatever power they could call upon if they were to survive. His mind raced as he rallied his men. This was no forced entry. This was a betrayal from within. He would find those responsible later, he swore. He would deal with them personally.

At the top of the main stairs, the Druid Guard made its stand. Elves, Dwarves, Trolls, and one or two Gnomes, they stood shoulder to shoulder, ordered and ready, united in their determination. Caerid Lock stood foremost in the center of their ranks, sword drawn. He did not try to fool himself; this was a holding action at best and doomed eventually to fail. Already he was considering his options when they were defeated. There was nothing he could do about the outer walls; they were lost already. The inner walls and the Keep were theirs for the moment, the entries sealed off, his men rallied in their defense. But these efforts would only slow a determined attacker. There were too many ways into and over and under the inner wall for the Druid Guard to hold for very long. Sooner or later their attacker would break through from behind. When that happened, they would have to flee for their lives.

An attack was mounted from below under the direction of the Skull Bearer, and crooked-limb monsters ascended the stairs in a knot of teeth and claws and weapons. Caerid led his guards in a counterattack, and the rush was repulsed. The monsters came again, and again the Druid Guard threw them back. But by now half of the defenders were either dead or injured, and no more had appeared to replace them.

Caerid Lock looked around in despair. Where were the Druids? Why weren't they responding to the alarm?

The monsters attacked a third time, a bristling mass of thrashing bodies and windmilling limbs, shrieks and cries rising out of gaping throats. The Druid Guard counterattacked once more, cutting into the monsters, beating them back down the stairway, leaving half their number sprawled lifeless on the blood-slicked steps. In desperation Caerid dispatched another man to summon help from wherever he could find it. He grabbed the man by his tunic as he was about to leave and pulled him close. "Find the Druids and tell them to flee while there is still time!" he whispered so that no other might hear. "Tell them Paranor is lost! Go quick, tell them! Then flee yourself!"

The messenger's face drained of blood, and he sprinted away wordlessly.

Another assault massed in the shadows below, a congealing of dark forms and guttural cries. Then, from somewhere higher up within the Keep, where the Druids slept, a piercing scream rose.

Caerid felt his heart sink. It's finished, he thought, not frightened or sad, but simply disgusted.

Seconds later, the creatures of the Warlock Lord surged up the stairway once more. Caerid Lock and his failing command braced to meet them, weapons raised.

But this time there were too many.

KAHLE RESE WAS ASLEEP in the Druid library when the sounds of the attack woke him. He had been working late, cataloging reports he had compiled during the past five years on weather patterns and their effects on farm crops. Eventually he had fallen asleep at his desk. He came awake with a start, jolted by the cries of wounded men, the clash of weapons, and the thudding of booted feet. He lifted his graying head and looked about uncertainly, then rose, took a moment to steady himself, and walked to the door.

He peered out guardedly. The cries were louder now, more

terrible in their urgency and pain. Men rushed past his door, members of the Druid Guard. The Keep was under attack, he realized. Bremen's warning had fallen on deaf ears, and now the price of their refusal to heed was to be exacted. He was surprised at how certain he was of what was happening and how it would end. Already he knew he was not going to live out the night.

Still he hesitated, unwilling even at this point to accept what he knew. The hall was empty now, the sounds of battle centered somewhere below. He thought to go out for a better look at things, but even as he was contemplating the idea, a shadowy presence emerged from the back stairway. He pulled his head inside quickly and peered out through his barely cracked door.

Black, misshapen creatures lurched into view, things that were unrecognizable, monsters from his worst nightmare. He caught his breath and held it. Room by room, they were working their way down the corridor to where he waited.

He closed the library door softly and locked it. For a moment he just stood there, unable to move. A rush of images recalled themselves, memories of his early days as a Druid in training, of his subsequent tenure as a Druid Scribe, of his ceaseless efforts to collect and preserve the writings of the old world and of faerie. So much had happened, but in so short a time. He shook his head in wonder. How had it all gone by so quickly?

There were screams close at hand now, freshly raised, come from just beyond his door, in the hall where the monsters prowled. Time was running out.

He moved quickly to his desk and took out the leather pouch that Bremen had given him. Perhaps he should have gone with his old friend. Perhaps he should have saved himself while he had the chance. But who would have protected the Druid Histories if he had done so? Who else could Bremen have relied upon? Besides, this was where he belonged. He knew so little of the world beyond anymore; it had been too long since he had gone out into it. He was of no use to anyone beyond these walls. Here, at least, he might still serve a purpose.

He walked to the bookcase that doubled as a hidden doorway to the room that concealed the Druid Histories and triggered its release. He entered and looked around. The room was filled with huge, leather-bound books. Row after row, they sat in numbered, ordered sequence, reservoirs of knowledge, of all the lore the Druids had gathered since the time of the First Council from the ages of faerie, Man, and the Great Wars. Each page of each book was crammed with information gained and recorded, some of it understood, some of it a mystery still, all that remained of science and magic past and present. Much of what was written in these books had been done so in Kahle's own hand, the words painstakingly inscribed, line by line, for more than forty years. Their recordings were the old man's special pride, the summation of his life's work, the accomplishment he favored most.

He crossed to the nearest bank of shelves, took a deep breath, and opened the drawstrings to Bremen's leather pouch. He mistrusted all magic, but there was no other choice. Besides, Bremen would never mislead him. What mattered to both was the preservation of the Histories. They must survive him, as they were intended to. They must survive them all.

He took a generous handful of the glittering, silver dust he found inside the pouch and threw it across one section of the books. Instantly, the entire wall on which the books were housed began to shimmer, taking on the look of a mirage in deep summer heat. Kahle hesitated, then threw more of the dust across the liquid curtain. The shelves and books disappeared. He moved on quickly then, using handfuls of the dust on each set of shelves, each section of books, watching them shimmer and fade away.

Moments later, the Druid Histories had vanished completely. All that remained was a room with four blank walls and a long reading table at its center.

Kahle Rese nodded in satisfaction. The Histories were safe now. Even if the room was discovered, its contents would remain concealed. It was as much as he could hope for.

He walked back through the door, suddenly weary. There was a scraping at the library door as unwieldy claws tried to fasten on the handle and turn it. Kahle turned and carefully closed the bookcase door. He placed the nearly empty leather pouch into the pocket of his robe, walked to his desk, and stood there. He had no weapons. He had no place to run. There was nothing to do but wait.

Heavy bodies threw themselves against the door from without, splintering it. A second later it gave way, crashing open against the wall. Three crook-backed beasts slouched into the room, red eyes narrow and hateful as they fixed on him. He faced them without flinching as they approached.

The closest held a short spear. Something in the bearing of the man before him infuriated him. When he was right on top of Kahle Rese, he drove the spear through his chest and killed him instantly.

WHEN IT WAS FINISHED, when all who remained of the guards had been hunted down and slaughtered, the Druids who had survived were herded from their hiding places into the Assembly and made to fall upon their knees, ringed by the monsters who had undone them. Athabasca was found, still alive, and brought to stand before the Skull Bearer. The creature stared at the imposing, white-haired First Druid, then ordered him to bow down and acknowledge him as Master. When Athabasca refused, proud and disdainful even in defeat, the creature seized him by his neck, looked into his frightened eyes, and burned them out with fire from his own.

As Athabasca lay writhing in agony on the stone floor, a sudden hush fell over the Assembly. The hissing and chittering died away. The scraping of claws and grinding of teeth faded. A silence descended, dark and foreboding, and all eyes were drawn to the hall's main entry, where the heavy double doors hung shattered and broken from their bindings.

There, within the jagged opening, the shadows seemed to come together, a coalescing of darkness that slowly took shape and grew into a tall, robed figure that did not stand upon the floor as normal men, but hung above it in midair, as light and insubstantial as smoke. A chill permeated the air of the Assembly at its coming, a cold that swept through the chamber and penetrated to the bones of the captured Druids. One by one their captors dropped to their knees, heads bowed, voices a rough murmur.

Master, Master.

The Warlock Lord looked down upon the beaten Druids and was filled with satisfaction. They were his, now. Paranor was his. Revenge was at hand, after all this time.

He brought his creatures back to their feet, then stretched his cloaked arm toward Athabasca. Unable to help himself, blinded and in pain, the First Druid was jerked upright as if by invisible wires. He hung above the floor, above the other Druids, crying out in terror. The Warlock Lord made a twisting motion, and the First Druid went ominously still. A second twisting motion, and the First Druid began to chant in terrible, croaking agony, *"Master, Master, Master."* The Druids huddled about him turned their eyes away in shame and rage. Some wept. The massed creatures of the Warlock Lord hissed with pleasure and approval, lifting their clawed limbs in salute.

Then the Warlock Lord nodded, and the Skull Bearer struck with terrible swiftness, tearing Athabasca's heart from his chest while he still lived. The First Druid threw back his head and shrieked as his chest exploded, then slumped forward and died.

For several long moments, the Warlock Lord held him suspended over his fellows like a rag doll, the blood draining from his body. He swung him this way and that, back and forth, and finally let him drop to the stone in a sodden mass of ruined flesh and bone.

Then he had all the captured Druids taken from the Assembly, herded like cattle to the deepest regions of Paranor's cellars, and walled away alive.

As the last of their screams died into silence, he went up through the stairways and corridors of the Keep in search of the Druid Histories. He had destroyed the Druids; now he must destroy their lore. Or take with him what he could use. He went swiftly now, for already there were stirrings from somewhere down within the Keep's bottomless well that hinted of magic coming awake in response to his presence. In his own domain, he was a match for anything. Here, within the haven of his greatest enemies, he might not be. He found the library and searched it through. He uncovered the bookcase that opened on the hidden chamber beyond, but that chamber was empty. There was magic in use, he sensed, but he could not determine its origin or purpose. Of the Histories, there was no sign.

From within the depths of the Druid Well, the stirrings grew stronger. Something had been set loose in response to his coming, and it was rising to seek him out. He was disturbed that this should be, that power of this sort should be set at watch to challenge him. It could not have originated with these pitiful mortals he had so easily subdued. They were no longer able to invoke such power. It must have come instead from the one who had penetrated his domain so recently, the one his creatures had tracked, the Druid Bremen.

He went back down to the Assembly, anxious to be gone now as swiftly as possible, his purpose here accomplished. He had the three who had betrayed Paranor brought before him. He did not speak to them with words, for they were not worthy of this, but let his thoughts speak for him. They cringed and prostrated themselves like sheep, poor foolish creatures who would be more than they were able.

Master! they whimpered in placating voices. *Master, we serve only you!*

Who among the Druids escaped the Keep besides Bremen?

Only three, Master. A Dwarf, Risca. An Elf, Tay Trefenwyd. A Southland girl, Mareth.

Did they go with Bremen?

Yes, with Bremen.

No others escaped?

No, Master. None.

They will return. They will hear of Paranor's fall and want to make certain it is so. You will be waiting. You will finish what I have begun. Then you will be as I am.

Yes, Master, yes!

Stand.

They did so, rising hastily, eagerly, broken spirits and minds that were his to command. Yet they lacked the strength to do what was required of them and so must be altered. He reached out to them with his magic, wrapped them about with strands as thin as gossamer and as unyielding as iron, and stole away the last of what was human.

Their shrieks echoed through the empty halls as he relentlessly shaped them into something new. Arms and legs flailed. Heads jerked wildly and eyes bulged.

When he was done, they were no longer recognizable. He left them thus, and with the remainder of his minions trailing obediently after he stole back into the night, abandoning the castle of the Druids to the dying and the dead.

CHAPTER

7

BREMEN GAVE HIS HAND to Risca in parting, and the Dwarf clasped it firmly in his own. They stood just outside the grotto in which they had taken shelter upon leaving the Hadeshorn and its ghosts. It was nearing midday now, the rain had dwindled to a fine mist, and the skies were beginning to clear west above the dark peaks of the Dragon's Teeth.

"It seems we no sooner meet up again and it's off our separate ways," Risca grumbled. "I don't know how we manage to stay friends. I don't know why we bother."

"We have no choice," Tay Trefenwyd offered from one side. "No one else would have anything to do with us."

"True enough." The Dwarf smiled in spite of himself. "Well, this should test the friendship, sure enough. Scattered Eastland to Westland and then some, and who knows when we'll meet again?" He gave Bremen's hand a hard squeeze. "You watch out for yourself."

"And you, my good friend," the old man replied.

"Tay Trefenwyd!" the Dwarf shouted over his shoulder. He was already striding down the trail. "Don't forget your promise! Pack up the Elves and bring them east! Stand with us against the Warlock Lord! We'll be counting on you!"

"Goodbye for now, Risca!" Tay called after him.

The Dwarf waved, hitching up his pack on his broad shoulders, his broadsword swinging at his side. "Luck to you, Elf ears. Keep alert! Watch your backside!"

They bantered back and forth good-naturedly, the Elf and the Dwarf, old friends comfortable with each other's joshing, accustomed to exchanges that teased and chided and masked emotions that lay just beneath the surface of the words. Kinson Ravenlock stood to one side listening to the verbal byplay and wished there were time to know them better. But that would have to wait. Risca had departed, and Tay would leave them at the mouth of the Kennon, when they turned north toward Paranor and the Elf continued west to Arborlon. The Borderman shook his head. How hard this must be for Bremen. It had been two years since he had seen Risca and Tay. Would it be two more before he saw them again?

When Risca had disappeared from view, Bremen led the three remaining members of the little company down a secondary trail to the base of the cliffs and then west along the north bank of the Mermidon, retracing the steps that had brought them there. They walked until well after sunset, camping finally in the lee of a copse of alder on a cove where the Mermidon branched south and west. The skies had cleared and were brilliant with stars, the light reflecting in a kaleidoscopic sparkle off the placid surface of the water. The company gathered on the riverbank and ate their dinner staring out into the night. No one said much. Tay cautioned Bremen to be wary at Paranor. If the vision he had been shown had come to pass and the castle of the Druids had fallen, there was reason to believe that the Warlock Lord and his minions might yet be in residence. Or if not, the Elf added, he might have left traps to ensnare any Druids who had escaped and were foolish enough to return. He said it lightly, and Bremen responded with a smile. Kinson noted that neither bothered to dispute the likelihood of Paranor's destruction. It must have been a bitter realization for both, but neither showed anything of what they were feeling. They made it a point not to dwell on the past. It was the future that mattered now.

To that end, Bremen talked at some length with Tay about his vision of the Black Elfstone, going over the particulars of what he had been shown, what he had sensed, and what he had deduced. Kinson listened idly, glancing now and again at Mareth, who was doing the same. He wondered what she was thinking, knowing as she did now that the Druids of Paranor were probably gone. He wondered if she realized how dramatically her role as a member of this company had changed. She had said barely a word since coming out of the Valley of Shale, keeping apart during the exchanges between Bremen, Risca, and Tay, watching and listening. Not unlike himself, Kinson thought. For she, too, was an outsider, still looking to find her place, not a Druid like the others, not yet proven, not entirely accepted as an equal. He studied her, trying to gage her toughness, her resilience. She would need both for what lay ahead.

Later, when she was sleeping, Tay sprawled close to her and Bremen at watch, Kinson rolled out of his cloak and walked over to sit with the old man. Bremen said nothing as he came up, looking out into the darkness. Kinson seated himself, crossed his long legs before him, and wrapped his cloak comfortably about his shoulders. The night was warm, more in keeping with the season than of late, and the air was filled with the smell of spring flowers and new leaves and grasses. A breeze blew down out of the mountains, rustling the limbs of the trees, rippling the waters of the river. The two men sat in silence for a time, listening to the night sounds, lost in their separate thoughts.

"You are taking a great risk in returning," Kinson said finally.

"A necessary risk," Bremen amended.

"You feel certain Paranor has fallen, don't you?"

Bremen did not respond for a moment, as still as stone, then nodded slowly.

"It will be very dangerous for you if that is so," Kinson pressed. "Brona hunts you already. He probably knows you have been to Paranor. He will expect you to return."

The old man's face turned slightly toward his younger companion, creased and browned by weather and sun, etched by a lifetime of struggle and disappointment. "I know all this, Kinson. And you know that I know, so why are we discussing it?"

"So that you will be reminded," the Borderman declared firmly. "So that you will be doubly cautious. Visions are fine, but they are tricky as well. I don't trust them. You shouldn't either. Not entirely."

"You refer to the vision of Paranor, I presume?"

Kinson nodded. "The Keep fallen and the Druids destroyed. All clear enough. But the sensation of something waiting, something dangerous—that's the tricky part of this matter. If it's accurate, it won't come in any form you expect."

Bremen shrugged. "No, I don't suppose it will. But it doesn't matter. I have to make certain that Paranor is truly lost—no matter the strength of my own suspicions—and I have to recover the Eilt Druin. The medallion is to be an integral part of the talisman needed to destroy the Warlock Lord. The vision was clear enough on that. A sword, Kinson, that I must shape, that I must forge, that I must imbue with magic that Brona himself cannot withstand. The Eilt Druin is the only part of that process that I have been shown; the medallion's image was clearly visible on the sword's handle. It is a place to begin. I must recover the medallion and determine what is needed from there."

Kinson studied him a moment in silence. "You have already constructed a plan for this, haven't you?"

"The beginnings of one." The old man smiled. "You know me too well, my friend."

"I know you well enough to anticipate you now and then." Kinson sighed and looked out across the river. "Not that it helps me in my efforts to persuade you to take better care of yourself."

"Oh, I wouldn't be so sure of that."

Wouldn't you? Kinson thought wearily. But he did not challenge the statement, hoping that perhaps it was at least partly true, that the old man did listen to him about a few things, particularly those that argued for caution. It was funny that Bremen, now in the twilight of his life, was so much more reckless than the younger man. Kinson had spent a lifetime on the border learning that a single misstep was the difference between life and death, that knowing when to act and when to wait kept you safe and whole. He supposed that Bremen appreciated the distinction, but he didn't always act as if he did. Bremen was far more apt to challenge fate than Kinson. The magic was the difference, he supposed. He was swifter and stronger than the old man, and his instincts were surer, but Bremen had the magic to sustain him, and the magic had never failed. It gave Kinson some small measure of reassurance that his friend was cloaked in an extra layer of protection. But he wished the measure could be larger.

He unfolded his long legs and stretched them out in front of him, leaning back, bracing himself with his arms. "What happened back there with Mareth?" he asked suddenly. "At the Hadeshorn, when you collapsed and she reached you first?"

"Interesting young woman, Mareth." The old man's voice was suddenly soft. He turned to face Kinson once more, a faraway look in his eyes. "Remember how she claimed to have magic? Well, the claim is a valid one. But perhaps it is not the sort of magic I envisioned. I'm still not sure. I do know something of it, though. She is an empath, Kinson. Her healing art is buttressed by this power. She can take another's pain into herself and lessen it. She can absorb another's injury and speed its healing. She did that with me at the Hadeshorn. The shock of seeing the visions and being touched by the shades of the dead rendered me unconscious. But she lifted me—I could feel her hands—and brought me awake, strong again, healed." He blinked. "It was very clear. Did you happen to see what effect it had on her?"

Kinson pursed his lips thoughtfully. "She seemed to lose strength momentarily, but it didn't last long. But her eyes. On the bluff, when you disappeared in the storm while talking with the shade of Galaphile, she said she could see you when the rest of us could not. Her eyes were white."

"Her magic seems quite complex, doesn't it?"

"Empathic, you said. But not in any small way."

"No. There is nothing small about Mareth's magic. It is very powerful. Probably she was born with it and has worked to develop her skills over the years. Certainly with the Stors." He paused. "I wonder if Athabasca realizes she possesses this skill. I wonder if any of them realize it."

"She isn't one to give much away about herself. She doesn't want anyone to get too close." Kinson pursed his lips thoughtfully. "But she does seem to admire you. She told me how important it was to her that she come with you on this journey."

Bremen nodded. "Yes, well, there are secrets yet to be revealed about Mareth, I think. You and I, we shall have to find a way to draw them out into the open."

Good luck to you on doing that, Kinson wanted to say, but kept the thought to himself. He remembered Mareth's reticence to accept even the small comfort of his cloak when he had offered it. It would take an unusual set of circumstances for her to give away anything about herself, he suspected.

But, then, nothing usual lay ahead for any of them, did it?

He sat with Bremen on the banks of the Mermidon, not speaking, not moving, looking out across the water, projecting images from the dark recesses of his mind of what he feared might come to pass.

THEY ROSE AT SUNRISE and walked through the day in the shadow of the Dragon's Teeth, following the Mermidon west. The weather turned warmer still, the temperature soaring, the air thickening with moisture and heat. Travel cloaks were discarded and water consumed in increasing quantities. They rested more frequently in the afternoon hours, and it was still light when they reached the Kennon. There Tay Trefenwyd left them to continue on across the grasslands to the forests of Arborlon.

"When you find the Black Elfstone, Tay, do not think to use it," Bremen cautioned on parting. "Not for any reason. Not even if you are threatened. Its magic is powerful enough to accomplish anything, but it is dangerous as well. All magic exacts a price for its use. You know that as well as I. The price for use of the Black Elfstone is too high."

"It might destroy me," Tay finished, anticipating.

"We are mortal beings, you and I," Bremen observed quietly. "We must tread lightly where the use of magic is concerned. Your task is to recover the Elfstone and to bring it to me. We do not seek to use it. We seek only to prevent the Warlock Lord from using it. Remember that."

"I will remember, Bremen."

"Warn Courtann Ballindarroch of the danger we face. Convince him that he must send his army to aid Raybur and the Dwarves. Don't fail me."

"It will all be done." The Druid Elf clasped his hand, released it, and was off with a jaunty wave. "Another memorable reunion, wasn't it? Watch out for him, Kinson. Take care, Mareth. Good luck to you all."

He whistled happily, smiling back at them one final time. Then his long stride lengthened, and he disappeared into the trees and rocks and was gone.

Bremen huddled then with Kinson and Mareth to decide whether they should continue on through the pass or wait until morning. It appeared another storm was approaching, but if they waited it out they might lose another two days. Kinson could tell that the old man was anxious to continue, to reach Paranor and discover the truth of what had happened. They were rested and fit, so he urged that they go on. Mareth was quick to give her support. Bremen smiled his appreciation and beckoned them forward.

They hiked into the pass as the sun dropped steadily toward the horizon and slipped from view. The skies remained clear and the air warm, so travel was comfortable and they made good time. By midnight, they were through the top of the pass and starting down into the valley beyond. The wind had picked up, howling out of the southwest in a steady rush, spinning dirt and gravel off the trail in small funnels, clouding the air with debris. They walked with their heads lowered until they were below the rim of the mountains and the wind had tailed off. Ahead, the black silhouette of the Druid's Keep was clearly visible against the starlit sky, rising out of the trees, towers and parapets stark and jagged. No lights burned in its windows or from its battlements. No movement or sound disturbed its silence.

They reached the valley floor and were swallowed by the forest. Moon and stars lit their way through the deep shadows, guiding them on toward the Keep. Massive old growth hemmed them about, rising over them like the pillars of a temple. Glades softened by thick grasses and small streams came and went. The night continued still and sleepy about them, empty of sound and movement save for the wind, which had picked up again, blowing past their faces in small, hard gusts, rustling their cloaks and the branches of the trees like shaken bedding. Bremen led them swiftly, steadily on, the pace belying his age and challenging theirs. Kinson and Mareth exchanged glances. The Druid had tapped into a hidden reservoir of strength. He had turned as hard and unyielding as iron.

It was not yet dawn when they reached Paranor. They slowed as the fortress came into view, materializing through breaks in the trees, lifting toward the starlit heavens, a massive black husk. Still, no light shone. Still, there was no sound or movement from within. Bremen stopped the Borderman and the Healer where they were hidden by the forest shadows. Silent, stone-faced, he scanned the walls and parapets of the Keep. Then, staying within the concealment of the woods, he took them left about the castle perimeter. The wind whipped across the battlements and around the spiraling towers in a mournful howl. Within the trees where they crept, it was a giant's breath that warned of its owner's approach. Kinson was sweating freely, his nerves on edge, his breathing harsh in his lungs.

They arrived at the main gates and stopped once more. The gates stood open, the portcullis raised, the entry left black and gaping and vaguely reminiscent of a mouth frozen in a death scream.

There were bodies by the shattered doors, twisted and lifeless.

Bremen hunched forward in concentration, staring at the Keep, but not really seeing it, looking somewhere beyond. His gray hair whipped about his head, as wispy as corn silk. His mouth moved. Kinson reached beneath his cloak and pulled forth his short sword. Mareth's eyes were wide and dark, and her small body rigid, poised to bolt.

Then Bremen took them forward. They crossed the open space separating the forest from the Keep, walking slowly, steadily, not bothering to hurry or conceal their approach. Kinson's eyes flicked left and right apprehensively, but Bremen did not seem concerned. They reached the gates and the dead men, and stooped to identify them. Druid Guards, most of them looking as if they had been torn apart by animals. Blood stained the ground beneath them, soaked from their bodies. Their weapons were drawn; many were shattered. They looked to have fought hard.

Bremen moved into the shadow of the wall, past the sagging gates and raised portcullis, and there he found Caerid Lock. The Captain of the Druid Guard was slumped against the watchtower door, blood dried and crusted on his face, his body pierced and slashed in a dozen places. He was still alive. His eyes flickered open, and his mouth moved. Hurriedly, Bremen bent to listen. Kinson could hear nothing, the wind obscuring the words.

The old man looked up. "Mareth," he called softly.

She came at once, bending over Caerid Lock. She did not need to be told what was required. Her hands ran quickly over the wounded man's body, searching for ways to help. But she was too late. Not even an empath could save Caerid now.

Bremen pulled Kinson down so that the two were huddled close, their faces almost touching. About them, the wind continued to howl softly as it twisted and turned about the walls. "Caerid said Paranor was betrayed from within, at night, while most slept. Three Druids were responsible. Everyone was killed but them. The Warlock Lord left them to deal with us. They are inside, somewhere. Caerid dragged himself here, but could go no further."

"You are not going in there?" Kinson asked hurriedly.

"I must. I must secure the Eilt Druin." The old man's seamed face was set and his eyes were hard and angry. "You and Mareth will wait for me here."

Kinson shook his head stubbornly. Dust and grit blew into his eyes as the wind whipped through the dark opening. "This is foolish, Bremen! You will need our help!"

"If something happens to me, I will need you to get word to the others!" Bremen refused to yield. "Do as I say, Kinson!"

Then he was on his feet and moving away, a ragged bundle of stick limbs and blowing robes, hastening from the gates and across the courtyard to the inner wall. In seconds, he had passed through a doorway and was lost from view.

Kinson stared after him in frustration. "Shades!" he muttered, furious at his own indecision.

He glanced over at Mareth. The young woman was closing Caerid Lock's eyes. The Captain of the Druid Guard was dead. It was a miracle, Kinson thought, that he had lasted this long.

Any of his wounds would have finished a normal man on the spot. That he had lived until now was a testament to his toughness and determination.

Mareth was on her feet, looking down at him. "Come on," she said. "We're going after him."

Kinson stood up quickly. "But he said . . ."

"I know what he said. But if anything happens to Bremen, what difference do you think it will make whether we get word to the others or not?"

His lips compressed in a tight line. "What difference, indeed?"

Together they hurried across the empty, windswept courtyard toward the Keep.

WITHIN PARANOR, Bremen moved swiftly down the empty halls, as silent as a cloud crossing the sky. He explored as he went, attuned to the tastes and smells and sounds of the Keep. He reached out with his senses and instincts to uncover the danger of which Caerid Lock had warned, wary of its presence and intent. But he could not find it. Either it was very well concealed or it had departed.

Be cautious, he urged himself. Be alert.

Everyone within the Keep was dead—of that much he was certain. All of the Druids, all of their guards, all who had lived and worked and studied here for so many years, all those he had left behind just four days ago. The shock of it was like a blow to the stomach; it took the wind and the strength from him and left him numb with disbelief. All dead. He had known it could happen, had believed it possible, had even seen the vision of it. But the reality was much worse. Bodies lay strewn everywhere, twisted in death. Some had died by the sword. Some had been torn apart. Some, he sensed, had been taken to the lower depths of the Keep and killed there. But none had survived. No heartbeat reached his ears. No voice called. No living thing stirred. Paranor was a charnel house. It was a tomb.

He worked his way through the echoing corridors to the Assembly and there found Athabasca, his face frozen with the moment of his death, his corpse a sad and ruined thing. Bremen stooped to look for the Eilt Druin and did not find it. He straightened and paused. He felt only sadness for the High Druid, only regret. Seeing him thus, seeing all of them dead and the castle of the Druids empty, made him wish he had tried harder in his efforts to persuade them of the danger. Guilt washed through him. He could not help himself. He was in some way to blame for this. His was the knowledge and the power, and he had failed to use either in a convincing way. This was the result. He drew Athabasca's robes across his face and walked away.

He climbed then to the library, keeping his back to the wall as he moved through the castle's dead shell, listening for the betraying sounds of danger, cautious and alert. It was here, the danger of which Caerid Lock and the vision both had warned. The traitor Druids, in some form, waiting. So be it. But the Warlock Lord was gone, and his creatures with him. The cauldron of magic that had been stirred with their coming—Bremen's trip wire set in place within the Druid Well—had bubbled and boiled just enough to cause them to fear and to persuade them not to linger. Listening, he could hear it now, a faint hiss, the magic sunk back within the pit, the magic that gave life to the Keep, that gave power to most of the Druid spells. Vast and mercurial, it gave back only a portion of what it promised, and that so small it paled in the face of Brona's monstrous power. Still, it had served its purpose this once, driving the rebel Druid from the Keep.

Bremen sighed. There was no pleasure to be taken from so small a victory. Brona had his revenge, and that was what mattered. He had destroyed those who had opposed him, who would have challenged him, and he had savaged their safehold. Now there was no one to stop him save one old man and a handful of followers.

Perhaps. Perhaps.

He reached the library and found Kahle Rese. He cried silently on seeing him, unable to help himself. He covered his old friend as well, unable to look upon him more than once, and went through the hidden doorway to the room in which the Druid Histories were concealed. The room was empty of everything but the worktable and chairs, and the dust that Bremen had given Kahle as a last resort lay scattered on the floor, dull now and lifeless, evidence that it had been put to the use for which it was intended. Bremen tried momentarily to see Kahle in those last few moments of his life. He could not manage it. It was enough to know that the Druid Histories were safe. That would have to serve as his old friend's epitaph.

He heard something then, a sound that came from somewhere far below, a sound so soft that he detected it with his instincts rather than his ears. He hastened from the room, sensing that whatever time had been allotted him in Paranor was running out. He must find the Eilt Druin now. Locating the medallion was all that was left. Athabasca had not been wearing it. It might have been taken from his body, but Bremen did not think so. The attack had come at night, Caerid Lock had said, and no one had been ready. Athabasca would have been roused from his bed. He would not have taken time to put on the medallion. It was probably in his chambers.

Bremen climbed the stairs to the High Druid's office, a soundless, voiceless ghost among the dead. He felt as if he had no weight, no substance, no presence. He was inconsequential, a madman playing with fire and having no cure for the burns it was sure to inflict. He felt tired, lost to his fears for the world. It was such a hopeless task he had set himself—creating a magic, forging a talisman to contain it, finding a champion to wield it. What chance did he have to accomplish all this? What hope?

He found the door to Athabasca's rooms open and entered cautiously. He scanned the shelves and desktop without result. He opened doors to cabinets and files and found nothing. Fearful now that he had come too late even for the medallion, he hastened into the High Druid's bedchamber.

There, sprawled on a night table, forgotten in the rush that had carried Athabasca from his sleep to his death, was the Eilt Druin.

Bremen picked it up and examined it, making sure it was real. The burnished metal glimmered back at him. He ran his fingers over the raised surface of hand and burning torch. Then he tucked it quickly into his robes and hurried from the room.

He went down the corridors and stairs once more, still listening and watching, still wary. He had gotten this far without encountering anything. Perhaps he could slip past whatever had been set at watch. Cloud silent, he eased through the gloom and the dead, past shadows pooling in narrow corners and bodies flung through doorways and across stone floors. He caught sight suddenly of a faint brightening in the sky east, visible though tall, latticed glass windows. Night was fading, the dawn at hand. Bremen breathed deeply of the musty, stale air, and longed for the smell and taste of the green forest beyond.

He reached the main stairway and started down. He was midway between floors when he caught sight of movement on the broad landing below. He slowed, stopped, and waited. The movement detached itself from the shadows, a new kind of shadow, a different form. The thing that showed itself was human, but only vaguely. Arms, legs, torso, and head, all were covered in thick black hair, bristling and stiff, all crooked and bent like bramble wood, elongated and misshapen. There were claws and teeth that glimmered like the jagged ends of old bones, and eyes that flickered with bits of crimson and green. The thing whispered to him, called out to him, begged and wheedled with a wretchedness that was palpable.

Breeemen, Breeemen, Breeemen.

The old man glanced quickly to the upper landing, also visible within the wide, open stairwell, and another of the creatures appeared, a mirror image of the first, creeping from the gloom.

Breeemen, Breeemen, Breeemen.

Both came onto the stairs, one ascending, one descending. They had trapped him between them. There were no doors leading off, there was no way to go but up or down, past one or the other. They had waited him out, he realized. They had let him go about his business, let him collect what he chose, then closed in on him. The Warlock Lord had planned it thus, wanting to know what was important enough to bring him back, what treasure, what bit of magic could be precious enough to salvage. Find out, the Warlock Lord had ordered, then steal it from his lifeless body and bring it to me.

Bremen looked from one to the other. Druids once, these creatures, now altered into unspeakable things. Ravers, berserk-ers, beings stripped of their humanity and made over so that they might serve one last purpose. It was difficult to feel sorrow for them. They had been human enough when they had betrayed the Keep and its occupants. They had been free enough to choose then.

But there were supposed to be three, he realized suddenly. Where was the third?

Warned by a sixth sense, by instincts honed to a fine edge, he looked up just as it dropped from its hiding place in a stone niche in the stairwell wall. He flung himself aside, and it thudded to the stairs with a snapping of broken bones. Still, it didn't quit. It rose in a flurry of teeth and claws, shrieking and spitting, and launched itself at him. Bremen acted instinctively, throwing up the Druid fire that served as his defense in a blue curtain that engulfed the creature. Even then, it did not stop. It came on, burning, the black hair of its body flaring like a torch, the skin beneath peeling and melting away. Bremen struck at it again, frightened now, amazed that it could still stand. The thing careered into him, and he twisted away, falling back upon the stairs, kicking out in desperation.

Then, at last, the creature's strength failed. It lost its footing and tumbled away, rolling to the edge of the stairwell and dropping from view, a bright flare in the inky black.

Bremen lurched to his feet, singed by flames and raked by the creature's claws. The other two attackers continued their approach with slow, mincing steps, like cats at play. Bremen tried to call up his magic in defense, but he had exhausted himself defending against the first attack. Startled by its ferocity, he had used too much of his strength. Now he had almost nothing left.

The creatures seemed to know this. They eased smoothly toward him, mewling anxiously.

Bremen put his back to the stairwell wall and watched them come.

AS HE DID SO, Kinson and Mareth crept silently through the corridors of the Keep, searching for him. The dead lay everywhere, but there was no sign of the old man. Though they watched and listened for his passing, they could detect nothing.

Kinson was growing worried. If there was something evil hidden within the Keep, waiting for intruders, it might find them first. It might find them before they found Bremen, and Bremen would be forced to come to their rescue. Or had the Druid already fallen victim without their hearing? Were they already too late?

He should never have let Bremen go on alone!

They passed through the bodies of the Druid Guard who had made their last stand at the top of the stairs on the Keep's second level, and continued up. Still nothing showed itself. The stairs wound upward into the black, endless in number. Mareth was pressed against the wall, trying to get a better look at what lay ahead. Kinson kept glancing behind them, thinking an attack would come from there. His face and hands were slippery with sweat.

Where was Bremen?

Then something stirred on the next landing up, a faint altering of light, a detaching of shadows. Kinson and Mareth froze. An odd whispery wail drifted down to where they stood.

Breeemen, Breeemen, Breeemen.

They glanced at each other, then cautiously eased ahead.

Something dropped onto the stairs above them, a heavy body, too far away yet to see, but close enough to imagine. Blue fire exploded through the darkness. Shrieks rang out, and bodies thudded. Seconds later, a flaming ball hurtled over the edge of the stairs and fell past them, a living thing, if only barely, thrashing in agony as it crashed to the floor below.

Caution forgotten, Mareth and Kinson charged ahead. As they climbed, they caught sight of Bremen higher up on the stairs, trapped between two hideous creatures that were advancing on him from the landings above and below. The old man was bloodied and burned and clearly exhausted. Druid fire flared at his fingertips, but would not ignite. The creatures who stalked him were taking their time.

All three turned at the approach of the Borderman and the girl, startled.

"No! Go back!" Bremen cried on seeing them.

But Mareth raced up the stairs and onto the lower landing

with a sudden burst of speed, leaving a surprised Kinson be-hind. She planted her feet and hunched down within her cloth-ing like a coiled spring. Her hands came up, her arms stretched wide, and her palms turned upward as if to beseech help from the heavens. Kinson exhaled in dismay and rushed after her. What was she doing? The monster closest to the girl hissed in warning, whirled, and came at her, bounding down the stairs as swift as thought, claws extended. Kinson cried out in anger. He was still too far away!

Then Mareth simply exploded. There was a huge, booming cough, and the shock wave threw Kinson against the wall. He lost sight of Mareth, Bremen, and the creatures. Fire burst up-ward from where Mareth had been standing, a blue streak that burned white-hot. It ripped into the closest creature and tore it apart. Then it found the second, where it was closing on Bre-men, and bore it away, a leaf upon the wind. The creature shrieked in dismay and was consumed. The fire raced on, burn-ing along the stone walls and stairs, swallowing the air and turning it to smoke.

Kinson shielded his eyes and struggled to his feet. The fire disappeared, gone in an instant. Only the smoke remained, thick clouds of it filling the stairwell. Kinson charged up the steps and found Mareth collapsed on the landing. He lifted her, cradling her limp body. What had happened to her? What had she done? She was as light as a feather, her small features pale and streaked with soot, her short dark hair a damp helmet about her face. Her eyes were half-closed and staring. Through the slits, he could see they had turned white. He bent close. She didn't seem to be breathing. He couldn't find a pulse.

Bremen appeared abruptly before him, materializing out of the haze, disheveled and wild-eyed. "Take her out of here!" he shouted.

"But I don't think she's . . ." he tried to argue.

"Quick, Kinson!" Bremen cut him short. "Now, if you want to save her, get out of the Keep! Go!"

Kinson turned without a word and hastened down the stairs, Mareth in his arms, Bremen trailing in a ragged swirl of torn robes. Down through the Keep they stumbled, coughing and choking on the smoke, eyes tearing. Then Bremen heard something rumbling in the earth beneath. It was the sound of something waking, something huge and angry, something so vast it was unimaginable.

"Run!" Bremen cried once more, needlessly.

Together, the Borderman and the Druid fled through the smoky gloom of dead Paranor toward daylight and life.

THE

SEARCH

FOR THE

BLACK
ELFSTONE

CHAPTER

8

FTER LEAVING BREMEN, Tay Trefenwyd proceeded west along the Mermidon through the mountains that formed the southern arm of the Dragon's Teeth. Sunset arrived, and he camped for the night still within their shelter, then set out again at daybreak. The new day was clear and mild, last night's winds having swept the land clean, the sun dazzling. The Elf worked his way down out of the foothills to the grasslands below the Streleheim and prepared to cross. Ahead, he could see the forests of the Westland, and beyond, their tips coated in white, the peaks of the Rock Spur. Arborlon was another day's walk, so he traveled at a leisurely pace, his thoughts occupied by all that had happened since Bremen's arrival at Paranor.

Tay Trefenwyd had known Bremen for almost fifteen years, longer even than Risca. He had met him at Paranor, before his banishment, Tay newly arrived from Arborlon, a Druid in training. Bremen had been old even then, but with a harder edge to his personality and a sharper tongue as well. Bremen in those days had been a firebrand burning with truths self-evident to him but incomprehensible to everyone else. The Druids at Paranor had dismissed him as being just this side of mad. Kahle Rese and one or two others valued his friendship and listened patiently to what he had to say, but the rest mostly looked for ways to avoid him.

Not Tay. From the first moment they met, Tay had been mesmerized. Here was someone who believed it was important—even necessary—to do more than talk about the problems of the Four Lands. It wasn't sufficient simply to study and converse on issues; it was necessary to act on them as well. Bremen believed that the old ways were better, that the Druids of the First Council had been right in involving themselves in the progress of the Races. Noninvolvement was a mistake that would end up costing everyone dearly. Tay understood and believed. Like Bremen, he studied the old lore, the ways of the faerie creatures, and the uses of magic in the world before the Great Wars. Like Bremen, he accepted that power once subverted was twice as deadly, and that the rebel Druid Brona lived on in another form and would return again to subvert the Four Lands. It was an unpopular and dangerous view, and in the end it cost Bremen his place among the Druids.

But before that happened, he made an ally of Tay. The two formed an immediate bond, and the older man took the younger for his pupil, a teacher with a store of knowledge so vast that it defied cataloging. Tay did the tasks and completed the studies that were assigned him by the Council and his elders, but his spare time and enthusiasm were reserved almost exclusively for Bremen. Though exposed from an early age to the peculiar history and lore of their race, few of the Elves at Paranor who had taken up the Druid pledge were as open as Tay to the possibilities that Bremen suggested. But then, few were as talented. Tay had begun to master his magic skills even before he arrived at Paranor, but under Bremen's tutelage he progressed so rapidly that soon no one, save his mentor, was his equal. Even Risca, after his arrival, never reached the level that Tay attained, too wedded, perhaps, to his martial skills to embrace fully the concept that magic was an even more potent weapon.

Those first five years were exciting ones for the young Elf, and his thinking was shaped irrevocably by what he learned. Most of the skills he mastered and the knowledge he gained he kept secret, forced to do so by the Druid ban against personal involvement in the use of magic except as an abstract study. Bremen thought the ban foolish and misguided, but he was in the minority always, and at Paranor the Council's decisions governed all. So Tay studied privately the lore that Bremen was willing to share, keeping it close to his heart and concealed

from other eyes. When Bremen was exiled and chose to travel
west to the Elves to pursue his studies there, Tay asked to go,
too. But Bremen said no, not forbidding, but requesting that he
reconsider. Risca was of a like mind, but for both there were
more important tasks, the old man argued. Stay at Paranor and
be my eyes and ears. Work to master your skills and to persuade
others that the danger of which I have warned is real. When it
is time for you to leave, I will come back for you.

So he had, five days earlier—and Tay and Risca and the
young Healer Mareth had escaped in time. But the others, all
those he had tried to convince, all those who had doubted and
scorned, probably had not. Tay did not know for certain, of
course, but he felt in his heart that the vision Bremen had revealed to them had already come to pass. It would be days before the Elves could verify the truth, but Tay believed that the
Druids were gone.

Either way, his leaving with Bremen marked the end of his
time at Paranor. Whether the Druids were dead or alive, he
would not return now. His place was out in the world, doing
the things that Bremen had argued they must do if the Races
were to survive. The Warlock Lord had come out of hiding, revealed to those who had eyes to see and instincts to heed, and
he was coming south. The Northland and the Trolls were his already, and now he would attempt to subjugate the other Races.
So each of them—Bremen, Risca, Mareth, Kinson Ravenlock,
and himself—must be held accountable. Each must stand and
fight on what ground was given.

His was the Westland, his home. He was returning for
the first time in almost five years. His father had died in that
time. His younger brother had married and moved into the
Sarandanon. His sister's second child had been born. Lives had
changed while he was away, and he would be coming back into
a world different from the one he had left. More to the point,
he would be bringing change to it that dwarfed anything that
had occurred in his absence. It was the beginning of change for
all the lands, and there were many who would not welcome it.
He would not be well received when it was known why he had
come. He would have to approach things cautiously. He would
have to choose his friends and his ground well.

But Tay Trefenwyd was good at that. He was an affable, easygoing man who cared about the problems of others and had always done his best to give what help he could. He was not confrontational like Risca or stubborn like Bremen. While at Paranor, he had been genuinely well liked, even given his association with the other two. Tay was governed by strong beliefs and an unmatched work ethic, but he did not hold himself up to others as an example of how to be. Tay accepted people as they were, isolating what was good and finding ways to make use of it. Even Athabasca had not quarreled with him, seeing in Tay what he hoped was hidden even in the most troublesome of his friends. Tay's big hands were as strong as iron, but his heart was gentle. No one ever mistook his kindness for weakness, and Tay never let the first suggest the second. Tay knew when to stand his ground and when to yield. He was a conciliator and a compromiser of the first order, and he would need those skills in the days ahead.

He ran over the list of what he must accomplish, laying out each item, one by one.

He must persuade his king, Courtann Ballindarroch, to mount a search for the Black Elfstone.

He must persuade his king to send his armies in support of the Dwarves.

He must convince him that the Four Lands were about to be altered by circumstance and events in a way that would change them all irrevocably and forever.

He strode across the open grasslands thinking of what this meant, heading north and west toward the forestlands that marked the eastern boundary of his country, smiling easily, whistling a tune. He did not yet know how he was going to accomplish any of this, but that didn't matter. He would find a way. Bremen was counting on him. Tay did not intend to let him down.

The daylight hours slipped away, and the sun passed west into the distant mountains and disappeared. Tay left the Mermidon at the edge of the Westland forests below the Pykon and turned north. Because it was night and he could no longer see well on the flats, he stayed within the concealment of the trees as he continued on. His skills as a Druid aided him. Tay was an elementalist, a student of the ways in which magic and science interacted to balance the principal components of his world—earth, air, fire, and water. He had developed an understanding of their symbiosis, the ways in which they related to each other, the ways they worked together to maintain and further life, and the ways they protected each other when disturbed. Tay had mastered the rules for changing one to the other, for using one to destroy the other, for using any to give life to another. His talents had grown quite specialized. He could read movement and detect presence from the elements. He could sense thoughts. On a broad basis, he could reconfigure history and predict the future. It wasn't the same as having a vision. It wasn't linked to the dead or to the spiritual. It was tied instead to earth laws, to the power lines that encircled the world and tied all things together with linkage of acts and counteracts, of cause and effect, of choice and consequence. A stone thrown into a still pond produced ripples. So, too, everything that happened to shift the world's balance, no matter how small, resulted in change. Tay had learned to read those changes and to intuit what they meant.

So now, as he walked in the shadow of the forest night, he read in the movement of the wind and the smells still clinging to the trees and the vibrations borne on the surface of the earth that a large party of Gnomes had passed this way earlier and now waited somewhere ahead. He tasted their presence more strongly the farther along he went. He eased deeper into the trees, listening for them, reaching down periodically to touch the earth in search of their lingering body heat, the magic that served him rising within his chest in small, feathery trailers that flowed outward to his fingertips.

Then he slowed and went still, sensing something new. He held himself perfectly still, waiting. A chill settled deep inside, an unmistakable warning of what it was that he had sensed, of what it was that approached. A moment later it appeared in the sky overhead, just visible through breaks in the trees, one of the winged hunters, the Skull Bearers that served the Warlock Lord. It soared slowly, heavily across the velvet back, hunting, but not for anything in particular. Tay held himself in place, resisting the natural impulse to bolt, calming himself so that the other could not detect him. The Skull Bearer circled and came back, winged form hanging against the stars. Tay slowed his breathing, his heartbeat, his pulse. He disappeared into the still darkness of the forest.

Finally the creature moved on, flying north. To join those it commanded, Tay reasoned. It was not a good sign that the Warlock Lord's minions were this far south, daring to nudge up against the kingdom of the Elves. It strengthened the likelihood that the Druids were no longer perceived as a threat. It suggested that the long anticipated invasion of the Warlock Lord was at hand.

He took a deep breath and held it. What if Bremen had been wrong, and the invasion was to be directed not at the Dwarves, but at the Elves?

He mulled over the possibility as he proceeded on, still searching for the Gnomes. He found them twenty minutes later, camped within the fringe of Drey Wood. There were no fires in the camp and sentries at every turn. The Skull Bearer circled overhead. A raiding party of some sort, but Tay could not imagine what they were after. There was not much to raid this close to the grasslands save a few isolated homesteads, and the intruders would hardly be interested in those. Still, it was not comforting to find Eastland Gnomes, let alone a Skull Bearer, this far west and so close to Arborlon. He eased ahead until he could see them clearly, watched them for a time to see if he could detect anything, failed in his attempt, took a careful head count, and eased away again. He retraced his steps a safe distance, found a secluded stand of fir, crawled beneath the sheltering boughs, and fell asleep.

It was morning when he woke, and the Gnomes were gone. He checked carefully for them from within his shelter, then emerged and walked to their camp. Their footprints led west into Drey Wood. The Skull Bearer had gone with them.

He debated going after them, then decided against it. He had enough to deal with at this point without taking on anything else. Besides, where there was one raiding party there were likely others, and it was important to alert the Elves to their presence as quickly as possible.

So Tay continued north, staying back within the trees, his

long strides eating up the distance. It was not yet noon when he reached the Valley of Rhenn and turned west down its long, broad corridor. The Rhenn was the doorway to Arborlon and the west, and the Elves would be at watch at its far end. The eastern exposure was inviting, a gentle stretch of grasslands spread between two clusters of low foothills. But the valley quickly narrowed, the floor sloped upward, and the hills rose to become steep bluffs. By the time you reached the other end, you were looking into the jaws of a vise. The Rhenn provided the Elves with a natural defensive position against an army approaching from anywhere east. Because the forests were thick and the terrain mountainous coming down from the north or up from the south, the Rhenn was the only way into or out of the Westland for any sizable force.

It was always guarded, of course, and Tay knew that he would be met. He didn't have long to wait. He was barely halfway down the valley's green corridor when Elven horsemen thundered out of the pass ahead to challenge him, reining in with shouts of recognition as they neared. The riders knew him, and he was greeted warmly. He was given a horse and taken up through the pass to the Elven camp, where the watch commander sent word of his coming to Arborlon. He told the commander about the raiding party, mentioning the Gnomes but not the Skull Bearer, preferring to save that information for Ballindarroch. The commander had received no report of Gnomes and immediately dispatched riders south to make a search. The commander then ordered food and drink for Tay and sat with him while he ate, answering his questions about Arborlon and bringing him up to date on events about which he asked.

The talk was casual and passed quickly. There were rumors of Troll movements on the Streleheim, but nothing definite. No sightings had been reported this far south. Tay avoided mention of anything concerning the Warlock Lord or Paranor. When he was done with his meal, he asked to go on. The commander provided him with a horse and a two-man escort. He accepted the former, declined the latter, and was on his way once more.

He rode from the valley toward Arborlon, lost in thought. Rumors, no sightings. Ghosts and shadows. The Warlock Lord was as elusive as smoke. But Tay had seen the Skull Bearer and the Gnomes, and Bremen had seen the Warlock Lord at his safehold in the Northland, and they were real enough. Bremen seemed certain of what was about to happen, so now it was up to Tay to find a way to persuade the Elves that it was so.

The road he followed wound through the Westland forests with serpentine precision, avoiding the thick stands of old growth, sidling past small lakes and along winding streams, rising and falling with the lay of the land. Sunlight dappled the woods, streaking the tall trunks and stands of tiny wildflowers, long fingers of light amid the shadows. Like banners and pennants, they welcomed Tay Trefenwyd home again. The Elf shrugged off his cloak in response, feeling the sun fall like a warm mantle across his broad shoulders.

He encountered other travelers on the roadway, men and women journeying between villages and homes, traders and craftsmen bound for jobs in other places. Some nodded or waved in greeting; some simply passed him by. But all were Elves, and he had not been in a place where the people were his own for a long time. It seemed strange to him now—so many like himself and no others.

He was nearing Arborlon in the languid, slow hours of mid-afternoon, the heat of the late spring day heavy and insistent even within the cool forest, when a horseman appeared ahead of him. The newcomer rode out of a shimmer of light at the crest of a rise and bore down on him at a gallop, his cloak whipping and his hair blowing. One hand waved vigorously and a riotous cry of greeting broke the silence. Tay knew him at once. A huge smile widened on his face, and he waved back eagerly, spurring his own mount ahead. The two met in a swirling cloud of dust, reining in their horses and jumping down, racing to embrace each other.

"Tay Trefenwyd, as I live and breathe!"

The newcomer wrapped his arms around the tall, lanky Tay and lifted him like a child, swinging him once about and then setting him down again with a grunt.

"Shades!" he roared. "You must do nothing but eat while you're away! You're as heavy as any horse!"

Tay clasped his best friend's hand. "It isn't me who's grown heavy! It's you who's grown weak! Layabout!"

The other's hand tightened in response. "Welcome home, anyway. I have missed you!"

Tay stepped back for a good, long look. Like all those he had left behind in Arborlon, it had been five years since he had seen Jerle Shannara. He had missed Jerle the most, he supposed, even more so than the members of his family. For this was his oldest friend, his constant companion while they were boys growing up together in the Westland, the one person to whom he could tell anything, the one to whom he would entrust his life. The bonds had been formed early and had survived even the years the two had spent apart while Tay was at Paranor and Jerle had remained behind, Courtann Ballindarroch's first cousin, his service to the throne predetermined from his birth.

Jerle Shannara was born a warrior. He was physically imposing for an Elf, big and strong-limbed, with cat-quick reflexes that belied his size, and a fighter's instincts. He was training with weapons almost from the time he could walk, in love with combat, enthralled by the excitement and challenge of battle. But there was a great deal more to him than strength and size. He was quick. He was cunning. He was a relentless adversary. His work ethic was prodigious. He never expected less from himself than the best he had to offer, no matter the importance of the task, no matter if anyone was there to see. But most important of all, Jerle Shannara was fearless. It was in his blood or in the way he grew or perhaps in both, but Tay had never known his friend to back down from anything.

They made an odd pair, he reflected. Of similar size and look, both larger than average, blond and long-limbed, and reared with high expectations from their families, they were nevertheless entirely different. Tay was easygoing and always the compromiser in difficult situations; Jerle was quick-tempered and confrontational and maddeningly unwilling to back down in any dispute. Tay was cerebral, intrigued by difficult questions and complicated puzzles that challenged and confused; Jerle was physical, preferring the challenge of sports and combat, relying on quick answers and intuition. Tay always knew he wanted to travel and study with the Druids at Paranor; Jerle always knew he wanted to become Captain of the Home Guard, the elite unit of Elven Hunters that protected the king and his family. They were different personalities with different intents and goals, yet something of who and what they were bound them together as surely as ties of blood or the dictates of fate.

"So you're back," Jerle announced, releasing Tay and stepping clear. He brushed at his curly blond hair with one massive hand and gave his friend a rakish smile. "Have you come to your senses at last? How long will you stay?"

"I don't know. But I won't be going back to Paranor. Things have changed."

The other's smile dimmed. "Is that so? Tell me about it."

"All in good time. But let me do it in my own way. I am here for a specific purpose. Bremen sent me."

"Then it must be serious, indeed." Jerle knew the Druid from his time in Arborlon. He paused. "Does it involve this creature they call the Warlock Lord?"

"You were always quick. Yes, it does. He marches south with his armies to attack the Dwarves. Did you know?"

"There are rumors of Troll movement on the Streleheim. We thought they might march west against us."

"The Dwarves first, you later. I am sent to persuade Courtann Ballindarroch to send the Elves to lend their support. I will need help in this, I expect."

Jerle Shannara reached for his horse's reins. "Let's move off the roadway and sit in the shade while we talk. Do you mind if we don't continue on to the city just yet?"

"I would rather speak to you alone, first."

"Good. You look more like your sister every time I see you." They walked their mounts into the trees and tied them to a slender ash. "That's a compliment, you know."

"I do." Tay smiled. "How is she?"

"Happy, settled, content with her family." Jerle gave him a wistful look. "She did well enough without me, after all."

"Kira was never for you. You know that as well as I. Look at how you live. What would you do in her life? What would she do in yours? You have nothing in common but your childhood."

Jerle snorted. "That's true of us as well, yet we remain close."

"Close is not married. And it's different with us."

Tay settled himself on the grass, long legs folded before him. Jerle hunkered down on a stump worn smooth by time and weather and looked at his boots as if he had never seen them before. His sun-browned hands were crisscrossed with white scars and small red nicks and scratches. Tay could not remember a time when they hadn't looked like that.

"Are you still Captain of the Home Guard?" he asked his friend.

Jerle shook his head. "I'm considered too important for that these days. I am Courtann's chief advisor in military matters. His de facto general, second-guessing all the real generals. Not that it matters much just now, since we're not at war with anyone. But I suppose all that could change, couldn't it?"

"Bremen believes that the Warlock Lord will attempt to subjugate the other Races, beginning with the Dwarves and then moving on. The Troll army is powerful. If the Races do not join together to stand against it, they will be overwhelmed, one by one."

"But the Druids won't let that happen. Moribund as they are these days—no offense, Tay—they wouldn't stand still for that."

"Bremen thinks that Paranor has fallen and the Druids have been destroyed."

Jerle Shannara straightened slightly, his mouth tightening in response to the news. "When did this happen? We've heard nothing."

"A day or two ago at most. Bremen went back to Paranor to make certain, but sent me to Arborlon, so I can't be sure. It would help if you would send someone to see if it's true before I speak with the king. Someone dependable."

"I will do that." The other shook his head slowly. "All the Druids are gone? All of them?"

"All but Bremen, myself, a Dwarf named Risca, and a young woman from Storlock who is still in training. We left Paranor together before the attack. Maybe someone else escaped later."

Jerle gave him a sharp look. "So you've come back to warn us, to tell us of Paranor's fall and to ask for help against the Warlock Lord and his Troll armies?"

"And one thing more. One very important thing. This is

where I need your help the most, Jerle. There is a Black Elf-stone, a magic of great power. This Elfstone is more dangerous than all the others, and it has been hidden since the time of faerie in the Breakline. Bremen has uncovered clues as to where it might be found, but the Warlock Lord and his creatures search for it as well. We must find it first. I intend to ask the king to mount an expedition. But he might be more disposed to grant the request if it came from you."

Jerle laughed, a big, booming howl. "Is that what you think? That I can help? I wouldn't stand too close to me if I were you! I've stepped on Courtann's toes a time or two of late, and I don't think he holds me in very high regard at the moment! Oh, he likes my advice on troop movement and defensive strategy well enough, but that is about as far as it goes!" His laugh died away, and he wiped at his eyes. "Ah, well, I'll do what I can." He chuckled. "You make life interesting, Tay. You always did."

Tay smiled. "Life makes itself interesting. Like you, I'm just along for the ride."

Jerle Shannara reached across, and they clasped hands once more, holding the grip firm for a long moment. Tay could feel the other's great strength, and it seemed as if he could draw from it something of his own.

Still maintaining the grip, he rose to his feet and pulled his friend up with him. "We had better get started," he advised.

The other nodded, and the smile he offered was bold and confident and filled with mischief. "You and me, Tay," he said. "The two of us, just like it used to be. This is going to be fun."

He meant something else entirely, of course, but Tay Trefenwyd supposed he understood.

CHAPTER

9

ONCE ARRIVED IN ARBORLON, Tay spent his time visiting with family and friends while he waited impatiently for confirmation from Jerle Shannara that Paranor and the Druids had fallen. His friend reassured him on parting that someone would be sent at once to discover if Bremen's suspicions were correct. When that was done, a meeting with the Elf King, Courtann Ballindarroch, and the Elven High Council would be arranged. Tay would be given a chance to make his plea for help for the Dwarves and for a search for the Black Elfstone. Jerle promised to stand with him. For now, neither would say or do anything further about the matter.

This was difficult for Tay, who recalled vividly the urgency in Bremen's admonition to seek Ballindarroch's help. The old man's voice whispered to him in the scrape of shoes on loose stone, in the voices of strangers he could not see, and even in his dreams. But Bremen did not himself appear or send news of any sort, and Tay knew that there was nothing to be gained by speaking out until word of Paranor's condition had been received. Formal announcement of Ballindarroch's pleasure at hearing of his return arrived almost at once, but no summons to appear before the king or High Council accompanied it. By all but Jerle Shannara, Tay's return to Arborlon was thought to be solely a visit to family and friends.

Tay stayed in the home of his parents, both grown old now, concerned mostly with the passing of the days and the welfare of their children. His parents asked him of his life at Paranor, but tired easily and did not press him for details when he gave his answers. Of the Warlock Lord and his Skull Bearers, they knew nothing. Of the Troll army, they had heard only rumors. They lived in a small cottage at the edge of the Gardens of Life along the Carolan, and their days were spent working in their tiny garden and at their individual crafts, his father's screen painting and his mother's weaving. They spoke to him while they worked, taking turns at asking questions, absorbed in their efforts, listening with half an ear. Small, brittle, fading away before his eyes, they reminded him of the frailty of his own life, the one he had assumed until so recently to be secure.

Tay's brother and family lived in the Sarandanon, miles to the west and south, and so Tay learned what he could of them from his parents. He had never been close to his brother and had not seen him in more than eight years, but he listened dutifully and was pleased to hear that he was doing well with his farming.

His sister Kira was another matter. She lived in Arborlon, and he went to see her on his first day home, finding her wrestling clothes onto her smallest child, her face still young and fresh, her energy still boundless, her smile as warm and heartbreaking as birdsong. She came to him with a welcoming laugh, flinging herself into his arms and hugging him until he thought he might explode. She took him into the kitchen and gave him cold ale, sitting him down at the old trestle bench, asking him of his life and telling him of hers, all at once. They shared concerns about their parents, and swapped stories of their childhood, and it was dark before they knew it. They met again the following day, and with Kira's husband and the children went into the woods along the Rill Song for a picnic. Kira asked if he had seen Jerle Shannara yet, and then did not mention him again. The hours slipped away, and Tay was almost able to forget he had come home for any other reason. The children played games with him, tired eventually, and sat on the riverbank kicking their feet in the cold water while he talked with their parents of the ways in which the world was changing. His brother-in-law was a maker of leather goods and traded regularly with the other Races. He no longer sent his traders into the Northland, now that the nations had been subjugated and made one. There were rumors, he said, of evil creatures, of winged monsters and dark shades, of beasts that would savage humans and Elves alike. Tay listened and nodded and affirmed that he had heard the rumors, too. He tried not to look at Kira too closely when he spoke. He tried not to let her see what was in his eyes.

He saw old friends as well, some of whom had been barely grown when he had seen them last. Some had been close once. But they had traveled down different roads, and all had gone too far to turn back. Or perhaps it was he who had gone too far. They were strangers now, not in appearance or voice, for those were still familiar, but in choices made that long since had shaped their lives. He shared nothing with them but memories of what had once been. It was sad, but not surprising. Time stole away commitments and loosened ties. Friendships were reduced to tales of the past and vague promises for the future, neither strong enough to recover what was lost. But that was what life did—it took you down separate roads until one day you found yourself alone.

Arborlon seemed strange as well, though not in a way he would have expected. Physically, it was the same, a village grown into a city, full of excitement and expectation, become the crossroads of the Westland. Twenty years of steady growth had made it the largest and most important city in the northern half of the known world. The conclusion of the First War of the Races had altered irrevocably the role of the Elven people in the future of the Four Lands, and with the decline of the Southland as a major influence, Arborlon and the Elves had become increasingly important. But while the city and its surroundings were familiar to Tay, even with his long absence and infrequent visits, he could not escape the feeling that he no longer belonged. This was not his home now; it hadn't been for the better part of fifteen years, and it was too late to change that. Even if Paranor was destroyed and the Druids gone, he was not sure he could ever come back. Arborlon was a part of his past, and somehow he had grown beyond it. He was a stranger here, as much as he tried to convince himself otherwise, and it made him feel awkward when he tried to fit in again.

How quickly everything slipped away when you weren't

paying attention, he thought more than once in his first few days back. How swiftly your life changed.

On the fourth day of his return, Jerle Shannara came to him in the late-afternoon hours accompanied by Preia Starle. Tay hadn't seen Preia yet, although he had wondered about her more than once. She was easily the most astonishing woman he had ever known, and if she hadn't been in love with Jerle for as far back as anyone could remember but had been in love with Tay instead, he might have changed his life for her. She was beautiful, with small, perfect features, cinnamon hair and eyes to match, a dusky tone to her skin that glowed like the surface of water caught in a sunrise, and a body that curved and flowed with the grace and supple ease of a cat's. That was Preia at first glance, but it didn't begin to tell you about her. Preia was as much a warrior as Jerle, trained as a Tracker, skilled at her chosen craft beyond anyone Tay had ever known, tough and steady and as certain as sunrise. She could track a ferret in a swamp. She could tell you the size and number and sex of a herd of goats crossing rocks. She could live out in the wilderness for weeks on literally nothing but what she scavenged. She disdained to follow the life most Elven women chose, forsaking the comforts of a home and the companionship of a husband and children. Preia was distanced from all that. She was happy enough with the life she was leading, she had told Tay once. Those other things would come to her when Jerle was ready for them. Until then, she would wait.

Jerle, for his part, was content to let her. He was ambivalent, Tay thought, about what he felt for her. He loved her in his way, but it was Kira that he had loved first and best and was unable to forget, even after all these years. Preia must have known that—she was too smart to miss it—but she never said anything. Tay had expected their relationship to have changed since his last visit, but it did not appear that it had. There had been no mention of Preia in his conversations with Jerle. Preia was still standing outside the gates of the fortress of self-sufficiency and independence that Jerle Shannara had erected around himself, waiting to be let in.

She came to Tay with a smile as he looked up from the

Westland maps he was studying at a small table in his parents' garden. He rose to meet her, his throat tightening at the sight of her, and he bent to receive her welcoming embrace and kiss.

"You look well, Tay," she greeted, stepping back to view him more closely, hands resting lightly on his arms.

"Better, now that I'm seeing you," he replied, surprising himself with the boldness of his response.

Preia and Jerle took him from the house to the Carolan, where they could talk privately. They sat at the edge of the Gardens of Life, looking out across the bluff to the tips of the tall trees beyond the Rill Song. Jerle had chosen a circular bench that allowed them to face each other and close out the distractions of passersby. He had said almost nothing since he had come for Tay, his look distant and preoccupied, and he faced Tay squarely now for the first time.

"Bremen was right," he said. "Paranor has fallen. All the Druids within are dead. If any escaped besides those who went with you, they are in hiding."

Tay stared at him, letting the weight of the announcement settle in, then glanced at Preia. There was no surprise in her face. She already knew.

"You sent Preia to Paranor?" he asked quickly, suddenly realizing why she was there.

"Who better?" Jerle asked matter-of-factly. And he was right. Tay had asked him to send someone dependable, and there was no one more dependable than Preia. But it was a dangerous task, filled with personal risk, and Tay would have chosen someone else. It pointed up the difference in their feelings for Preia, he realized. But it did not make his the more noble.

"Tell him what you saw," Jerle urged her quietly.

She faced Tay, her coppery eyes soft and reassuring. "I crossed the Streleheim without incident. There were Trolls, but no sign of the Gnomes and Skull Bearer you saw. I entered the Dragon's Teeth at dawn on the second day and went directly to the Keep. The gates were open and there was no life within. I entered without challenge. All the guards lay slaughtered, some by weapons, some by claws and teeth, as if animals had gotten them. The Druids lay within, all of them dead. Some had been killed in battle. Some had been dragged from the Assembly and taken to the cellars and walled away. I was able to read their passage and find their tombs."

She paused, seeing the look of horror and sadness that crept into his eyes as he remembered those he had left behind. One slender hand closed on his own. "There were signs of a second battle as well, one fought on the stairs leading up from the main entry. This one happened more recently, several days after the other. Several creatures were destroyed, things I could not identify. Magic was used. The entire stairwell was seared black by it, as if a fire had burned it clean, leaving only the ashes of the dead."

"Bremen?" he asked.

She shook her head. "I don't know. Perhaps." Her hand tightened over his. "Tay, I'm sorry."

He nodded. "Even knowing it these few days past, even preparing myself to accept it, it is still difficult hearing you speak the words. All dead. All those I worked and lived with for so many years. Maybe even Bremen. It makes me feel hollow inside."

"Well, it's over and done, and there's no help for it." Jerle was ready to move on. He rose. "We must speak with the Council now. I will go to Ballindarroch and set a meeting. He may fuss a bit, but I will find a way to make him listen. Meanwhile, Preia can tell you anything else you need to know. Be strong, Tay. We will have our own back from them in the end."

He strode off without looking back, finding purpose in action as always. Tay watched him go, then looked at Preia. "How have you been?"

"Good." She regarded him quizzically. "You were surprised I went to Paranor, weren't you?"

"Yes. It was a selfish reaction."

"But a nice one." She smiled. "I like having you home, Tay. I missed being with you. You were always interesting to talk to."

He stretched his long legs and looked out across the Carolan to where a unit of Black Watch were moving toward the Gardens. "Less so now, I'm afraid. I don't know what to say anymore. I am back four days and already thinking of leaving. I feel rootless."

"Well, you've been away a long time. It must seem strange."

"I don't think I belong here anymore, Preia. Maybe I don't belong anywhere, now that Paranor is gone."

She laughed softly. "I know that feeling. Only Jerle never has those doubts because he won't let himself. He belongs where he wants to belong; he makes himself fit in. I can't do that."

They were silent a moment. Tay tried not to look at her.

"You will be going west in a few days when the king gives you leave to search for the Stone," she said finally. "Maybe you will feel better when you do that."

He smiled. "Jerle told you."

"Jerle tells me everything. I am his life companion, even if he doesn't acknowledge it."

"He is a fool not to."

She nodded absently. "I will be coming with you when you go."

Now he looked directly at her. "No."

She smiled, enjoying his discomfort. "You can't tell me that, Tay. No one can. I don't allow it."

"Preia . . ."

"It is too dangerous, it is too hard a journey, it is too something or other." She sighed, but the sound did not chide. "I have heard it all before, Tay—although not from anyone who cares about me like you do." She met his gaze. "But I will be going with you."

He shook his head in admiration and smiled in spite of himself. "Of course. And Jerle won't object, will he?"

Her smile was dazzling, her face bright with undisguised pleasure. "No. He doesn't know yet, you understand, but when he does he will shrug like he always does and tell me I am welcome." She paused. "He accepts me for who I am better than you do. He treats me as an equal. Do you understand?"

Tay shifted on the bench, wondering if he did. "I think he is very lucky to have you," he said. He cleared his throat. "Tell me a little more about what you found at Paranor, anything you think might be of interest, anything you think I might want to know."

She tucked her legs beneath her on the bench, as if to ward off the unpleasantness of the words she must speak, and did so.

* * *

WHEN PREIA LEFT HIM, he remained sitting for a time trying to picture the faces of the Druids he would never see again. Strangely enough, his memory of some was already beginning to fade. It worked like that, he supposed, even with those that mattered most.

It was approaching evening, and he rose and walked along the edge of the Carolan and watched the sunset, the sky coloring gold and silver as the light faded toward darkness. He waited until torches began to brighten the city behind him, then turned and walked back toward his parents' home. He felt alienated, disconnected. Paranor's destruction and the death of the Druids had cut him loose from his moorings, leaving him adrift. All that remained for him was to fulfill Bremen's admonition to seek out the Black Elfstone, and he was determined to do that. Then he would start his life over again. He wondered if he could do that. He wondered where he would begin.

He was approaching his destination when a king's messenger stepped out of the shadows and advised him that he was to come at once. The urgency of the summons was apparent, so Tay did not argue. He turned from the pathway and followed the messenger back toward the Carolan and the palace that housed the king and his considerable family. Courtann Ballindarroch was the fifth of his line, and the size of the royal family had grown larger with each new coronation. Now the palace housed not only the king and queen, but five children and their spouses, more than a dozen grandchildren, and numerous aunts, uncles, and cousins. Among them was Jerle Shannara, although he spent most of his time at the Home Guard quarters, where he felt decidedly more comfortable.

The palace came in sight, a blaze of light against the darker backdrop of the Gardens of Life. But as they neared the front entry, the messenger took him left down a pathway that led to the summerhouse at one end of the compound. Tay glanced across the broad, dark sweep of the grounds, searching for the Home Guard that kept watch. He could sense them, could count their numbers if he chose by using his magic, but could see nothing. Inside the palace, framed against the lighted windows, shadows came and went like faceless wraiths. The messenger showed no interest, directing him past the main house to where Ballindarroch had chosen to receive him. Tay wondered at the abruptness of the summons. Had something new occurred? Had there been another tragedy? He forced himself not to speculate, but to wait for his answer.

The messenger took him directly to the front door of the summerhouse and told him to go inside. He entered alone, passed through the foyer to the living area beyond, and found Jerle Shannara waiting.

His friend shrugged and held up his hands helplessly. "I have no more idea than you. I was summoned, and here I am."

"You told the king what we know?"

"I told him you needed an immediate audience with the High Council, that you had urgent news. Nothing more."

They stared at each other, speculating on the matter. Then the front door opened, and Courtann Ballindarroch appeared. Tay wondered where he had come from—if he had walked down from the main house or had been listening outside the window in the gardens. Courtann was unpredictable. Physically, he was a man of average height and build, comfortably middle-aged, slightly stooped, graying a bit at the temples and along the edges of his beard, a series of deep creases beginning to show in his face and neck. There was nothing distinctive about Courtann; he looked very ordinary. He did not have an orator's voice or a leader's charm, and he was quick to admit confusion when beset by it. He had become king in the usual fashion, the eldest child of the previous king, and he neither sought power nor shied away from it. What he brought with him to his rule as leader of the Elves was a reputation of not being given to unexpected or outrageous behavior, of not being inclined to dramatic or precipitous change, so that he was accepted by his people in the manner of a favorite uncle.

"Welcome home, Tay," he greeted. He was smiling and relaxed and did not seem at all distressed as he came up to the younger man and clasped his hand. "I thought we might discuss your news in private before you present it to the High Council." He ran his hand through his thick shock of hair. "I prefer to keep surprises at a minimum in my life. And, should you need an ally, perhaps I might serve. No, don't look to your confidant—he hasn't said a word. Even if he had, I wouldn't listen to him. Too unreliable. Jerle is here only because I have never known either of you to keep secrets from the other, so there probably isn't much point in trying to start now."

He beckoned. "Let's sit over here, in these padded chairs. My back has been bothering me. Grandchildren will do that to you. And let's not be formal. First names will do. We've all known each other too long for anything else."

It was true, Tay thought, seating himself across from the king and next to Jerle. Courtann Ballindarroch was older by a good twenty years, but they had been friends for their entire lives. Jerle had always lived at court, and Tay had spent much of his time there and so had seen much of Courtann. When they were boys, Courtann had taken them fishing and hunting. Special events and feasts had often brought them together. Tay had been present when Courtann had been crowned some thirty years ago. Each of them knew what to expect from the other.

"I am afraid I was skeptical from the first that you had returned for no better reason than to visit us," the king advised with a sigh. "You have always been much too directed to squander a visit home on social pleasures. I hope you don't take offense." He rocked back. "So what news do you have for us? Come now, let's have it all."

"There is a great deal to tell," Tay replied, leaning forward to better hold the other's gaze. "Bremen sent me. He came to Paranor almost two weeks ago and tried to warn the Druid Council that they were in danger. He had gone into the Northland and confirmed the existence of the Warlock Lord. He had determined that it was the rebel Druid Brona, still alive after several hundred years, kept so by the magic that had subverted him. It was Brona who found a way to unite the Trolls and subjugate them so that they would serve as his army. Before traveling to Paranor, Bremen tracked that army south toward the Eastland."

He paused to choose his words carefully. "The Druid Council would not listen. Athabasca sent Bremen away, and a handful of us went with him. Caerid Lock was asked to come as well, but declined. He stayed behind to protect Athabasca and the others against themselves."

"A good man," the king advised. "Very able."

"With Bremen leading us, we went to the Valley of Shale. There, at the Hadeshorn, Bremen spoke with the spirits of the dead. I watched him do so. They told him several things. One was that Paranor and the Druids would be lost. Another was that the Warlock Lord would invade the Four Lands, and that a talisman must be constructed to destroy him. A third concerned the location of a Black Elfstone, a magic the Warlock Lord searches for, but that we must find first. When the spirits of the dead departed, Bremen sent the Druid Risca to warn the Dwarves of their danger. He sent me to warn you. I was instructed to persuade you to bring your army east across the Borderlands to join forces with the Dwarves. Only by combining our strength can we defeat the Warlock Lord's army. I was also instructed to request help in undertaking a search for the Black Elfstone."

Ballindarroch was no longer smiling. "You are being very candid in relating all this," the king advised, not bothering to hide his surprise. "I would have expected you to take a more subtle approach in seeking my help."

Tay nodded. "That was my intention. And I would have done so if I were speaking to you before the High Council. But I am not. I am speaking to you alone. There are only the three of us present, and as you have pointed out we know each other well enough not to pretend at things."

"There is a better reason than that," Jerle interjected quickly. "Tell him, Tay."

Tay folded his hands before him, but did not drop his gaze. "I have waited until now to speak to you because I wanted to confirm Bremen's suspicions about Paranor and the Druids. I asked Jerle to send someone back to see what had happened, to make sure. He did so. He sent Preia Starle. She returned this afternoon and spoke to me. Paranor has indeed fallen. All the

Druids and those who guarded them are dead. Caerid Lock is gone. Athabasca is gone. There is no one left—no one, Courtann, who possesses the power necessary to stand against Brona."

Courtann Ballindarroch stared at him wordlessly, then rose, walked to the window, looked out into the night, walked back, and seated himself once more. "This is troubling news," he said quietly. "When you told me of Bremen's vision, I thought it would turn out to be a trick, a subterfuge, something other than the truth. Anything. All the Druids dead, you say? So many of them our own people? But they have always been there, for as long as history records. And now they are gone? All of them? I can hardly believe it."

"But they are gone," Jerle declared, not willing to let the king dither over the matter. "Now we need to act quickly to prevent the same thing from happening to us."

The Elf King rubbed his beard. "But not too quickly, Jerle. Let us think this through a moment. If I do as Bremen has asked and march the Elven army east, I leave Arborlon and the Westland undefended. That is a dangerous course of action. I know the history of the First War of the Races well enough to avoid its mistakes. Caution is necessary."

"Caution suggests delay, and we don't have time for that!" Jerle snapped.

The king fixed him with an icy glare. "Do not press me, cousin."

Tay could not risk an argument between them at this point. "What do you suggest, Courtann," he interjected quickly.

The king looked at him. He rose and walked to the window once more and stood with his back to them. Jerle glanced at Tay, but Tay did not acknowledge him. The matter was now between himself and the king. He waited for Courtann to turn back again, to cross the room and seat himself once more.

"I am convinced by everything you have told me, Tay, so do not look upon my response as a contradiction. I have great faith in Bremen's word. If he says that the Warlock Lord lives and is the rebel Druid Brona, then it must be so. If he says that the land's magic is being pressed into evil's service, then it must be true. But I am a student of history, and I know that Brona was never a fool, and we must not assume that he will do what we expect. He surely knows that Bremen, if still alive, must try to stop him. He has eyes and ears everywhere. He may know what we intend, even before we intend it. We must make sure of what is needed before we act."

There was a moment's silence as his listeners absorbed his words. "What will you do then?" Tay asked finally.

Courtann smiled his fatherly smile. "Go with you before the High Council and give you my support, of course. The Council must be made to see the necessity of acting on your news. It should not be hard. The loss of Paranor and the Druids will be enough to persuade them, I think. Your request to go in search of the Black Elfstone will be approved at once, I expect. There is no reason to delay action on that. Of course your shadow, my cousin, will insist on going with you, and as you might suspect, I would prefer that he did."

He rose, and they stood up with him. "As for your second request, that our army march to the aid of the Dwarves, I must consider that a while longer. I will dispatch scouts to see what we can determine of the Warlock Lord's presence in the Four Lands. When they report back, and after I have thought this matter through and the High Council has had time to debate it, a decision will be made."

He paused, waiting for Tay's response. "I am grateful, my lord," Tay acknowledged quickly. In truth, it was more than he had expected.

"Then show it by making a strong argument to the Council." The king put his hand on Tay's shoulder. "They wait for us now in the Assembly. They will want to know that the time they gave up with their families this evening was in a good cause." He glanced at Jerle. "Cousin, you may come with us if you think you can manage to hold your tongue. Your voice is well respected in these matters, and we may require your insight. Agreed?"

Jerle nodded that it was. They went out of the summerhouse into the night and walked down to the Assembly. Members of the Home Guard materialized out of nowhere, front and back, dark shadows against the distant torchlight of the palace. The king didn't seem to notice them, humming softly as he walked, glancing at the stars with mild fascination. Tay was surprised, but pleased that the king had acted as quickly as he had. He breathed the night air, taking in the fragrance of jasmine and lilac, and gathered his thoughts for what lay ahead. He was already planning the trip west, thinking through what they would need, which routes they would choose, how they would proceed. How many should they be? A dozen should be sufficient. Enough to stay safe, but not so many as to draw attention. He was conscious of Jerle at his elbow, a large, impassive presence, lost in his own thoughts. It felt good to have him there, steady and reliable. It brought back memories of what had once been, when they were boys. There was always an adventure waiting to be undertaken then, a new cause to consider, a different challenge to be met. He had missed that, he guessed. It felt good having it back again. For the first time since his return, he thought he might be home.

He spoke that night before the High Council with a conviction and persuasiveness that surpassed anything of which he believed himself capable. All that Bremen had asked of him he accomplished. But it was Bremen himself, even absent, who made the difference. The old man was liked and respected in Arborlon, and during his time there he had won many friends with his work on the recovery of Elven history and magic. If he sought the help of the Elves, especially given the destruction of Paranor and the Druids, the Council would see that he got it. Permission was granted to mount a search for the Black Elfstone. A company would be formed under the joint leadership of Tay Trefenwyd and Jerle Shannara. Swift consideration was promised on the request for aid to the Dwarves. Support was strong and enthusiastic—more so than Courtann Ballindarroch had anticipated. The king, seeing the effect that Tay's words were having on the members of the Council, added his support as well, careful to stress that there were still questions to be resolved before aid could be sent to the Dwarves.

It was midnight when the High Council adjourned. Tay stood outside the Assembly and clasped hands with Jerle Shannara in silent congratulation. The king brushed past them with a smile and was gone. Overhead, the sky was pinpricked with stars, and the air about them was sweet and warm. Success was a heady intoxicant. Things had gone the way Tay had hoped, and he wished impulsively that he could get word of it to Bremen. Jerle was talking nonstop, flushed with excitement, anticipating the journey west, a new adventure to be undertaken, an escape from the boring routine of his court life in Arborlon.

In that moment of high jubilation, it felt to them both as if all things were possible and nothing could go wrong.

CHAPTER

10

HEN THE OTHERS HAD GONE and they were all that were left, Tay and Jerle walked up together from the Assembly to the palace. They took their time, still caught up in the euphoria of their success before the High Council, neither of them ready for sleep. The night was still, the city about them at peace, the world a place of dreams and rest. Torches flickered in doorways and at the intersections of roads, beacons against the onslaught of shadows made deeper by the fading of the moon south below the horizon. Buildings loomed out of the darkness like great beasts curled up in sleep. The trees of the forest lined the walkways and surrounded the Elven homes, sentinels standing shoulder to shoulder, motionless in the dark. It gave Tay, as his gaze wandered idly across the open spaces and through the shadows, an odd sense of comfort, as if he were being watched over and protected. Jerle talked on, working his way from subject to subject in eager consideration of the events that lay ahead, arms gesturing, laugh booming out. Tay let him go, swept along in his wake, detached enough that he could listen and still let his thoughts wander, thinking of how his past had come around to his present, of how perhaps what had been left behind could be reclaimed again.

"We will need horses to cross the Sarandanon," Jerle was musing. "But we can travel faster through the forest leading up to the valley, and then again once we are into the Breakline, if we are afoot. We'll have to pack differently for each portion of the journey, carry different provisions."

Tay nodded without answering. No answer was required.

"A dozen of us at the minimum, but perhaps two would be better. If we're forced to stand and fight, we can't be caught shorthanded." His friend laughed. "I don't know what I'm worried about. What would dare come against the two of us!"

Tay shrugged, looking down the walk to where the lights of the palace had come into view through the trees. "I am hopeful that we won't have to find out."

"Well, we'll be cautious, you can be sure. Leave quietly, stick to the cover of the trees, stay away from dangerous places. But . . ." He stopped and brought Tay about to face him. "Make no mistake—the Warlock Lord and his creatures will be hunting us. They know that even if Bremen did not escape the Druid's Keep, a handfull of his followers did. Quite possibly they suspect he penetrated their Northland safehold. They know we will be looking for the Black Elfstone."

Tay thought it over. "Expect the worst. That way we won't be surprised. Is that it?"

Jerle Shannara nodded, suddenly solemn. "That's it."

They started back up the path. "I'm not sleepy," the big man complained. He stopped again. "Where can we go for a glass of ale? One, to celebrate."

Tay shrugged. "The palace?"

"Not the palace! I hate the palace! All those parents and children rummaging about, family everywhere. No, not there. Your house?"

"My parents are asleep. Besides, I feel as much a stranger there as you do at the palace. How about the Home Guard barracks?"

Jerle beamed. "Done! A glass or two, then bed. We have much to talk about, Tay."

They walked on, glancing together at the palace as they passed. The downstairs was dark and the grounds quiet. There was no sign of movement anywhere. From an upstairs room, a single light burned behind a curtained window, a candle lit in a child's room to give promise of another morning.

From somewhere distant, a night bird cried out in a series of shrill calls that echoed forlornly before dying back into the silence.

Jerle slowed and stopped, bringing Tay up short with him. He stared at the palace.

"What is it?" Tay asked after a moment.

"I don't see any guards."

Tay looked. "Any guards where? I thought you weren't supposed to see them."

Jerle shook his head. "You aren't. But I am."

Tay stared with him, seeing nothing against the black of the buildings or across the tree-canopied sweep of the grounds. No shapes even vaguely human. He searched for movement and did not find any. Elven Hunters were trained to fade away. Home Guard were better still. But he should still be able to find them as easily as Jerle.

He used his magic then, a small sending that raked the whole of the palace enclosure from end to end, fingers of disclosure that picked at everything. There was movement now, discovered in his search, swift and furtive and alien.

"Something is wrong," he said at once.

Jerle Shannara started forward wordlessly, heading for the palace entry, picking up speed as he went. Tay went with him, a strange sense of dread welling up inside. He tried to give it definition, to place its source, but it slipped away from him, elusive and defiant. Tay searched the shadows to either side, finding everything suddenly black and secretive. His hands tested the air, the tips of his fingers releasing his Druid magic in a widening net. He felt the net close on something that twisted and squirmed and then darted away.

"Gnomes!" he exclaimed.

Jerle broke into a run, reaching down to his belt and yanking out his short sword, the blade gleaming faintly against the dark as it slipped free. Jerle Shannara never went anywhere without his weapons. Tay hurried to keep up. Neither of them spoke, falling in beside each other as they neared the front doors, glancing left and right warily, ready for anything.

The doors stood open. No light shone from within. From the walkway, it had been impossible to tell this. Jerle did not slow. He went through the doors in a crouch, sword held ready. Tay followed.

The hall stretched away before them like a cavernous tunnel. There were bodies everywhere, strewn about like sacks of old clothing, bloodied and still. Elven Hunters, slain to a man, but a scattering of Gnome Hunters as well. The floor was slick with their blood. Jerle motioned Tay to one side while he went to the other, and together they worked their way down the hall to the main rooms. The rooms were quiet and empty of life. The companions backtracked, moving swiftly toward the stairs leading up. Jerle did not speak, even now. He did not ask Tay if he wanted a weapon. He did not try to tell him what to do. He did not need to. Tay was a Druid and knew.

They went up the stairs like ghosts, listening to the silence, waiting for a betraying sound. There was none. They reached the upstairs landing and looked down the darkened corridors beyond. More guards lay dead. Tay was astonished. There had been no outcry of any kind! How could these men, these trained Elven Hunters, have died without sounding an alarm?

The hall branched both ways, burrowing into the darkness and angling off into the wings of the palace where the royal family slept within their bedrooms. Jerle glanced at Tay, eyes bright and hard, motioned him right, and went left himself. Tay glanced after his friend, crouched against the gloom like a moor cat, then turned swiftly away.

He moved ahead, hands clenched into fists, the magic called up and gathered within his palms like a hard pulse, waiting to be released. Fear mingled with horror. There were sounds now, small voices, sobs and little cries that went still almost as quickly as they came, and he raced toward them, heedless. Shadows moved in the hallway before him as he turned the corner to the back wing. Blades glinted wickedly, and gnarled forms came at him. Gnomes. He stopped thinking and simply reacted. His right hand lifted and opened, and the magic exploded into his attackers, picking them up and throwing them against the walls so hard that he could hear their bones snap. He went through them as if they were not there, past open doorways where the occupants lay sprawled in death—mothers, fathers, and children alike—to where the doors still stood closed and there might yet be hope.

A new clutch of attackers burst from hiding as he rushed past, flinging themselves onto him and bearing him to the floor.

Weapons rose and fell with desperate purpose, edges sharp and deadly. But he was a Druid, and his defenses were already in place. The blades slid off him as if come up against armor, and his hands fastened on the wiry bodies and threw them away. He was strong, even without his magic, and with his magic to aid him the Gnomes were no match. He was back on his feet almost immediately, his fire sweeping about him in a deadly arc, cutting apart those few still standing. New cries rose, and he went on, horror-stricken at what he knew was happening. An attack, a deadly strike against the whole of the Elven royal family. He knew immediately that it was the same band of Gnome Hunters he had encountered and bypassed on the plains below the Streleheim, that they were neither scouts nor foragers but assassins, and that somewhere close by was the Skull Bearer who led them.

He passed door after door of slain Ballindarrochs, large and small alike, killed in their sleep or immediately on waking. Once past the Home Guard, there was nothing to stop the Gnomes from completing their deadly mission. Tay hissed in frustration. Magic had been used in this. Nothing less would have gained the assassins entry without warning being given. Rage boiled through him. He reached another door and found the Gnomes within killing a man and woman they had backed against their bedroom wall. Tay threw his magic into the attackers and burned them alive. Cries rose up now as if in response, the warning he had wished for finally given, coming not from his wing, but from the other, where Jerle Shannara would be fighting as well.

He left the man and woman slumped against the wall and went on, unable to help them. There were only a few doors left. One, he realized suddenly, despairingly, was where Courtann Ballindarroch slept.

He went to that one first, desperate now, losing hope that he would be in time for anyone. He went past a closed door on his left and an open one on his right. Through the open door, a pair of Gnomes appeared, bloodied weapons raised, yellow eyes glinting, surprise revealed on their cunning faces. He gestured at them and they vanished in an explosion of fire, dead before they knew what was happening. Tay could feel his

strength diminished by the expenditure of power. He had not
been tested like this before, and he must be cautious. Bremen
had warned him more than once that use of the magic was
finite. He must hoard what remained for when it was truly
needed.

He saw now that the door to the king's bedroom was open
as well, cracked slightly from where it had been forced.

Tay did not hesitate. He rushed to the door and flung it
open with a crash, leaping inside. There were no lights in the
room, but broad windows set along the far wall let in a dull
glimmer from the street lamps below. Shadows rose up against
the hangings and drapes, distorted and grotesque. Courtann
Ballindarroch had been flung against a wall to one side. He lay
revealed in the half-light, his face and chest bloodied, one arm
bent horribly awry, his eyes open and blinking rapidly. The
Skull Bearer stood a dozen steps away, bent within the fold of
its leathery wings, hooded and caped. It had taken hold of the
queen, lifting her away from the tattered covers of the bed. Her
body was broken and lifeless, her eyes staring. The creature
flung her away as Tay appeared, a careless gesture, and wheeled
to face the Druid, hissing in challenge. Gnomes attacked as
well, coming out of the shadows, but Tay swatted them aside
like gnats and turned the full force of his power on their leader.
The Skull Bearer was caught unprepared, expecting perhaps another guard, another helpless victim. Tay's magic exploded into
the monster in a burst of fire that burned half its face away. The
Skull Bearer shrieked in rage and pain, clawing futilely at its
skin, then threw itself at Tay. Its speed was astonishing, and
now it was Tay who was surprised. The Skull Bearer slammed
into him before he could brace himself, thrust him aside, and
was out the door and gone.

Tay struggled to his feet, hesitated only a moment as he
glanced at Courtann Ballindarroch, then gave chase.

He went back down the darkened hallway, avoiding the
bodies of the dead and the slick of their blood, senses straining
to pick up the presence of other attackers. Ahead, the Skull
Bearer was a vague shadow lumbering through the gloom.
Shouts had risen from outside, and there was a thudding of
boots and a clash of weapons as Home Guard flooded the

grounds, arrived from their barracks in response to the alarm. Tay's pulse pounded in his ears as he ran. He threw off his cloak so that he could move more easily. At the bend in the hall, the Skull Bearer turned instinctively toward the opposite wing, avoiding the knot of Elven Hunters who rushed up the stairway. Tay called down to his countrymen as he raced past, summoning their help.

He called as well for Jerle Shannara.

The Skull Bearer glanced back, disfigured features a sodden, red mess in a sudden glimmer of torchlight. Tay called out to it in challenge, taunting it, rage and spite giving an edge to his voice. But the winged hunter did not slow, turning now onto a narrow set of stairs that led to a roof walk. The monster was faster than Tay and pulling steadily away from him. Tay swore in fury.

Then abruptly a solitary figure materialized at the far end of the hall, come from the gloom beyond, a lithe, tigerish form that dodged with ease through the bodies of the dead and turned up the stairs in pursuit of the Skull Bearer.

It was Jerle.

Tay charged ahead, forcing himself to run faster, his breath a ragged, harsh sound in his ears. He reached the stairs moments behind his friend and followed him up. He stumbled and fell in the pitch black of the stairwell, scrambled up determinedly, and went on.

On the parapets of the walk, he found Jerle locked in battle with the Skull Bearer. It should have been a mismatch, the winged hunter far more powerful than the Elf, but Jerle Shannara seemed possessed. He was fighting as if it made no difference to him whether he lived or died so long as his adversary did not escape. They surged back and forth across the walk, up against the balustrades, twisting and turning from darkness into light. Jerle had his arms locked about the monster's wings so that it could not fly. The Skull Bearer tore at the Elf with its claws, but Jerle was behind it, and it could not reach him.

Tay cried out to his friend and raced to help. He brought the magic to his fingertips, calling it up as Bremen had taught him, bringing the strength of his body into joinder with the elements of the world that had birthed him, a quickening of life's fire. The Skull Bearer saw him approaching, and wheeled away, placing Jerle between them so that the Druid could not use his magic. Below, on the palace grounds, Elven Hunters looked up, seeing the combatants for the first time, recognizing Jerle. Arrows were notched in longbows, and strings were drawn back and made ready.

Then the monster broke Jerle's grip, leaped onto the balustrade, and took wing. It hung momentarily against the light, huge and dark and nightmarish, a harried beast in search of any haven. Tay struck at it with everything he had, sending the Druid fire burning into its hated form. Below, bowstrings released, and dozens of arrows buried themselves in the creature's body. The Skull Bearer shuddered, faltered, and struggled on, streaming fire and smoke like kite tails, bristling with arrows. A second barrage of missiles from the bowmen flew into it. Now one wing collapsed, and in a final desperate effort it threw itself toward the tops of a stand of trees. But its strength was gone, and its body would no longer respond. Down it went, thrashing as it struck the ground and swordsmen swarmed over it.

Even then, it took a long time to die.

A SEARCH OF THE GROUNDS, the city, and the forests beyond did not turn up any further trace of the attackers. All had been killed, it seemed. Perhaps they had expected to die. Perhaps they had come to Arborlon knowing they would. It didn't matter now. What mattered was that they had succeeded in what they had come to do. They had destroyed the Ballindarroch family. Men, women, and children, the Ballindarrochs had died in their sleep, some never waking, some waking just long enough to realize what was happening before their lives were taken from them. The scope of the disaster was stunning. Courtann Ballindarroch still lived, but only barely. The Healers worked on him all night, but even after they had done everything they could to save him there was little hope. One son still lived, the next to youngest, Alyten, who had been hunting west with friends and by chance alone had avoided the fate of the others in his family. Two small grandchildren had survived as well, sleeping in the bedroom that Tay had passed on his way to the king's, saved because the Gnome assassins had not yet gotten to them. Even during the attack, they did not wake. The older was barely four, the younger not yet two.

Within hours, the city was transformed into an armed camp. Elven Hunters were dispatched to all quarters to set up watch. Patrols were sent down every trail and roadway and on to the Valley of Rhenn to give warning. The people of the city were roused and told to make ready for a full-scale assault. No one was certain what might happen next, appalled and terrified by the assassination of the royal family in their own beds. Anything seemed possible, and everyone was determined that whatever catastrophe might occur next, they would be ready for it.

By dawn the weather had changed, the temperature dropping, the skies clouding over, the air turning heavy and still. Soon a long, slow drizzle filled the air with mist and gloom.

Tay sat with Jerle Shannara on a window seat in a small alcove off the entry to the palace and watched the rain fall. The bodies of the dead had been removed. All the rooms had been searched twice over for assassins trying to hide. The blood and gore of the attack had been washed away, and the bedrooms where the carnage had occurred had been stripped and cleaned. All of it had been done in darkness, before dawn's light, as if to hide the travesty, as if to conceal the horror. Now the palace stood empty. Even Courtann Ballindarroch's two small grandchildren had been taken to other homes until it could be decided what to do with them.

"You know why this was done, don't you?" Jerle asked Tay suddenly, breaking a silence that had gone on for some time.

Tay looked at him. "The killings?"

Jerle nodded. "To disrupt things. To throw us off balance. To stop us from mobilizing the army." He sounded tired. "In short, to prevent us from sending help to the Dwarves. With Courtann dead, the Elves will not do anything until a new king is chosen. The Warlock Lord knows this. That's why he sent his assassins to Arborlon with orders to kill everyone. By the time we are regrouped sufficiently even to make a decision about ourselves, it will be too late for the Dwarves. The Eastland will have fallen."

Tay took a deep breath. "We can't let that happen."

Jerle snorted derisively. "We can't stop it! It's done!" He gestured dismissively. "Courtann Ballindarroch will be lucky to live out another day. You saw what was done to him. He's not a strong man, Tay. I don't know why he's still alive."

Jerle pushed himself back against the wall, feet drawing up on the seat before him, looking a little like a small boy being kept indoors against his will. His clothes were in tatters; he hadn't changed them since the fight. A wicked slash ran down the left side of his jaw. He had washed it and forgotten it. He looked a wreck.

Tay glanced down at himself. He didn't look any better. They were both in need of a bath and sleep.

"What else will he do to stop us, do you think?" Jerle asked softly.

Tay shook his head. "Nothing here. What else is there to do? But he will go after Risca and Bremen, I expect. Maybe he already has." He looked out into the rain, listening to its patter on the glass. "I wish I could warn them. I wish I knew where Bremen was."

He thought of what had been done this night to the Elves—their royal family decimated, their sense of security shattered, their peace of mind lost. Much had been taken from them, and he was not at all certain that any of it could be regained. Jerle was right. Until the king recovered or died and was replaced, the High Council would do nothing to help the Dwarves. No one would take responsibility for such a decision. It wasn't clear if anyone could. Alyten might attempt to act in his father's place, but it was unlikely. Not strong like his father, he was a reckless, impulsive youth who had not been given a lot of responsibility in his life. Mostly, he had served as his father's aide and done what he was told. He had no experience at leading. He would be king if Courtann died, but the High Council would not be quick to support his decisions. Nor would Alyten be quick to make them. He would be cautious and indecisive, anxious not to err. It was the wrong time for him to be king. The Warlock Lord would be quick to take advantage.

The size and complexity of the dilemma was depressing. The Elves knew who was responsible for the attack. The Skull Bearer had been clearly seen before its destruction, and the Gnome Hunters had been identified. Both served the Warlock Lord. But Brona was faceless and omnipresent in the Four Lands, a force that lacked a center, a legend bordering on myth, and no one knew how to reveal him. He was there, and yet he wasn't. He existed, but to what extent? How were they to proceed against him? With the Druids destroyed at Paranor, there was no one to tell them what to do, no one to advise them, no one they respected enough to heed. In two swift strikes, the Warlock Lord had destroyed the balance of power in the Four Lands and rendered the strongest of the Races immobile.

"We can't just sit here," Jerle observed pointedly, as if reading Tay's thoughts.

Tay nodded. He was thinking that time was slipping away, that he was suddenly in danger of failing to accomplish what Bremen had required of him. He stared out into the rain, a gray haze that rendered the world beyond his window seat muddy and indistinct. Where once so much had seemed certain, now nothing was assured.

"If we can do nothing for the Dwarves, we must at least do something for ourselves," he said quietly. His eyes fixed on Jerle's. "We must go in search of the Black Elfstone."

His friend studied him a moment, then nodded slowly. "We could, couldn't we? Courtann has already given his approval." A hint of excitement flickered in the hard blue eyes. "It will give us something to do while we wait out events here. And if we find the Stone, it will give us a weapon to use against the Warlock Lord."

"Or at least deprive him of one he might use against us." Tay was mindful of Bremen's warning about the power of the Black Elfstone. He straightened on the window seat, shrugging off his depression, his sense of purpose returning.

"Well, well, look at you, my friend," Jerle observed archly. "I like you better this way."

Tay stood up, anxious. "How soon can we leave?"

A smile played at the corner of Jerle Shannara's lips. "How soon can you be ready?"

CHAPTER

11

HEY SET OUT AT DAWN of the following day, Tay and Jerle and the few they had chosen to go with them, leaving the city quietly, while its citizens were still waking and their departure would go unnoticed. They were only fifteen in number, so it was not difficult to slip away without being seen. Tay and Jerle had advised the others of the little company only the night before. They were not being underhanded in their stealth; they were simply being cautious. The fewer who knew of their departure or who saw them leave, the fewer who could talk about it. Even idle conversation had a way of reaching the wrong ears. The High Council knew of their plans. Alyten, still not returned from his hunting trip, would be told later. That was enough. Even their immediate families did not know where they were going or what they were about. After what had happened to the Ballindarrochs, no one was taking any unnecessary chances.

It was a worrisome situation they were leaving behind. Ballindarroch hovered near death, and it was not clear yet whether he would recover. The High Council would manage the affairs of state in his absence, as Elven law required, but as a practical matter would do little until the king's fate was determined. Alyten, as the only surviving son, would rule in his father's place, but only nominally until a formal coronation became necessary. Life would go on, but the business of governing would slow to a near halt. The army would stay on alert, its commanders doing what was necessary to protect the city and

its people and to a lesser extent the Elves living in the countryside beyond. But the army's actions would be strictly defensive
in nature, and no one would advocate forays beyond the Westland borders until Ballindarroch recovered or his son took his
place. That meant no aid would be sent to the Dwarves. So
hidebound was the High Council on this matter that it refused
even to commit to sending word to the Dwarves about what
had befallen. Both Tay and Jerle separately begged the Council
to do so, but they were told only that their request would be
considered. Suddenly, secrecy became the order of the day.
Since there was nothing more they could do about the matter,
Tay and Jerle chose not to delay their departure. The king
would live or he would die, Alyten would become king or he
wouldn't, and the High Council would send word to the
Dwarves or stay silent—all of it would work out one way or
the other, and their presence in Arborlon would change nothing. It was better to get on with their search for the Black
Elfstone and make a difference where they could.

There were other reasons for leaving as well. Two unexpected issues had surfaced as a result of the assassinations, one
affecting Tay, the other Jerle. Both lent urgency to their plans
to depart the city.

As to the first, there were some who had begun wondering
aloud why the attack on the Elven royal family coincided so
closely with Tay's return from Paranor. The Druids were respected, but they were also mistrusted. The ones who mistrusted them were few, but in the wake of such a frightening
and unexpected disaster, their voices were commanding more
attention. The Druids wielded power and their ways were mysterious, a combination that was inherently disturbing, especially
with their decision to isolate themselves from the general populace following the First War of the Races. Wasn't it possible,
the voices whispered, that the Druids were somehow involved
in what had happened to the Ballindarrochs? Tay had gone to
see the king and to speak before the High Council the very
night of the killings. Had there been an argument that angered
Tay—that thereby angered all the Druids? Hadn't he been the
first to enter the king's chamber while the killings were taking
place? Was this simply a coincidence? Did anyone see what

happened? Did anyone see what he did? It didn't matter that the questions had already been addressed in one forum or another, by one official or another, and that no one in the High Council or army seemed the least concerned about Tay's conduct. What mattered was that there were no definitive answers being offered and no indisputable facts being supplied, and in their absence wild theories were bound to flourish.

The second issue was even more troubling. Because almost the entire Ballindarroch family had been wiped out, there were some who were saying that if Courtann Ballindarroch died, too, Jerle Shannara should be king. It was all well and good to adhere to the rules of ascendancy, but Alyten was weak and indecisive and not well liked by the people he would govern. And if he should falter, the next in line to rule would be a child of four. That meant years of regency rule, and no one wanted that. Besides, these were dangerous, demanding times, and they required a strong ruler. This attack on the royal family signaled the start of something bad. Everyone recognized that much. The Northland was already conquered by the Warlock Lord and his winged hunters and demon followers. What if he turned on the Elves next? There were rumors that his armies were on the move already, traveling south. Jerle Shannara was the king's first cousin and next in line to rule if the Ballindarrochs were wiped out. Perhaps it would be best if he ruled now, regardless of who was left after Courtann. A former Captain of the Home Guard, a strategist to the army's high command, an advisor to the High Council and the king, he was well suited. Perhaps the choice should be made regardless of precedent and protocol. Perhaps it should be made quickly.

Tay and Jerle heard of these rumors soon enough, saw where they might lead, and realized that the best way to deal with them was to remove themselves from the scene until things settled down. This loose talk provided additional impetus beyond the urgency of their quest for them to hasten their departure, and they were quick to do so. In twenty-four hours, they put together their company, their supplies, their transportation, and their travel plans, and set out.

It was raining when they departed, a cool, misty drizzle that had begun falling several hours earlier and was showing no signs of abating. The roads and trails were already sodden, and the limbs and trunks of the trees were stained black. Mist crept out of the forest, risen from the still warm earth, filling the gaps and crevices with strange movement. Gloom and damp shrouded everything, and the company moved through the early dawn like wraiths chasing after night. They traveled afoot, carrying only their weapons and the food and clothing they would require for twenty-four hours. After that, they would wash what they wore and hunt for their meals until they reached the Sarandanon, a hike of approximately three days. There they would be provided with horses, fresh clothing, and supplies for the remainder of the journey west to the Breakline.

They were a diverse group. Jerle Shannara had selected all but one. He had done so with Tay's approval, because Tay had been gone too long from Arborlon and the Elves to know who was best suited to help them in their quest. Elven Hunters were needed, fighters of the first rank, and Jerle selected ten, which brought their number to twelve. Preia Starle had already announced that she was going, as certain of herself as ever, and neither Tay nor Jerle cared to challenge her. Jerle chose another Tracker as well, a weathered veteran named Retten Kipp, who had served with the Home Guard for better than thirty years. More than one Tracker would be necessary if they were to keep close watch of their rear as well as their front. Besides, if anything happened to Preia, they would need a replacement. Tay did not like hearing the words, but he could not find fault with them.

That brought their number to fourteen. Tay asked for one more.

The man he wanted was Vree Erreden. It was an odd choice at first glance, and Jerle was quick to say so. Vree Erreden was not well regarded among the Elves, a reclusive, distracted, shy man with little concern for anything besides his work. What he did was a source of ongoing controversy. He was a locat, a mystic who specialized in finding people who were missing and objects that were lost. How successful he was at what he did was the subject of much debate. Those who believed in him possessed an unshakable faith. Those who didn't found him foolish and misguided. He was tolerated because he enjoyed occasional, verifiable success, and because the Elven people were understanding of differences in general, having themselves been the subject of much suspicion over the years in the eyes of the other Races. Vree Erreden did not himself make any claims about his accomplishments; the claims were provided by others. But the origin of the claims did nothing to improve the image of the man in the eyes of his detractors.

Tay was not among them. Tay identified closely with Vree Erreden, though he had never said so to anyone. They were kindred spirits, he believed. Had Vree chosen to do so, he might have become a Druid. His skills would have allowed for the possibility, and Tay would have recommended him. Both were possessors of talents developed through years of practice, Tay the elementalist, Vree the locat. Tay's was the more visibly demonstrable talent, however, utilizing magic and science culled from the earth's resources, a harnessing of power that gave clear evidence of what it was he could do. Vree Erreden's talent, on the other hand, resided almost entirely within, was passive in nature, and was difficult to verify. Mystics operated on prescience, intuition, even hunches, all of them stronger than the instincts normal men and women might experience, all of them impossible to see. Locats were once heavily in evidence, in a time when Elves and other faerie creatures exercised such power routinely. Now only a handful remained, the others lost with the passing of the old world and the irrevocable change in the nature of magic. But Tay was a student of the old ways and understood the origins of Vree Erreden's power, and it was as real to him as his own.

He went to see the locat late on the afternoon of the day before the scheduled departure and found him in his yard, bent over a tattered collection of maps and writings, his small, slender form hunched protectively, his hands tracing lines and words across the paper. He looked up as Tay came through the gate of the small, unremarkable cottage, peering myopically at him as he approached. The locat squinted against the sunlight and his own failing sight. Each year, it was rumored, his eyes failed a little more—but as his eyes failed, his intuition sharpened.

"It is Tay Trefenwyd," Tay announced helpfully, coming over so that the light fell on his face.

Vree Erreden peered up at him without recognition. Tay had been gone for five years, so it was possible the man no longer remembered him. Nor was Tay wearing the robes of his order, having reverted to the loose-fitting Elven garb preferred by the Westland people, so it was possible the locat was unable to identify him as a Druid either.

"I need your help in finding something," Tay continued, undaunted. The other's thin face cocked slightly in response. "If you agree to help me, you will have the opportunity of saving lives, many of them Elven. It will be the most important finding you will ever undertake. If you succeed, no one will ever doubt you again."

Vree Erreden looked suddenly amused. "That is a bold claim, Tay."

Tay smiled. "I am in a position where I must make bold claims. I leave tomorrow for the Sarandanon and beyond. I must convince you to go with me when I do. Time doesn't allow for a more subtle persuasion."

"What is it you are looking for?"

"A Black Elfstone, lost since the end of the world of faerie, thousands of years ago."

The small man looked at him. He did not ask Tay why he had come to him or question the strength of his belief. He accepted that Tay had faith in his power, perhaps because of who he was, perhaps because of what he did. Or perhaps because it didn't matter. But there was curiosity in his eyes—and a hint of doubt.

"Give me your hands," he said.

Tay stretched out his hands, and Vree Erreden clasped them tightly in his own. His grip was surprisingly strong. His eyes met Tay's, held them for a moment, then looked through them and beyond, losing focus. He stayed like that for a long time, as still as stone, seeing something hidden from Tay. Then he blinked, released his grip, and sat back. A small smile played across his thin lips.

"I will come with you," he said, just like that.

He asked where they were to meet and what he was required to bring, then turned back to his maps and writings without another word, the matter forgotten. Tay lingered just long enough to make certain there was no further reason to stay, and then left.

So they numbered fifteen in the end as they departed Arborlon in the slow rain of early dawn, cloaked and hooded and faceless in the gloom, and they had come for reasons best known to themselves. No one would speak hereafter of these reasons. No one would believe it made a difference. A decision made was a decision accepted. Armored in that conviction, they wound down out of the Carolan to where the Rill Song churned within its banks, crossed on a ferry raft kept in service for the city, and struck out west through the shadowed corridors of the ancient woods.

They marched all day through the rain, which did not cease, though after a time it lessened. They stopped once for lunch and twice at springs to refill their water skins, but they did not rest otherwise. No one tired, not even Vree Erreden. They were Elves and used to walking long distances, and all of them were fit enough to keep up with Jerle Shannara's moderate pace. The way was muddied and the footing uncertain, and on more than one occasion they were forced to find a way across a ravine which had flooded because of the rains. No one complained. No one said much of anything. Even when they stopped to eat, they sat apart from each other, withdrawn into their cloaks from the weather, thinking their separate thoughts. Once Tay stopped Vree Erreden to tell him how much he appreciated his decision to come with them, and the locat looked at him as if he had lost his mind, as if he had just made the most ridiculous statement in the history of mankind. Tay smiled and backed off and did not try to approach the other man again.

They moved steadily farther away from the mountains that warded Arborlon and closer to the Sarandanon. Night came, and they made camp. No fire was built, and the evening meal was eaten cold. It was dark and still within the trees, and there was no movement save for the steady falling of the rain. Another day or so would pass before they were free of the woods and onto the open grasslands of the valley. The country would change dramatically then as they traveled through the farmlands that produced the crops and livestock that fed the Elven nation. Beyond, the better part of a week's ride farther, waited the Breakline and their destination.

Damp, chilled, and lost in thought, Tay sat by himself when the meal was finished and stared out into the gloom. Hoping to find something he had missed, he replayed in his mind the vision of the Black Elfstone that Bremen had been shown at the Hadeshorn. The details of the vision were familiar by now, smoothed out like wrinkled paper so that they might be reexamined and considered at leisure. Bremen had given him the description of the talisman's hiding place just as it had been revealed by the shade of Galaphile, so that all that remained was to find it again in real life. There were several ways that might happen. The Trackers Preia Starle and Retten Kipp might discover the Black Elfstone through an accumulation of physical evidence in the course of their scouting. Tay might discover it as an elementalist, finding the breaks in the lines of power caused by the talisman's magic. And Vree Erreden might discover it by employing his special skill as a locat, tracing the Elfstone as he would any other lost object, through prescient thought and intuition.

Tay looked over at the locat, who was already asleep. Most of the others were sleeping as well by now, or in the process of drifting off. Even Jerle Shannara was stretched out, rolled into his blanket. A single Elven Hunter kept watch at one end of the camp, walking the perimeter, drifting through the gloom, just another of night's shadows. Tay watched him for a moment, thinking of other things, then looked again at Vree Erreden. The locat had spied out Bremen's vision when he had taken hold of his hands on that first visit. He was certain of it now, though he hadn't realized it at the time. It was what had decided the locat on coming, that momentary glimpse of a place lost in time, of a magic that had survived a world now gone, of what once was known and might now be revealed again. The theft was a clever piece of work, and Tay admired the other man's audacity in committing it. It was not everyone who would dare to pick the lock on a Druid's mind.

He rose after a while, still not sleepy, and walked out to stand where the guard patrolled. The Elven Hunter noted him, but made no move to approach, continuing his rounds as before. Tay looked out into the sodden trees, his eyes adjusting to the light, seeing strange shapes and forms in the rain, even in the absence of moon and stars. He watched a deer pass, small and delicate in the concealment of the gloom, eyes watchful, ears pricked. He saw night birds speed swiftly from branch to branch, hunters in search of food, finding it now and again, diving with shocking quickness to the forest floor and then lifting away, small creatures clutched tightly by claws and beaks. He saw in these victims an image of the Elven people if the Warlock Lord prevailed. He imagined how helpless they would be when Brona began his hunt. Already there was a sense of being sought out, of being considered prey. While he did not like to contemplate it, he did not think the feeling would diminish any time soon.

He was still considering what this meant when Preia Starle appeared out of nowhere at his elbow. He gasped in spite of himself, then forced himself to recover as he saw the smile twitch at the corners of her mouth. She had been gone all day, leaving early with Retten Kipp to scout the land ahead. No one had known when either of them would be back, Trackers having the freedom to do whatever they felt they must and to keep to their own schedule. She winked as she saw the shock leave his face, replaced by chagrin. Saying nothing, she took his arm and led him back off the perimeter and into the camp. She was wearing loose-fitting forest clothing, with gloves and soft boots, and all of it was soaked through. Rain plastered her curly, short-cropped, cinnamon hair to her head and ran down her face. She didn't seem to notice.

She sat him down some yards away from where the other members of the company were sleeping, choosing a dry spot beneath an oak where the thickness of the grass offered some comfort. She removed the brace of long knives, the short sword, and the ash bow she carried, looking altogether too fragile and young to be bearing such weapons, and sat next to him.

"Can't sleep, Tay?" she asked quietly, squeezing his arm.

He folded his long legs before him and shook his head. "Where have you been?"

"Here and there." She brushed the rain from her face and smiled. "You didn't see me, did you?"

He gave her a rueful look. "What do you think? Do you enjoy shortening people's lives by scaring them so? If I wasn't able to sleep before, how will I ever be able to sleep now?"

She suppressed a laugh. "I expect you will manage. You are a Druid after all, and Druids can manage anything. Take heart from Jerle. He sleeps like a baby all the time. He refuses to stay awake, even when I would have it otherwise."

She blinked, realizing what she had implied, and looked quickly away. After a moment, she said, "Kipp has gone on ahead to the Sarandanon to make certain that the horses and supplies are ready. I came back to tell you about the Gnome Hunters."

He looked sharply at her, waiting. "Two large parties," she continued, "both north of us. There might be more. There are a lot of tracks. I don't think they know about us. Yet. But we need to be careful."

"Can you tell what they are doing here?"

She shook her head. "Hunting, I would guess. The pattern of their tracks suggests as much. They are keeping close to the Kensrowe, north of the grasslands. But they may not stay there, especially if they learn about us."

He was silent for a moment, thinking it through. He could feel her waiting him out, studying his face in the gloom. Amid the sleepers, a snore turned into a cough, and a bundled form shifted. Rain fell in a slow patter, a soft backdrop against the black.

"Did you see any of the Skull Bearers?" he asked finally.

She shook her head once more. "No."

"Strange tracks of any kind?"

"No."

He nodded, hoping that was indicative of something. Perhaps the Warlock Lord had left his monsters at home. Perhaps Gnome Hunters were all they faced.

She shifted beside him, rising to her knees. "Give Jerle my report, Tay. I have to go back out."

"Now?"

"Now is better than later if you want to keep the wolf from the door." She grinned. "Do you remember that saying? You used it all the time when you were talking about going to Paranor and becoming a Druid. It was your way of saying you would protect us, the poor, homebound friends you were leaving behind."

"I remember." He took her arm. "Are you hungry?"

"I've eaten already."

"Why not stay until dawn?"

"No."

"Don't you want to give your report to Jerle yourself?"

She studied him a moment, reflecting on something. "What I want is for you to give it for me. Will you do that?"

The tone of her voice had changed. She was not open to a discussion on this. He nodded wordlessly and took his hand away.

She rose, strapped the knives and sword back in place, took up the bow, and gave him a quick smile. "You think about what you just asked of me, Tay," she said.

She slipped back into the gloom, and a moment later she was gone. Tay sat where he was for a time, considering what she had said, then climbed to his feet to wake Jerle.

RAIN FELL ALL THE FOLLOWING DAY, a steady downpour. The company continued on through the forest, keeping watch for Gnomes, staying alert to everything. The hours passed slowly, sunrise easing toward sunset, the whole of the day marked by graying half-light filtered through banks of clouds and water-laden boughs. Travel was slow and monotonous. They came upon no one in the woods. In the sodden gloom, nothing moved.

Night came and went, and neither Preia Starle nor Retten

Kipp returned. By dawn of the third day, the company was nearing the Sarandanon. The rain had stopped and the skies had begun to clear. Sunlight peeked through gaps in the departing clouds, narrow shafts of light come out of the bright blue. The air warmed, and the earth began to steam and bake.

In a clearing bright with sunlight on spring wildflowers, they came upon Preia Starle's ash bow, broken and muddied. There was no other sign of the Elf girl.

But the boot prints of Gnome Hunters were everywhere.

CHAPTER

12

DAYLIGHT WAS FADING and darkness edging out of the Anar as the last of the Warlock Lord's vast army spilled from the Jannisson Pass onto the grasslands of the northern Rabb. It had taken all day for the army to come down out of the Streleheim, for the Jannisson was narrow and winding and the army encumbered by a train of pack animals, baggage, and wagons that stretched for nearly two miles when set end to end. The fighting men moved at varying rates, the cavalry swift and eager astride their horses, the light infantry, bowmen, and slingers slower, and the heavily armored foot soldiers slower still. But none of the army's various components was as plodding or trouble-plagued as the pack train, which lumbered through the pass with an agonizing lack of progress, stopped every few minutes by broken wheels and axles, by the constant need for an untangling of traces and the watering of animals, and by collisions, mix-ups, and traffic jams of all sorts.

It gave Risca, watching from the concealment of the Dragon's Teeth half a mile to the south, a grim sense of satisfaction. Anything to slow the dark ones, he kept thinking. Anything to delay their hateful progress south toward his homeland.

Trolls made up the greater part of the army, stolid, thick-skinned, and virtually featureless, looking more like beasts than like men. The largest and most fierce were the Rock Trolls, averaging well over six feet in height and weighing several hundred pounds. They formed the core of the army, and their disciplined, precision-executed march testified to their efficiency in battle. Other Trolls were there mostly to fill the gaps. Gnomes dominated the cavalry and light infantry, the small, wiry fighters a tribal race like the Trolls though less skilled and more poorly trained. They served in the army of the Warlock Lord for two reasons. First and foremost, they were terrified of magic, and the Warlock Lord's magic exceeded anything they had believed possible. Second and only slightly less compelling, they knew what had happened when the larger, fiercer, and better armed Trolls had tried to resist, and they had quickly decided to jump to the winning side before the decision was made for them.

Then there were the creatures that had no name, beings brought over from the netherworld, things come out of the black pits to which they had been consigned in centuries past, freed now through the Warlock Lord's magic. In daylight, they stayed cloaked and hooded, indistinct shapes in the shifting, swirling dust of the march, outcasts by breeding and common consent. But as the twilight descended and the shadows lengthened, they began to shed their concealments and reveal themselves—terrible, misshapen monsters that all avoided. Among them were the Skull Bearers, the winged hunters that served as Brona's right arm. Men themselves once, the Skull Bearers were Druids who had tested the magic too frequently and deeply and been subverted. These last took flight now, lifting off into the dying light to begin casting about for prey to feed their hunger.

And in the center of all, set squarely amid the hordes that swept it inexorably onward like a raft on storm-tossed waters, was the huge, black, silk-covered litter that bore the Warlock Lord himself. Thirty Trolls carried it forward through the army's ranks, its coverings impenetrable in the brightest light, its iron stays studded with barbs and razors, its pennants emblazoned with white skulls. Risca watched the creatures about it bow and scrape, conscious that while they could not see him, their Lord and Master could easily see them.

Now, with night descending and the entire army down out of the Northland and poised to march south to invade the Anar and conquer the Dwarves, Risca sat back wearily within his rocky crevice and let the shadows envelop him. Bremen had been right, of course—right about everything. Brona had survived the First War of the Races and stayed hidden all these years merely to gain strength so that he might strike once again. Now he was returned, this time as the Warlock Lord, and the Trolls and Gnomes belonged to him, subjugated and made servants in his cause. If the Druids were destroyed as Bremen had foreseen they would be—and Risca now believed it so—there was no one left to intervene on behalf of the free Races, no one left to wield the magic. One by one, they would fall—Dwarves, Elves, and Men. One by one, the Four Lands would be subjugated. It would happen quickly. No one yet believed it was possible, and by the time anyone did, it would be too late. Risca had seen now for himself the size of the Warlock Lord's army. A juggernaut, unstoppable, monstrous. Only by uniting could the free Races hope to prevail. But it would take time for them to decide to do this if left to their own devices. Politics would slow any decision making. Self-interest would generate an ill-advised caution. The free Races would debate and consider and be made slaves before they realized what had happened to them.

Bremen had foreseen it all, and now it was left to the handful who had believed him to find a way to prevent the inevitable from happening.

Risca reached into his pack, pulled out a piece of day-old bread he had bought at the edge of the border settlements, and began to chew absently on it. He had left Bremen and the others of the little company three days earlier at the mouth of the Hadeshorn. He had come east out of Callahorn to carry word to the Dwarves of the Warlock Lord's approach, to warn them of the danger, and to persuade them that they must make a stand against the Northland army. But by the time he had reached the western edge of the Rabb, he had decided that his task would be made considerably easier if he could report that he had seen the approaching army with his own eyes. Then he could offer an estimate of its size and strength and thereby be more persuasive in his appeal. So he had turned north and used a second day to reach the Jannisson. There, on this third day, he had crouched in hiding in the foothills of the Dragon's Teeth, and watched the army of the Warlock Lord come down out of the Streleheim; it had grown larger and larger until it seemed there would be no end to it. He had counted units and commands, animals and wagons, tribal pennants and standards of battle until he had its measure. It might as well have been the whole Troll nation come to call. It was the largest army he had ever seen. The Dwarves could never stand alone against it. They could slow it, delay it perhaps, but they could not stop it. Even if the Elves came to stand with them, they would still be badly outnumbered. And they had no magic of the sort wielded by Brona and the Skull Bearers and the netherworld creatures. They had no talismans. They had only Bremen, Tay Trefenwyd, and himself, the last of the Druids.

Risca shook his head, chewing and swallowing. The odds were too great. He needed to find a way to even them up.

He finished his bread and drank deeply from the aleskin he carried strapped across his shoulder. Then he rose and moved back to the precipice, where he could look down on the encamped army. Fires had been lit by now, the descent of night's darkness nearly complete, and the plains were bright with clusters of flame and the air thick with smoke. The army sprawled for almost a mile, bustling with activity, alive with sound and movement. Food was being prepared and bedding unrolled. Repairs were being undertaken and plans laid. Risca stared down from his perch, disheartened and angry. If strength of will and rage alone could have stopped this madness, his would have been sufficient. He caught a glimpse of a pair of Skull Bearers as they circled the inky skies beyond the aura of the firelight, searching for spies, and he hunched down into the concealing rocks, becoming one with the mountains, another colorless piece of the rough terrain. His eyes wandered the length and breadth of the campsite, but kept returning to the black silken litter in which the Warlock Lord reposed. It had been lowered to the ground now, set deep within the army's midst, surrounded by Trolls and other creatures less human, a small island of silence within the teeming mass of activity. No fires were lit close to it. No creatures approached from the light. Blackness pooled about it like a lake, leaving it solitary and marked as inviolate.

Risca's face hardened. The trouble begins and ends with the

monster who occupies that tent, he was thinking. The Warlock Lord is the head of the beast that threatens us all. Cut off the head, and the beast dies.

Kill the Warlock Lord, and the danger ends.

Kill the Warlock Lord . . .

It was a wild, reckless, impulsive thought, and he did not allow himself to pursue it. He shoved it aside and forced himself to consider his responsibilities. Bremen was depending on him. He must bring word of this army to the Dwarves so that they could prepare for the invasion of their homeland. He must persuade the Dwarves to engage an army many times its size in a battle they could not hope to win. He must convince Raybur and the Elders of the Dwarf Council that a means would be found to destroy the Warlock Lord and that the Dwarves must buy with their lives the time that was needed to accomplish this. It was a tall order and would require a great sacrifice. It would be up to him to lead them, the warrior Druid who could stand against any creature the Warlock Lord might employ.

For Risca had been born to battle. It was all he knew. He grew to manhood in the Ravenshorn, the son of parents who had lived their entire lives in the Eastland wilderness. His father was a scout and his mother a trapper. There had been eight brothers and sisters on his father's side and seven on his mother's. Most of them lived within a few miles of one another still, and Risca had been raised by all at one time or another. Over the years of his boyhood, he saw as much of his aunts and uncles and cousins as he did his parents. There was a sharing of responsibility for raising the young in his family. The Dwarves of this part of the world were constantly at war with the Gnome tribes, and everyone was always at risk. But Risca was equal to the challenge. He was taught to fight and hunt at an early age, and he discovered that he was good at it—better than good, in fact. He could sense things the others could not. He could spy out what was hidden from them. He was quick and agile and strong beyond his years. He understood the art of survival. He stayed alive when others did not.

At twelve, he was attacked by a Koden and killed the beast. He was thirteen when one of a company of twenty that was ambushed by Gnomes. He alone escaped. When his mother was killed setting lines, he was only fifteen, but he tracked down those responsible and dispatched them single-handedly. When his father died in a hunting accident, he carried his body deep into the heart of Gnome country and buried it there so that his spirit could continue the fight against their enemies. Half of his brothers and sisters were dead by then, lost to battle or sickness. He lived in a violent, unforgiving world, and his life was hard and uncertain. But Risca survived, and it was whispered when they thought he could not hear, for he was superstitious where fate was concerned, that the blade had not been forged that could kill him.

When he was twenty he came down out of the Ravenshorn to Culhaven and entered into the service of Raybur, newly crowned King of the Dwarves and a much admired warrior himself. But Raybur kept him in Culhaven only a short time before sending him to Paranor and the Druids. Raybur recognized Risca's special talents and believed the Dwarf people would be best served if the young man with the warrior's heart and the hunter's skills was trained by the Druids. He, too, like Courtann Ballindarroch of the Elves, knew of Bremen and admired him. So a note was addressed to the old man, asking that he consider giving young Risca special consideration as a student. Thus bearing the note, Risca traveled to Paranor and the Druid's Keep and stayed, becoming a staunch follower of Bremen and a believer in the ways of the magic.

His eyes stayed fixed on the black silken tent in the enemy camp below as he thought of the ways in which the magic now served him. His was the strongest after Bremen's—stronger these days perhaps, given his youth and stamina and the other's age. That was what he firmly believed, though he knew Tay Trefenwyd would certainly argue the matter. Like Tay, Risca had studied assiduously the lessons taught by Bremen, working at them even after the old man was banished, testing himself over and over again. He studied and trained virtually alone, for no others among the Druids, even Tay Trefenwyd, considered themselves warriors or sought to master the battle arts as he did. For Risca, the magic had but a single useful purpose—to protect himself and his friends and to destroy his enemies. The other uses of magic were of no interest to him—healing, divin-

ing, prescience, empathics, mastery of the sciences, elemental-
ism, history, and conjuring. He was a fighter, and strength of
arms was his passion.

The memories came and faded, and his thoughts returned to
the matter at hand. What should he do? He could not abandon
his responsibilities, but he could not ignore who he was either.
Below, the silken folds of the tent seemed to ripple in the faint
dance of the firelight. One blow was all it would take. How easily their problems would be solved if he could deliver it!

He took a deep breath and let it out slowly. He was not
afraid of Brona. He was aware of how dangerous the other was,
how powerful, but he was not afraid. He possessed considerable
magic himself, and if he employed it in a direct strike, he did
not think that anyone or anything could withstand it.

He closed his eyes. Why was he even considering this? If he
failed, there would be no one to give warning to the Dwarves!
He would have given his life for nothing!

But if he were to succeed . . .

He eased back into the rocks, slipped off his travel cloak,
and began to strip away his weapons. He supposed his mind
had been made up from the moment the idea had entered his
head. Kill the Warlock Lord and put an end to this madness.
He was the best suited of any of them to make the attempt.
This was the ideal time, when the Northland army was still
close to home and Brona believed himself safe from attack.
Even if he died too, it would be worth it. Risca was willing to
make that sacrifice. A warrior was always prepared to make that
sacrifice.

When he was down to his boots, pants, and tunic, he
shoved a dagger in his belt, picked up his battle-axe, and started
down through the rocks. It was nearing midnight by the time
he reached the foot of the mountains and started across the
plains. Overhead, the Skull Bearers still circled, but he was behind them by now and cloaked in magic that concealed him
from their spying eyes. They were looking outward for enemies
and would not see him. He walked easily, loosely, his approach
silent in the black, the light of the campfires masking him from
those who might notice his approach. Their sentry system was
woefully inadequate. A perimeter of guards, a mix of Gnomes

and Trolls, had placed themselves too far apart and too close to the light to be able to see anything coming in out of the dark. The skies were clouded and the night air was hazy with smoke, and it would take sharp eyes under the best of circumstances to catch sight of any movement on the plains.

Still, Risca took no chances. He came in at a crouch when the cover of grasses and scrub thinned, picking his place of approach carefully, choosing one of the Gnome sentries as a target. Leaving the battle-axe in the long grass, he went in with only the dagger. The Gnome sentry never saw him. He dragged the body back out into the grasses, concealed it, wrapped himself in the fellow's cloak, pulled up the hood to hide his face, picked up the axe again, and started in.

Another man would have thought twice about just walking right up to an enemy camp. Risca gave it barely any thought at all. He knew that a direct approach was always best when you were trying to catch someone off guard, and that you tended to notice less of what was right before your eyes than of what lurked at the fringes of your vision. The tendency was to discount what didn't make sense, and a lone enemy strolling right past you into the center of your own heavily armed camp made no sense at all.

Nevertheless, Risca stayed at the edges of the firelight as he entered, and he kept the cloak in place. He did not skulk or lower his head, for that would signal that something was wrong. He moved as if he belonged and did not alter his approach. He passed the outer perimeter of guards and fires and moved into the center of the camp. Smoke wafted past him, and he used it like a screen. Shouts and laughter rose all about, men eating and drinking, telling tales and swapping lies. Armor and weapons clinked, and the pack animals stamped and snorted in the hazy dark. Risca moved through them all without slowing, never losing sight of his destination, now a ragged jut of poles and dark pennants lifting above the swarm of the army. He carried the battle-axe low against his side, and he projected himself through his magic as a soldier of no consequence, as just another Gnome Hunter on his way to somewhere unimportant.

He passed deep into the maze of fires and men, skirting

wagons and stacks of supplies, tethered lines of pack animals and menders engaged in repair of traces and equipment, and vast racks of pikes and spears, their shafts and armored tips angling skyward. He kept to the portions of the camp that were occupied by Gnomes when he could, but now and again was forced to pass through clusters of Trolls. He shied from them as a Gnome might, deferential, wary, not showing fear, but not challenging either, turning away from them as he approached, not quite meeting the craggy, impersonal faces, the battle-hardened stares. He could feel their eyes settle on him and then move away. But no one stopped him or called him back. No one found him out.

Sweat ran down his back and under his arms, and it was not from the heat of the night. Now men were beginning to sleep, to roll themselves into their cloaks next to the fires and go quiet. Risca went more swiftly. He needed the noise and the bustle to mask his movements. If everyone slept, he would seem out of place still moving about. He was closing on the Warlock Lord's haven now—he could see its canopy lifting against the darkness ahead. The number of fires was thinning out as he approached, and the number of soldiers about them was dwindling. No one was allowed to come too close to the quarters of the Warlock Lord and none wished to. Risca stopped at the edge of a fire where a dozen men lay sleeping. Trolls, huge, hard-featured fighters, their weapons lying next to them. He ignored them, studying the open ground ahead. A hundred feet separated the black tent on all sides from the sleeping army. There were no sentries to be seen. Risca hesitated. Why were there no guards? He glanced about carefully, searching for them. There were none to be found.

At that moment, he almost turned back. There was something wrong with this, he sensed. There should be guards. Did they wait within the tent? Were they somewhere he could not see? To find out, he would have to cross the open ground between the closest of the watch fires and the tent. There was enough light to reveal his coming, so he would have to use magic to cloak his approach. He would be all alone out there, and there would be nowhere to hide.

His mind raced. Would there be Skull Bearers? Were they all out hunting or did some remain behind to protect the Master? Did other creatures stand guard?

The questions burned through him, unanswerable.

He hesitated a moment longer, glancing about, listening, testing the air. Then he tightened his grip on the battle-axe and started forward. He brought the magic up to shield him, to help him blend into the night, to make him one with the darkness. Just a shading, so that even someone familiar with the magic would not be warned. Determination swept through him. He could do this. He must. He crossed the open ground, as silent as a cloud scudding across a windswept sky. No sounds reached out to him. No movement caught his eye. Even now, he could find no one protecting the tent.

Then he was beside it, the air about him gone deathly still, the sounds and smells and movements of the army faded away. He stood close to the black silk and waited for his instincts to warn him of a trap. When they did not, he brought the edge of the battle-axe, sharp as a razor, down the fabric's dark skin and slit it open.

He heard something then—a sigh, perhaps, or a low moan. He stepped quickly through the opening.

Despite the blackness of the enclosure, his eyes were able to adjust immediately. There was nothing there—no people, no furniture, no weapons, no bedding, no sign of life. The tent was empty.

Risca stared in disbelief.

Then a hiss rose out of the silence, low and pervasive, and the air began to move in front of his face. The blackness coalesced, coming together to form a thing of substance where a moment earlier there had been nothing. A black-cloaked figure began to take shape. Risca realized what was happening and a terrible chill swept through him. The Warlock Lord had been there all along, there in the darkness, invisible, watching and waiting. Perhaps he had even known of Risca's coming. He was not, as the Dwarf had believed, a creature of flesh and blood that could be killed with ordinary weapons. He had transcended his mortal shell through his magic and could now as-

sume any form—or no form at all. No wonder there were no
guards. None were needed.

The Warlock Lord reached out for him. For a second Risca
found that he could not move and believed he would die without being able to lift a finger to save himself. Then the fire of
his determination broke through his fear and galvanized him.
He roared in defiance at the terrible black shape, at the skeletal
hand that reached for him, at the eyes as red as blood, at his
terror, at fate's betrayal. His battle-axe came up in a huge
sweep, the fire of his own magic sweeping its length. The Warlock Lord gestured, and Risca felt as if iron bands had fastened
themselves about his body. With a tremendous effort, he
snapped them asunder and flung the battle-axe. The weapon
smashed into the cloaked form and exploded in flames.

Risca did not wait to see the result of his strike. He knew
instinctively that this was a battle he could not win. Strength of
arms and fighting skills alone were not enough to defeat this
enemy. The moment he released the axe, he dove back through
the opening in the tent, scrambled to his feet, and broke for
freedom. Already shouts were rising out of the firelight, and
men were waking from their sleep. Risca did not look behind
him, but he could feel Brona's presence like a black cloud,
reaching out for him, trying to drag him back. He raced across
the open ground and leapt through the nearest fire, kicking at
the dying flames, scattering sparks and brands in every direction. He snatched up a sword from a sleeping man and dodged
left into the haze of smoke from the scattered fire.

Alarms rose from every quarter. The hand of the Warlock
Lord still reached for him, tightening about his chest, but it
grew weaker as he widened the distance between them. His
wits had scattered, and he tried to regain them. A Troll appeared before him, challenging his passage, and he left the dagger buried in the other's throat. He reacted instinctively, unable
to think clearly yet. Men were swirling all about him, running
in every direction, searching for the cause of the uproar, still
unaware that it was him. He forced himself to slow, to ignore
the frantic beat of his pulse and the tightness about his chest.
Shades! He had come so close! He moved swiftly now, but he

no longer ran. By running, he drew attention to himself. He summoned his magic, abandoned at the moment of his flight, realizing for the first time that he had almost lost control of it completely, that he had almost given way to his fear. He cloaked himself swiftly, then angled left toward the open plains, a different direction than he had come, a direction in which they would not think to look. If he was discovered and had to fight his way clear, he would be killed. There were too many for him. Too many for any man, Druid or no.

Down through the camp he hastened, the heat of his encounter with the Warlock Lord threatening to suffocate him. He forced himself to breathe evenly, to ignore the turmoil of the waking camp, the shouts and cries, and the thudding of booted feet as squads of armed soldiers were dispatched in every direction. Ahead, he could see the blackness of the plains appear, the sweep of emptiness that lay beyond the ring of campfires. Guards were standing all about the perimeter, but they were looking out into the darkness in expectation of an attack from that direction. He had an almost irresistible urge to look back over his shoulder, to see what might be following, but something warned him that if he did so he would reveal himself. Perhaps the Warlock Lord would see his eyes and know who he was, even from within his concealment. Perhaps he would recognize his face. Maybe that would be enough to undo him. Risca did not turn. He continued ahead, slowing to choose the point of his escape as he neared the perimeter of the camp.

"You and you," he said to a pair of Gnomes as he passed between them, not bothering to slow so that they could see his face, using their own language to address them, a language he had spoken fluently since he was ten. He beckoned. "Come with me."

They did not question. Soldiers seldom did. He had the appearance and look of an officer, and so they went without argument. He strode out into the darkness as if he knew what he was about, as if he had a mission to perform. He took them far into the night, then dispatched them in opposite directions and simply walked away. He did not try to go back for his weapons and cloak, knowing it was too dangerous. He was fortunate to be alive, and it would not do to tempt fate further. He breathed the night air deeply, slowing his pulse. Did Bremen know the nature of their enemy? he wondered. Did the old man realize the power that the Warlock Lord possessed? He must, for he had gone into the monster's lair and spied on him. Risca wished he had asked a few more questions of the old man when he had the chance. Had he done so, he would never have considered attempting to destroy Brona on his own. He would have realized that he lacked the weapons. No wonder Bremen sought a talisman. No wonder he relied on the visions of the dead to advise him.

He searched the skies for the Skull Bearers, but he did not see them. Nevertheless, he kept his magic in place so that he remained concealed. He walked out into the Rabb and turned southeast for the Anar. Before morning's light could reveal him, he would be safely within the concealment of the trees. He had escaped to fight another day and could count himself lucky to be able to say so.

But what sort of fight could he manage against an enemy like the Warlock Lord? What could he tell the Dwarves to give them hope?

The answers eluded him. He walked on into the night, searching for them.

CHAPTER

13

WO DAYS LATER the Northland army was encamped within twenty miles of Storlock. The army had crossed the plains unhindered, angling east toward the Anar, staying clear of the entangling forests, a huge, sluggish worm inching its way steadily closer to the haven of the Dwarves. Watch fires burned in the distance against a twilight sky, a bright yellow haze that stretched for miles across the flats. Kinson Ravenlock could see the glow from as far away as the edge of the Dragon's Teeth below the mouth of the Valley of Shale. The army would have spent the afternoon crossing the Rabb River before settling in. At sunrise it would resume its march south, which meant that by sunset tomorrow it would reach a point directly opposite the village of the Stors.

Which meant in turn, the Borderman realized, that he and Mareth must cross the Rabb tonight, ahead of the army's advance, if they wished to avoid being trapped on the wrong side of the plains.

He stood motionless in the shadow of a cleft in the rocks some fifty feet above the plains and found himself wishing they had been able to get this far a day earlier so that a night crossing would not have been necessary. He knew that with the coming of darkness Brona's winged hunters would be abroad, prowling the open spaces that lay between them and safety. It was not an appealing thought. He glanced back to where Mareth sat rubbing her feet in an effort to alleviate the ache of the day's forced march, her boots dumped unceremoniously on the ground along with her cloak and their few provisions. They could not have come faster than they had, he knew. He had pushed her hard just to get this far. She was still weak from her experience in the Druid's Keep; her stamina drained quickly and she required frequent rests. But she had not complained once, not even when he had insisted they must forgo sleep until they reached Storlock. She had great determination, he acknowledged grudgingly. He just wished he understood her a little better.

He looked back out at the plains, at the watch fires, at the darkness as it rolled out of the east and descended in gathering layers across the landscape. Tonight it was, then. He wished he had magic to hide them on their passage, but he might as well wish he could fly. He could not ask her to use hers, of course. Bremen had forbidden it. And Bremen himself was absent still, so there was no help to be found there.

"Come eat something," Mareth called to him.

He turned and walked down out of the rocks. She had set out plates with bread, cheese, and fruit, and poured ale into metal cups. They had bartered for their provisions with a farmer above Varfleet yesterday evening, and this was the last of what they had acquired. He sat down across from her and began to eat. He did not look at her. They were two days gone from fallen Paranor, having come down out of the Kennon once more and turned east along the Mermidon, following it below the wall of the Dragon's Teeth to here. Bremen had sent them ahead, had given them strict orders to go on without him, to follow the Mermidon to the Rabb and then cross to Storlock. There they were to inquire after a man the Druid believed was living somewhere within the Eastland wilderness of the Upper Anar, a man of whom Kinson had never heard. They were to determine where he might be found, and then they were to wait until Bremen could rejoin them. The Druid did not explain what it was that he would be doing in the meantime. He did not explain why they were looking for this unknown man. He simply told them what to do—told Kinson what to do, more to the point, since Mareth was still sleeping at that juncture—and then disappeared into the trees.

Kinson believed that he had gone back into the Druid's

Keep, and the Borderman once more wondered why. They had
fled Paranor in a maelstrom of sound and fury, of magic un-
leashed and gone wild, some of it Mareth's and some the Keep's
itself. It was as if a beast had risen to devour them, and it had
seemed to Kinson that he could feel its breath on his neck and
hear the scrape of its claws as it pursued them. But they had escaped to the forests without and hidden there in night's fading
dark while the rage of the beast vented itself and died away.
They had remained in the shelter of the trees all the next day
and let Mareth sleep. Bremen had tended her, obviously concerned at first, but when she had come awake long enough to
drink a cup of water before sleeping again, he had ceased to
worry.

"Her magic is too powerful for her" was how he had explained it to Kinson. They were keeping watch over her in the
late-morning hours after she had awakened and gone back to
sleep again. The sun was high overhead, and the dark memory
of the night before was beginning to fade. Paranor was a silent
presence beyond the screen of the trees, gone as still as death,
emptied of life. "It seems obvious that she came to the Druids
in an effort to find a way to better understand it. I suppose she
was not with them long enough to do so. Perhaps she asked to
come with us believing we might help her."

He shook his gray head. "But did you see? She summoned
her magic to protect me from the creatures Brona had left to
ward against my return, and instantly she lost all control! She
seems unable to judge the measure of what is needed. Or perhaps judgment is not an issue at all, and what happens is that
on being summoned, her magic assumes whatever form it
chooses. Whatever the case, it rolls out of her like a flood! In
the Druid's Keep, it swallowed those creatures as if they were
gnats. It was so powerful that it alerted the magic the Keep
maintains for its own protection, the earth magic set in place by
the first Druids. This was magic I tested on my return to make
certain it could still guard against an attempt to destroy the
Keep. I could not protect the Druids from the Warlock Lord,
but I could ward Paranor. Mareth's magic was so pervasive in its
destruction of Brona's creatures that it suggested that the Keep

itself was in danger and thereby conjured forth the earth magic as well."

"Hers is innate magic, you once said," Kinson mused. "Where would it have come from to be so strong?"

The old man pursed his lips. "Another Druid, perhaps. An Elf who carries the old magic in his blood. A faerie creature, survived from the old world. It could be any of those." He arched one eyebrow quizzically. "I wonder if even she knows the answer."

"I wonder if she would tell us if she did" was Kinson's reply.

Thus far, she had barely spoken of it. By the time she came awake, Bremen had gone. It was left to Kinson to advise her that she was not to use her magic again until Bremen had returned and counseled her. She accepted the edict with little more than a nod. She said nothing of what had happened in the Keep. She seemed to have forgotten the matter entirely.

He finished his meal and looked up again. She was watching him.

"What are you thinking?" she asked.

He shrugged. "I was wondering about the man we are sent to find. I was wondering why Bremen considers him so important."

She nodded slowly. "Cogline."

"Do you know the name?"

She did not respond. She seemed not to have heard.

"Perhaps one of your friends at Storlock will be able to help us."

Her eyes went flat. "I have no friends at Storlock."

For a moment he simply stared at her, uncomprehending. "But I thought you told Bremen . . ."

"I lied." She took a breath and her gaze fell away from his. "I lied to him, and I lied to everyone at Paranor before him. It was the only way I could gain acceptance. I was desperate to study with the Druids, and I knew they would not let me if I did not give them a reason. So I told them I had studied with the Stors. I gave them written documents to support the claim, all false. I deliberately misled them." Her gaze lifted. "But I would like to stop lying now and tell the truth."

The darkness was complete about them, the last of the daylight faded, and they sat cloaked within it, barely able to make each other out. Because they would cross the Rabb that night, Kinson had not bothered with a fire. Now he wished he had so that he could better see her face.

"I think," he said slowly, "that this might be a good time for the truth. But how am I to know if what you tell me is the truth or simply another lie?"

She smiled faintly, sadly. "You will know."

He held her gaze. "The lies were because of your magic, weren't they?" he guessed.

"You are perceptive, Kinson Ravenlock," she told him. "I like you for that. Yes, the lies were made necessary because of my magic. I am desperate to find a way to . . ." She hesitated, searching for the right word. "To live with myself. I have struggled with my power for too long, and I am growing weary and despairing. I have thought at times that I would end my life because of what it has done to me."

She paused, looking off into the dark. "I have had the magic since birth. Innate magic, as I told Bremen. That much was the truth. I never knew my father. My mother died giving birth to me. I was raised by people I did not know. If I had relatives, they never revealed themselves. The people who raised me did so for reasons that I have never understood. They were hard, taciturn people, and they told me little. I think there was a sense of obligation, but they never explained its source. I was gone from them by the time I was twelve, apprenticed to a potter, sent to his shop to fetch and haul materials, to clean up, to observe if I wished, but mostly to do what I was told. I had the magic, of course, but like myself it had not yet matured and was still just a vague presence that manifested itself only in small ways.

"As I grew to womanhood, the magic blossomed within me. One day the potter tried to beat me, and I defended myself out of instinct, calling on the magic for protection. I nearly killed him. I left then, and went out into the border country to find a new place to live. For a time, I lived in Varfleet." Her smile returned. "Perhaps we even crossed paths once upon a time. Or were you already gone? Gone, I suppose." She shrugged. "I was attacked again a year later. There were several men this time, and they had more in mind than a beating. I called up the magic again. I could not control it. I killed two of them. I left Varfleet and went east."

Her smile turned mocking and bitter. "You see a pattern to all this, I imagine. I began to believe I could live with no one because I could not trust myself. I drifted from community to community, from farm to farm, earning my way however I could. It was a useful time. I discovered new things about my magic. It was not merely destructive; it was also restorative. I was empathic, I found. I could apply the magic and bring healing to those who were injured. I discovered this by accident when a man I knew and liked was injured and in danger of dying from a fall. It was a revelation that gave me hope. The magic used in this way was controllable. I could not understand why, but it seemed governable when called upon to heal and not to destroy. Perhaps anger is inherently less manageable than sympathy. I don't know.

"In any case, I went to live with the Stors, to ask to be allowed to study with them, to learn to use my skills. But they did not know me and would not accept me into their order. They are Gnomes, and no member of another race has ever been allowed to study with them. They refused to make an exception for me. I tried for months to persuade them otherwise, staying in their village, watching them at their work, taking meals with them when they would let me, asking for a chance and nothing more.

"Then one day a man came down out of the wilderness to visit with the Stors. He wanted something from them, something of their lore, and they did not seem concerned in the least about giving it to him. I marveled. After months of begging for scraps, I had been given nothing. Now this man appears out of nowhere, a Southlander, not a Gnome, and the Stors can't wait to help him. I decided to ask him why."

She scuffed her boot against the earth as if digging at the past. "He was strange-looking, tall and thin, all angles and bones, pinch-faced and wild-haired. He seemed constantly distracted by his thoughts, as if it were the most difficult thing in the world to hold a simple conversation. But I made him speak with me. I made him listen to my story. It became clear as I went along that he understood a great deal about magic. So I told him everything. I confided in him. I don't know why to this day, but I did. He told me the Stors would not have me, that there was no point in remaining in the village. Go to Paranor and the Druids, he suggested. I laughed. They would not have me either, I pointed out. But he said they would. He told me what to tell them. He helped me make up a story and he wrote the papers that would gain me acceptance. He said he knew something of the Druids, that he had been a Druid once, long ago. I was not to mention his name, though. He was not held in favor, he said.

"I asked his name then, and he told it to me. Cogline. He told me that the Druids were no longer what they once were. He told me that with the exception of Bremen they did not go out into the Four Lands as they once had. They would accept the story he had provided for me if I could demonstrate my healing talents. They would not bother to check further on me because they were trusting to a fault. He was right. I did as he told me, and the Druids took me in."

She sighed. "But you see why I asked Bremen to take me with him, don't you? The study of magic is not encouraged at Paranor, not in any meaningful way. Only a few, like Risca and Tay, have any real understanding of it. I was given no chance to discover how to control my own. If I had revealed its presence, I would have been sent away at once. The Druids are afraid of the magic. *Were* afraid rather, for now they are all gone."

"Has your magic grown more powerful?" he asked as she paused. "Has it become more uncontrollable? Was it so when you called it up within the Keep?"

"Yes." Her mouth tightened in a hard line, and there were sudden tears in her eyes. "You saw. It overwhelmed me completely. It was like a flood threatening to drown me. I could not breathe!"

"And so you look to Bremen to help you find a way to master it, the one Druid who might have an understanding of its power."

She looked directly at him. "I do not apologize for what I have done."

He gave her a long look. "I never thought for a minute that you would. Nor do I propose to judge you for your choice. I have not lived your life. But I think the lies should end here. I think you should tell to Bremen when we see him next what you have told to me. If you expect his help, you should at least be honest with him."

She nodded, wiping irritably at her eyes. "I intend that," she said. She looked small and vulnerable, but her voice was hard. She would give up nothing further of herself, he realized. She must have agonized over telling him as much as she had.

"I can be trusted," she said suddenly, as if reading his mind.

"With everything but your magic," he amended.

"No. Even with that. I can be trusted not to use it until Bremen tells me to."

He studied her wordlessly for a moment, then nodded. "Fair enough." He was thinking suddenly, unexpectedly, that they were much alike. Both had traveled far to leave the past behind, and for neither was the journey finished. Both had bound themselves to Bremen, their lives inextricably intertwined with his, and neither could envision now that there had ever been any other choice.

He glanced at the sky and climbed to his feet. "Time for us to be on our way."

They blackened their faces and hands, tied down their metal implements and weapons so they would not clink, went down from their hiding place in the rocks, and set out across the Rabb. The night air was cool and soft, a small breeze blowing out of the foothills and carrying with it the scents of sage and cedar. Clouds drifted overhead, screening away the half-moon and stars so that their light was diffused and they appeared only in brief glimpses. Sound traveled far on such a night, so Kinson and Mareth walked softly, carefully in the tall grasses, avoiding the loose rock that might betray their presence. North, the light of the encamped army was a blaze of smoky saffron against the dark, stretched between the Dragon's Teeth west and the Anar east. Every so often Kinson would stop and listen, picking out the sounds that belonged, wary of those that didn't. Mareth followed a step behind and did not speak.

Kinson could feel her there without having to look, a shadow at his back.

The hours passed, and the plains stretched away about them, lengthening as they crossed so that for a time it appeared they were making no headway. Kinson kept watch over the clouded skies, wary of the winged hunters that would be prowling the night. He kept watch out of habit and not because he expected to see the dark ones. He had learned from experience that he would feel them first, and when he did he must hide at once, for if he waited until he saw them it would be too late. But the unpleasant tingling, the rush of chilling trepidation, the warning of something untoward did not come, and with Mareth following dutifully, he pressed on.

They stopped once to drink from their aleskins, crouching down in a twisting gully choked with brush, sitting close together in the dark. Kinson found himself wondering what it must have been like for her, bereft of family and friends, made outcast by her magic, left homeless by circumstance and choice alike. She showed courage, he thought, in persevering, in not giving up when it would have been easy for her to do so. Nor had she compromised herself or others in choosing her path. He wondered how much of this Bremen had deduced in making his decision to allow her to accompany them. He wondered how well Mareth had succeeded in deceiving the old man. Not so well as she thought, he suspected. He knew from experience that Bremen could look inside you as if you were made of glass and see all the working parts. That was one reason he had managed to stay alive all these years.

Sometime after midnight one of the Skull Bearers crossed their path. He came out of the east, from the direction in which they were proceeding, surprising Kinson, who was thinking any danger would come from the north. He sensed the creature and went down on his face in a patch of brush immediately, dragging Mareth after him. He could tell from the look on her face that she knew what was happening. He pulled her close against him, deep within the concealment.

"Do not look up," he whispered. "Do not even think of what flies above us. It will sense us if you do."

They lay against the earth as the creature flew closer and the fear within them grew until it rushed through them like the sun's heat at midday. Kinson forced himself to breathe normally and to think of days gone when he was a boy hunting with his brothers. He held himself quiet, his body still, his muscles relaxed, his eyes closed. Pressed against him, Mareth matched his breathing and his poise. The Skull Bearer passed overhead, circling. Kinson could feel it, knowing how close it was from experience, from his days spent scouting in the Northland, when the winged hunters had scoured the land in which he traveled every night. Bremen had taught him how to avoid them, how to survive. The feelings the monsters generated could not be avoided, but they could be endured. The feelings alone, after all, could not cause harm. Mareth understood. She did not shift or tremble within the crook of his arm. She did not attempt to rise or bolt from their hiding place. She lay as he did, patient and determined.

At last the Skull Bearer flew on, moving to another part of the plains, leaving them shaken, but relieved. It was always like this, Kinson thought, climbing to his feet. He hated the feeling, hated the shame it generated within him to have to cower so, to have to hide. But he would have hated dying more.

He gave Mareth a reassuring smile, and they walked on into the night.

THEY REACHED STORLOCK just before dawn, wet and bedraggled from a sudden shower that had caught them only a mile or so from the village. Sad-faced and deferential, the white-robed Stors came out to meet them and take them inside. Hardly a word was spoken; words did not seem necessary. The Stors appeared to recognize them both and asked no questions. It was possible they were remembered from before, Kinson thought as he was led in out of the weather. Mareth had lived among the Stors, and he had visited them on several occasions with Bremen. In any case, it made things simpler. Though typically aloof and preoccupied, the Stors were generous with both food and shelter. As if they had been expecting their guests all along, the Stors provided hot soup, dry clothes, and beds in guest rooms in the main building. Within an hour of their arrival, Kinson and Mareth were asleep.

When they woke, it was late afternoon. The rain had stopped, so they stepped outside to look around. The village was quiet, and the surrounding forest felt empty of life. As they walked the roadways from one end to the other, Stors passed wraithlike and silent in pursuit of their tasks, barely looking up at the strangers. No one approached them. No one spoke. They visited several of the hospitals where the Healers were at work on the people who had come to them from various parts of the Four Lands. No one seemed concerned that they were there. No one asked them to leave. While Mareth stopped to play with a pair of small Gnome children who had been burned in a cooking accident, Kinson walked outside and stood looking off into the darkening trees, thinking of the dangers posed by the approach of the Northland army.

At dinner, he told Mareth of his concern. The army would have reached a point on the Rabb close to where the village lay. If there was a need for food or supplies, as there almost always was, scouts would be sent to forage and Storlock would be in real danger. Most knew of the Stors and the work they did, and they respected their privacy. But Brona's army would be held to a different code of conduct, a different set of rules, and the protections normally afforded the village would likely be absent. What would become of the Stors if one of the Skull Bearers came prowling? The Healers had no means of protecting themselves; they knew nothing of fighting. They relied solely on their neutrality and disinterest in politics to keep them safe. But where the winged hunters were concerned, was that enough?

While mulling this dilemma over, they asked after Cogline and discovered almost immediately where he could be found. It seemed not to be any great secret. Cogline kept in regular contact with the Stors, preferring to deal with them to obtain what he needed as opposed to the trading posts that dotted the fringes of the wilderness into which he had retreated. The once-Druid had made his home deep within the Anar, in the seldom traversed tangle of Darklin Reach at a place called Hearthstone. Even Kinson had never heard of Hearthstone, though he knew of Darklin Reach and regarded it as a place to be avoided. Spider Gnomes lived there, wiry, barely human creatures so wild and primitive they communed with spirits and sacrificed to old gods. Darklin Reach was a world frozen in time, unchanged since the advent of the Great Wars, and Kinson was not pleased to learn that they would probably have to travel there.

After dinner was completed and the Stors had drifted back to whatever work commanded their attention, the Borderman sat with the girl on a hard-backed bench on the dining-hall porch and looked out at the gathering gloom. His thoughts were distracting to him. Bremen had not appeared. Perhaps he was still at Paranor. Perhaps he was trapped on the other side of the Rabb, with the Northland army settled between them. Kinson did not like the uncertainty of it. He did not like being forced to await the Druid's arrival, kept idle when he would rather be active. He could wait when it was necessary, but he questioned the reason for waiting now. It seemed to him that Bremen should have sent him on ahead to look for Cogline, even if it meant going into Darklin Reach. It felt to him as if time was slipping away from them all.

A line of Stors appeared from the hall, cloaked and hooded, withdrawn and secretive. They went down the porch steps and across the roadway to another building, their white forms slowly fading into the gray haze of twilight, ghosts in the night. Kinson wondered at their single-mindedness, at the peculiar mix of dedication to work and obliviousness to the world beyond their tiny village. He glanced at Mareth, trying to picture her as one of them, wondering if she still wished she had been accepted into their order. Would the isolation better agree with her, beset by the dictates of her magic's use, by the threat of its escape? Would she feel less constrained here than at Paranor? The puzzle of her life intrigued him, and he found himself thinking of her in ways he had never thought of anyone else.

He slept poorly that night, plagued by dreams rife with faceless, threatening creatures. When he came awake shortly before dawn, he was on his feet and had his sword in hand almost before he realized what he was doing. There were voices without, harsh and guttural, and he could hear the ring and scrape of armor. He knew at once what had happened. Leaving his boots behind, taking only his sword, he eased from his bedroom and slipped down the hallway to the front entry where a bank of windows opened onto the main street. Keeping to the shadows, he peered out.

A large Troll raiding party had appeared in the roadway and was facing a small cluster of Stors who stood on the steps of the main healing center across the way. The Trolls were armed and threatening; their gestures made it clear that they intended to go inside. The Stors were not opposing them in an overt manner, but neither were they giving way. The angry voices belonged to the Trolls; the Stors were silent and stoic in the face of the intruders' threats. Kinson could not tell what the Trolls wanted—whether it was food and supplies or something more. But he could tell that the Trolls were not going to give up on their demands. They understood as clearly as he did that there was no one in the village to oppose them.

Kinson stared from darkened building to shadowed walkway, from heavy forest to open road, and considered his options. He could stay where he was and hope that nothing happened. If he did that, he was condemning the Stors to whatever fate the Trolls decided upon. He could attack the Trolls from the rear and probably kill as many as four or five before the rest overpowered him. Not much would be accomplished with that. Once he was killed, as he surely would be, the Trolls would be free to do as they chose with the Stors anyway. He could try a diversion. But there was nothing to guarantee that he would draw all of the Trolls away from the village or that they would not return later.

He thought suddenly of Mareth. She had the power to save these people. Her magic was powerful enough to incinerate the entire Troll raiding party before even one could blink. But Mareth was forbidden to use her magic, and without her magic she was as vulnerable as the Stors.

Across the way, one of the Trolls had begun to climb the steps onto the porch, his huge pike lowered menacingly. The Stors waited for him, white-robed sheep in the path of a wolf. Kinson gripped his sword tighter and moved to the front door, easing it carefully open. Whatever he was going to do, he was going to have to do it quickly.

He was ready to step out from the shadows of the doorway when a shriek arose from the midst of the beleaguered Stors. Someone pushed through them from out of the building they warded, a shambling, half-clothed figure that tottered and flailed as if beset by a form of madness. Rags trailed from the figure, the bindings for wounds that now lay open and weeping. The creature's face was ravaged by sores and lesions, the body made frail by a wasting disease that had left the bones taut against the mottled and withered skin.

The figure stumbled from the midst of the Stors to the edge of the porch, wailing in despair. The Trolls brought up their weapons guardedly, the foremost falling back a step in shock.

"Plague!" the ravaged creature howled, the word rising up in the silence, harsh and terrible. A swarm of insects rose off the creature's back, buzzing madly. "Plague, plague everywhere! Flee! Flee!"

The creature swayed and dropped to its knees. Bits of flesh fell from it, and blood dripped from its open wounds onto the wooden steps, steaming in the cool night air. Kinson winced in horror. The disease was causing it quite literally to fall apart!

It was all too much for the Trolls. Soldiers to the core, they were brave in the face of enemies they could see, but as terrified of the invisible as the meekest shopkeeper. They fell back in disarray, trying not to show fear, but determined not to stay another moment in close proximity to the disaster that had collapsed on the steps before them. Their leader waved off the Stors and their village in a gesture of anxious defiance, and the entire patrol hurried back down the roadway in the direction of the Rabb and disappeared into the trees.

When they were gone, Kinson stepped into the light, sword lowering as the pulse of his body slowed and the heat of his blood cooled. He looked back at the Stors across the way, finding them clustered about the strange apparition, heedless of the disease that ravaged it. Forcing himself to ignore his own fear, he crossed to see if he could be of help.

On reaching them, he found Mareth standing in their midst.

"I broke my promise," she said, her large dark eyes anxious, her smooth face troubled. "I'm sorry, but I could not stand by and see them harmed."

"You used your magic," he guessed, amazed.

"Just a little. Just that part that goes into the healing, the part I use as an empath. I can reverse it to make what is well appear sick."

"Appear?"

"Well, mostly." She hesitated. He could see the weariness now, the dark circles about her eyes, the lines of fading pain etched at the corners of her mouth. Sweat beaded her forehead. Her fingers were crooked and rigid. "You understand, Kinson. It was necessary."

"And dangerous," he added.

Her eyelids fluttered. She was on the verge of a real collapse. "I am all right now. I just need to sleep. Can you help me walk?"

He shook his head in dismay, picked her up without a word, and carried her back to her room.

THE FOLLOWING DAY, the Northland army decamped and moved south. One day later, Bremen appeared. Mareth had recovered from the effects of her magic and looked strong and well again, but Bremen appeared to have taken her place. He was haggard and worn, dust-covered and spattered with mud, and clearly angered. He ate, bathed, dressed in fresh clothing, and then told them what had kept him. After making certain that the magic that warded the Druid's Keep was returned to its safehold and that the Keep was intact, he had gone once more to the Hadeshorn to speak with the spirits of the dead. He was hoping that he might learn more of the visions he had been shown on his last visit, that something further might be revealed to him. But the spirits would not speak, would not even appear, and the waters of the lake rose up in such fury at his summons that they threatened to inundate him, to drag him down into their depths for the audacity of his intrusion. His voice took on an edge as he described his treatment. He had been given all the help he was going to get, it appeared. Their fate, from here forward, was largely in their own hands.

On being asked of Cogline, he demurred. Time enough for that later. For now, they would have to be patient and let an old man catch up on his sleep.

Kinson and Mareth knew better than to argue. A few days of rest were clearly necessary to restore the old man's strength.

But before the sun had risen the following day, the Druid collected them from their beds and in the deep, predawn silence took them out of the still sleeping village of the Stors toward Darklin Reach.

CHAPTER

14

ITH PREIA STARLE and Retten Kipp still absent and the Sarandanon drawing near, Tay Trefenwyd now assumed the point position for the little company from Arborlon. Jerle Shannara objected, but not strongly, conceding Tay's argument that with his Druid skills he was best suited to keep watch against whatever threatened. Tay spun out a faint webbing of magic, strands that extended like nerve endings to warn him of what waited ahead. Using his Druid training, he drew upon his command of the elements to test for the presence of intruders.

Nothing revealed itself.

Behind him, the others fanned out, keeping watch left and right. The morning warmed, the dampness of the past two days dried, and the trees ahead thinned so that the valley of the Sarandanon grew visible, its broad sweep spreading away into the haze of the mountains farther west.

Tay's mind wandered. For the first time since his return from Paranor, he allowed himself to consider what losing Preia Starle might mean. It was an odd exercise, since she had never really been his to lose in the first place. To the extent that she belonged to anyone, she belonged to Jerle. She had always belonged to him, and Tay had known it. But he realized that he had thought of her as his anyway, that he had loved her steadfastly and without bitterness toward Jerle, accepting as settled her relationship with his best friend, content to keep her as he might a memory that he could call up and admire but never really possess. He was a Druid, and Druids did not take mates, their lives given over to the pursuit of knowledge and the dissemination of learning. They lived apart and they died alone. But their feelings were the same as those of other men and women, and Tay understood that somehow he had always been sustained by his feelings for Preia.

What would it mean for him if she was gone?

The question burned through him like fire, heating his blood, searing his skin, threatening to immolate him. He could barely get through the question, let alone address the answer. What if she was dead? He had always been prepared to lose her in other ways. He knew that she would marry Jerle one day. He knew that they would have children and a life apart from him. He had separated himself from any other possibility long ago. He had left all that behind when he had gone to live among the Druids, to be a member of their order. He recognized that what he felt for her could find no expression in real life, but must remain a fantasy locked within his imagination— that she was never to be more to him than a close friend.

But thinking of her dead, of her life ended, forced him to concede what before he could never admit—that he had always harbored the hope, however faint, that somehow the impossible might happen and she would forsake Jerle to become his.

The realization was so strong that for a moment he lost track of where he was, let loose the strands of his seeking magic, gave up the sweep of the dark places that waited ahead, and was made blind to everything but this single truth. Preia his—he had kept the dream alive and carefully protected in the secretmost corner of his mind. Preia his, because he could not stop himself from wanting her.

Oh, shades!

He recovered himself in the next instant, gathered up the lines of his magic, and pushed on. He could not afford such thoughts. He did not dare to think further of Preia Starle. The admonishments of Bremen came rushing back, words spoken with the iron weight of armor being fastened to his body. Persuade the Elves to come to the aid of the Dwarves. Find the Black Elfstone. Those two charges ruled his life. Nothing else mattered. There were lives beyond his own and those of the

FIRST KING OF SHANNARA

people he loved that depended on his perseverance, on his diligence, on his resolve. He looked off into the haze of the valley ahead and carried himself out from the present and into the future by strength of will alone.

By midday, they had crossed into the Sarandanon. Twice more, they encountered the tracks of Gnome Hunters in large numbers without seeing the Gnomes themselves. The Elves were edgy now, anxious to gain the mounts they had been promised and to be gone from this region. If they were caught out in the open by a superior force with no way to flee, they would be in serious trouble. Tay searched the earth and air for Gnomes and found signs of their passing all about, but still no actual presence. The Gnomes, he decided, were crisscrossing the valley's east end in search of them. If they had found Preia, they would know she was not alone. A Tracker would be with a larger party, scouting ahead for them. Had they found Preia then? Was he conceding as much? It seemed an unavoidable conclusion, given the discovery of her broken bow amid the cluster of enemy footprints. All of which led once more to the inevitable second question he was so desperately trying to avoid.

Jerle knew all of the valley outposts where horses were kept quartered for Elven Hunter use, and he made for the closest. The land was rolling and thick with tall grasses where the crop fields did not extend. They kept to these, staying down off the hills. When they were less than a mile from their destination, Tay gained a strong sense of Gnome Hunters and brought the party to a stop. Somewhere close ahead, a trap had been set. The Gnomes were expecting them. Leaving the others to await their return, Tay and Jerle went on alone, working their way south and then north again to come in from a different direction than the one from which they were expected. Tay's magic sheltered them from discovery and gave them eyes with which to see. By the time they neared the small cluster of buildings that formed the outpost, Tay had determined that it was here the trap had been laid. The wind, no more than a soft breeze, blew into their faces, and both could smell the enemy clearly, a rough mix of body oil and earth, heavy and pungent. No effort was being made to disguise it. Tay was instantly alarmed.

Gnome Hunters would normally be more cautious than this. They crawled to where they could see one side of the barn and the whole of the paddock in which the horses were kept. There was nothing there. The paddock was empty. No one moved in the yard. No sounds came from the house.

Yet something was hidden there. Tay was certain of it.

Unwilling to leave without determining what had happened, both of them thinking separately and without saying so that Preia Starle might be involved, they eased their way along a drainage ditch behind a pasture of new wheat, so that they could see the front of the house and barn. Tay could now sense movement in both buildings, restless and furtive. Gnome Hunters, waiting. He tried to sense the presence of anything else, of anything more dangerous. Nothing. Tay breathed slowly, easily, following Jerle's lead as his friend slipped silently ahead. He was conscious of the wheat stalks singing faintly with their movement in the wind and of the deep, vast silence of the land beyond. He was reminded of what it had felt like when they had slipped into the house of the Ballindarrochs on the night of the slaughter—of the sense of foreboding, of the whisper of doom.

Then they were where Jerle wanted them, still concealed within the wheat, but close enough to see the front of the outpost. Jerle lifted his head slightly and then dropped quickly down again, his face ashen. Tay stared at him a moment, searching his eyes, then rose cautiously to look for himself.

Retten Kipp hung spread-eagled from the barn door, where nails had been driven through his hands and feet to hold him in place. Blood dripped from his wounds and stained the splintered wood. Hair and clothes drooped limply, as if from the stick frame of a scarecrow. But then Kipp's head lifted slightly. The old Tracker, though dying, was still alive.

Tay sank down, eyes closing momentarily. Rage and fear coursed through him, struggling for control of his reason. No wonder the Gnomes had not worked harder at hiding their presence. With Retten Kipp to bait their trap, they knew the Elves must show themselves. He fought to bring his feelings under control, staring grim-faced at Jerle Shannara.

His friend's blue eyes were cold and steady as he bent close. "Do they have Preia as well?" he whispered.

Tay did not reply. He did not trust himself. Instead, he closed his eyes a second time and sent his threads of magic into the house and barn, searching for the Elf girl. There was risk in this, but he saw no other way. He took his time, going deep inside each building to make certain.

Then he let his eyes open again. "No," he breathed.

Jerle nodded, letting nothing show in his face of what that meant to him. His mouth twisted. His words were barely audible. "We cannot save Retten Kipp—but we cannot leave him either."

He stared at Tay, waiting. Tay nodded. He knew what Jerle was asking. "I understand," he breathed softly.

This would be dangerous, he knew. The Gnome Hunters might not sense his use of the magic, but a Skull Bearer most certainly would. He had not discovered any of the winged hunters in his search for Preia, but they might be deliberately concealing themselves. This trap might have been designed specifically for him, one of the Druids they hunted, to bring him to them and then to draw him out. If a Skull Bearer was present and he did what Jerle wanted, they were lost. Still, there was little choice. Jerle was right. They could not leave Kipp to die this way.

He summoned his magic and wrapped himself in its dark cloak, stirring the air about him with its power, feeling the heat of its passion rise within his chest. He kept his eyes open, for this time his use of the magic would require sight and direction. His face altered and assumed the character of a death mask. He watched Jerle shrink from him, dismayed. He understood the look.

Then he lifted his head just high enough so that he could see Retten Kipp's ragged, tortured form and spun the magic toward him along the slender thread of his life line. He proceeded cautiously, testing the ether he penetrated, wary of what he might find waiting. But nothing revealed itself, and so he continued on. When he reached Retten Kipp's heart, when he could feel his pain and suffering, when he could hear the sound of his ragged breathing as if it were his own, he drew away the air that fed the old man's failing lungs and then waited patiently until his breathing stopped.

When it was finished, he slid down next to Jerle, his face shiny with sweat. There were tears in his eyes. "Done," he whispered.

Jerle Shannara put a hand on his shoulder and squeezed gently to comfort him. "It was necessary, Tay. He was in pain. We could not simply leave him."

Tay nodded wordlessly, knowing Jerle was right, but knowing as well that his friend would not have to live with the memory of Retten Kipp's life thread pulsing gently between his fingers and then going still. He felt cold and empty. He felt ravaged and abandoned.

Jerle beckoned to him, and together they made their way back along the ditch and through the fields, leaving the outpost and its inhabitants, living and dead, behind.

It TOOK THEM the better part of an hour to reach their comrades. By now it was nearing midafternoon, and the sun was lowering toward the jagged tips of the Breakline. They walked into its burning glare, half-blind when they were forced to move out of the shadow of the fields and hills and along the flats. Tay continued to lead, his magic spread out before them in a wide net, searching. He had checked for pursuit after their return from the farmhouse, but found none. Ahead, however, there were hints of Gnome Hunters at almost every turn. He could not tell how strong the parties were, but there were several. They had discussed waiting until dark before proceeding, but had decided it was more dangerous to remain in one place than to go on. Jerle stayed close, guiding him toward the secondary outpost that lay a few miles farther on, hopeful that this one might not have been discovered. Neither spoke. All about them, the others of the company scanned the countryside for enemies.

Then suddenly Vree Erreden was at Tay's elbow, his small, slight form pressing close, his pinched face eager. "There!" He pointed sharply left. "Horses, a dozen or more, hidden in that draw!"

Tay and Jerle stopped and stared, seeing nothing beyond a line of fields planted thick with early corn.

The locat's eyes darted from one face to the other, his impatience obvious. "Don't waste your time looking! You can't see them from here!"

"Then how do you know?" Jerle asked quickly.

"Intuition!" the other snapped. "How else?"

The big man glanced over doubtfully. "The outpost we seek lies just ahead. Are there horses there as well?"

Vree Erreden's voice was sharp with urgency. "I only know what my intuition tells me! There are horses left, in a draw beyond those hills!" He pointed again for emphasis.

Jerle Shannara frowned, irritated by the other's insistence. "What if you are wrong, locat? How far is it to this draw that none of us can see?"

Tay held up his hand quickly to forestall Vree Erreden's angry reply. He stood silent a moment, weighing the choice, then gazed out across the fields one final time. "Are you sure about the horses?" he asked the small man quietly.

The look the other gave him was withering. Tay's smile cocked slightly, and he nodded. "I think we should see what lies left."

Despite Jerle's continued misgivings, they changed course, making their way across the flats. The central bowl of the Sarandanon spread away before them, the planting fields a sprawling patchwork quilt of raw earth and new crops. They were out in the open now and clearly visible to whoever might be looking for them. There was no help for it. Whichever way they traveled they were exposed, and Tay took what comfort he could from that, because they were moving away from the outpost and if Vree Erreden was mistaken or had somehow been misled, their chances of escape were diminished considerably. Tay tried not to worry. It was for this that he had brought the locat—his ability to sense what even Druid magic could not. The little man would not have said anything if his instincts were not strong. He knew the risks of their situation as well as Tay.

Tay's net of magic spread wider in search of enemies, and now he found them. They came swiftly from the north, a Gnome patrol on horseback, still some distance away, but racing across the flats. He could not see them yet, but there was no mistaking their intent. He shouted a quick warning to Jerle, and the members of the little company began to run. Ahead, the fields abutted a line of low hills. The draw must lie beyond, Tay thought. And the horses as well, he prayed, for they were too far now from the outpost to escape any other way.

Then more Gnomes appeared, a new band, this one spilling out of its hiding place within the outpost, which now barely visible through the stalks of corn. These Gnomes were afoot, but began a determined charge forward to intercept the Elves, obviously intent on slowing them until the arrival of their mounted brethren. Tay gritted his teeth as he ran. There was no help to be had from the outpost. Now there was only Vree Erreden's intuition and the draw.

Jerle Shannara sprinted past him effortlessly, feet flying across the plowed earth as he tore through the cornrows for the hills. Others surged ahead as well, swifter afoot than Tay. Laboring heavily, his breath a sharp pain in his chest, the Druid suddenly panicked. What if the horses that Vree Erreden had sensed were part of another trap? What if there were Gnomes sitting astride them, waiting? Frantically, he tried to cast his net of magic beyond the hills to discover if there was cause for his fear, but his strength was failing and he could not manage the reach.

Shouts, raucous and jarring, rose from the pursuing Gnomes. Tay ignored them. Vree Erreden appeared beside him again, running close, in better shape than Tay would have imagined. Tay yelled at him in warning, but he did not seem to hear. He passed Tay by and went on. Tay now trailed everyone. It was the price you paid for living a sedentary life, he thought ironically.

Then Jerle Shannara broke from the cornfield and began to race up the line of hills. As he did so, a shrill whinny and a pounding of hooves rose from behind the crest. Dust lifted in a cloud in the clear afternoon air. Jerle slowed, unsure of what he faced, reached quickly for his sword, and drew it free. His Elven Hunters raced to protect him. Metal blades glittered in the sun, the light dancing from their polished surfaces in sudden explosions of brightness.

In the next instant a line of horses surged into view, charging out of the sun's glare in a burst of sound and color. There were a dozen, maybe more, all roped together, galloping out of the late-afternoon swelter to take shape like a mirage brought to life.

A single rider led them, bent low over the lead mount.

Tay Trefenwyd slowed to a ragged halt at the edge of the cornfield, his heart beating wildly, his pulse pounding in his head.

The rider was Preia Starle.

She swept by Jerle Shannara without slowing, releasing several of the mounts as she did, the ropes tossed to his waiting hands. She rode on, dropping off the horses one by one to the Elven Hunters she passed. Straight for Tay she came and reined to a wild halt before him.

"Climb on, Tay Trefenwyd, and we'll ride for our lives! The Gnomes are all about!" Blood flecked her face and tunic. He could see cuts and bruises on her face. She wheeled her mount into him so hard she nearly knocked him down. "Get on!" she screamed.

There was no time to think about it. The others of the little company were already mounted and racing away. Tay stepped into the stirrup she had kicked free and swung up behind her. "Hold tight to me!" she cried.

In a whirlwind of dust and grit and a pounding of hooves, they charged after the others.

IT WAS A TERRIFYING FLIGHT. The Gnomes afoot had spread out across the fields before them in an effort to block their escape, some with slings, some with bows. North, visible now for the first time, the Gnomes on horseback appeared. Together, they outnumbered the Elves nearly four to one. They were clearly too many to defeat in a pitched battle.

Jerle Shannara took the lead and rode straight at the Gnomes afoot. The reason for his decision was obvious. The only hope for the Elves was to outdistance the Gnomes on horseback, and the only way to do that was to get ahead of them and stay there. If they swung left, which was what the Gnomes on foot were trying to make them do, they would be forced back up into the low hills and slowed, allowing the Gnomes on horseback to cut them off. If they swung right, they would be heading directly at their mounted pursuers. There was, of course, no point in turning back. What was left, then, was to go forward, to break past the Gnomes afoot and ride west, because everyone knew, Elves and Gnomes alike, that the Gnome didn't live who could outride an Elf.

Down through the cornrows raced the Elven Hunters, some in one field, some in another, spread out as far as they could manage so as to thin the ranks of the enemy archers and slingers, to confuse and divide, to break free of the trap. The Gnomes darted here and there, calling out wildly, trying to track their prey. The Elves stayed low astride their mounts, presenting the smallest targets possible. Only Jerle defied the odds, rising in his stirrups, howling like a madman at the Gnomes before him, his sword swinging above his head like a deadly scythe. From his position far to the left, Tay could just make him out, charging into the teeth of the Gnome line, the big bay he rode leaping recklessly through the furrowed rows. Tay knew what his friend was doing. He was trying to draw as many of the Gnomes as possible to him to give his companions a better chance.

Then Preia hissed at him to stay down, and the burly sorrel she rode swerved sharply along a shallow draw, breaking out of the field close against the line of hills. Tay thought he heard something whip past his head. He lowered himself over Preia's slender back, a protective cloak, hanging tightly to her waist. He could feel her body move in front of him, leaning this way and that, her horse responding each time. He had a glimpse of someone running toward them, a blur of arms and legs amid the cornstalks. Something small and hard slammed into his shoulder, and he felt his arm go numb. His grip on Preia loosened, and he thought he might fall, but she reached back for him with one arm, helping him keep his seat. They reached the west end of the field, vaulted a drainage ditch to a wide swath of grassland, and galloped into the open. Tay risked a glance over

his shoulder. Gnomes knelt at the edge of the corn and slung
their stones and fired their arrows in obvious rage. But already
the missiles were falling short of their mark.

Tay looked ahead again. Elven riders streamed out abreast
of them in a ragged line, racing toward the sunset, past the
abandoned outpost buildings and into the grasslands beyond.
Tay tried to count their numbers, tried to determine if Jerle in
particular was all right, but the landscape was clouded by dust
and cloaked in a damp shimmer of late-afternoon heat, and he
quickly gave up and concentrated all of his efforts on not falling
off the horse.

The Elves joined up again not far beyond the outpost and
began to pace their horses against the demands of their flight.
Miraculously, all had escaped, most uninjured. Jerle Shannara
was barely scratched. Tay discovered that he had been struck
on the shoulder by a slinger's stone and sustained a deep bruise.
The numbness was already fading, replaced by a dull pain.
Nothing broken, he decided, and pushed the matter aside. The
Gnomes on horseback chased after them, swinging west across
the grasslands when they realized that their quarry had broken
through the trap in the cornfields. But they had already ridden
their horses a long way to get this far, and they did not know
the country as the Elves did. Taking the lead once more, Jerle
Shannara chose the path most advantageous to his company.
This was his homeland, and he knew it well. Where the land
dipped suddenly, he could find the high passage. Where sink-
holes or bogs threatened, he was forewarned to swing wide.
Where rivers flowed swift and broad, he could point to the
shallows. The chase wore on, but the Gnomes fell steadily farther behind, and by nightfall they were no longer visible
against the darkening horizon.

Even so, and after they had slowed their horses to a walk to
guard against injury in the dimness of the clouded night sky,
they went on for a time, unwilling to risk a chance discovery.
Jerle took them north along a creek bed, hiding their passing
while changing their direction. The darkness cloaked them, a
welcome friend. The heat of the day seeped away and the air
cooled. A thin rain fell for a time, then passed on. They rode
in silence, save for the splashing of the horses in the shallow

water and, when they left the stream, the muffled thud of their hooves in the soft earth.

When he could do so safely, Tay bent close to Preia's ear and whispered, "What happened to you?"

She glanced back at him, her eyes startlingly bright amid the crosshatched damage to her face. "A trap." Her voice was a low, angry hiss. "Kipp had gone on ahead to secure the horses at the first outpost. I was scouting against discovery by the Gnome Hunters we had determined were in the area. But they were waiting for us. I was lucky. Kipp wasn't."

"We found Kipp, Jerle and I," he said softly.

She nodded, no response. He wanted to tell her what he had done and why, but he could not bring himself to speak the words.

"How did they know?" he pressed.

He could feel her shrug. "They didn't. They guessed. The outposts are no secret. The Gnomes knew we would come searching for the Black Elfstone. They simply waited for us. They are waiting at all of the outposts, I imagine." She paused. "If they had known our plans exactly, if they had known how to find us, they would have gotten me as well as Kipp. But I found them just before they found me."

"You had to fight to get away, though. We found your bow."

She shook her head. "I was afraid you would. It could not be helped."

"We thought . . ."

"I dropped it fleeing them," she cut him off before he could say what they had thought. "Then I went after Kipp. That was where the fighting took place. At the outpost, just after they seized him. But there were too many for me. I had to leave him."

The words were edged with bitterness. It had cost her to tell him this. "We had to leave him as well," he admitted.

She did not turn. "Alive?"

He shook his head slowly.

He felt her sigh. "I could not get back to warn you. There were too many Gnomes between us. I had to go on ahead to try to secure the horses. I knew that without horses, we were finished. I thought, too, that I could draw some of them off." Her laugh was small and hollow. "Wishful thinking, I'm afraid. Anyway, I was able to steal a horse from under their noses last night while they slept, ride it south to an outpost beyond the valley that I knew they would not have discovered, secure these horses we ride now, herd them back again, and hide until you appeared."

Tay stared at her, astonished. "How in the world did you manage all that in one day?"

She shrugged. "It wasn't that hard." There was a long pause, with only the soft thud of the horses' hooves. "Not as hard as what you had to do." She looked back at him once more, her smile sad and uncertain. "You did well, Tay."

He forced himself to smile back. "You did better."

"I wouldn't want to lose you," she said suddenly, and turned away.

He sat silent behind her, unable to offer a reply.

THEY RODE ON THROUGH the night and made camp just before dawn in a shallow ravine grown thick with slender-boughed ash and white birch. They slept only a few hours, rose, ate, and went on. The rain had returned, a steady drizzle, and with it a mist that clouded the whole of the land in roiling gray. The mist and the rain hid them, and so they pressed on through that day and the next and deep into the second day's night, hidden from those who searched for them. Tay rode point with Preia Starle, using his magic to scan the heavy gloom, worried not so much that they might be discovered by Gnome Hunters as that they might accidentally stumble across them. They walked their horses most of the time, anxious to save their strength for when it would be needed and to guard against missteps in the rain-soaked earth.

Tay and Preia did not talk, concentrating on keeping watch, he with his magic, she with her eyes. But they pressed close against each other in the rain, and for Tay, that was enough. He allowed himself to imagine they meant more to each other than they did. It was a pointless exercise, but it made him feel for a short time as if he had found a place for himself in the world beyond Paranor. He thought that if he tried hard enough, perhaps he could find a way to belong again, even without Preia. He knew that she could not accompany him, but perhaps she could help him find a path. He held her loosely about the waist, shielding her from the weather with his taller frame, feeling the heat of her body seep into his. He wondered at how he had gotten to where he was in life. He wondered at the choices he had made and whether, if made over again, they might be different.

They slept near dawn of the third day, finding shelter this time in a grove of towering hardwoods set back within a blind draw at the edge of the Kensrowe. They had traveled far north of where they had come into the valley, and were now close to its west end. Ahead lay the dark stretch of the Innisbore and the pass through Baen Draw that would take them to the Breakline. Tay had found no trace of Gnomes that day. He was beginning to believe they had outdistanced their pursuers and would lose them for good in the tangle of the mountains ahead.

Tay rose early and found Jerle Shannara already awake, standing at the edge of the camp looking out into the new day. It was gloomy and dark once more, the weather unchanged.

The big man turned at his approach. "Tay. Too short a night, wasn't it?"

Tay shrugged. "I slept well enough."

"Not like you're used to sleeping, though. Not like you did at Paranor with the Druids, in a bed, in a dry room, with hot food waiting when you rose."

Tay moved up beside him, avoiding his gaze. "It doesn't matter. The Druids are all dead. Paranor is gone. That part of my life is over."

His friend's blue eyes studied him shrewdly. "Something bothers you. I know you too well to miss it. You've been distracted these past few days. Is it Retten Kipp? Is it what you had to do to release him from his pain?"

"No," Tay answered truthfully. "It is more complicated than that."

Jerle waited a moment. "Am I to guess or would you rather I simply left the matter alone?"

Tay hesitated, not certain he wanted to give any answer at

all. "It has to do with coming back to something after being away for too long," he replied finally, choosing his words with care. "I was gone from the Westland for fifteen years. Now I am back, but I don't seem to belong anymore. I don't know where I should be or how I should act or what I should do. If it were not for this search, I would be completely lost."

"Maybe the search is enough for now," his friend suggested gently. "Maybe the rest will come with time."

Tay shook his head. "I don't think so. I think I am changed and cannot change back again. Those years at Paranor shaped me in ways I did not begin to understand until now. I feel caught between who I was and who I am. I don't feel like I am either one or the other."

"But you have just come home, Tay. You cannot expect everything to feel the same at first. Of course it feels strange."

Tay looked at his friend. "I think maybe I shall have to go away again, Jerle, when this is over."

Jerle Shannara pushed back his blond hair from his eyes, the mist's dampness glistening on his face. "I would be very sorry to see that happen." He paused. "But I would understand, Tay. And we will still be friends forever."

He put his hand on Tay's shoulder and kept it there. Tay smiled in response. "We will always be friends," he agreed.

THEY RODE WEST once more into the damp haze. The rain quickened and turned heavier as the day wore on. They made their way across the last quarter of the Sarandanon, riders cloaked in the gloom, all but invisible even to each other. It was as if the world from which they had come and into which they were going had melted away. It was as if nothing remained but the small bit of earth across which they rode, materializing ahead, disappearing behind, never there for longer than the few moments it took to pass by.

They came to Baen Draw, the entrance through the Kensrowe to the Breakline, at dusk, came upon it as the light was failing completely. There they found the Gnome Hunters once more, and again the Gnomes were ahead of them. A large contingent had settled into the draw, blocking it against all passage.

It was a different group from those who had attacked them in the east valley; these Hunters had been settled here for a long time. Preia Starle scouted ahead and found their camp. The camp, she reported, was old and established. The sentry lines stretched across the mouth of the draw, and there was no way to get past unseen. Avoiding the draw would do the job, but would add three days to the journey, and the Elves could not afford the delay. They would have to find a way to go through here.

After some consideration, they settled on a plan that relied mostly on surprise. They waited until midnight, then mounted up and rode directly for the pass. Hooded and cloaked, shrouded by night and the weather, they were barely visible to each other, let alone to the Gnome sentries watching for them. They rode without hurry, seemingly at ease, giving the impression that they belonged where they were. When they were near enough to the mouth of the pass to be challenged, Tay, who spoke any number of languages learned from his time at Paranor, called out to the Gnomes in their own tongue, behaving as if they were expected. Reinforcements, he advised casually, and the Elves rode closer.

By the time the Gnomes thought to act on their uncertainty, the Elves were on top of them, putting heels to their horses, and surging ahead into the draw. They rode directly through the camp, scattering fires and Gnomes in all directions, howling as if they were a hundred instead of a handful. The surprise was complete. The Gnomes rolled out of their bedding and gave chase, but by then the Elves were safely away.

But then their luck ran out. As a precaution against just such a breakdown, the Gnomes had established a second line at the far end of the draw, and these Hunters heard the warning cries of their comrades and were waiting as the Elves rode into them. Spears, arrows, and slingers' stones flew at the Elves as they raced toward the end of the pass. There was no time to slow, to rethink their strategy, to do anything but bend low and hope they would break free. Jerle Shannara charged right into the thickest knot of attackers, fearless and unyielding. Weapons swung toward him and a hail of missiles sought to bring him down. But he was charmed, as always, and somehow he kept astride his horse and his horse stayed upright. Together they careered into the Gnomes, and Tay Trefenwyd watched bodies spin away like pieces of deadwood. Then Jerle Shannara was clear.

Tay and Preia escaped as well, the Tracker girl's sturdy pony barreling past the crush of attackers along the left bank of the draw, then leaping a trip line that was meant to bring it down. Shouts of hunters and hunted alike mingled with the screams of horses. Riders shot past, disembodied shapes charging back and forth in the gloom. In desperation Tay used his magic to throw a screen around the remaining Elves in an effort to hide them from the Gnomes.

But when they reassembled several miles beyond the draw, six among them were missing. Now their number was reduced to eight, and the hundreds of Gnome Hunters that were scattered throughout the Sarandanon would converge on the pass and track them into the Breakline.

They would track them until they were found.

CHAPTER

15

B Y NIGHTFALL of the following day, the Elves were deep
within the mountains. They had ridden on through the
previous night after escaping the Gnome Hunters at
Baen Draw, working their way up into the rugged foothills that fronted the Breakline, pressing on until the dawn light
began to creep out of the east and spill down into the bowl of
the Sarandanon. They had rested then for a few hours, risen,
eaten, and gone on. The rains had ceased, but the skies remained clouded and gray, and mist hung across the hills in a
thick blanket. There was a dampness in the air that carried the
smell of earth and rotting wood. As they climbed higher, the
hills turned barren and rocky, and the smell dissipated. Now
the air was cool and sharp and clear, and the mist began to
break apart.

Noon came, and they left the hills behind and wound their
way up into the mountains. Jerle Shannara had already told the
company that they would ride until dark, anxious to put distance between themselves and their pursuers, determined that
before they stopped they would be on terrain that would not
leave a trail that could be easily followed. No one argued the
point. They rode obediently through the gloom and silence,
watching as the mist cleared and the mountains rose before
them. The Breakline was a wall of jagged rock, of peaks that
soared skyward until they disappeared into the clouds, of cliffs
that fell away in sheer drops of thousands of feet, of massive
outcroppings and ragged splits formed by pressure in the earth

from a time when the world was still forming. The mountains lifted to the heavens as if trying to climb free of the world, an outstretching of the arms of giants frozen by time. As far north and south as the Elves could see, the Breakline was visible against the sky, a barrier forbidding passage, a fortress against encroachment.

The Elves stared at the mountains in silence, and in the face of such permanence felt an unmistakable sense of their own mortality.

By nightfall, they had passed beyond the lower peaks and could no longer look back on either the foothills that had brought them up or the more distant valley of the Sarandanon. They camped in a grove of spruce cradled in a narrow valley tucked between barren peaks on which snow glistened in a thin, white mantle. There was fresh water and grass for the horses, and wood for a fire.

As soon as they were settled and had eaten, Preia Starle departed to backtrack their trail to determine if a pursuit had been mounted. While they waited for her return, Tay conferred with Jerle and Vree Erreden about the vision that had revealed the location of the Black Elfstone. Once more, he recounted its specifics, taking care to describe everything related to him by Bremen. Jerle Shannara listened carefully, his strong face intense, his gaze fixed and unwavering. Vree Erreden, on the other hand, seemed almost disinterested, his eyes straying frequently, looking off into the night in search of something beyond what Tay's words could offer.

"I have never been to this part of the Westland," he remarked when Tay had finished. "I know nothing of its geography. If I am to divine the hiding place we seek, I must first get closer to it."

"How helpful," Jerle ventured irritably. He had been watching the locat's eyes stray as well and was clearly displeased with his attitude. "Is that the best you can do?"

Vree Erreden shrugged.

Jerle was incensed. "Perhaps you could do better if you had paid closer attention to what Tay was saying!"

The locat looked at him, squinting myopically. A slow fire kindled in his eyes. "Let me tell you something. When Tay

Trefenwyd came to me to ask my help, I read his mind. I can do that sometimes. I saw Bremen's vision, the one Tay just described, and my memory of it is quite clear. That vision is real, my friend. If it were not, I would not be here. It is real, and the place it shows is real, and of that much I am certain. Even so, I cannot find it without more than what I know right now!"

"Jerle, you have traveled this country often," Tay broke in quickly, anxious to avoid a confrontation. "Is there nothing of what I have described that is at all familiar?"

His friend shook his head, a disgruntled look settling over his broad features. "Most of my travel has been confined to the passes—to Halys Cut and Worl Run, and what lies beyond. This particular formation of mountains—the twin peaks split like two fingers, in particular—sounds like it could be any of a dozen pairs I have seen."

"But you're not sure which?"

"What does it sound like to you?" his friend snapped.

"Which way do you think we should go, then?" Tay pressed. He could not understand the other's uncharacteristic display of temper.

Jerle climbed to his feet. "How would I know? Ask 'my friend' the locat here to give you his best guess!"

"One minute," Vree Erreden said quickly, and rose as well. He stood facing Jerle, small and slight in the other man's shadow, but unintimidated. "Would you be willing to try something? I might be able to help you remember if you've seen this particular formation."

Tay jumped up as well, realizing at once what the locat intended. "Can you do for Jerle what you did for me?" he asked quickly. "Can you recover his memory like you did Bremen's vision?"

"What are you talking about?" Jerle snapped, looking from one to the other.

"Perhaps," Vree Erreden answered Tay, then looked at Jerle Shannara. "I told you before. Sometimes I can read minds. I did so earlier with Tay to get a look at Bremen's vision. I can try it with you to see if your subconscious retains some memory of this formation we seek."

Jerle flushed. "Try your magic out on someone else!"

He wheeled away, but Tay grabbed his arm and brought him about. "But we don't have anyone else, do we, Jerle? We only have you. Are you afraid?"

The big man stared at him with something very close to rage. Tay held his ground, mostly because he didn't have any choice. The night sky had cleared, and its broad expanse was filled with stars. Their brightness was almost blinding. Standing beneath their light in the shadow of the mountains, locked in this unexpected confrontation with his best friend, Tay felt oddly exposed.

Jerle carefully freed his arm from Tay's grip. "I'm not afraid of anything, and you know it," he said softly.

Tay nodded. "I do know it. Now please let Vree try."

They sat down again, grouped close together in the silence. Vree Erreden took Jerle Shannara's hands in his own, holding them loosely, looking boldly into the other's eyes. Then he closed his own. Tay watched the pair uneasily. Jerle was as tense as a cat prepared to spring, ready to bolt at the first indication that he was in any kind of danger. The locat was by contrast calm and detached, especially now, gone somewhere deep inside himself to find what he was looking for. They remained like that for a few moments, locked together, an odd alliance, neither revealing anything of what was happening.

Then Vree Erreden released Jerle Shannara's hands and gave a short nod. "I have it. A place to start, anyway. Your memory is very good. The twin peaks in the form of a V are called the Pinchers—at least by you."

"I remember now," the big man said softly. "Five or six years ago, when I was scouting for a third passage onto Hoare Flats. Back in the mountains north of Worl Run, deep in the thickest mass. There was no chance that a pass would go through there, so we gave it up. But I remember the formation. Yes, I do remember!"

Then his enthusiasm seemed to diminish, and the hard edge of his irritation returned. "Enough of this." He nodded curtly, more to himself than to them, and rose. "We have our starting point. I hope everyone is happy. Now perhaps I can get some sleep."

He turned and stalked away. Tay and Vree Erreden watched

him go, neither of them speaking. "He's not usually like this," Tay said finally.

The locat rose. "He just lost six men who trusted him to an attack he feels he should have better anticipated." Tay stared at him, and he shrugged. "It's what he's thinking about right now. He couldn't hide it from me, even though he clearly wanted to."

"But those men dying, that wasn't his fault," Tay declared. "It wasn't anyone's fault."

The locat squinted down at him. "Jerle Shannara doesn't look at it like that. If you were in his shoes, would you?"

Then he turned and walked off, leaving Tay to ponder the matter alone.

THE COMPANY set off again at daybreak, working its way north through the mountains toward Worl Run. Preia Starle had returned during the night to report that there was no sign of a close pursuit. None of them believed for a moment that this meant they were safe. It only meant that they had gained a little extra breathing room. The Gnomes were still out there searching for them, but the Elves would be hard to find in these mountains, where tracks had a tendency to disappear amid the jumbled boulders and twisting passes. If they were lucky, they might avoid discovery just long enough to find what they were looking for.

It was wishful thinking, Tay supposed, but it was the best they could hope for. They rode north for the remainder of the day without seeing anything of their pursuers, following a line of deep valleys that cut through the eastern edge of the mountains snakelike to the entrance to Worl Run. They camped that night on a flat overlooking the pass and the valleys leading in from the Sarandanon, close now to where Jerle remembered seeing the V formation he called the Pinchers. He was in a somewhat better mood this day, still withdrawn and taciturn, but no longer curt, helped perhaps by the fact that they now had a better idea of where they were going. He actually apologized to Tay in a rather offhanded way, commenting lightly at one point on the unfortunate shortness of his temper. He said nothing to Vree Erreden, but Tay let the matter lie.

Preia Starle seemed unfazed by Jerle's shift in attitude and spent her time talking to him as if everything were fine. Tay thought she must know his friend's moods well enough by now to have developed an appropriate way of responding to each. He felt a pang of jealousy, for there was no such closeness between them. Again he was reminded that he was the outsider, come back into his old life from another, still trying to make himself fit in. He did not know why this bothered him so except that his life at Paranor was completely gone and his life here seemed to revolve around the duplicity of his relationship with Preia and Jerle. He couldn't claim it was an honest one, because he hid so much of what he felt for Preia from both of them. Or thought he did. Perhaps they knew far more than they were letting on, and he was playing a game of secrets where the secrets were all known.

They rode out again at sunrise and reached the Pinchers by midday. Tay recognized the peaks immediately, a clear match for the rendering provided by Bremen's vision. The peaks rose in a sharp V against the horizon, breaking apart in a deep split fronted by a tangle of small mountains worn by age and the elements and left bare save for sparse stands of fir and alder and struggling patches of grasses and wildflowers. Beyond, through the gap in the V, rose a wall of mountains so misty that their features were unrecognizable.

Jerle brought the company to a halt at the low end of a pass leading up into the peaks and dismounted. Overhead, hunting birds soared against the blue, wings spread as they circled in long, graceful sweeps. The day was clear and bright; the rain clouds had moved east into the Sarandanon. Tay felt the sun on his face, warm and reassuring as he stared upward into the vast expanse of cliffs and defiles and wondered at their secrets.

"We'll leave the horses here and walk in," Jerle announced. He smirked, seeing the look on Tay's face. "We could only ride them a short distance farther in any event, Tay. Then they would be left exposed to any who follow us. If we leave them now, we can hide them in the forest. We may have to make a run for it before we're finished."

Preia added her support, and Tay knew they were right, although it made him feel uncomfortable to give up the animals that had carried them past so many close calls. It had been hard enough to gain possession of them in the first place. But those who pursued them would have to proceed afoot as well if they reached this point, so he supposed that was as much as could be hoped for.

Jerle chose one of the Elven Hunters to remain behind with the horses, a grizzled veteran named Obann, instructing him to take the animals and hide them where they would not be found, then to keep watch for the company's return. Obann wanted to rejoin them after concealing the horses, but Jerle pointed out that it might prove necessary to change the hiding place if a Gnome search party drew too close and that it might further be necessary for Obann to bring the horses to his comrades if they were attacked coming down out of the peaks. Obann reluctantly agreed, took the horses in hand, and departed.

Then Jerle led those who remained, their number now reduced to seven—himself, Tay, Preia, Vree Erreden, and the last three Elven Hunters—up through the tangle of rock and trees toward the dark cleft of the Pinchers.

They climbed for the remainder of the day. As they proceeded, Tay found himself pondering anew the task that lay ahead. He might argue that the others of the company shared his responsibility for recovering the Black Elfstone, but the fact remained that Bremen's charge had been given expressly to him, not to them. Moreover, he was a Druid, the only one among them, the only one who commanded use of magic—of the sort, at least, that could offer them any real protection—and the one best equipped to find and secure the Elfstone. He had not forgotten the part of Bremen's vision that hinted at the danger that surrounded the Elfstone's hiding place, the suggestion of dark coils that warded it from those who would steal it away, the unmistakable sense of evil. He was aware that finding the Black Elfstone was only the first step. Securing it was the second, and it would not be done easily or without risk. If the Elfstone remained undisturbed after all these centuries, it must be strongly protected. Vree Erreden and Preia Starle might assist in finding it. Jerle Shannara and his Elven Hunters might aid in retrieving it. But ultimately the burden fell to him.

Which was as it should be, he supposed on reflection. He

had trained for this for the better part of fifteen years, for what constituted almost the whole of his adult life. His time at Paranor had been for this, if it had been for anything. Nothing else he had accomplished was in any way comparable to what was required of him now. Like other Druids, he had spent his time at Paranor immersed in his studies, in the pursuit of knowledge, and the fact that he had continued to develop his skills with magic did not alter the fact of his mostly sedentary existence. For fifteen years he had lived in an isolated, cloistered fortress, neither involved with nor engaged by the world without. Now, with his tenure at Paranor ended, his life was to be forever changed, and it began here, in these mountains, amid the ruins of another age, with a talisman unseen by anyone since the coming of Mankind.

So he must not fail, of course—that was of paramount importance. Failure meant an end to any hope of defeating the Warlock Lord, to any chance of creating a weapon that would destroy him, and, most likely, to Tay Trefenwyd's life. There would be no second chance in a matter like this, no opportunity to go back and try again. This effort would mark the culmination of years of believing in and practicing the Druid magic. It would vindicate both what the magic had been created to accomplish and the purpose of his life as a Druid. It was, he imagined, the defining point of everything.

His concerns bridged outward from there. The company was weary from being chased, from running and hiding, from escaping traps, from lack of sleep and long hours of travel. They had not eaten well in over a week, bereft of the supplies they had hoped to obtain, living off what they hunted and scavenged during their flight. They were disheartened by the loss of their comrades and by the fear, steadily eroding the hard surface of their determination, that their quest would not succeed. No one spoke of these things, but they were there, in their faces, in their eyes, in the way they moved, apparent to anyone who bothered to look for them.

Time was slipping from them, Tay Trefenwyd thought. Like water through cupped hands, it was draining away, and if they were not careful they would find it suddenly gone.

By nightfall, they were at the mouth of the pass, and they camped within a thin copse of alder in the lee of the mountains. It was cool here, farther up on the slopes, but not so cool as to be chill. The rock walls seemed to collect and hold the day's heat within the pass, perhaps because it dipped sharply into a low valley that spanned the east and west reaches. Eating sparingly, their water supply still good, they rolled into their blankets and slept undisturbed.

At daybreak, they went on. The sunrise poured down into the valley and lit their path with hazy streamers that flashed over the eastern horizon like beacons. Preia Starle led them, scouting several hundred yards forward of the main group, coming back now and again to report, warning of obstacles, advising of smoother paths, keeping them all safe. Tay walked with Jerle, but neither of them said much. They climbed out of the valley through its west end, leaving the shadow of the twin peaks, and promptly found their forward passage blocked by a massive berm that looked to have been formed of vast plates of earth cracked and gathered by a giant's hands. Ahead, the wall of the Breakline rose skyward, its broken peaks gathered together by those same giant's hands into bundles, all stacked together in haphazard and incomprehensible fashion, all waiting for someone to sort them out and put them back together again.

Preia returned to take them left along the berm for almost a mile to a trail that wound upward into the jagged rocks. By now, Jerle had exhausted what little there was of his recovered memory, and there was nothing for any of them to do but to press on until something in Bremen's vision recalled itself. They scrambled onto the berm, avoiding fissures that dropped straight down into blackness, staying back from the thin edges of drops and off the steep crests of slopes where, if you lost your footing, you could slide away forever. Jerle had been right, Tay realized, in leaving the horses behind. They would have been useless here.

At the crest of the berm, they encountered a slender, twisting trail, barely discernible from the land about it, that led through a narrow defile into the larger rocks ahead. They followed it cautiously, Preia going on ahead, the Elf girl stepping lightly through the mix of light and shadows, there one moment and gone completely the next.

When they came upon her again, she stood at the defile's end, looking out at the mountains beyond. She turned on their approach, and her excitement was palpable. She pointed, and Tay saw at once the cluster of mountains directly left of where they stood, spires jutting skyward at awkward angles, encircled at their base by a broad, high span of collapsed rock.

Like fingers jammed together, crushed into a single mass.

Tay smiled wearily. It was the landmark they were looking for, the ragged gathering of peaks that hid somewhere within their crumpled depths a fortress lost since the time of faerie—a fortress, Bremen's vision had promised, that concealed the Black Elfstone.

IT HAD BEEN easier than Tay Trefenwyd had expected, finding first the twin peaks in the shape of a V and then the clustered mountains that resembled crushed fingers. Vree Erreden's recovery of a forgotten memory and Preia Starle's tracking had brought them to their destination with a speed and efficiency that defied logic. Had it not been for the intrusion of the Gnome Hunters at various points along the way, they would have arrived almost without effort.

But now, just as quickly, things grew difficult. They searched all that day and the next for the entrance to the fortress hidden within the peaks and found nothing. The massed rock, boulders and plates alike, stacked all about the jammed peaks, offered dozens of openings that led nowhere. Slowly, painstakingly, the members of the little company explored each pathway, following it into shadow and cool darkness, tracing it to a slide or cliff face or drop that ended all further approach. The search wore on, extending into the third day, and then the fourth, and still the Elves found nothing.

Tempers grew short. They had come a long way and at great cost, and to now find themselves completely stymied was almost more than they could stand. There was a nagging feeling of time running out, of danger approaching from the east as the Gnomes continued their inevitable search, of expectations losing momentum and disappointment settling in.

Jerle Shannara kept them going. He did not turn dark and moody as Tay expected or revert to the temper he had displayed toward Vree Erreden after the loss of the Elven Hunters at Baen Draw, but stayed steady and determined and calm. He drove them relentlessly, of course—even Tay. He insisted they press on with their search. He made them retrace their steps. He forced them to look into each opening in the rocks again and again. He refused by strength of will alone to let them lose hope. He was, Tay thought on reflection, quite remarkable in his leadership.

Vree Erreden did not provide the help that Tay had hoped for. There were no visions, no hunches, no displays of instinct, nothing that would give insight into where the fortress or its entrance might lie. The locat did not seem unsettled by this; indeed, he seemed quite sanguine. But Tay supposed that he was used to failure, that he had accepted the fact that his talent did not come on command, but mostly at times and places of its own choosing. At least he did not sit back and wait on its arrival. Like everyone else in the company, he went out searching, probing the recesses of the collapsed rock, poking into this nook and cranny, into that crevice and defile. He did not comment on the failure of his talent to aid them, and Jerle Shannara, to his credit, did not comment on it either.

In the end, it was Preia Starle who made the discovery. Although the area they searched was sprawling and mazelike, after four days they had covered the better part of it. It became clear to everyone by then that if the vision had not misled them, then the fortress was concealed in a way they had not considered. Preia rose before dawn on the fifth morning of their search and went down to stare at the jagged crush of monoliths. She did it out of frustration and a need to study the landscape anew. She sat back within the shadows of a cliff face east, watching the light ease out of the peaks behind her, lifting to chase the darkness, to change the gray of fading night to the silver and gold beginnings of the new day. She watched the sun's bright rays fall across the towering span of the mountains, seeping down the faces of the cliffs like a paint stain down wooden walls, the color dipping into each dark crevice, etching out the shape and form of each rock wall.

And then she saw the birds. They were large, angular, white fishers, seabirds miles from any visible water, rising out of a cleft in the rock face of a peak centered within the cluster, several hundred feet above where she sat. The birds appeared in a rush, more than a dozen of them, lifting away with the coming of the light as if by unspoken command, soaring skyward and disappearing into the new day east.

What, Preia Starle wondered instantly, were seabirds doing in those barren peaks?

She went to the others at once with her report. She described what she had seen, convinced it was worth investigating, and immediately Vree Erreden cried, as if shown a revelation, Yes, yes, this was what they were looking for! The company was galvanized into action, and though stiff and sore from the efforts of their search and from sleeping on the stone of the mountains for five nights straight, and though hungry for food they did not possess and weary of eating the food they did, they went out of their camp and up the mountainside with a determination that was heartening.

It took them until midmorning to reach the cleft from which the white birds had flown. There was no direct route up, and the path they were forced to follow twisted laboriously back and forth across the cliff face, its navigation requiring deliberation and care with every step. Preia, leading the way as always, got there first and disappeared into the opening. By the time the others had arrived to stand upon a narrow shelf fronting the cleft, she was back with news of a pass that cut through the rock.

They went forward in single file. The walls of the cleft narrowed where the searchers walked, hemming them in. The warmth of the sun turned to dank, cool shadow, and the light faded. Soon overhangs and projections formed a ceiling that shut them away entirely. That there was any light at all was due solely to the fact that the defile was so rife with fissures that small amounts of illumination penetrated at virtually every turn. Their eyes adjusted to the gloom, and they were able to continue. The birds, they realized, were able to maneuver easily at the higher elevations, where the walls broadened. They found white feathers and bits of old grass and twigs that might have been carried in for nests. The nests, of course, would be farther on, where there was better light and air. The company pressed ahead.

After a time, the overhangs dropped so low that they were forced to proceed at a crouch. Then the defile branched left and right. Preia told them to wait and went right. She returned after a very long time and took them left. After a short distance the defile widened again, and they were able to stand once more. Ahead, the light grew brighter. They were nearing the passageway's end.

Fifty yards farther on, the cleft opened out onto the edge of a vast lake. The lake was so unexpected that everyone stopped where they were and stood staring at it. It rested within a vast crater, its waters broad and still, undisturbed by even the faintest ripple. Overhead, the sky was visible, a cloudless blue dome that channeled light and warmth to the crater. Sunlight reflected off the lake, and the lake mirrored the rock walls surrounding it in perfect detail. Tay scanned the cliffs and found the nests of the seabirds, set high in the rocks. No birds were visible. Within the shelter of the mountain walls and across the flat expanse of the lake, nothing moved, the silence vast and complete and as fragile as glass.

After a short, hushed conference with Jerle, Preia Starle took them left along the edge of the lakeshore. The shoreline was a mix of crushed rock and flat shelves, and the scrape of their boots as they proceeded echoed eerily in the crater's cavernous depths. Tay cast his magic forward of where they walked, hunting for pitfalls, exploring for hidden dangers. What he found were lines of earth power so massive and so old that they tore apart his fragile net and forced him to rebuild it. He drew Jerle close to him and gave warning. There was tremendous magic at work here, magic as old as time and as settled. It warded the crater and everything that lay within. He could find no specific danger from it, but could not trace its source or discover its use. He did not think them threatened by it, but they would be smart to proceed with caution.

They went on until they were nearly halfway around the lake. Still there was no sign of life, no indication of anything beyond what they could see before them. Neither Tay with his Druid magic nor Vree Erreden with his locat talent could discover what they searched for. The sun had moved out of the shadow of the cliff rim so that it blazed directly down on them, a burning orb against the blue. They could not look up at it without being blinded, and so kept their gaze lowered as they walked.

It was then, with the advent of high noon, that Tay Trefenwyd saw the shadow.

He had moved off the waterline momentarily to higher ground, trying to see the far shore through the dazzling reflection of the sun on the lake's still surface. As he searched for a position that would lessen the brightness, he saw how the sun had thrown the shadow of a rock projection far overhead across the length of the lake onto the cliff face several hundred yards ahead. The point of the shadow climbed the rock wall to a narrow fissure and stopped. Something about the fissure caught his eye. He sent his magic to probe the opening.

What he found, carved into the rock above, was writing.

He went forward quickly to catch Preia, and together they turned the company inland. Moments later they stood before the fissure, staring upward in silent contemplation of the writing. It was ancient and indecipherable. It was Elven, but the dialect was unfamiliar. The carving itself was so weathered it was almost worn away.

Then an inspired Vree Erreden stepped forward, had Tay and Jerle boost him, and reached up to run his fingers over the writing. He remained suspended for a moment, eyes closed, hands moving, stopping, moving on. Then he slid down again. As if in a trance, he bent to the rock on which they stood, and without seeming to look at what he was doing, his eyes focused somewhere beyond what they could see, he scratched words onto a smooth surface with a piece of jagged rock.

Tay bent close to read.

THIS IS THE CHEW MAGNA. WE LIVE HERE STILL. TOUCH NOTHING. TAKE NOTHING.

OUR ROOTS ARE DEEP AND STRONG.
BEWARE.

"What does it mean?" Jerle whispered.

Tay shook his head. "That magic wards what lies beyond this opening. That any disturbance will bring unpleasant consequences."

"It says they are still alive," Vree Erreden observed, his voice a hiss of disbelief. "That can't be! Look at the carving! The writing is out of the time of faerie!"

They stood staring at the writing, the fissure, and each other. Behind them, the Elven Hunters and Preia Starle waited. No one spoke. There was a sense of time dropping away, of past and present joining and transcending the passing of lives and history. There was a sense of standing at the edge of a cliff, knowing that one false step would send you hurtling to your death. Tay's awareness of the magic's presence was so strong that it seemed he could feel its touch against his skin. Old, powerful, iron-willed, and conjured out of purpose and need, it filled up his senses and threatened to overwhelm him.

"We did not come this far to turn back," Jerle Shannara observed quietly, looking over at him. "Not for any reason."

Tay nodded. He was determined as well. He glanced at Vree Erreden, at Preia Starle, at the Elven Hunters who stood behind her, and finally once again at Jerle. He gave his friend a crooked smile.

Then he took a deep breath and stepped forward into the dark mouth of the fissure.

CHAPTER

16

HE FISSURE WIDENED immediately into a corridor broad enough for the Elves to stand two abreast. Steps wound downward into darkness so complete that not even Tay Trefenwyd's keen vision could penetrate to what lay beyond. He moved forward several yards, feeling his way along the wall, and encountered a metal plate. When he touched it, light appeared across its flat surface, pale yellow and cool. He stared at the plate in surprise; here was a magic he had never encountered. The light revealed another plate, just at the edge of the darkness farther on. He walked over to it, placed his hand on it, and it, too, brightened. Amazing, he thought. He could hear the footsteps of the others coming up behind him. He wondered what they must be thinking. But no one spoke, and he did not look back at them. Instead, he continued on, touching the metal plates, lighting their way through the darkened corridor.

Their descent took a long time. Tay could not measure it, the whole of his concentration given over to the casting of his Druid magic before him to ferret out hidden traps. The metal plates that gave off light revealed a sophistication he had not expected. Faerie magic was not well known, for most of the lore had been lost with time's passage, but Tay had always assumed that magic to be grounded more in nature and less in technology. Yet the plates suggested he was mistaken, and that made him uneasy. Take nothing for granted here, he warned himself. Riding the air currents, skimming through the seams in the rock, bouncing across the dust motes that were stirred with their passing, his Druid magic hunted. With swift precision, he sorted and defined the secrets of the world through which they passed. He found no trace of human life, though the warning above the door had suggested it should be otherwise. He found no trace of another's passing, not in years, perhaps centuries. But, in spite of this, he experienced a sharp feeling of being watched, of his measure being taken, of something waiting farther on, patient and inexorable in its purpose.

The stairway ended at a massive iron door. No locks bound it. No magic warded it. Above its rusted, pitted frame, the words CHEW MAGNA were carved in stone—but those words only and nothing else of what had been written on the wall above the fissure into which they had entered. The others of the little company crowded close. On hands and knees, Preia Starle examined the ground before the doors, then rose and shook her head. No one had passed this way in a very long time.

Tay probed the doors and the spaces between. Nothing revealed itself. He stepped forward then, seized the great iron handles, and pulled down.

The handles gave easily, the latches released, and the doors swung inward as if perfectly balanced. Misty light poured through the opening, streaming down in a surreal shimmer, as if filtered through a pane of rain-streaked glass.

A massive fortress stood before them, its stone blocks so ancient the edges were worn smooth and its surface so cracked it seemed as if spiderwebs had covered it over. It was a wondrous construction, a balancing of towers atop battlements, an interlinking of parapets that cantilevered forward and back at every turn, and a spiraling of catwalks that suggested the intricacy of tapestry threads woven on a loom. The castle rose high and then higher, until its farthest reaches were barely discernible. Mountains ringed the castle, opening to the sky through a ceiling of clouds and mist. Trees and scrub grew thick along the rock walls at the higher elevations, branches and vines drooping inward toward the castle spires, letting daylight slip through in a ragged seam. It was from here that the light took its odd cast, spilling down through the filter of the leafy canopy and swirling haze to coat the fortress stone in its watery illumination.

Tay moved through the doors and into a vast courtyard that spread to either side and toward the central structure of the keep. He discovered now that he had passed through the castle's outer walls, which abutted the peaks themselves. He stared back at the walls in astonishment, realizing that with the passing of time, the mountains had shifted, closing and tightening about the ancient fortress until its walls had begun to crack and crumble. Inch by inch, the mountains were reclaiming the ground on which the fortress had been built. One day they would close about it for good.

The company advanced farther into the courtyard, glancing about guardedly. The air was damp and fetid, smelling of swamp and decay, strange for where they were, so deep in the mountains. But they had descended a long way since coming through the fissure in the crater wall, and Tay felt they might again be nearing sea level, far enough down to encounter marshy conditions. He glanced up again at the trees and scrub and vines growing high above them on the cliffs, and realized that the mist was almost a rain. He could feel the damp on his face. He looked at the fortress doors and windows, black holes in the gray haze. Iron hinges and locks hung empty and useless; the wood had rotted away at every turn. Moisture worked at the stone and mortar as well, wearing it down, eroding it. Tay walked to the wall of the nearest tower and rubbed his hand across the stone. The surface crumbled like sand under his fingers. This ancient keep, this Chew Magna, had the unpleasant feel of a place that would collapse under a strong wind.

Then Tay saw Vree Erreden. The locat was on his knees at the center of the court, head lowered between his shoulders, arms braced to keep himself from collapsing completely, his breath a harsh gasp in the near silence. Tay hurried over and knelt beside him. Preia appeared as well, then Jerle, their faces anxious and intent.

"What is it?" Tay asked the stricken man. "Are you sick?"

The locat nodded quickly, pulling his arms into his body,

sagging against Tay for support, shivering as if struck with a terrible chill.

"This place!" he hissed. "Shades, can you feel it?"

Tay held him close. "No. Nothing. What do you feel?"

"Such power! Evil, harsh as grit against my skin! I felt nothing and then, suddenly, it was everywhere! It overwhelmed me! For a moment, I could not breathe!"

"What is its source?" Jerle asked quickly, edging close.

The locat shook his head. "I cannot tell! This is nothing I am familiar with, nothing I have experienced before! It wasn't a vision, or a hunch, or . . . anything. It was blackness, a wave of blackness, then a feeling of . . ."

He took a deep, steadying breath, closed his eyes, and went still. Tay glanced down hurriedly, thinking he had lost consciousness. But Preia touched him and shook her head; Vree Erreden was only resting. Tay let him be. He remained kneeling, holding the locat in his arms, and the entire company waited with him.

Finally the stricken man opened his eyes once more, exhaled a long, deep breath, eased away from Tay, and climbed to his feet. He was steady as he faced them, but his hands still shook. "The Black Elfstone," he whispered, "is here. That was what I sensed, the source of the evil." He blinked, then looked sharply at Tay. "Its power is immense!"

"Can you tell where it is?" Tay asked, trying to stay calm.

The locat shook his head, arms folding against his chest defensively. "Ahead, somewhere. In the keep."

So they went on, moving cautiously into the fortress proper. Tay led once more, his magic sent before him in a sweeping net to guard against all dangers. They went through a doorway at the center of the keep and began to wind their way along the corridors beyond. Tay felt Jerle brush against his elbow, then Preia, a step behind. They were protecting him, he realized. He shook his head. He was disturbed by his lack of awareness of the Black Elfstone's proximity when it had been so clear to Vree Erreden. His Druid magic had failed him. Why was that? Was his magic rendered useless in this keep? No, he answered himself, because he had sensed a presence earlier on entering, eyes keeping watch. Whose, then? The Elfstone could not possess intelligence, but there was clearly something that lived here. What could it be?

They pressed on through the fortress, working their way deeper into its catacombs. Shadows lay over everything in dark layers of musty velvet. Dust rose from beneath their feet to cloud the air. The furnishings that had once graced this castle had crumbled. Nothing remained but scraps of metal and shreds of cloth. Nails poked from the walls, where once tapestries and paintings had hung. There had been artistry and craftsmanship at work in another time, but nothing they had produced remained. Rooms opened off hallways and passages, some vast and regal, some small and intimate, all empty of life. Benches lined a corridor they traversed, but when Tay put his hand on one it crumbled into dust. Glass lay shattered in niches. Weapons lay broken and rendered useless, stacks of rotted wood and rusted metal. Ceilings lifted into clouds of gloom, and windows gaped like the ruined sockets of blinded eyes. Everything was still, the silence of a crypt.

At a juncture of several broad corridors, Vree Erreden brought them to a sudden stop. He was holding his head with one hand, pain etched on his thin features, his slender body taut. "Go left!" he gasped, pointing raggedly.

They turned as he directed. Preia Starle dropped back to take his arm, lending her support. He was breathing rapidly again, his eyes blinking as if to rid themselves of an irritation. Tay glanced back at him, then ahead once more. He still sensed nothing. He felt oddly defenseless, as if his magic had abandoned him and he could no longer rely on it. He gritted his teeth against his perceived inadequacy and forced himself to go on. His magic would never desert him, he admonished himself. Never.

They passed down a broad stairway that wound about the outer wall of a vast rotunda. Their footsteps echoed faintly in the muffling silence, and now Tay sensed the eyes again, more strongly this time, more evident. What lived within this keep was close.

They reached the bottom of the stairway and stopped. A courtyard opened before them, broad and bright with misty sunlight. Shadows fell away, tattered and frayed. The musty staleness of the dark corridors faded. The dust and grit that hung upon the captured air disappeared.

At the center of the courtyard was a garden.

The garden was rectangular in shape, encircled by a broad walkway constructed of painted tiles and stone, the colors still resonant. Flowers grew along the outer border, a variety Tay could not identify, multicolored, profuse. The central portion of the garden was given over to a grove of slender trees and vines so closely intertwined as to be virtually inseparable, their leaves bright green and shiny, their limbs and trunks a curious mottled pattern.

A garden! Tay Trefenwyd marveled. Excitement washed through him. A garden, deep within the bowels of this ancient fortress, where nothing should grow, where no sunlight should reach! He could hardly believe it!

Almost without thinking, he came down off the stairs and hurried toward the garden's edge. He was within several yards when Jerle Shannara caught hold of his arm and yanked him firmly back.

"Not so quick, Tay," his friend warned.

Startled, Tay looked at the other, then saw Vree Erreden down on one knee again, shaking his head slowly from side to side as Preia held him. He realized suddenly how strong the impulse had been to go forward, how anxious he had been to explore. He realized as well that he had abandoned his defenses entirely. So eager had he been that he had released the protective shield of his Druid magic without a thought.

Saying nothing, he walked quickly to where Vree Erreden knelt. The locat grasped him immediately, sensing rather than seeing him, drawing him close. "The Black Elfstone," he hissed through teeth clenched against some inner pain, "lies there!"

His hand, shaking, pointed at the garden.

Preia touched Tay's arm gently so that he would look at her. Her ginger eyes were wary, guarded. "He went down the moment you left the stairs. Something attacked him. What's happening?"

Tay shook his head. "I'm not sure."

He reached for Vree Erreden's hands and took them in his own. The locat flinched, then went still again. Tay summoned his magic, called up a healing balm, and sent it flowing into the other's slender arms and body. Vree Erreden sighed and went still, his head drooping.

Preia looked at Tay, one eyebrow cocked. "Just hold him for a moment," he said to her.

Then he rose again to stand with Jerle. "What do you suppose this garden is doing here?" he asked softly.

His friend shook his head. "Nothing good, if that's where the Black Elfstone lies. I wouldn't walk in there if I were you."

Tay nodded. "But I cannot reach the Elfstone if I don't."

"I wonder if you can reach it even if you do. You said yourself that the vision warned that something wards the Stone. Perhaps it is this garden. Or something that lives within it."

They stood close, staring into the tangle of vines and limbs, trying to detect something of the danger they sensed waiting. A soft wind seemed to ruffle the shiny leaves momentarily, but nothing else moved. Tay stretched out his arm and sent a feeler of Druid magic to probe the garden's interior. The feeler snaked its way inward, searching carefully. But there was only more of what he could already see—the slender trees and vines with their shiny leaves and the earth from which they grew.

Yet he could feel life there, life beyond what the plants suggested, a presence strong and ancient and deadly.

"Walk with me," he said to Jerle finally.

They left the company and began a slow, cautious exploration of the garden's perimeter. The walkway was broad and unobstructed, so they were able to keep a wary eye in all directions as they proceeded. The garden ran for several hundred feet down one side, another hundred across, then several hundred back again. On each side, it looked the same—flowers along its border, trees and vines within. There were no paths. There were no indications of other life. There was no sign of the Black Elfstone.

When they were back where they started, Tay walked over to Vree Erreden once more. The locat was conscious again and crouched next to Preia. His eyes were open, and he was staring fixedly at the garden, although it seemed to Tay that he was looking at something else entirely.

Tay knelt beside him. "Are you certain the Black Elfstone is here?" he asked quietly.

The locat nodded. "Somewhere in that maze," he whispered, his voice rough and thick with fear. His eyes shifted suddenly to Tay. "But you must not go in there! You will not come out again, Tay Trefenwyd! What wards the Elfstone, what lives in this place, waits for you!"

One hand came up to knot before his pain-etched face. "Listen to me! You cannot stand against it!"

Tay rose and walked over to Jerle Shannara. "I want you to do something," he said. He was careful to make certain Vree Erreden could not hear. "Call the other Hunters over. Leave Preia with the locat."

Jerle studied him a moment, then beckoned the remaining Elven Hunters to his side. When they were gathered about, he looked questioningly at Tay.

"I want you to take hold of my arms," he told them. "Two on each side. Take hold, and no matter what I say or do, you are to keep hold. Do not release me. Do not react to anything I say. Do not even look at me if you can help it. Can you do that?"

The Elven Hunters looked at one another and nodded. "What are you going to do?" Jerle demanded.

"Use Druid magic to find what lies within the garden," Tay answered. "I will be all right if you remember to do as I said."

"I'll remember," his friend answered. "We all will. But I don't like this much."

Tay smiled, his heart pounding. "I don't like it much either."

He closed his eyes then and washed the others of the company from his consciousness. Gathering his magic to him, he went down inside himself. There, deep within the core of his being, he formed of the magic an image of himself, a thing of spirit and not substance, and dispatched it forth in a long, slow exhale of his breath.

He emerged from his corporeal body an invisible wraith, a bit of ether against the pale gray light of the ancient fortress. He slipped past Jerle Shannara and the Elven Hunters, past Preia Starle and Vree Erreden, toward the thick, green tangle of the silent garden. As he went, he came to sense more clearly the magic buried there. Old, wily, and established, it rooted deeper than the trees and vines that concealed it. It was the entity to which the lines of power that warded this fortress were attached. They grew from it as gossamer threads, entwining stone and iron, reaching from outer walls to tallest spires, from deepest cellars to highest battlements. They stretched across the chasm of the mountains where they breached against the sky, a vast concentration of thought and feeling and strength. He came up against their webbing and eased his way carefully past, sliding by without touching to continue on.

Then he was within the garden, wending his way through its maze, into the lush mustiness of earth and the sweet tang of leaves and vines. Everywhere, the garden was the same, deep and secret and enveloping. He sailed weightless and substanceless on a current of air, avoiding the lines of power that stretched everywhere, doing nothing to trigger a disturbance that might alert whatever watched to his presence.

He had penetrated so far into the garden that he thought he must be close to passing all the way through when he encountered an unexpected tightening of the lines of power at a place where the light seemed to diminish and the shadows to encroach once more. Here, the slender trees and vines disappeared. Here, darkness held sway. Bare earth lay revealed in a space where nothing grew and the diffuse light was absorbed as if water soaked into a sponge. Something unseen throbbed with the vibrancy and consistency of a beating heart, layered in protective magic, wrapped in blanketing power.

Tay Trefenwyd eased close, peering into the suffocating shadows, stealing past the warding lines. Within his guise, he stilled himself, and even the beating of his pulse, the whisper of his breath, and the shudder of his heart slowed to silence. He withdrew all but the smallest part of himself and became one with the darkness.

Then he saw it. Resting on an ancient metal frame into which runes had been scrolled and strange creatures wrought was a gem as black as ink, so impenetrable that no light reflected from its smooth surface. Opaque, depthless, radiating power that was beyond anything Tay Trefenwyd had imagined possible, the Black Elfstone waited.

For him.

Oh, Shades! For him!

A moth drawn to a flame, he reached for it—impulsive, unthinking, unable to resist. He reached for it with the desperation and need of a drowning man, and this time Jerle Shannara was not there to stop him. An image only, a wraith without substance, he gave no thought to what he did. In that moment, reason was lost to him and his need was all that mattered.

That he was a ghost and nothing more was what saved him. The moment his hand closed about the Elfstone, he was known. He could feel the lines of power shimmer in response to his presence, feel them vibrate and whine in warning. He tried to draw back, to flee what was coming, but there was no escape. The watcher he had not been able to identify, the thing that lived within the ruins of the Chew Magna, took sudden, hideous shape. The earth trembled in response to its waking, and the vines that grew throughout the garden, limp and flaccid a moment earlier, thrust upward—become the coils of death of which Galaphile's shade had warned. They whipped through the spaces between the slender trees like snakes, searching. Magic drove them, fed them, gave life to them, and Tay Trefenwyd, even in his spirit form, knew them for what they were instantly. They fastened on his arms and legs, about his body and head, dozens strong, come from everywhere. They fastened, and then they began to squeeze. Tay could feel the pressure. He should not have been able to do so—he had made himself a spirit. But the garden's magic had the power to ferret him out even in this elusive form. Magic to hold magic—magic to destroy even a Druid. Tay felt himself being ripped apart. He heard himself scream in response—the pain a reality within his psyche. Gathering himself within the core of his shattered form, bringing the small part that mattered into a particle no larger than a dust mote, he hurtled out through a gap in the writhing mass of vines and into the light.

Then abruptly he was back inside his body, twisting and screaming, arching as if electrified, struggling so hard to break free that it was all Jerle Shannara and the Elven Hunters could do to hold him. He gasped, shuddered, and collapsed finally into their arms, spent. He was drenched in sweat, and his clothes were ripped from his efforts to rid himself of their hands. Before him, the garden undulated with life, an ocean of deadly intent, a quagmire that nothing caught within could hope to escape.

Yet he had done so.

His eyes closed and tightened into slits. "Shades!" he whispered, fighting down his memory of the tenacious vines as they crawled over him, tightening.

"Tay!" Jerle's voice was harsh, desperate. The big man held him, arms wrapped about his body. He trembled violently. "Tay, do you hear me?"

Tay Trefenwyd gripped his friend in response and his eyes snapped open. He was all right now, he told himself. He was safe, unharmed. He took a long, slow, steadying breath. He was returned to the living, and of the horror of the Black Elfstone's dark magic he had discovered all that he needed to know.

HE TOLD THE OTHERS of the company what he had learned. He gathered them close, all of them, for there was no reason they should not all know, and told them what had occurred. He did not lie, but he kept from them the darkest of the truths he had uncovered. He tried not to show how frightened he was, though his fear worked through him anew as he recounted the experience, a river vast and wide and deep. He kept his voice calm and steady and his story brief. When he was finished, he told them he needed to think awhile about what they should do next.

They left him alone save for Vree Erreden. The locat came away with him unbidden, and as soon as they were out of hearing of the others, he took Tay's arm.

"You said nothing of the watcher. You did not name it, yet you must know its identity." The thin, strong fingers tightened. "I sensed it waiting for you—you, in particular, as if you were special to it. Tell me what it is, Tay Trefenwyd."

They moved onto the spiral staircase and sat together in the echoing silence of the fortress depths. Before them, the garden had gone still again, a garden once more, and nothing else. It was as if nothing had happened.

Tay glanced at the locat and then looked away. "If I tell you, it must remain between us. No one else is to know."

Vree Erreden nodded. "Is it the Warlock Lord?" he whispered.

Tay shook his head. "What rules here is older than that. What lives in the garden is what once lived in this castle. It is a compendium of lives, a joining of faerie creatures, Elves mostly, that centuries ago were just as you and I. But they coveted the power of the Black Elfstone. They coveted it, and their need was so desperate that they could not resist. They used the Stone, all of them, together perhaps, or separately, and they were destroyed. I can't tell how, but their story was made known to me. I could feel their horror and their madness. They are transformed, become the substance of this garden, a collective conscience, a collaborative power, their magic sustaining what remains of the fortress, gathered here, where all that is left of them has taken root in the form of these trees and vines."

"They were human?" the locat asked in horror.

"Once. No more. They lost what was human when they summoned the power of the Elfstone." Tay fixed him with a haunted gaze. "Bremen warned me of the danger. He told me that whatever happened, whatever the cause, I must not use the Black Elfstone. He must know what it would cost me if I did."

Vree Erreden's thin face lowered into shadow. His eyes blinked rapidly. "I could feel what lives here waiting for you—I told you that. But *why* does it wait? Does it seek its own kind, creatures of power, beings who have use of the magic in some form? Or does it ward against them? What drives it? It passed me by, I think, because my magic lacks definition and strength. My magic is instinct and vision, and it has no use for that. But, Shades, I could feel the darkness of it!"

He turned back to Tay. "You have a Druid's power, and such power is infinitely more compelling. There can be no question that it either fears or covets your magic."

Tay's mind raced. "It protects the Black Elfstone because the

Elfstone is the source of its power. And of its life. I threatened it by coming into the garden and disturbing the lines of power it has established. Does it know me as a Druid, though? I wonder."

"It knows you as an enemy, certainly. It must, since it tried to destroy you. It knows you are not subverted." The locat exhaled, a long, ragged breath. "It will be waiting for you to try again, Tay. If you go back into that garden, you will be devoured."

They stared at each other wordlessly. *It knows you as an enemy,* Tay thought, repeating Vree Erreden's words. *It knows you are not subverted.* He was reminded of something suddenly, but he could not think what. He wrestled with it for a moment before remembering. It was Bremen, changing his appearance, his form, his very thinking, so that he could penetrate the stronghold of the Warlock Lord. It was Bremen, altering himself so that he became one with the monsters that dwelled within.

Could he do that here?

His breath caught in his throat, and he turned away, unwilling to let Vree Erreden see what was in his eyes. He could not believe what he was thinking. He could not imagine he was giving the idea even the smallest consideration. It was insane!

But what other choice was left to him? There was no other way—he knew that already. He looked at the others sitting grouped at the edge of the deadly garden. They had come a long way to find the Black Elfstone, and none of them would turn back now. It was pointless to think otherwise. The stakes were too great, the price too high, for them to fail. They would die first.

Oh, but there must be another way! His mind tightened with the pressure of iron bands drawn taut. How could he make himself do it? What chance did he have? This time, should he fail, there would be no escape. He would be consumed . . .

Devoured.

He rose, needing to stand if he was to face this decision, needing to move away from his fear. He stepped down from the stairway, leaving the perplexed locat staring after him. He walked away from the others as well—from Jerle and Preia and the Hunters—to collect himself and take measure of his strength. A tall, gangly figure, he felt as worn and bent as the stone about him, and no less vulnerable to time. He knew himself for what he was—a Druid first, last, and always, but one of only a handful, one of an order that was in all probability moving toward extinction. The world was changing, and some things must pass. It might be so with them, with Bremen, Risca, and himself.

But they should not pass in quiet complacency, he thought angrily. They should not pass as ghosts, fading into mist with the coming of the new day, inconsequential things and only half-believed.

We should not be less than what we are.

Empowered by his words and armored in the strength of his convictions, he summoned up the last of his courage and called to Jerle Shannara.

CHAPTER

17

HERE IS A WAY to reach the Black Elfstone," Tay said quietly to Jerle Shannara. "But only I can do it, and I have to do it alone."

They stood apart from the others, Tay's crooked smile belying the knot that tightened his throat. The day was beginning to fade toward nightfall, the sun already gone west beyond the rim of the mountains surrounding them. He did not want to be caught down here in the dark.

Jerle studied him wordlessly for a moment. "You require some use of the Druid magic, I gather?"

"I do."

The shrewd eyes fixed him. "A disguise?"

"Yes. Of a sort." Tay paused. "I would rather not explain the specifics. I would rather you simply trusted me. I need to be left alone, no matter what happens. No one must come near me until I say it is permitted. This will be hard, because you will want to do otherwise."

"This will be dangerous." Jerle made it a statement of fact.

Tay nodded. "I must go into the garden. If I do not come out, you are to take the company and return to Arborlon. Wait, hear me out," he said, cutting short the other's protest. "If I am killed, there is no one else who stands a chance. You have a brave heart, Jerle, but no magic, and you cannot overcome what lives in the garden without magic. You must go back to Arborlon and wait for Bremen. He will be able to help. We have found the Black Elfstone, so it only remains to discover a way to retrieve it. If I cannot, he must."

Jerle Shannara put his hands on his hips and looked away in disgust. "I am not much good at standing around while someone else risks his life—especially when it is you."

Tay folded his arms across his chest and looked down at his feet. "I understand. I would feel the same way if our positions were reversed. Waiting is hard. But I have to ask it of you. I will need your strength later, when mine is gone. One thing more. When I come out again, when you see me, even if you are not sure it is me, speak my name."

"Tay Trefenwyd," the other repeated dutifully.

They stared at each other, thinking back on the years they had been friends, measuring what was being asked against their private expectations of themselves.

"All right," Jerle said finally. "Go. Do what you must."

At Tay's request, he took the other members of the company to stand with him at the bottom of the spiral staircase, well back from the edge of the garden. Tay glanced at them only once, locking eyes momentarily with Preia Starle before turning away. He had distanced himself from his feelings for her since coming into the Chew Magna, knowing he could not afford the distraction. He did so anew now, focusing on his life as a Druid, on the years given over to the study of his special talents, on the disciplines and skills he had mastered. He pictured Bremen: the lean, creased face; the strange, commanding eyes; the sense of purpose stamped everywhere. He repeated the charge the old man had given him, the charge he had accepted in coming here.

He faced the garden then, the deadly tangle of vines, the shadowed recesses, the invisible life force that waited somewhere deep within. He stilled himself, slowed his heartbeat and his pulse, quieted his thoughts, and enveloped himself in a blanket of calm. He reached out for the elements that fueled his magic—for air, water, fire, and earth, for the tools of his trade. He summoned what he could find of them, searched them out and retrieved them, and surrounded himself in their heady mix. He breathed them in, infused himself with their feel, and slowly began to change.

He worked carefully to achieve the result he desired, taking small steps as he invoked his Druid magic, altering himself without haste. He stripped away his own identity layer by layer, removing his features, changing his look. He scrubbed himself clean so that nothing of his physical identity remained. Then he went down inside his body to change what was there as well. He locked away feelings and beliefs, emotions and thoughts, codes of conduct and values of life—everything that marked him for who and what he was. He gathered them up and hid them where they could not be found, where nothing would release them save Jerle Shannara speaking his name.

Then he began to rebuild himself. He drew from the life of the garden to accomplish this. He drew from the creatures that had once been human but were no longer so. He found the essence of what they were, the core of what the Black Elfstone's magic had made of them, and he let it blossom within himself. He became as they were, as dark and lost, as ravaged and barren, a replica of their madness and their evil. He became like them, save for the fact that he retained the basic substance of his form so that he might walk among them. He was one step removed from their fate, so close there was no difference beyond the taking of that step.

The Elves watching could see him change. They could see his tall, slightly stooped form shrink and curl. They could see his gangly arms and legs turn gnarled and bent. They could feel the foulness creep over him and into him until there was nothing else. They could smell the decay. They could taste the ruin. He was anathema to anything good, to anything human, and even Jerle Shannara, steeled as he was to face what his friend was about to do, shrank from him.

Madness buzzed within Tay Trefenwyd's head, full-blown and obsessive. He reeked of the crippling effects of the garden's dark magic, of the ruin brought to those who infused it with their lives, who had made it their home. For an instant Tay thought he understood the magic, how it had derived from misguided use of the Black Elfstone, but the proximity of his understanding threatened the last vestige of his sanity, the small kernel of what held him to his purpose, and he was forced to back away.

He went into the garden now, a fellow to the creatures it had absorbed. He went boldly, for no other approach made sense. He went as one of them, still tending to the duties they had abandoned on changing form, still inhabiting the world they had left behind. He slid between the slender trees and brushed up against the flaccid vines, a serpent come to a serpent's refuge. He was as poisonous as they, and nothing of what they had become was any worse than what reflected in him. He slipped into the shadowed depths, seeking their comfort, easing sinuously into their embrace, soulless.

The garden and the creatures that fed it reacted as he had hoped. They welcomed him. They embraced him as one of their own, recognizable and familiar. He immersed himself in their foulness, in their decay, letting the tendrils of their collective thought worm into his mind so that they might see his intent. He was their keeper, they saw. He was a tender of the garden. He was come to bring them something, a change that would inspire new growth, that would satisfy some unspoken need. He was come to give them release.

He went deep into the garden, so deep that he lost himself completely in what he had become. All else faded and would not be remembered if he did not come out. He twisted down into a knot that squeezed away his life in small, scarlet drops. He was all madness and itch, a ravaged specter without a trace of his former identity. He was lost to everything he had been.

But he was driven, too, by the unalterable and compelling sense of purpose to which he had given himself over. He had come for the Black Elfstone, and he was determined, even in his madness, that he would have it. With single-mindedness and inexorable need, he approached it. The lines of power brushed against him and slid away. The vines shuddered, but with appreciation rather than rage. The life of the garden let him bend to the Elfstone, let him take it in his hands, let him lift it to his breast. He had come to care for the Stone, they saw. He had come to draw new magic from it, magic they would share, that would feed and satisfy anew their hunger.

For this was the guise that Tay Trefenwyd had assumed. The creatures that composed the garden could no longer invoke the power that had subverted them, could no longer feed upon it, but were locked in what it had made of them, trapped within the vines and trees and flowers of this rectangular patch of earth, deep within the fortress that had once been their home, rooted in place forever. They guarded the stone as they would a lock to their shackles, waiting for the time when a key would be brought to release them. Tay was the bearer of that key. Tay was the chance and the hope and the promise their madness allowed.

So he went, step by step, back through the garden, bearing in his hands—or what passed for hands—the Black Elfstone. Lines of power trailed after him, the webbing of the garden's power, played out to give him room, its tendrils releasing so that he might proceed. They snapped softly with his passing, and he could feel the garden shudder with the pain. But the pain fed back into him, the feeling delicious. Pain gave promise of agony, agony of transformation. Dark intent rode his footsteps, riddled his heart, and spurred him on through the shadows. A new power worked on his ravaged form, a tentative probe, like the touching of silken fingers against skin. It was the dormant magic of the Black Elfstone stirring to life, anxious for a new release, waking to give promise of what might be. It caressed Tay Trefenwyd as a lover. It stroked his ruined form and filled him with joy. He could have its power for his own, it whispered. He could command it as he wished, and it would give him anything.

He broke from the shadows of the garden into the light, free of the vines, of the voices, of the touch of those that dwelled there. He was a terrible, wasted thing, not in any way human, but something so dark and vile as to be unrecognizable. He slouched and oozed his way onto the stone of the walkway, the Black Elfstone clutched to him, the lines of power trailing invisibly behind, strings that only he could see, threads that could pull him back in an instant's time. Ahead, the Elves who had come with him into the Chew Magna watched in horror. On seeing him emerge, they drew their weapons with a cry and braced themselves to meet his attack. He looked at them and did not know who they were. He looked at them and did not care.

Then Jerle Shannara held up his hand to stay the weapons

of his companions. He came forward alone, unaided, staring fixedly at the apparition before him. When he was within only a few yards, he stopped and whispered in the stillness, his voice ragged and harsh and filled with despair. "Tay Trefenwyd?"

The sound of his name being spoken by Jerle Shannara gave Tay back his life. The Druid magic, held in check within the deepest, most impenetrable core of his being, surged through him, exploded out of him. It freed him from the trappings of the guise he had assumed, brought him out from the darkness that had enveloped him, from the quagmire into which he had sunk. It burned away the shell of the creature he had made himself. It burned away the madness that had consumed him. It rebuilt him in an instant's time, his features and identity restored, his reason and beliefs given back.

Then it severed the lines of power that trailed after him, giving him sole possession of the Black Elfstone.

The garden went berserk. Vines and trees surged out of the earth with such force that they threatened to tear loose from their roots. They lunged for the Black Elfstone and Tay Trefenwyd, first to recover, then to destroy. But Tay was shielded by his Druid fire, the magic set in place at the moment of his release, preordered to protect him from the garden's rage. Vines hammered down at him, wound about him, and tried to drag him back into the shadowy depths. But the fire held them at bay, burned them to ash, and kept the Druid safe.

Jerle Shannara and the rest of the company rushed forward, swords and knives slicing at the waving mass of vines. *No!* thought Tay as he struggled to slow them. *No, stay clear!* He had told them not to come near him, had warned Jerle expressly that they must not! But the Elves were unable to help themselves, seeing him returned and bearing the prized Elfstone, believing he was in need. So they charged bravely, recklessly ahead, weapons drawn, heedless of the magnitude of the danger they faced.

Too late they realized their mistake. The garden turned on them as swiftly as thought. It caught the closest Elven Hunter before he could leap clear, bore him away from his fellows, and ripped him to shreds. Frantically Tay extended the protection of the Druid fire to his beleaguered friends, allowing his own shield to weaken. Then he broke for the safety of the stairs, yelling at the others to follow after him. They did so, all but one—another of the Hunters, too slow to react, caught from behind as he turned and dragged to his doom.

Tay reached the stairs and bolted up their broad sweep. He could feel the collapse of the lines of power all about him. He could feel the ebbing of the garden's magic. Stealing the Black Elfstone had caused irretrievable damage deep within the life force of the Chew Magna, and the fabric of its skin was rent beyond repair. Beneath his feet, he could feel the earth begin to shudder.

"What is it? What's happening?" Jerle cried out, coming abreast of him.

"The fortress is collapsing!" Tay shouted. "We must get out!"

They sprinted into the corridors of the keep, through the tangle of halls, down the shadowed, empty passageways, and back toward the fissure that had admitted them. A strange and unsettling mix of elation and discomfort roiled through Tay's breast. He was free, his gambit a success, and his blood raced with the thought. But the measure of its cost had not yet been taken. He did not feel right; something had been done to him in the garden, something he could not yet identify. He looked down at himself, as if thinking to find some piece missing. But he was whole, he saw, unharmed. The damage was inside.

Cracks appeared along the ancient walls of the fortress, splitting and widening before them. Stone blocks shook violently and crumbled. Tay had destroyed the power of the Chew Magna, the carefully constructed magic that sustained the garden and the keep more fragile than he had realized. The Chew Magna was coming down. Its time in the world, extended for so long, was at an end.

Preia Starle bolted past him and sprinted ahead, shouting back over her shoulder. She was resuming her place as scout for the company once more. She flew across the shuddering stone, slender limbs and cinnamon hair flying. Tay peered after her, unable to see her as clearly as he should. His vision was blurred, and he was having trouble breathing. He gulped mouthfuls of air, and still it was not enough.

He was stumbling when Jerle Shannara caught up with him,

slowed, wrapped one powerful arm about his sagging body, and pulled him on. Behind them charged Vree Erreden and the last of the Elven Hunters.

Walls and ceilings were collapsing as they broke from the keep and raced across the courtyard to the outer wall and the gates that had brought them in. Tay felt a fire burning in his chest. Some part of the garden's foul magic, he realized, was still inside him. He tried to seal it off, to close it away from the rest of his body, using his own magic to suffocate it. He glanced down at himself, trying to draw reassurance from what he saw.

To his horror, the Black Elfstone was pulsing softly against his chest. He wrenched his glance away, covering the dark gem hurriedly so that the others would not see.

The five dashed through the fortress gates and up the stairs that led back to the fissure's entry. The rumbling behind them had grown louder, infused with the sound of stone cracking and sliding away. Dust clogged the passageway, and they could scarcely breathe. Vree Erreden was beginning to lag as well, and the Elven Hunter who ran beside him slowed to help. Like old men, the four stumbled ahead, coughing and choking, trying to keep up with Preia Starle.

There was an explosion deep within the mountain, and a vast cloud of debris hammered into them from behind, knocking them from their feet to sprawl on the stairs. Shaken and dazed, they scrambled up determinedly and went on.

Tay's strength was failing badly. The pain inside him was spreading. He could feel the pulse of the Black Elfstone grow stronger as it throbbed against his chest. That part of the garden's magic still locked within him was feeding into the magic of the Elfstone. He had disguised himself too well. He had altered himself too thoroughly. He had thought he would be able to recover from what he had done, but the sickness with which he had invested himself would not be so easily dispelled. He gritted his teeth and pressed on. It was a risk he had accepted. There was nothing to be done about it now.

Then they were clear of the fissure and back out onto the slide leading down to the lake within the mountain crater. Preia Starle stood frozen directly before them, only yards away.

"Shades!" hissed Jerle Shannara.

Before them, arrayed in a broad semicircle that cut off any possibility of escape, were dozens of Gnome Hunters. At their center, black-cloaked and hunched down like wraiths awaiting night, were a pair of the dreaded Skull Bearers.

Their pursuers had caught up with them at last.

The Elves stumbled to a ragged halt behind Preia. Tay counted quickly. They were five matched against almost a hundred. They stood no chance. Preia backed carefully to Jerle's side. She had not drawn a weapon.

"They were waiting when I came out," she said quietly. There was no fear in her voice. She glanced at Tay, and her face was oddly calm. "They are too many for us."

Jerle nodded. He glanced at Tay, grim-faced. Behind them, the fissure belched grit and dust as a new explosion tore through the mountain. The earth shuddered beneath them, still reacting to the fall of the Chew Magna and the giving up of its magic.

"We'll have to go back," Jerle whispered. "Maybe we can find another way out."

But there was no other way, Tay knew. There was only this way, through the Skull Bearers and the Gnome Hunters. Going back into the fissure was suicide. The entire mountain was collapsing, and anything caught within its tunnels would be crushed. Behind and to his left, the remaining Elven Hunter released his grip on Vree Erreden and let the other man slide to the rock floor. The locat was just barely conscious. There was blood on his head and face. When had that happened? Tay wondered. How had he missed it?

The Elven Hunter came forward to stand beside him.

Hopeless, Tay thought.

He eased himself away from Jerle then, testing his strength to stand on his own. He found he could do so. He straightened, then looked directly at his friend. Jerle stared back at him suspiciously, and Tay smiled at the other in spite of himself. Preia Starle watched him curiously. Her eyes were bright and challenging, and he thought that maybe she saw what Jerle did not.

"Wait here for me," he said.

"What are you going to do?" Jerle demanded at once, stepping forward to take hold of his arm, to restrain him.

Carefully, Tay freed himself. "I'll be all right," he said. "Just wait here."

He went down the slope, picking his way carefully on the smooth, loose rock, feeling long tremors rumble through the mountain as the destruction of the Chew Magna continued. He glanced upward along the cliff face to the sky, taking in the expanse of the crater's walls and its still, captured lake, the mountain peaks, and the fading sun. He allowed his thoughts to drift. He thought of Bremen and Risca, far away now in some other part of the Four Lands, waging their own fight. He imaged how it must be for them. He thought about his family and his home in Arborlon, his parents and Kira, his brother and wife and children, his friends of old, the places he had lived. He thought of doomed Paranor and the Druids. He took the measure of things past and present in a few brief moments, scattered his musings out before him, swept them up again, and put them away for good.

He stopped when he was only a dozen yards from the Skull Bearers. They had risen from their crouch and were watching him with baleful red eyes, their faces hidden within the darkness of their hooded cloaks. He lacked the magic necessary to stand against them, he knew. He had used himself up in the Chew Magna, and he was sick and worn. He accepted this calmly. The quest for the Black Elfstone was finished. All that remained was to see the Stone safely returned to Arborlon. Those with him must be given the chance to complete their journey home. He must see to it. Where once he would have been enough to protect them all, now he was barely able to protect himself. Yet he would have to do. He was all they had.

He looked down at his tightly clutched hand. The power of the Black Elfstone lay within. Bremen had warned him not to invoke it, and he had given his word to the old man that he would not. But things did not always work out the way you wanted.

He brought up his fist in a sudden sweep, feeling the dark pulse of the Elfstone against his palm. Summoning every last ounce of strength and determination that remained to him, he reached down into the heart of the dark magic and called forth its power. Already the Skull Bearers were reacting. Realizing the danger, they summoned their own deadly fire, a wicked green brilliance they launched at him with deadly efficiency. But they were not quick enough. The Black Elfstone had been awaiting Tay's summons, anticipating it, linked to him from the moment of its taking, master to slave with the roles not yet determined. Pulsing with expectation, its magic surged from between his fingers in a swath of non-light, a black void that swallowed up everything in its path. It smashed the fire of the Skull Bearers. It smashed the Skull Bearers themselves. It smashed the Gnome Hunters, all of them, even those who tried to flee, down to the last terrified man. It devoured everything. It burned men and monsters to ash, then stole away their lives and fed them back into the holder of the Stone.

Tay shuddered and cried out as the Elfstone's magic returned to him, imbued with the lives of its victims. Deep into his body went the evil of the Skull Bearers and the killing force of their fire. All of their dark intent and wicked need surged through him, filling him, ravaging him. He recognized in that instant the secret of the Black Elfstone's power—to negate the power of other magics, to steal them away, to make them its own. But the price was hideous, for the power stolen became the power of the Elfstone's holder and changed the holder forever.

It was over in seconds. The whole of the enemy force that had confronted them was destroyed. On the sweep of the crater slope there were only bits of clothing and weapons and small piles of ash. In the air, there was the smell of burning flesh. Across the surface of the still crater waters, there were ripples from the passing of the Black Elfstone's heat.

Tay dropped to his knees, the expended magic roiling through him. He could feel it eating away at his body and spirit, reducing them to dust. There was nothing he could do to stop it. He was being destroyed and made over. The Black Elfstone tumbled from his nerveless fingers onto the rocks and lay still. Its non-light had gone out. Its pulsing had ceased. Tay stared fixedly at it, trying to find a way to concentrate his magic in an effort to stop what was happening to him. He squeezed his eyes shut against the pain. Nothing could have prepared him for this—nothing. He had disobeyed Bremen, and this was the price.

Then Jerle Shannara was holding him, bending close and saying something. Preia was there, too. He could hear their voices, but he could not understand the words. He kept his eyes closed, fighting off the Black Elfstone's magic. He had gone back into the garden one time too many. The magic had seeded in him, taken root, and waited for him to succumb to its lure. It was a trap he had not foreseen. There had been too many other considerations, too many distractions.

"Tay!" he heard Preia cry.

Something dark was growing inside him now, something vast and unimaginably evil. He was being cast anew in the wake of the infusion of magic that had brought with it the foul essence of the Skull Bearers. He was being subverted. He could not fight it off. He was too badly damaged to do so.

"Preia!" he whispered. "Tell Bremen . . ."

Then he was drifting, lost in another time and place. It was summer in Arborlon, and he was a child again. He was at play with Jerle and had fallen while trying to scale a wall. He had struck his head hard and was lying in the grass. Jerle was beside him, saying, Oh, don't be such a baby! That fall was nothing! You aren't hurt! And he was struggling to rise, partially stunned, scraped about the elbows and face, when Preia, who was playing with them, took him in her arms and held him, saying, Stay quiet, Tay. Wait a moment until the dizziness passes. There's no hurry.

He opened his eyes. Jerle Shannara was cradling him in his arms, his strong face stricken. Preia knelt close, her eyes filled with tears, her face streaked with them.

His hand found hers and held it.

Then, as he had done with Retten Kipp, he used his magic to draw the air from his lungs. Slowly he felt his heart and his pulse slow. He felt the destruction of his body slow as well, thwarted. He grew sleepy. It was all that was left him. Sleep.

Darkness filmed his eyes and stole away his sight. He sighed once. Death came swiftly, gently, and bore him away.

THE

OF THE

18

REMEN, Mareth, and Kinson Ravenlock took the better part of a week to reach Hearthstone. They walked the entire way, both the Druid and the Tracker believing that they would make better time afoot than on horseback. This was country they both knew, having traveled it often, and the shortcuts they had discovered over the years could not be navigated on horseback. There would come a point early in the journey when the horses could go no farther on any trail and would have to be abandoned. It was better simply to go on foot from the beginning and not complicate matters.

All well and good for them, Mareth thought. They were used to walking long distances. She was not. But she said nothing.

Kinson led the way, setting a pace he thought would be comfortable for all three. He knew Mareth wasn't as conditioned to foot travel as Bremen and himself, but she was tough enough. He kept them on even ground for the first two days, when the roads and trails were still visible and the terrain relatively flat. He stopped often to let Mareth rest, making certain she took water each time. At night, he checked her boots and feet to make certain both were sound. Surprisingly enough, she let him do this without arguing. She had retreated within herself a bit since Bremen's return, and Kinson assumed she was preparing for the moment when she would tell the Druid the truth about herself.

Meanwhile, they pressed on through the passes of the Wolfsktaag into Darklin Reach. Much of the time they followed the Rabb River, for it provided a recognizable reference point and a means for locating drinking water. The days were slow and sunny, and the nights were calm. The deep woods sheltered and soothed, and the journey proceeded without incident.

On their third night out, Mareth kept her promise and told Bremen she had lied to him about her time at Storlock. She had not been one of the Stors, had not been accepted into their order, and had not studied healing with them. What she knew of magic, whether healing or otherwise, she had taught herself. Her skills had been mastered through laborious and sometimes painful experience. It seemed to her that her magic worked best when it was employed for healing, that she did better in those instances at keeping it under control.

She revealed as well her relationship with Cogline. She admitted Cogline had urged her to go to the Druids at Paranor, had told her to seek help with her magic there, and had assisted her in forging the necessary documents to gain admission.

Somewhat to Kinson's surprise, Bremen was not angry with her. He listened attentively as she spoke, nodded in response, and said nothing. They were seated around the cooking fire, dinner consumed, the flames burned almost to coals, and the night about them bright with moon and stars. He did not glance at Kinson. He seemed, in fact, to have forgotten the Borderman was even there.

When the girl had finished, Bremen smiled encouragingly. "Well, you are a bold young lady. And I appreciate your confidence in both Kinson and myself. Certainly, we will try to help you. As for Cogline, this business of sending you off to Storlock to learn about your magic, giving you false references, encouraging you to dissemble—that sounds exactly like him. Cogline has no love for the Druids. He would tweak their collective noses at the slightest provocation. But he also knew, I think, that if you were determined enough to discover the truth about your magic, if you were the genuine article, so to speak, you would eventually find your way to me."

"Do you know Cogline well?" Mareth asked.

"As well as anyone knows him. He was a Druid before me.

He was a Druid in the time of the First War of the Races. He knew Brona. In some ways, he sympathized with him. He thought that all avenues of learning should be encouraged and no form of study forbidden. He was something of a rebel himself in that respect. But Cogline was also a good and careful man. He would never have risked himself as Brona did.

"He left the Druid order before Brona. He left because he grew disenchanted with the structure under which he was required to study. His interest lay in the lost sciences, in sciences that had served the old world before its destruction. But the High Druid and the Druid Council were not supportive of his work. In those days, they favored magic—a power that Cogline distrusted. For them, the old sciences were better left in peace. They might have served the old world, but they had also destroyed it. Uncovering their secrets should be done slowly and cautiously and for limited use only. Cogline thought this nonsense. Science would not be contained, he would argue. It would not be revealed according to Man's agenda, but according to its own."

Bremen rocked back slightly, arms clasped about knees drawn up, all bones and angles, his smile one of reminiscence. "So Cogline left, infuriated at what had been done to him—and at what he had done to himself, I imagine. He went off into Darklin Reach and resumed his studies on his own. I would see him now and then, cross paths with him. We would talk. We would exchange information and ideas. We were both outcasts of a sort. Except that Cogline refused to consider himself a Druid any longer, while I refused to consider myself anything less."

"He's been alive longer than you have," Kinson observed casually, poking at the coals of the fire with a stick, refusing to meet Bremen's gaze.

"He has use of the Druid Sleep, if that's what you are getting at," Bremen replied quietly. "It is the one indulgence of magic's use that he permits himself. He is mistrustful of the rest. All of it." He glanced at Mareth. "He thinks the magic dangerous and uncontrollable. He would have taken some delight, I expect, in learning that you found it that way as well. In sending you to Paranor, he was hoping to make a point. The trouble is, you hid your secret too well, and the Druids never discovered what you were capable of doing."

Mareth nodded, but said nothing. Her dark eyes looked off into space thoughtfully.

Kinson stretched. He felt impatient and irritated with both of them. People complicated their own lives unnecessarily. This was just another example.

He caught Bremen's eye. "Now that we have all our secrets and past history on the table, tell me this. Why are we going to Hearthstone? What is it that we want with Cogline?"

Bremen studied him a moment before replying. "As I said, Cogline has continued his study of the old sciences. He knows secrets lost to everyone else. One of those secrets might be of use to us."

He stopped, smiled. He had said all he was going to say, Kinson could tell. There was probably a reason for this beyond irritating the living daylights out of the Borderman, but Kinson did not care either to speculate or to ask what it was. He nodded as if satisfied and rose.

"I will take the first watch," he announced, and stalked off into the dark.

He sat brooding over the matter until after midnight when Bremen came to relieve him. The old man materialized out of nowhere—Kinson never heard him coming—and sat down next to the Borderman. They kept each other company for a long time without speaking, looking out into the night. They were seated on a low bluff that overlooked the Rabb as it snaked its way through the trees, its surface flat and silver with moonlight. The woods were quiet and sleepy, and the air smelled of juniper and spruce. Darklin Reach began just west of where they camped. Starting tomorrow, the terrain would turn rugged and travel would grow much more difficult.

"What Cogline can give us," the old man said suddenly, his voice soft and compelling, "is the benefit of his knowledge of metallurgy. Do you remember the visions? They are centered around the creation of a weapon of magic that will destroy the Warlock Lord. The weapon is a sword. The sword will be borne in battle by a man we have not yet met. The sword requires many things to endow it with sufficient strength to withstand the power of Brona. One of those things is a forging process that will make it the equal of any weapon ever shaped. Cogline will give us that process."

He looked at Kinson and smiled. "I thought it best to keep that piece of information between ourselves."

Kinson nodded and did not reply. He looked down at his feet, nodded again, and then rose. "Good night, Bremen."

He started to walk away.

"Kinson?"

The Borderman turned. Bremen was looking away again, staring out over the river and the woods. "I would not be so sure that all the secrets and past history are on the table yet, either. Mareth is a very cautious and deliberate young woman. She has her own reasons for doing what she does, and she keeps them to herself until she thinks it prudent to reveal them." He paused. "As you already know. Good night."

Kinson held his ground a moment more, then walked away.

They pushed on for another three days through country so rough and tangled that the only trails they encountered were those made by animals. They saw no other humans, and they found no human tracks. The country had turned hilly, serrated by ravines and ridgelines, eroded by flash floods from spring-time cresting of the Rabb, choked by scrub and grasses grown waist-high. The river broke out of its channel in a dozen places, forming loops and sloughs, and they could no longer rely on its banks to provide either a footpath or a reference point. Kinson took them away from the jumble of waterways into the deep woods, choosing country where the shade of the old growth kept the scrub and grass from growing so thick and thereby offered better passage across the drops and splits. The weather stayed good, so they were able to make reasonable progress, even with the changing topography.

As they traveled, Bremen walked with Mareth, speaking about her magic and counseling on its use.

"There are ways in which you can control it," he offered. "The difficulty lies in identifying the ways. Innate magic is more complicated than acquired magic. With acquired magic, you learn its usage through trial and error, building on your knowledge as you go. You discover what works and what doesn't; it is predictable, and usually you come to understand the why of things. But with innate magic, that isn't always possible. Innate magic is simply there, born to you, a part of your flesh and blood. It does what it will, when it will, often how it will, and you are left to discover the why of things as best you can.

"The problem of controlling innate magic is further complicated by other factors which influence the way magic works. Your character can affect the results of the magic's implementation. Your emotions, your mood. The makeup of your body—you have built-in defenses to anything that threatens your health, and these can affect the way the magic responds. Your view of the world, Mareth, your attitude, your beliefs, your reasoning—they can all determine results. The magic is a chameleon. Sometimes it simply gives up and goes away, will not try to breach your defenses or the obstacles you place in its path. Sometimes it mounts a rush to overcome them, to break through and work its will in spite of all you do to stop it."

"What is it that so affects me?" she asked him.

And he replied, "That is what we have to discover."

On the sixth day of their journey, they reached Hearthstone. It was just after midday, and they had come down out of a range of broad, steep hills and rugged valleys that heralded the approach of the Ravenshorn Mountains. They were hot and footsore, and having left the Rabb and its tributaries far behind, they had not bathed in two days. No one was doing much talking this day; they were concentrating all their energies on reaching their destination before nightfall, as Kinson had promised they would. Despite the fearsome reputation of Darklin Reach, nothing had threatened them on their journey and, if anything, they were growing bored with the tedium of their travel. So it was a relief to catch sight of the solitary, chimney-shaped spire that jutted skyward in the bright sunlight that lit the far end of the small valley directly before them. They emerged from a stretch of spruce and hemlock where the shadows were so thick they had to grope their way clear, and there it was. Kinson pointed, but Bremen and Mareth were already nodding and smiling in recognition.

They went down off the hills through patches of wildflowers to the cool shadow of the woods that filled the valley floor. It was silent as they passed through towering stands of hard-woods—red elm, white and black oak, shagbark hickory, and birch. Conifers grew there as well, shaggy, hoary, and ancient, but the hardwoods dominated. Hemmed in by a canopy of limbs and a wall of trunks, they quickly lost sight of Hearth-stone. Kinson led, still looking for tracks, still not finding any, but now wondering why. If Cogline lived in the valley, didn't he ever walk around in it? There were no signs of human habita-tion. There were birds and small ground animals, but not much of anything else.

They crossed a stream, a spray of cold mist washing over them from where the waters tumbled down a rapids. Kinson brushed at his face, closed his eyes against the coolness, and wiped the sweat from his brow. He blinked away the damp as he walked, listening to the silence, glancing back at Bremen and Mareth, who followed a few steps behind. He felt a twinge of uneasiness, but he couldn't identify its source. His Tracker's in-stincts told him something was wrong, but neither of his com-panions seemed bothered.

He dropped back a step to walk with them. "Something doesn't feel right," he muttered.

Mareth looked at him blankly. Bremen only shrugged. Irri-tated, Kinson strode on ahead once more. They crossed a broad clearing to a stand of fir and pushed through the curtain of boughs. Suddenly Kinson smelled smoke. He slowed and turned to warn the other two.

"Keep your eyes forward," Bremen warned. He glanced past Kinson, and as he did so, the Tracker saw Mareth's eyes grow huge.

Kinson whirled back and found himself face-to-face with the biggest moor cat he had ever seen. The moor cat was stand-ing six feet away, staring at him. The lantern eyes were a lumi-nous yellow, and the muzzle was black, but the rest of the cat was a curious brindle patchwork. Moor cats were rarely seen, and it was commonly said that seeing one was usually the last event in a person's life. Moor cats kept mostly to themselves, living out their lives in the Eastland swamps. They were difficult to spy out because they could change color to blend into their surroundings. They ran on average six to eight feet long and up to three feet tall at the shoulder, but this one was a dozen feet from nose to tail and at least four feet at the shoulder. It was nearly eye level with Kinson, and if it chose it would be on top of him before he could blink.

"Bremen," he said softly.

From behind him, he heard a strange chittering sound, and the moor cat cocked its massive head in response. The sound came again, and now Kinson realized that its source was Bremen. The moor cat licked its muzzle, made a similar noise in response, turned, and walked away.

Bremen came up beside the stunned Borderman and put a reassuring hand on his shoulder. "That's Cogline's cat. I'd say we're close to our man, wouldn't you?"

They walked out of the stand of fir, crossed a glade bisected by a meandering stream, and angled past a massive old white oak. All the while the moor cat padded on ahead, neither hurrying nor lagging, seemingly disinterested, but at the same time letting them keep it in sight. Kinson looked questioningly at Mareth, but she shook her head. Apparently, she didn't know any more about this than he did.

Finally they reached a broad clearing in which a small cabin had been built. The cabin was rustic and weathered, badly in need of repairs, pieces of clapboard siding come loose, shutters off their hinges, planks on the narrow porch splintered and cracked. The roof looked solid enough and the chimney was sound, but a vegetable garden planted just south was in disarray and weeds nuzzled the cabin foundation expectantly. A man stood in front of the cabin waiting for them, and Kinson knew at once from Mareth's description of him that this was Cogline. He was tall and stooped, a bony, ragged figure, rather disheveled and unkempt, in clothes that looked to be in about the same shape as the cabin. His hair was dark, but shot through with gray, and it stuck out from his angular head like a hedgehog's spines. A narrow, pointed beard jutted from his chin, and a mustache drooped off his upper lip. Lines creased his weathered face, furrows that marked more than the passing of his years. He put his hands on his hips and let them come to him, a broad smile twisting his face.

"Well, well, well!" he exclaimed enthusiastically. "The girl from Storlock comes calling. Wouldn't have thought to see you again. You've got more spunk than I'd given you credit for. Found the true master of the lore, too, have you? Well met, Bremen of Paranor!"

"Well met, Cogline," Bremen replied, extending his hand, letting the other clasp it momentarily in his own. "Sent your cat to greet us, I see. What's his name? Shifter? Startled my friend so badly he may have lost five years off his life."

"Hah, we have the remedy for that, and if that's Kinson Ravenlock who's with you, he probably knows it already!" Cogline gave the Borderman a wave. "Druid Sleep will give you back those years in a blink!" He cocked his angular face. "You know what the cat's for, my friend?" Kinson shook his head. "He screens out unwelcome guests, which includes just about everyone. The only ones who get this far are the ones who know how to talk to him. Bremen knows how, don't you, old man?"

Bremen laughed. "Old man? Pot and the kettle there, wouldn't you say?"

"I wouldn't say yes, and I wouldn't say no. So the girl found you, did she? Took her long enough. Mareth, isn't it?" Cogline bowed slightly. "Lovely name for a lovely girl. Hope you drove all those Druids to distraction and a bad end."

Bremen came forward a step. The smile disappeared from his face. "The Druids found a bad end all on their own, I'm afraid. Not two weeks past, Cogline. They're all dead at Paranor save myself and two more. Hadn't you heard?"

The other man stared at him as if he were mad, then shook his head. "Not a word. But I haven't been out of the valley for a while either. All dead? You're certain of that, are you?"

Bremen reached into his robes and brought forth the Eilt Druin. He held it up for the other to see, letting it dangle in the light.

Cogline screwed up his mouth. "Sure enough. You wouldn't have possession of that if Athabasca lived. All dead, you say? Shades! What did them in? Him, was it?"

Bremen nodded. There was no need to speak the name. Cogline shook his head again, folded his arms across his chest, and hugged himself. "I didn't wish that for them. I never wished that. But they were fools, Bremen, and you know it. They built up their walls and closed up their gates and forgot their purpose. They drove us out, the only two who had an ounce of sense, the only two who understood what mattered. Galaphile would have been ashamed of them. But all dead? Shades!"

"We've come to talk about it," Bremen said quietly.

The other's sharp eyes snapped up to meet those of the old man. "Of course you did. You came all this way to give me the news and talk about it. Kind of you. Well, we know each other, don't we? One old, the other older. One a renegade, the other a castoff. Neither one the least bit devious. Hah!"

Cogline's chuckle was dry and mirthless. He looked at the ground a moment, then his gaze swept up to Kinson. "Say, Tracker—you see the other one on your way in, sharp-eyed as you are?"

Kinson hesitated. "Other what?"

"Hah! Thought so! Other cat, that's what! Didn't see it?" Cogline snorted. "Well, all I can say is, it's a good thing Bremen likes you or you'd probably be someone's meal by now!" He chuckled, then lost interest and threw up his hands. "Well, come on, come on! No point standing around out here. There's food waiting on the fire. I suppose you'll want a bath, too. More work for me, not that it matters to you. But I'm a good host, aren't I? Come on!"

Mumbling and grousing, he turned and loped up the steps and into the cabin, his visitors trailing obediently behind.

THEY WASHED THEMSELVES and their clothes, dried as best they could, dressed anew, and were sitting down to dinner by the time the sun set. The sky turned orange and gold, then crimson, and finally an indigo-amethyst that left even Kinson staring out through the screen of the trees in amazement. The meal Cogline served them was better than the Borderman would have expected, a stew of meat and vegetables, with bread, cheese, and cold ale. They ate at a table set out in back of the cabin with the night sky visible above, its collection of stars laid out in kaleidoscopic order. Candles lit the table, giving off some sort of incense that Cogline claimed kept the insects away. Maybe his claim was well founded, Kinson conceded, because there didn't seem to be anything flying about while they ate.

The moor cats joined them, wandering in with the darkness to curl up close to the table. As Cogline had advised, there were two—a brother and a sister. Shifter, the male, whom they had encountered on their way in, was the larger of the pair, while the female, Smoke, was smaller and leaner. Cogline said he had found them as kittens, abandoned in the swamp regions of Olden Moor and prey at that age to the Werebeasts. They were hungry and frightened and clearly in need, so he took them home. He laughed at the memory. Little bits of fur then, but they grew up quick enough. He hadn't done anything to make them stay; they chose to do that on their own. Probably liked his companionship, he opined.

Twilight came and went, and night deepened into warm breezes and soft silence. The meal concluded, and as they sat back to sip ale from fired clay mugs, Bremen told Cogline what had befallen the Druids at Paranor. When he was finished, the once-Druid sat back with ale glass in hand and shook his head in disgust.

"Fools all, down to the last man," he said. "I'm sorry for them, sorry they came to such an end, but mad, too, because they wasted the opportunities Galaphile and the others gave them in forming the First Council. They lost sight of their purpose, of the reason for their being. I can't forgive them that."

He spit into the darkness. Smoke looked up at him and blinked, startled. Shifter never moved. Kinson looked from one to the other, wild-haired recluse and his pet moor cats, and wondered what living out here for any length of time did to your mind.

"When I left the Druids, I went to the Hadeshorn and spoke with the spirits of the dead," Bremen went on. He sipped at his ale, the creases of his weathered face deepening with the memory. "Galaphile himself came to me. I asked him what I might do to destroy Brona. In response, he showed to me four visions." He described them one by one. "It is the vision of the man with the sword that brings me to you."

Cogline's angular face squinched down on itself like a fist. "Am I supposed to help you find this man? Am I supposed to know him?"

Bremen shook his head. His gray hair looked as fine as silk in the candlelight. "It is not the man, but the sword that requires your attention. This is a talisman that I must forge. The vision reveals that the Eilt Druin will be transformed by the forging and made part of the weapon. The weapon will be anathema to Brona. I don't pretend to understand the particulars as yet. I only know the nature of the weapon that is needed. And I know that special care must be taken in its forging if it is to be strong enough to overcome Brona's magic."

"So you've come all the way here to ask me about it, have you?" said the other, as if the curtain had just been raised and the truth revealed.

"No one knows more about the science of metallurgy than you. The forging process must be a fusion of science and magic if it is to be successful. I have the magic—my own and that of the Eilt Druin—to incorporate into the process. But I need your knowledge of science. I need what science alone can provide—the proper mix of metals, the correct temperatures of the furnace at each melding, and the exact times of curing. What form of tempering must be used if the metal is to be strong enough to withstand whatever force is directed against it?"

Cogline dismissed the matter with a wave of his hand. "You can just stop right there. You've already missed the point. Magic and science do not mix. We both know that. So if you want a weapon forged of magic, then use magic. You don't need anything from me."

Bremen shook his head. "We have to bend the rules a bit, I'm afraid. Magic is not enough to accomplish the task. Science is needed as well. Science brought out of the old world. Brona is a creature of magic, and magic is what he has armored himself against. He does not know science, does not care about it, has no regard for it. For him, as for so many, science is dead and gone, a part of the old world. But we know differently, don't we? Science lies dormant as magic once did. Magic is favored now, but that does not mean that science has no place. It may be necessary in the forging of this sword. If I can implement the best techniques of old world science, I have one more strength on which to rely. I need that strength. I am alone with Kinson and Mareth. Besides us, there are only two more who are allied with us, one gone east, the other west. We are all. Our magic is but a fraction of that of our enemy. How shall we prevail against the Warlock Lord and his minions without a weapon against which they cannot defend?"

Cogline sniffed. "There is no such weapon. Besides, there is nothing to say that a weapon forged of science—in whole or in part—would stand any better chance than one forged of magic. It might just as easily be true that magic is all that can prevail against magic, and that any form of science is useless."

"I do not believe that."

"Believe what you choose." Cogline rubbed irritably at his hair. A scowl twisted his thin mouth. "I left the world and its more conventional beliefs behind me a long time ago. I haven't missed them."

"But both will catch up with you sooner or later, just as they catch up with us all. They won't go away or cease to be simply because you reject them." Bremen's eyes fixed on the other. "Brona will come here one day, after he has finished with those of us who have not hidden away. You must know that."

Cogline's face hardened. "He will rue that day, I promise you!"

Bremen waited, saying nothing, not choosing to challenge the statement. Kinson glanced at Mareth. She met his gaze and held it. He knew she was thinking the same thing he was—that Cogline's posturing was vain and foolish, that his thinking was patently ridiculous. Yet Bremen did not choose to challenge him.

Cogline shifted uneasily on the bench. "Why do you press me so, Bremen! What is it that you expect of me? I want no part of the Druids!"

Bremen nodded, his face calm, his gaze steady. "Nor they of you. The Druids are gone. There is no part of them left to be had. There are only the two of us, Cogline, old men who have stayed alive longer than they should, conjurers of the Druid Sleep. I grow weary, but I shall not rest until I have done what I can for those who have not lived so long—the men, women, and children of the Races. These are the ones who need our help. Tell me. Should we have no part of them either?"

Cogline started to answer and stopped. Everyone sitting at the table knew what he was tempted to say and how foolish the words would sound. His jaw muscles tightened in frustration. There was indecision in his sharp eyes.

"What cost to you if you choose to help us?" Bremen pressed quietly. "If you would truly have no part of the Druids, then consider this. The Druids would not have helped in this—indeed, chose not to help when they had the chance. They were the ones who determined that their order should stay separate and apart from the politics of the Races. That choice destroyed them. Now the same choice is given to you. The same choice, Cogline—make no mistake. Isolation or involvement. Which is it to be?"

They sat silent about the table, the Druid, the once-Druid, the Tracker, and the girl, the night enfolding deep and calm about them. The big cats lay sleeping, the sound of their breathing a soft, regular whistle of air through damp nostrils. The air smelled of burning wood, food, and the forest. There was comfort and peace all about. The four were cocooned away in the heart of Darklin Reach, and if you tried hard enough, Kinson Ravenlock thought, you might imagine that nothing of the outside world could ever reach you here.

Bremen leaned forward slightly, but the distance between himself and Cogline seemed to close dramatically. "What is there to think about, my friend? You and I, we have known what the right answer is all of our lives, haven't we?"

Cogline snorted derisively, brushed at the air in front of him, looked off into the darkness, then wheeled back irritably. "There is a metal as strong as iron, but far lighter, more flexible, and less brittle. An alloy really, a mix of metals, that was in use in the old world, conceived of the old science. Iron mostly, tempered by carbon at high temperature. A sword forged of that mix would be formidable indeed." He looked sharply at Bremen. "But the temperatures used in the tempering are far greater than what a smith can generate in his forge. Engines are needed to generate temperatures of this magnitude, and those engines are lost to us."

"Have you the process?" Bremen asked.

Cogline nodded and tapped his head. "Up here. I will give it to you. Anything to send you on your way and end this pointless lecturing! Still, I cannot see its use. Without a kiln or furnace hot enough . . ."

Kinson's gaze wandered back to Mareth. She was staring directly at him, her dark eyes huge and shadowed beneath her helmet of short-cropped black hair, her face smooth and serene. In that instant, he thought he was on the verge of understanding her as he had been unable to do before. It was something about the way she was looking at him, in the openness of her expression, in the intensity of her gaze. But then she smiled unexpectedly, her mouth quirking at the corners, and her eyes shifted from his face to something she saw behind him.

When he turned to look, he found Shifter staring at him, the big moor cat's face only inches from his own, the luminous eyes fixed on him as if he were the strangest thing the cat had ever seen. Kinson swallowed the lump in his throat. He could feel the heat of the cat's breath on his face. When had it come awake? How had it gotten so close without him noticing? Kinson held the cat's gaze a moment longer, took a deep breath, and turned away.

"I don't suppose you would want to come with us?" Bremen was asking their host. "A journey of a few days, just long enough to see the talisman forged?"

Cogline snorted and shook his head. "Take your games-playing elsewhere, Bremen. I give you the forging process and my best wishes. If you can make use of either, well and good. But I belong here."

He had scribbled something on a piece of old parchment, and now he passed it to the Druid. "The best that science can offer," he muttered. "Take it."

Bremen did, stuffing it into his robes.

Cogline straightened, then looked at Kinson and Mareth in turn. "Watch out for this old man," he warned. There was dismay in his eyes, as if he had suddenly discovered something that displeased him. "He needs more looking after than he realizes. You, Tracker, have his ear. Make sure he listens when he needs to. You, girl—what is your name? Mareth? You have more than his ear, don't you?"

No one spoke. Kinson's eyes shifted to Mareth. There was no expression on her face, but she had gone suddenly pale.

Cogline studied her bleakly. "Doesn't matter. Just keep him safe from himself. Keep him well."

He stopped abruptly, as if deciding he had said too much. He mumbled something they could not hear, then rose to his feet, a loose jumble of bones and skin, a rumpled caricature of himself.

"Spend the night, and then be on your way," he muttered wearily.

He looked them over carefully, as if expecting to find something he had missed previously, as if thinking perhaps they might be other than who they claimed. Then he turned and moved away.

Good night, they called after him. But he did not respond. He walked resolutely away from them and did not look back.

CHAPTER

19

CLOUDS SKIMMED THE EDGES of the quarter-moon, casting strange shadows that raced across the surface of the earth like night birds ahead of the advancing Dwarves. It was the slow, deep hour before sunrise, when death is closest and dreams hold sway in men's sleep. The air was warm and still, and the night hushed. There was a sense of everything slowing, of time losing half a tick in its clockwork progression, of life drifting momentarily from its inexorable pathway so that death, for a few precious moments, might be further delayed.

The Dwarves had slipped from the trees of the Anar in a wave of dark forms that seemed to flow like a river. They were several thousand strong, come down through the Wolfsktaag out of the Pass of Jade a dozen miles north of where the army of the Warlock Lord was encamped. It was two days since the army had passed south of Storlock, and while the Dwarves had watched its progress closely, they had determined to wait until now to attack.

They eased their way down the line of the trees to where the Rabb dropped away in a long, low swale close to a small river called the Nunne. It was there that the Northland army, unwisely, had chosen to make its camp. To be sure, there was water and grass and space to sprawl out, but it gave away the high ground to an attacker and exposed two flanks of the army to an enfilading strike. The army had set watch, but any watch

265

was easily dispatched, and even the presence of the roving Skull Bearers was no deterrent to men in a desperate situation.

Risca gave them cover when they were close enough that cover mattered. He sent images of himself south below the Nunne to distract the winged hunters, and when the clouds masked moon and stars completely, the Dwarves went in. They crept swiftly across the last mile separating their strike force from the sleeping army, killed the sentries before they could sound an alarm, took the high ground north and east above the river, and attacked. Stretched out across the ridge of the high ground for half a mile in either direction, they used longbows and slings, and they raked the Trolls and Gnomes and monsters of darkness with volley after volley. The army came awake, men screaming and cursing, racing to put on their armor and to take up their weapons, falling wounded and dead in midstride. A cavalry assault was mounted in the midst of the confusion, a doomed counterattack that was cut to pieces as it charged up the incline from the maelstrom of the camp.

One of the Skull Bearers circled out of the dark and swept down on the Dwarves in retaliation, claws and teeth exposed, a silent stalker. But Risca was expecting this, his attention given over to preparing for it, and when the Skull Bearer appeared, he let it come almost to the earth before he struck at it with his Druid fire and flung it away, burned and shrieking.

The strike was swift and measured. The damage inflicted was largely superficial and of no lasting consequence to an army of this size, so the Dwarves did not linger. Their primary purpose was to cause disruption and to draw the enemy away from its intended line of march. In that, the Dwarves were successful. They fled back into the trees, taking the most direct route, then turned north again for the Pass of Jade. The enemy was quick to give pursuit. A large force was mounted and gave chase, the size of the Dwarf party having not yet been determined. By sunrise, the pursuers were closing on the Dwarves as they neared the mouth of the Pass of Jade.

Everything was going exactly as Risca had planned.

* * *

"THERE," said Geften softly, pointing into the trees fronting the pass.

Below, the last of the Dwarf strike force was filing through the pass and dispersing into the rocks above, taking up positions next to the men already in place, four thousand strong. Behind them, less than a mile away, the first movements of their pursuers could be detected in the still, deep shadows of the predawn forest. Even as he watched, Risca could see the movement widen and spread, like a ripple from a stone thrown into the center of a still pond. It was a sizable force that had come after them, much too large for them to defeat in a direct engagement, even though a large part of the Dwarf army was assembled here.

"How long?" he asked Geften in response.

The Tracker shrugged, a small movement, spare like all his gestures, like the man himself, unobtrusive and restrained. Coarse, unruly gray hair topped an oddly elongated head. "An hour if they stop to debate the wisdom of coming into the pass without a plan."

Risca nodded. "They'll stop. They've been burned twice now." He smiled at the older man, a gnarled veteran of the Gnome border wars. "Keep an eye on them. I'll tell the king."

He abandoned his position and moved back into the rocks, climbing from where Geften monitored their pursuers' progress. Risca felt a wild excitement course through him, fueled by the knowledge that a second battle lay just ahead. The strike at the Northland camp had only whetted his appetite. He breathed the morning air and felt strong and ready. He had waited all his life for this, he supposed. All those years shut away at Paranor, practicing his warrior skills, his fighting tactics, his weapons mastery. All for this, for a chance to stand against an enemy that would challenge him as nothing at Paranor ever could. It made him feel alive in a way he could not ignore, and even the desperation of their circumstances did not lessen the rush of excitement he felt.

He had reached the Dwarves three days earlier and gone at once to Raybur. Already alerted to the presence of the Northland army, already certain of its intent, the king had received him. Risca merely confirmed what he knew and gave further impetus to his need to act. Raybur was a warrior king as Risca was a warrior Druid, a man whose entire life had been spent in battle. Like Risca, he had fought against the Gnome tribes when he was a boy, a part of the Dwarf struggle to prevent Gnome encroachment on those lands in the Lower and Central Anar that the Dwarves had considered theirs for as long as anyone could remember. When he became king, Raybur had pursued his cause with a single-mindedness that was frightening. Taking his army deep into the interior, he had pushed back the Gnomes and extended the boundaries of his homeland until they were twice their previous size, until the Gnomes were so far north of the Rabb and east of the Silver River that they no longer threatened. For the first time in centuries, all that lay between was safe for the Dwarves to settle and inhabit.

But now the challenge was mounted anew, this time in the form of the army that approached. Raybur had mobilized the Dwarves in preparation for the battle that lay ahead, the battle that everyone knew they could not win without help, yet must fight if they were to survive. Risca had told them that the Elves were coming. Bremen had charged that it must happen, and Tay Trefenwyd, whom he would trust with his life, had gone west to make it so. Yet it remained for the Dwarves to buy the time that was needed for that help to arrive. Raybur understood. He was close with Bremen and Courtann Ballindarroch, and he knew both to be honorable men. They would do what they could. But time was precious, and nothing could be taken for granted. Raybur understood that as well. So Culhaven was evacuated—it was there that the Northland army would come first, and the Dwarves could not defend their home city against so massive a force. Women, children, and old people were sent deep into the interior of the Anar, where they could be safely hidden away until the danger was over. The Dwarf army, in the meantime, went north through the Wolfsktaag to face the enemy.

Raybur turned as Risca approached, looking away from his commanders and advisors, from Wyrik and Banda, the eldest of his five sons, from the charts they studied and the plans they had drawn. "Do they come?" he asked quickly.

Risca nodded. "Geften keeps watch over their progress. He estimates we have an hour before they strike."

Raybur nodded and beckoned the Druid to walk with him. He was a big man, not tall, but broad and strong through the chest and shoulders, his head huge and his features prominent, his weathered face bearded and creased. He had a hooked nose and shaggy brows that gave him a slightly bestial look, but beneath his imposing exterior he was warm and exuberant and quick to laugh. Older than Risca by fifteen years, he was nevertheless as physically imposing as the Druid and more than a match for him in an even contest. The two were very close, more so in some ways than with their own families, for they shared common beliefs and experiences and had come from hard lives and close escapes to live as long as they had.

"Tell me again how you will make this happen," the king directed, putting his arm around Risca and steering him away from the others.

"You know that already," Risca responded with a snort. The plan was theirs, devised by Risca and approved by the king, and while they had shared it in general with the others, they had kept the specifics to themselves.

"Tell it to me anyway." The gruff face glanced at him, then looked away. "Humor me. I am your king."

Risca nodded, smiling. "The Trolls and Gnomes and what have you will converge on the pass. We will try to stop them from entering. We will make a good show of it, then fall back, apparently beaten. We will delay them through the mountains for the next day or so, slowing but not stopping them. In the meantime, they will have moved the rest of their army south to the Silver River. Dwarves will flee at their approach. They will find Culhaven abandoned. They will discover that no one challenges them. They will think that the whole of the Dwarf army must be fighting in the Wolfsktaag."

"Which is not far from the truth," Raybur grunted, rubbing at his beard with one massive hand.

"Which is not far from the truth," Risca echoed. "Sensing victory, because they know the geography of these mountains, they will seize the Pass of Noose and wait for their comrades to drive us south through the valleys into their arms. The Gnomes will have assured them that there are only two ways out of the Wolfsktaag—through the Pass of Jade north and the Pass of Noose south. If the Dwarf army is trapped between the two, they have no chance of escape."

Raybur nodded, worrying his upper lip and the edges of his mustache with his strong teeth. "But if they advance on us too quickly or too far . . ."

"They won't," Risca cut him short. "We won't let them. Besides, they will not take that kind of chance. They will be cautious. They will worry that we will find a way around them if they proceed too quickly. It will be easier to let us come to them. They will wait until they see us, and then strike."

They moved to a flat shelf of rock and sat down side by side, staring off into the interior of the mountains. The day was sunny and bright, but the Wolfsktaag, away from the entrance to the pass and deep into the valleys and ridges that crisscrossed its vast interior, was shrouded with mist.

"It is a good plan," said Raybur finally.

"It is the best we could devise," Risca amended. "Bremen might do better if he were here."

"He'll come to us soon enough," Raybur declared softly. "And the Elves with him. Then we'll have this invader in a place not so much to his liking."

Risca nodded wordlessly, but he was thinking back to his encounter with Brona not so many nights earlier, remembering what he had felt when he realized the extent of the Warlock Lord's power, remembering how the other had paralyzed him, had almost had him in his grasp. Such a monster would not be easily overcome, no matter the size or strength of the force sent against him. This was more than a war of weapons and men; it was a war of magic. In such a war, the Dwarves were at a decided disadvantage unless Bremen's vision of a talisman could be brought to pass.

He wondered where the old man was now. He wondered how many of his four visions were taking shape.

"The Skull Bearers will try to spy us out," Raybur mused.

Risca pursed his lips and considered. "They will try, but the Wolfsktaag will not be friendly to them. Nor will it make any difference what they see. By the time they realize what we have done, it will be too late."

The king shifted. "They will come for you," he said suddenly, and looked at the Druid. "They know you are their greatest threat—their only threat besides Bremen and Tay Trefenwyd. If they kill you, we have no magic to protect us."

Risca shrugged and smiled. "Then you had better take good care of me, my king."

IT TOOK THE NORTHLANDERS longer than Geften had estimated to launch their attack, but it was fierce when it came. The Pass of Jade was broad where it opened to the eastern Anar, then narrowed abruptly at the twin peaks that formed its entrance into the Wolfsktaag. Having determined beforehand that Dwarf resistance would be strong, the army of the Warlock Lord threw the whole of its force into the gap, intent on breaking through on the first try. Against a less well prepared defender, they would have succeeded. But the Dwarves had held the passes of the Wolfsktaag for years against Gnome raiders and in doing so had learned a trick or two. The size of the Northland force was already negated to some extent by the narrowness of the pass and the ruggedness of the terrain. The Dwarves did not try to block the Northland charge, but assailed it from the protection of the slopes. Pits had been dug into the winding floor. Massive boulders were tumbled from above and spiked barricades swung into place. Arrows and spears rained down. Hundreds of attackers died in the first rush. The Trolls were particularly determined, huge and strong and armored against the missiles sent to kill them. But they were ponderous and slow, and many fell into the pits or were crushed by the boulders. Still they advanced.

They were stopped finally at the far end of the pass. Raybur had caused a log wall to be built at the back of a trench filled with dead wood, and on the Northlanders' rush he had the whole of it fired. Pressed forward by those who followed and too heavy themselves to climb free, the Trolls died where they stood, burned to the bone. The screams and the stench of their ruined flesh filled the air, and the attack broke off.

They came again at midday, less reckless this time, and again they were beaten back. They attacked once more at nightfall. Each time the Dwarves were forced a little deeper into the pass. Positioned on both sides of the draw, Raybur and his sons directed the Dwarf defense, holding as long as they reasonably could before withdrawing, giving ground grudgingly, but judiciously, so that no more lives were lost than necessary. Raybur commanded the left flank in the company of Geften while Wyrik and Fleer commanded the right. Risca was left to choose his own ground. The Dwarves fought bravely, pressed at every turn by a force at least three times their size, seasoned from countless battles. No winged hunters or creatures of the netherworld came at them in daylight, so Risca did not waste his magic in support of their defense. The plan, after all, was not to win the battle. The plan was to lose it as slowly as possible.

Nightfall brought a break in the hostilities and a new quiet to the mountains. Mist slipped down from the higher elevations in the slow melting of the light to close about defender and attacker alike. The silence grew pervasive as vision narrowed and shortened, and small breezes, damp and cloying, slithered out of the rocks to caress and tease. There were living things in the touch of those breezes, invisible and shapeless, but as certain as midnight. They were creatures of the Wolfsktaag, beings formed of magic as old as time and as needful as men's souls. The Dwarves knew of them and were wary of their intent. They were forerunners of things larger and more powerful still and not to be listened to. They whispered lies and false promises, rendered dreams and treacherous visions, and to heed them in any way was to invite death. The Dwarves understood this. Knowledge was what protected them.

Not so with the Gnomes who camped opposite them at the head of the pass. The Gnomes were terrified of these mountains and the things that dwelled within. Superstitious and pagan, wary of all magic and particularly of the sort that resided here, they would have preferred to avoid the Wolfsktaag entirely. There were gods here to be prayed to and spirits to be appeased. This was sacred ground. But the power of the Warlock Lord and his dark followers frightened them even more, so they closed ranks with the more stolid and less impressionable Trolls. But they did so reluctantly and with little heart, and the Dwarves made ready to use their fear against them.

As Risca had foreseen, the Northland army mounted a new attack several hours before dawn, when darkness and brume still masked its movements. They came silently and in force, massing on the floor of the pass and along its higher slopes and ridges, intent on sweeping over the Dwarves through sheer strength of numbers. But Raybur had withdrawn his line of defense a hundred yards farther back into the pass from where the battle had ended at dusk. Between the two lines, the Dwarves had built piles of green wood and new leaves and left them ready to light. On the floor of the pass, fresh barricades and trenches had been readied, staggered at intervals between the fires. When the Northlanders reached the expected Dwarf line of defense, they found the position deserted. Had the Dwarves abandoned the pass? Had they fallen back under cover of darkness? Momentarily confused, they hesitated, milling about as their leaders deliberated. Finally, they started forward once more. But by now the Dwarves were alerted to the attack. Risca used his magic to light the fires that dotted the slopes and floor of the pass, and suddenly the Northlanders found themselves engulfed by a blanket of smoke that choked and blinded. Eyes tearing, throats clogging, they came doggedly on.

Then Risca sent the wraiths. He created some from magic, lured some from the mist, and sent all into the smoke to play. Things of tooth and claw, of red maw and black eye, of fears real and imagined, the wraiths closed on the gasping, half-blind Northlanders. The Gnomes went mad, shrieking in terror. Nothing would hold them against this. They broke ranks and ran. Now the Dwarves struck, slingers, throwers, and bowmen sending their deadly missiles into the heart of the attacking force. Steadily they pushed the attackers back. The assault stalled and fell apart as men died at every turn. By dawn, the pass belonged to the Dwarves once more.

The Northlanders attacked again the next day, refusing to give up, determined to break through. Their losses were frightful, but the Dwarves were losing men as well, and they had fewer lives to spare. By midafternoon, Raybur had begun making preparations to withdraw. Two days was long enough to stand against this army. Now it was time to retreat a bit, to draw the enemy on. They waited until nightfall, until darkness had closed down about them once again. Then they fired a last trench of deadwood topped with leaves and green saplings so that the smoke would mask their movements and slipped away.

Risca stayed behind to make certain they were not followed too quickly. With a small band of Dwarf Hunters, he defended the narrowest point of the deep pass against a tentative assault before falling back with the others. Once a Skull Bearer showed itself, trying to wing beneath the layers of mist and smoke, but Risca countered with the Druid fire and flung it away.

They marched all night after that, traveling deep into the mountains. Geften led them, a veteran of countless expeditions, familiar with the canyons and defiles, ridges and drops, knowing where to go and how to get there. They avoided the dark, narrow places where the monsters dwelled, the things that had survived since ancient times and lent substance to the superstitions of the Gnomes. They kept to the high open ground where possible, sufficiently concealed by darkness and mist that they remained hidden from their pursuers. The Northland army would have scouts as well, but they would be Gnomes, and the Gnomes would be cautious. Raybur's force moved swiftly and deliberately. When the army of the Warlock Lord found them, it would again be on ground of their choosing.

By the following day, after the Dwarves had stopped to rest for several hours at dawn and were again on the march, a messenger arrived from the smaller force that defended the Pass of Noose at the south end of the mountains. The balance of the army of the Warlock Lord had arrived, pressing inward from the lower end of the Rabb to set camp. An attack would probably be launched by nightfall. The Dwarves could hold the pass for at least a day before yielding. Raybur looked at Risca and smiled. A day would be long enough.

They let the Northland army coming down from the Pass of Jade catch up to them that afternoon, when the sun was already gone behind the peaks and the mist was beginning to creep down out of the higher elevations like vines in search of light.

They waited in a canyon where the floor rose steeply through a maze of giant rocks and treacherous drops, and attacked as the Northlanders climbed out of the exposed bowl. They held their ground just long enough to frustrate the advance, then fell back once more. Darkness descended, and their pursuers were forced to halt for the night, unable to retaliate.

By dawn, the Dwarves were gone. The Northlanders pressed on, anxious to end this game of cat and mouse. But the Dwarves surprised them again at midday, this time leading them into a blind pass, then tearing at their exposed flanks as they sought to withdraw. By the time the Northlanders had recovered, the Dwarves had disappeared once more. All day it went on, a series of strikes and withdrawals, the smaller force taunting and humiliating the larger. But the south end of the mountains was drawing near, and the Northlanders, furious at their inability to close with the Dwarves, began to take heart from the fact that their quarry was running out of places to hide.

The contest had grown serious. One false step and the Dwarves would be finished. Messengers raced back and forth between those who harassed the enemy coming down out of the north and those who still held the Pass of Noose south. Timing was important. The enemy south pressed hard to claim the Pass of Noose, but the Dwarves held firm. The Pass of Noose was more easily defended and difficult to take, no matter the size of the force at either end. But the Dwarves would yield it up at dawn and fall back, slowly, deliberately, letting the Northlanders believe they had prevailed. The army of the Warlock Lord would claim the pass and then wait for their comrades to drive the overmatched and beleaguered Dwarves onto their spearpoints.

Dawn arrived, and while one army of Northlanders occupied the Pass of Noose, the other drove relentlessly south. The Dwarves, caught between, had nowhere left to run.

ALL THAT DAY, Raybur's army fought to slow the southward advance. The Dwarf King used every tactic he had mastered in thirty years of Gnome warfare, hammering at the invaders when there was opportunity, creating opportunity when none presented itself. He divided his army in thirds, giving the largest of the three over to his generals to command so that they might provide an obvious target for the enemy to pursue. The two smaller companies, one commanded by himself, one by his eldest son Wyrik, became pincers that harried the Northlanders at every turn. Working in unison, they drew the enemy first one way and then the other. When a flank was exposed by one, the second would be quick to strike. The Dwarves twisted and wound about the larger army with maddening elusiveness, refusing to be pinned down, pressing the attack at every turn.

By nightfall, they were exhausted. Worse, the Dwarves from the north had been backed up against those from the south. The two joined and became one, both having retreated as far as they could, and suddenly there was no place left for either to go. Night and mist shrouded them sufficiently that running them to ground should have been postponed until morning. But instead, the hunt went on, in large part because the Northlanders were too angry and frustrated to wait. The Pass of Noose was only a few miles farther on. The Dwarves were trapped, bereft of room to maneuver or hide, and now, finally, the Northlanders were certain that their superior force would be able to exact a long-overdue retribution.

As night descended and the brume thickened along the last few miles of the valley into which the Dwarves had withdrawn, Raybur dispatched scouts to give warning of any enemy approach. Time was running out, and they must act quickly now. Geften was called, and the first of the Dwarf defenders prepared for the escape that had been intended from the beginning. The escape would commence under cover of darkness and be finished by midnight. It marked the culmination of a plan the king had settled on with Risca when the Druid had first returned from Paranor, a plan devised from knowledge possessed only by the Dwarves. Unknown to any but them, there was a third way out of the mountains. Close to where they were gathered, not far from the more accessible Pass of Noose, there were a series of connecting defiles, tunnels, and ledges that twisted and wound east out of the Wolfsktaag into the forests of the central Anar. Geften himself had discovered this hidden passage, explored it with a handful of others, and reported it to Raybur some eight years past. It was knowledge carefully protected and kept secret. A select number of Dwarves had used the passage now and again to make sure it was kept open, memorizing its twists and turns, but no others were shown the way. Risca had learned about it from Raybur on a visit home several years ago, the Dwarf King sharing the secret with the one man who was as close to him as his sons. Risca had recalled it when the Northland army had come east, and his plan had taken shape.

Now the Dwarves set the plan in motion. Slowly they began to reduce their numbers, siphoning off their strength in a long, steady line that withdrew east into the mountains, following the escape route meticulously laid out by Geften. The Northlanders approached the head of the valley, and the scouts began to report back. Yet the most dangerous part of the scheme remained. The Northlanders must be delayed until the Dwarves were safely away. With Risca accompanying him, Raybur took a small band of twenty volunteers north. They placed themselves in a jumble of rocks that overlooked the valley's broad passage in, and when the first of the Warlock Lord's army appeared, they attacked.

It was a precise, momentary strike, intended only to disrupt and confuse, for the Dwarves were vastly outnumbered. They used bows from the cover of the rocks, firing their arrows just long enough to draw attention to themselves before falling back. Even so, escape was difficult. The Northlanders came after them, furious. It was dark and treacherous in the rocks, a maze of jagged edges and deep crevices, and the light, as always in the Wolfsktaag, was poor. Mist curled down out of the taller peaks, masking everything on the valley floor. More familiar with the terrain than their pursuers, the Dwarves slipped quickly through the maze, but the Northlanders were everywhere, swarming over the rocks. Some of the defenders were overtaken. Some turned the wrong way. All of these were killed. The fighting was ferocious. Risca used his magic, sending Druid fire into the midst of the hunters, chasing them back. A handful of the netherworld grotesques hove into view, lurching mindlessly after the scrambling Dwarves, and Risca was forced to stand long enough to throw them back as well.

They nearly had him then. They closed on him from three

sides, drawn by the flare of his Druid fire. Weapons flew, and dark things launched themselves at him and tried to drag him down. He fought with fury and exhilaration, alive as he could not otherwise be, a warrior in his element. He was strong and quick, and he would not be overpowered. He threw back his attackers, fought off their strikes, used the Druid magic to shield his movements, and escaped them.

Then he was at the back side of the maze and racing after the last of the Dwarves. Their force had been halved, and those who remained were bloodied and exhausted. Raybur lingered until Risca caught up, grim-faced and sweating in the faint light. The battle-axe he carried had one blade shattered and was covered in blood.

"We'll have to hurry," he warned, lumbering forward. "They're almost on top of us."

Risca nodded. Spears and arrows flew at them from out of the rocks below. They charged up the valley slope, hearing the cries of the Northlanders chase after. Another of the Dwarves went down in front of them, an arrow in his throat. There were only a handful left of the twenty who had come. Risca whirled as he sensed something sweep out of the skies and sent a bolt of fire after one of the winged hunters as it swooped hurriedly away. The mist was growing thicker now. If they could stay clear of their pursuers for a few more minutes, they would lose them.

And so they did, pushing on until they were past exhaustion and running on determination alone. Eight in all, the last of the Dwarves reached the gathering place of the others, deserted now save for Geften. Wordlessly, they hastened after the anxious Tracker as he led them into the hills and the peaks beyond.

Behind them, the Northlanders swarmed into the valley, crashing through trees and brush, howling in fury. Somewhere the Dwarves were hidden and trapped. Soon they would be found. The hunt went on, moving farther south toward the Pass of Noose. With luck, Risca thought, the two halves of the War-lock Lord's army would run up against each other in the mist and dark and each would think the other was their quarry. With luck, each would kill large numbers of the other before they discovered their mistake.

He moved up into the boulders that marked the beginning of the high range. They would not be followed here, not in this darkness, and by morning they would have passed the point where their tracks could be found.

Raybur dropped back and clapped a congratulatory hand on his friend's broad shoulder. Risca smiled at the king, but inwardly he felt cold and hard. He had measured the size of the army that hunted them. He had judged the nature of the things that commanded it. Yes, the Dwarves had escaped this time. They had tricked the Northlanders into a prolonged and futile hunt, delayed their advance, and lived to fight another day.

But it would be a day of reckoning when it came.

And it would come, Risca feared, all too soon.

CHAPTER

20

RAIN WAS FALLING in Arborlon, a slow, steady downpour that draped the city in a curtain of shimmering damp and hazy gray. It was midafternoon. The rain had begun at dawn and now, more than nine hours later, showed no signs of lessening. Jerle Shannara watched it from the seclusion of the king's summer home, his current retreat, his present hideaway. He watched it spatter on the windowpanes, on the walkways, in the hundreds of puddles it had already formed. He watched it transform the trees of the forest, turning their trunks a silky black and their leaves a vibrant green. It seemed to him, in his despondency, that if he watched it long and hard enough, it would transform him as well.

His mood was foul. It had been so since his return to the city three days earlier. He had come home with the remnant of his battered company, with Preia Starle, Vree Erreden, and the Elven Hunters Obann and Rusk. He had carried back the Black Elfstone and the body of Tay Trefenwyd. He had brought no joy with him and found none waiting. In his absence, Courtann Ballindarroch had died of his wounds. His son, Alyten, had assumed the throne, his first order of business to sally forth on an expedition dedicated to tracking down his father's killers. Madness. But no one had stopped him. Jerle was disgusted. It was the act of a fool, and he was afraid that the Elves had inherited a fool for a king. Either that, or the Elves once again had no king at all. For Alyten Ballindarroch had departed Arborlon a week earlier, and there had been no word of him since.

He stood in the silence and stared out the window at the rain, at the space between the falling drops, at the grayness, at nothing at all. His gaze was empty. The summerhouse was empty as well—just him, alone in the silence with his thoughts. Not pleasant company for anyone. His thoughts haunted him. The loss of Tay was staggering, more painful than he could have imagined, deeper than he would let himself admit. Tay Trefenwyd had been his best and closest friend all his life. No matter the choices they had made, no matter the length of their occupational separations, no matter the events that had transformed their lives, that friendship had endured. That Tay had become a Druid while Jerle had become Captain of the Home Guard and then Court Advisor to the king had altered nothing. When Tay had come home from Paranor this final time, when Jerle had first seen his friend riding up the roadway to Arborlon, it was as if only a few moments had passed since last they had parted, as if time meant nothing. Now Tay was gone, his life given so that his friends and companions could live, so that the Black Elfstone could be brought safely to Arborlon.

The Black Elfstone. The killing weapon. A dark rage surged through Jerle Shannara as he thought of the cursed talisman. The cost of keeping the Elfstone had been his friend's life, and he still had no concept of its purpose. For what use was it intended? What use, that he could measure its worth against the loss of his dearest friend?

He had no answer. He had done what he must. He had carried the Elfstone back to Arborlon, keeping it from falling into the hands of the Warlock Lord, thinking all the way that it would be better if he were to rid himself of the magic, if he were to drop it down the deepest, darkest crevice he could find. He might have done so if he had been alone, so intense was his anger and frustration at the loss of Tay. But Preia and Vree Erreden accompanied him, and the care of the Stone had been given over to them as well. So he had carried it home as Tay had wanted, prepared to relinquish all claim to it the moment he arrived.

But fate worked against him in this as well. Courtann Ballindarroch was dead, and his successor son was off on a fool's mission. To whom, then, should he give the Elfstone? Not to the Elven High Council, a clutch of ineffectual, bickering old men who lacked foresight and reason, and were concerned mostly with protecting themselves now that Courtann was dead. Not to Alyten, who was absent in any case—the Elfstone had never been intended for him. Bremen then, but the Druid had not yet arrived in Arborlon—if he was to arrive at all.

So on Preia's advice and with Vree Erreden's concurrence, these two the only ones he could consult on the matter, he hid the Black Elfstone deep in the catacombs of the palace cellars, down where no one could ever find it without his help, away from the prying eyes and curious minds that might attempt to unlock its power. Jerle, Preia, and the locat understood the danger of the Elfstone as no other could. They had seen what the Elfstone's dark magic could do. They had witnessed firsthand the extent of its power. All those men, human and inhuman alike, burned to ash in the blink of an eye. Tay Trefenwyd, ruined by the backlash despite his Druid defenses. Such power was anathema. Such power was black and witless and should be locked away forever.

I hope it was worth your life, Tay, Jerle Shannara thought bleakly. *But I cannot conceive that it was.*

The chill of the rain worked through him, causing his bones to ache. The fire, the sole source of heat for the large gathering room, was dying in the hearth behind him, and he walked over to add a few more logs. He stared down into the rising flames when he had done so, wondering at the vagaries of circumstance and fate. So much had been lost these past few weeks. What purpose had these losses served? Where would it all culminate? In what cause? Jerle shook his head and brushed back his blond hair. Philosophical questions only confused him. He was a warrior, and what he understood best was what he could strike out against. Where was the hard substance of this matter to be found? Where was its flesh and blood? He felt ruined, battered without and empty within. The rain and the gray suited him. He was come back to nothing, to no purpose, to no recognizable future, to great loss and pain.

On the day of his return, he had gone to Tay's parents and Kira to tell them of his death. He would have it no other way.

Tay's parents, old and easily confused, had accepted the news
stoically and with few tears, seeing with the approach of the
end of their own lives the inevitability and capriciousness of
death. But Kira had been devastated. She had hung on Jerle as
she cried, clutching him in desperation, seeking strength he did
not have to give. He held her, thinking she was as lost to him
as her brother. She clung to him, a crumpled bit of flesh and
bone and cloth, as light as air and as insubstantial, sobbing and
shaking, and he thought in that moment that their grief for Tay
was all they would ever share again.

He turned from the fire and stared out the window once
more. Gray and damp, the day wore on, and nothing of its
passing gave hope.

The front door opened and closed, a cloak was removed
and hung, and Preia Starle walked into the room. Dampness
glistened on her face and hands, on the smooth, brown skin still
marred by the cuts and bruises of their journey to the Breakline.
She brushed at the water that beaded on her curly, cinnamon
hair, flicking it away. Honey-brown eyes studied him, as if surprised by what they saw.

"They want to make you king," she declared quietly.

He stared at her. "Who?"

"All of them. The High Council, the king's advisors, the
people on the streets, the Home Guard, the army, everyone."
She smiled wanly. "You are their only hope, they say. Alyten is
too unreliable, too reckless for the job. He has no experience.
He has no skills. It doesn't matter that he is already king, they
want him gone."

"But two grandchildren survive after him! What of them?"

"Babies, barely grown old enough to walk. Besides, the
Elven people don't want children sitting on the Ballindarroch
throne. They want you."

He shook his head in disbelief. "They haven't the right to
make that decision. No one has."

"You do," she said.

She crossed to the fire, her slim, supple body catlike in the
near gloom, all grace and efficiency. Jerle marveled at the ease
with which she moved. He marveled at her composure. He was

awed by the depth of her strength, even now, in the face of all that had happened. She stood before the fire, rubbing her hands to warm them. After a moment she stopped and just stared.

"I heard his voice today," she said. "On the streets. Tay's voice. He was calling after me, speaking my name. I heard it clearly. I turned, so eager to find him I collided with a man following me. I pushed past him, ignoring what he said, looking for Tay." She shook her head slowly. "But he wasn't there. I only imagined it."

Her voice died away in a whisper. She did not turn.

"I still can't believe he's gone," Jerle said after a moment. "I keep thinking that it's a mistake, that he's out there and any moment he will walk through the door."

He looked off into the shadows of the front entry. "I don't want to be king. I want Tay to be alive again. I want everything back the way it was."

She nodded wordlessly and watched the fire some more. They could hear the patter of the rain on the roof and against the window glass. They could hear the whisper of the wind.

Then Preia turned and walked over to him. She stood before him, motionless. He could not read the look she gave him. It was filled with so many emotions that it lacked definition. "Do you love me?" she asked directly, staring into his eyes.

He was so surprised by the question, so caught off guard, that he could not manage an answer. He just stared at her, openmouthed.

She smiled, laying claim to something that had eluded him. Her eyes filled with tears. "Did you know that Tay was in love with me?"

He shook his head slowly, stunned. "No."

"For as long as I can remember." She paused. "Just as you've always been in love with Kira." She reached up quickly and put a finger to his lips. "No, let me finish. This needs to be said. Tay was in love with me, but he would never have done anything about it. He wouldn't even speak of it. His sense of loyalty to you was so strong that he couldn't make himself. He knew I was pledged to you, and even though he was uncertain of your own feelings, he did nothing to interfere. He believed that you loved me and would marry me, and he would not jeopardize his relationship with either of us to change that. He knew of Kira, but he knew as well that she was not right for you—even when you did not."

She came a step closer. The tears were beginning to run down her cheeks now, but she ignored them. "That was a side of Tay Trefenwyd you never saw. You didn't see it because you didn't look. He was a complex man, just as you are. Neither of you understood the other as clearly as you thought. You were each the shadow of the other, but as different in some ways as the shadow is from the flesh. I know that difference. I have always known."

She swallowed. "Now you have to face up to it as well. And to what it means to be alive when your shadow is dead. Tay is gone, Jerle. We remain. What is to become of us? We have to decide. Tay loved me, but he is dead. Do you love me as well? Do you love me as strongly? Or will Kira always be between us?"

"Kira is married," he said softly, his voice breaking.

"Kira is alive. Life breeds hope. If you want her badly enough, perhaps you can find a way to have her. But you cannot have both of us. I have lost one of the two most important men in my life. I lost him without ever taking time to speak with him as I am speaking with you. I will not let that happen a second time."

She paused, uncomfortable with what she was about to say, but refusing to look away. "I am going to tell you something. If Tay had asked me to choose between you, I might have chosen him."

There was an endless silence between them. Their eyes locked and held. They stood in the center of the room, motionless. The fire in the hearth crackled softly and the rain beat down. The shadows in the room had begun to lengthen with the approach of nightfall.

"I do not want to lose you," Jerle said quietly.

Preia did not respond. She was waiting to hear more.

"I did love Kira once," he admitted. "I love her still, I suppose. But it's not the same as it was. I know I have lost her, and I no longer mourn that loss. I haven't for years. I care for her. I think of her when I think of Tay and our childhood. She was part of that, and I would be foolish if I tried to pretend that it was otherwise."

He took a deep breath. "You asked me if I loved you. I do. I haven't really thought about it in any deliberate way—I just always accepted it. I suppose I believed that you would always be there and so dismissed any further consideration as unnecessary. Why examine something that was so obvious? There seemed no need to do so. But I was wrong. I see that. I took you for granted without even realizing it. I thought that what we shared was sufficient as it was. I didn't allow for change or doubts or complacency.

"But I have lost Tay and a large part of myself with him. I have lost direction and purpose. I am come to the end of a road I have traveled for a long time and find no way to turn. When you ask if I love you, I am faced with the fact that loving you is perhaps all I have left. It is no small thing, no consolation to measure against my pain. It is much more than that. I feel foolish saying this. It is the one real truth I can acknowledge. It means more than anything else in my life. Tay let me discover this by dying. It is a high cost to pay, but there it is."

His big hands reached out and fastened gently on her shoulders. "I do love you, Preia."

"Do you?" she asked quietly.

He felt a vast distance open between them as she spoke the words. He felt an immense weight settle on his shoulders. He stood awkwardly in front of her, unable to think of what else he could do. His size and strength had always been a source of reassurance, but with Preia they seemed to work against him.

"Yes, Preia," he said finally. "I do. I love you as much as I have ever loved anyone. I don't know what else to say. This, I guess—that I hope you still love me."

She said nothing even then, standing there motionless before him, looking into his eyes. The tears had stopped, but her face was streaked and damp. A tiny smile lifted the corners of her mouth. "I have never stopped loving you," she whispered.

She stepped forward into his arms and let him hold her. After a while, she held him back.

* * *

THEY WERE SITTING TOGETHER before the fire when Vree Erred-
en appeared several hours later. It was dark by then, the last of
the daylight faded, the rain lessened to a drizzle that fell without sound on the already drenched woodlands. A silence had
fallen across the weary city, and lights had begun to appear
in the windows of buildings barely glimpsed through gaps in
the sagging, water-laden boughs of the trees. No one lived
in the palace now, the building empty while repairs were made
and a ruler determined, and only the summerhouse saw life
within the grounds. Even so, the Home Guard watched over
Jerle Shannara, come to protect one of their own as much as to
protect a member of the royal family and a rumored king-to-be.

The Guard stopped Vree Erreden three times before he
reached the door to the summerhouse, letting him pass then
only because Jerle had made certain that the locat was to be
given free access to him at all times. It was strange how their
relationship had changed. They had little in common, and Tay's
death might easily have ended any pretense at friendship between them, for the Druid Elf was the source of any bonding
they had forged on their journey west. With Tay dead, they
might have drifted apart again, each suspicious and disdainful of
the other, each drawing back into himself.

But that had not happened. Perhaps it was their unspoken,
individual resolve that it should not happen, that they owed
Tay this much. Perhaps it was a common need that bound
them, a need to understand the terrible events of their journey,
a need to make something good come out of their friend's
death. Tay had sacrificed himself for them—shouldn't they put
aside their differences for his sake? They talked of many things
on their return—of what their friend had done, of the importance he attached to carrying out Bremen's charge, of the
deadly nature of the Black Elfstone, of its place in the greater
scheme of things, of the darkening shadow of the Warlock Lord
hanging over them all. With Preia Starle, they talked of what
Tay had hoped to accomplish and how they must see that his
goals were realized—to see that the Black Elfstone reached
Bremen and that the Elven army was dispatched in aid of
the Dwarves. Their thoughts were not of themselves, but of the
greater world and the danger that threatened it.

Two nights out of Arborlon on their return from the Breakline, Jerle asked the locat if he would reveal to him any visions or whisperings hereafter that might affect what they had agreed to try to accomplish. It was not easy for him to ask, and Vree Erreden knew it. The locat said, after a few moments' reflection, that he would—that he would do anything in his power to help. He would like, in fact, to offer his services to Jerle personally, if the other thought he might have use of them. Jerle accepted the offer. They shook hands to seal their arrangement and, though they would not say so, the beginnings of their friendship.

So here was the locat come for the first time in two days, stepping in out of the rain like a beaten creature, his worn cloak soaked clear through, his small, thin form hunched and shivering. Preia met him at the door, took his cloak away and led him to the fire so that he might warm himself. Jerle poured a measure of strong ale and gave it to him. Preia wrapped him in a blanket. Vree Erreden accepted all with muttered thanks and furtive looks. His eyes were intense. He had come to them for a reason.

"I have something to tell you," he said to Jerle after the chill had left him sufficiently that he could speak without shaking. "I have had a vision, and it involves you."

Jerle nodded. "What have you seen?"

The locat rubbed his hands together, then drank some of the ale, a few sips only. His face was pinched and his eyes deep-set and hollow, as if he hadn't been sleeping well. But he had looked haunted ever since their return from the Breakline. The events in the Chew Magna had devastated his psyche. The fortress and its occupants had attacked him mercilessly, tried to crush him so that he would be of no use to Tay Trefenwyd, whom they had intended for their own. They had failed, but the damage to the locat from their attack was evident.

"When Tay first came to me to solicit my help in his search for the Black Elfstone, I used my skills to look into his mind." Vree Erreden shifted suddenly to face the other, his gaze unexpectedly steady. "It was a way to discover quickly and accurately what it was that he believed I might find. I did not tell him what I was doing; I did not want him to shade any truths that he possessed.

"What I discovered was more than what I sought. He had been told by the Druid Bremen of four visions. One was of the Chew Magna and the Black Elfstone. This was the one that I was supposed to see. But I saw the others as well. I saw the destruction at Paranor as Bremen searched for a medallion that hung from a chain. I saw the Druid again at a dark lake . . ."

He trailed off, then brushed aside what he was about to say with a quick, anxious wave of his hand. "Never mind either of those. It is the last that matters."

He paused, distracted. "I have heard talk. The Elves would make you king. They would be done with Alyten and the grandchildren and crown you."

"Just talk, nothing more," Jerle interjected quickly.

Vree Erreden folded into himself beneath his robes. "I don't think so." He let the words hang.

Preia edged forward beside Jerle. "What have you seen, Vree? Is Alyten Ballindarroch dead?"

The locat shook his head. "I don't know. I wasn't shown that. I was shown something else. But it impacts on the matter of kingship." He took a deep breath. "The vision, Bremen's last, that I glimpsed within Tay's memory, was of a man standing on a battlefield armed with a sword. The sword was a talisman, a powerful magic. The Eilt Druin's image of a hand holding forth a burning torch was graven on the pommel of the sword, clearly revealed. Across from the man was a wraith cloaked all in black, featureless and impenetrable save for eyes that were pinpricks of red fire. The man and the wraith were engaged in mortal combat."

He sipped again at his ale, and now his gaze dropped away. "I only had a single glimpse of this vision, and I did not pay it much mind. It was not important then. It gave credence to the rest of what Tay told me of his quest, nothing more. I had not really thought about it again until now."

The dark eyes lifted. "Today, I read my maps before the fire. The warmth of the flames and the rain falling outside in steady cadence caused me to doze, and as I slept I had a vision. It was sudden, intense, and unexpected. This is unusual, because mostly the visions, the hunches, the indicators of what is lost and might be found, are slower and more gentle in their coming. But this vision was sharp, and I recognized it immediately. It was Bremen's vision of the man and the wraith on the battlefield. But this time I knew them. The wraith was the Warlock Lord. The man, Jerle Shannara, was you."

Jerle wanted to laugh. For some reason, this struck him as ridiculous. Perhaps it was the impossibility of the idea. Perhaps it was his inability to believe that Tay had not recognized him in the vision, yet Vree Erreden had. Perhaps it was simply a reaction to the twinge of misgiving he felt on hearing the locat's words.

"There is more." The locat did not give him time to think. "The sword you carried bore the emblem of the medallion that Bremen carried in the vision of Paranor destroyed. The medallion is called the Eilt Druin. It is the symbol of office of the High Druids of Paranor. Its magic is very powerful. The sword was the weapon forged to destroy Brona, and the Eilt Druin was made a part of that weapon. No one told me these things, you understand. No one said they were so. I simply knew them to be true. Just as I knew, seeing you standing on that battlefield for that single moment in time, that you had become King of the Elves."

"No." Jerle shook his head stubbornly. "You are mistaken."

The locat faced him and did not look away.

"Did you see my face?"

"I did not need to see your face," Vree Erreden declared softly. "Or hear your voice. Or look about to see if others followed you as they would their king. It was you."

"Then the vision itself is false. It must be!" Jerle looked to Preia for help, but her response to his gaze was deliberate silence. His fists knotted angrily. "I do not want any part of this!"

No one spoke. The fire crackled softly, and the night was deep and still, as if listening covertly to what was taking place, an eavesdropper waiting to see what would happen. Jerle rose and walked to the window. He stood looking out at the trees and the mist. He tried to will himself to disappear. "If I were to let them make me king . . ."

He did not finish. Preia rose and stood looking across the room at him. "It would give you a chance to accomplish the things Tay Trefenwyd could not. If you were king, you could persuade the High Council to send the Elves to give aid to the Dwarves. If you were king, you could dispose of the Black Elfstone at a time and place of your own choosing and not be answerable to any. Most important of all, you would have an opportunity to destroy the Warlock Lord."

Jerle Shannara's head snapped around quickly. "The Warlock Lord destroyed the Druids. What chance would I have against a thing so monstrous?"

"A better chance than anyone else I can think of," she answered at once. "The vision has been shown twice now, once to Bremen, once to Vree. Perhaps it is prophetic. If so, then you have a chance to do something that not even Tay could do. You have a chance to save us all."

He stared at her. She was telling him she believed he would be king. She was saying that he must. She was asking him to agree with her.

"She is right," Vree Erreden said softly.

But Jerle wasn't listening to him. He continued to stare at Preia, thinking back to several hours earlier when she had demanded that he make his choice on a different matter. How much do I mean to you? How important am I? Now she was asking the questions again, the words altered only slightly. How much do your people mean to you? How important are they to you? He was aware of a sudden, precipitous shift in both the nature of their relationship and the direction of his life, both brought about by Tay Trefenwyd's death. Events he would never have dreamed possible had conspired to create this shift. Fate of a willful and deliberate sort had settled her hands squarely on his shoulders. Responsibility, leadership, and the hopes of his people—all hung in the balance of the decision demanded of him.

His mind raced in search of answers that would not come. But he knew, with a certainty that was terrifying, that whatever choice he made, it would haunt him always.

"You must stand and face this," Preia said suddenly. "You must decide."

He felt as if the world was spinning out of control. She asked too much of him. There was not yet need to decide anything. Any present need was fueled by rumors and speculation. No formal overture had been made concerning the kingship. Alyten's fate was not determined. What of Courtann Ballindarroch's grandchildren? Tay Trefenwyd himself had saved their lives. Were they to be cast aside without a thought? His own mind was not made up on any of this. He could barely conceive of what he was being asked to consider.

But his thoughts had a hollow and ill-considered ring to them, and in the silence of their aftermath he found himself face-to-face with the grinning specter of his own desperation.

He turned away from the two who waited for him to speak and looked out the window into the night.

No answer would come.

CHAPTER

21

T WAS SUNSET, and the city of Dechtera was bathed in blood-red light. The city sprawled across a plain between low-lying hills that ran north and south, the buildings a ragged, uneven jumble of walls and roofs silhouetted against the crimson horizon. Darkness crept out of the eastern grasslands, pushing back against the stain of the dying light, swallowing up the land in its black maw. The sun had settled behind a low bank of clouds, turning both sky and land first orange and then red, painting with vibrant, breathtaking colors, a defiant parting gesture as the day came to its reluctant close.

Standing east with Bremen and Mareth where the darkness already commanded the low heights and the plains below were beginning to streak with shadows, Kinson Ravenlock stared wordlessly down at the destination they had traveled so far to find.

Dechtera was an industrial city, easily reached from the other major Southland cities, set close to the mines that served its needs. It was large, far larger than any city that lay north, any of the border cities, any of the Dwarf or Elven cities, and any but the greatest of the Troll cities. There were people and homes and shops in Dechtera, but mostly there were the furnaces. They burned without ceasing, grouped in clusters throughout the city, defined in daylight by the plumes of thick smoke that rose from their stacks and at night by the bright, hot glow of their open mouths. They drank greedily of the wood and coal that fed the firings of the ores that passed into their bellies to be melted down and shaped. The hammers and anvils of the smiths clanged and sparked at all hours, and Dechtera was a city of never-ending color and sound. Smoke and heat, ash and grit filled the air and coated the buildings and the people. Amid the cities of the Southland, Dechtera was a grime-encrusted member of a family that needed more than wanted her, put up with more than embraced her, and never once thought to view her with anything approaching pride or hope.

It was an unlikely choice for the forging of their talisman, thought Kinson Ravenlock once more, for it was a city that cared nothing for imagination, a city that survived by toil and rote, a city notoriously inhospitable to Druids and magic alike. Yet it was here, Bremen had countered when the Borderman had first mentioned his concerns some days ago, that the man they needed would be found.

Whoever he was, Kinson amended, because although the Druid had been willing enough to tell them where they were going, he hadn't been willing to tell them who they were going to see.

It had taken them almost two weeks to complete their journey. Cogline had given Bremen the formula for the mixing of the metal alloy to be used in the forging of the sword that would be carried in battle against the Warlock Lord. Cogline had remained recalcitrant and skeptical to the moment of their parting, bidding farewell with the firm assurance that he expected never to see any of them again. They had accepted his dismissal with weary resignation, departing Hearthstone for Storlock, retracing their steps through Darklin Reach. That portion of their trek alone had taken them almost a week. Upon their arrival back in Storlock, they had secured horses and ridden out onto the plains. The Northland army had passed south by then, engaged in its hunt for the Dwarves in the Wolfsktaag. Nevertheless, Bremen was wary of those forces still deployed outside the Anar and took his companions all the way to the Mountains of Runne and then south along the shores of the Rainbow Lake. That far west of the Anar, he believed, they had less chance of encountering those who served the Warlock Lord. They passed down across the Silver River and skirted the Mist Marsh before passing onto the Battlemound. Travel was slow and cautious, for this was dangerous country even without the added presence of the creatures that served Brona, and there was no point in taking unnecessary chances. There were things born of old magic living in the Battlemound, things akin to those that resided in the Wolfsktaag, and while Bremen knew of them and of the ways in which they could be combated, the better choice was to avoid them altogether.

So the trio rode south along a line that angled between the barren stretches of the Battlemound, with its Sirens and wights, and the dark depths of the Black Oaks with its wolf packs. They traveled by day and kept close watch over one another by night. They sensed, rather than saw, the things they wished to avoid, things both native and foreign, things of land, water, and air alike, aware of the eyes that followed after them, feeling more than once a presence pass close by. But nothing challenged them outright or made any attempt to track them, and so they eased past the dangers of the Borderlands and moved steadily on.

So that now, at the close of the thirteenth day of this most recent leg of their odyssey, they stood looking down at the red welter of Dechtera's industrial nightmare.

"I hate this city already," Kinson offered glumly, brushing the dust from his clothes. The land about them was barren and dry, empty of trees and shade, thick with long grass and loose silt. If it rained in this part of the world, it did not do so regularly.

"I would not want to live in such a place," Mareth agreed. "I cannot imagine those who do."

Bremen said nothing. He stood looking down at Dechtera, his gaze more distant than the city itself. Then he closed his eyes and went still. Kinson and Mareth glanced at each other, waiting him out, letting him be. Below, the mouths of the furnaces glowed in white-hot spots amid the gathering dark. The red wash of the sunset had died away, the sun gone down below the horizon far enough that its light was just a dim streak barely visible through the clouds west. A silence had settled across the plains, and in its hush could be heard the hammering of metal on metal.

"We are here," Bremen said suddenly, his eyes open once more, "because Dechtera is home to the finest smiths in the Four Lands outside the Troll nation. The Southlanders have no use for the Druids, but they are more likely to provide us with what we require than the Trolls. All we need do is find the right man. Kinson, that will be your task. You will be able to pass through the city freely and without attracting attention."

"Fair enough," Kinson agreed, anxious to get on with matters. "Who is it I seek?"

"That will be up to you to decide."

"Up to me?" Kinson was astounded. "We came all this way to find a man we don't even know?"

Bremen smiled indulgently. "Patience, Kinson. And have faith. We did not come here blindly or without reason. The man we seek is here, known to us or not. As I said, the best smiths in the Four Lands reside in Dechtera. But we must choose among them and choose wisely. It will take some investigating. Your Tracker skills should serve you well."

"What exactly am I looking for in this man?" Kinson pressed; he was irritated by his own uncertainty.

"What you would look for in any other man—plus skill, knowledge, and pride of workmanship in his trade. A master smith." Bremen put one frail hand on the big man's shoulder. "Did you really have to ask me that?"

Kinson grimaced. Standing to one side, Mareth smiled faintly. "What do I do when I've found this master smith?"

"Return here for me. Then we will go down together to persuade him to our cause."

Kinson looked back at the city, at its maze of dark buildings and scattered fires, at the mix of black shadows and crimson glare. The workday had become the work night, and there was no dimming of the furnaces or slowing of the labor. The swelter of heat and body sweat hung above the city in a damp shimmer.

"A smith who understands the concept of mixing ores to make stronger alloys and of tempering metals to gain that strength." Kinson shook his head. "Not to mention a smith who thinks it is all right to help the Druids forge a weapon of magic."

Bremen tightened his hand on his friend's shoulder. "Do not be overly concerned with our smith's beliefs. Look for the other qualities instead. Find the master we seek—leave the rest to me."

Kinson nodded. He looked at Mareth, at the huge, dark eyes staring back into his. "What of you?"

"Mareth and I will wait here for your return. You will do better alone. You will be able to move more freely if not burdened by the presence of companions." Bremen took his hand from the Borderman's shoulder. "But be careful, Kinson. These are your countrymen, but they are not necessarily your friends."

Kinson stripped off his pack, checked his weapons, and wrapped his cloak carefully about his shoulders. "I know that."

He clasped the old man's hand and held it. Bird bones, more fragile than he remembered. He released his grip quickly.

Then, so impulsively he could not later decipher his reasoning, he bent to Mareth, kissed her lightly on the cheek, turned, and set off down the slope of the night-draped hill for the city.

HIS JOURNEY IN took him more than an hour. He did not set a hurried pace, but walked slowly and easily across the flats that led in. There was no reason to rush, and should anyone be watching he did not want to call attention to himself. He worked his way steadily out of the darkness and into the light, feeling the temperature of the air rise as he neared the buildings, hearing the sounds of hammer and tongs on metal grow louder and more intense. Voices rose, a cacophony that signaled the presence of ale houses, taverns, inns, and brothels amid the great furnaces and warehouses. Laughter rose out of the grunts and swearing, out of the clamor and din, and the mix of work and pleasure was pervasive and incongruous. No separation of life's functions in this city, the Borderman decided. No separation of any sort.

He thought briefly of Mareth, of that quiet way she had of looking at him—as if she was studying him in ways he could not understand, as if she was measuring him for something.

Strangely enough, it did not bother him. There was reassurance to be found in her gaze, a comfort to be taken from having her want to know him better. That had never happened before, not even with Bremen. But Mareth was different. They had grown close in the past two weeks, in the time they had traveled south to Dechtera. They had talked not of the present, but of the past, of when they were young and of what growing up had meant for them. They had told their separate stories and begun to discover they shared much in common. The sharing was not of events or of experiences so much as of insights. They had learned the same lessons in their lives and arrived at the same conclusions. Their view of the world was similar. They were content with who and what they were, accepting that they were different from others. They were content to live alone, to travel, to explore what was unknown, to discover what was new. They had given up their family ties long ago. They had shed their civilized skin and taken on the wanderer's cloak. They saw themselves as outcasts by choice and accepted that it was all right to be so.

But most important of all was their mutual willingness to allow themselves to keep what secrets they would and to reveal them as they chose. It meant more to Mareth, perhaps, than to Kinson, for she was the more closely guarded of the two and the one to whom privacy meant the most. She had harbored secrets from the beginning, and Kinson felt certain that despite her recent revelations she harbored them still. But he did not sense bad intent in this, and he believed strongly that everyone had the right to wrestle their personal demons without interference from others. Mareth was risking as much as they in coming with them. She had taken a gamble in allying herself with them when it would have been just as easy to go her own way. Perhaps Bremen would be able to help her with her magic and perhaps not—there was no guarantee. She had to know this. After all, he had barely mentioned the matter since leaving Hearthstone, and Mareth had not sought to press him.

In any event, they had drawn closer as a result of their confidences, their bonds forged selectively and with care, and now each possessed insight to help determine how best to measure the other's words and actions. Kinson liked that.

Yet there remained a distance between them that he could not close, a separateness that no words could transcend or actions breach. It was Mareth's choice to enforce this condition, and while it was not just Kinson whom she kept at arm's length it sometimes felt so to him when measured against the closeness they had otherwise achieved. Mareth's reasons, while unknown, seemed weighted by habit and fear. There was something within her that demanded she stay isolated from others, some flaw, some defect, or perhaps some secret more frightening than anything he might imagine. Now and again, he would sense her trying to break past her self-imposed prison with some small word or act. But she could not seem to manage it. Lines had been drawn in the sand, a box for her to stand inside, and she could not make herself step out.

That was why he felt some satisfaction now, he supposed, from surprising her as he had with that kiss, an act so unexpected that for one brief moment it had breached her defenses. He recalled the look on her face as he drew away. He recalled how her arms had wrapped protectively about her small body.

He smiled to himself as he walked, Dechtera drawing close now, its separate parts coming into focus—the walls and roofs of individual buildings, the lights shining out of windows and doorways, the alleys prowled by rats and the streets roamed by homeless, the working men and women moving through the screen of ash and heat in pursuit of their goals. He put his thoughts of Mareth aside, no longer able to dwell on them, the task that lay ahead demanding his full attention. There would be time for Mareth later. He let the image of her eyes linger before him a moment more, then brushed it away.

He walked into the city along one of several main streets, taking time to study the buildings and the people crowded around him. He was in a working district, amid a cluster of warehouses and storage sheds. Flat carts pulled by donkeys hauled pieces of metal scrap for melting and reshaping at the furnaces. He scanned the rusted, broken buildings, a neglected, mostly dilapidated collection, and then moved on. He passed through a section of smaller forges manned by single smiths, the tools and molds rudimentary, the firings meant for simple tasks, and did not slow. He passed slag heaps and scrap piles, stacks of old building timbers and rows of abandoned buildings. Smells rose out of the gutters and refuse, rank and pervasive. Kinson shied away. Shadows flickered and jumped in the glare of the furnace fires and street lamps, small creatures darting momentarily from hiding places and then disappearing back again. The men who passed him were bent and worn, laborers all their lives, trudging from payday to payday until death laid claim to their souls. Few eyes even bothered to look up as he passed. No one spoke.

He went down into the center of the city, the evening close and sluggish with heat, the hour edging toward midnight. He glanced through the doors and windows of the ale houses and taverns, debating whether he should enter. He did finally, choosing one or two that suited his purpose, staying long enough to listen to the talk, to ask a question or two, to buy a glass when it was called for, then moving on. Who did the finest metalwork in all the city? he would ask. Which of the smiths was master of his craft? The choices differed each time, and the reasons supporting the choices differed even more. Using the names he had heard mentioned more than once, Kinson stopped at a handful of midsize forges to test them on the smiths at work there. Some responded with little more than grunts of disinterest. Some had more voluble opinions to offer. One or two gave a thoughtful response. Kinson listened, smiled agreeably, and moved on.

Midnight came and went.

"HE WILL NOT BE BACK TONIGHT," Bremen said, looking down at the city from the hills, his cloak wrapped tightly about his spare form in spite of the heat.

Mareth stood next to him in silence. They had watched the Borderman until he could no longer be seen, a diminishing figure melting away in the gathering dark. Even then, they had not moved, continuing their vigil as if sentinels posted against the coming of the night. Overhead the skies brightened with stars and a quarter-moon, visible from the heights, but not from the smoke-shrouded city below.

Bremen turned away, walked a few steps to his left, and settled himself in a patch of soft, thick grass. Comfort for his aging bones. He sighed contentedly. It took less and less to satisfy him, he found. He thought to eat, but realized he wasn't really hungry. He looked up as Mareth came over to join him, seating herself unbidden, looking off into the dark as if something waited for her there.

"Would you like to eat?" he asked her, but she shook her head. Lost in her thoughts, gone back into the past again or perhaps speculating on the future—he had learned to recognize the look. More often somewhere other than where she was, possessed of a restless spirit and a dissatisfied heart, that was Mareth.

He left her alone for a time, gathering his own thoughts, not wanting to rush what he intended. It was a delicate matter, and if she felt she was being coerced, she would close herself off from him completely. Yet there must be a resolution, and it must come now.

"On nights like these, I think of my boyhood," he said finally, looking not at her, but at the summit of the hills and the stars that hung above them. He smiled. "Oh, I suppose it seems as if someone as old as I am could not ever have been young. But I was. I lived in the hill country below Leah with my grandfather, who was a metalworker of great skill. Even when he was old, his hands were steady and his eye keen. I would watch him for hours, amazed at his dexterity and patience. He loved my grandmother, and when she died, he said she took a part of him with her that he could never have back again, but that the loss was worth it for the time they had shared. He said I had been given him in her place. He was a fine man."

He looked at Mareth now and found her looking back, interested. "But my parents were another matter. They were nothing like my grandfather. They were never able to settle in one spot for long, not ever in their short lives, and nothing of my grandfather's dedication to his craft ever took root in them. They were always moving about, changing their lives, looking for something new, something different. They left me with my grandfather shortly after I was born. They had no time for me."

His aged brow wrinkled thoughtfully. "I resented it for many years, but eventually I came to understand. That's how it is with parents and children. Each disappoints the other in ways that neither recognizes nor intends, and it takes time to overcome that disappointment. It was so with my parents and their decision to leave me."

"But you have a right to expect your parents to stay with you through your childhood," Mareth declared.

Bremen smiled. "I used to believe that. But a child doesn't always understand the complexities of adult choices. A child's best hope in life is that its parents will try to do what is best for it, but deciding what is best is a difficult process. My parents knew I would not grow well traveling with them, for they were not able to give me the attention I needed. They could barely give it to each other. So they left me with my grandfather, who loved me and watched over me as they could not. It was the right choice."

She mulled it over for a moment. "But it marked you."

He nodded. "For a time, but not in any lasting way. Perhaps it even helped toughen me. I don't pretend to know. We grow as best we can under the circumstances given us. What good does it do to second-guess ourselves years after the fact? Better that we simply try to understand why we are as we are and then better ourselves by learning from that."

There was a long silence as they faced each other, the expressions on their faces lit well enough by the light of stars and moon to be clearly discernible.

"You are talking about me, aren't you?" Mareth said finally. "My parents, my family."

Bremen did not let his expression change. "You do not disappoint me, Mareth," he said softly. "Your insight serves you well."

Her small features hardened. "I do resent my parents. They left me to grow up with strangers. It wasn't my mother's fault; she died giving birth to me. I don't know about my father. Perhaps it wasn't his fault either." She shook her head. "But that doesn't change how I feel about them. It doesn't make me feel any better about being left."

Bremen eased forward, needing to shift his body to avoid cramping of muscles and joints. The aches and pains were more frequent and less easily dispelled these days. The very opposite of his hunger, he thought with irony. Welcome to old age. Even the Druid Sleep was losing its power to sustain him.

His eyes sought hers. "I would guess that you have reason to be angry with your parents beyond what you have told me. I would guess that your anger is a weight about your heart, a great stone you cannot dislodge. Long ago, it defined the boundaries of your life. It set you on your journey to Paranor. It brought you to me."

He waited, letting the impact of his words sink in, letting her see what was in his eyes. He wanted her to decide that he was not the enemy she sought, for seek her enemy she did. He wanted her to accept that he might be her friend if she would let him. He wanted her to confide in him, to reveal at last the truth she kept so carefully hidden.

"You know," she replied softly.

He shook his head. "No. I only guess, nothing more." He smiled wearily. "But I would like to know. I would like to offer some comfort to you if I could."

"Comfort." She said the word in a dull, hopeless way.

"You came to me to discover the truth about yourself, Mareth," he continued gently. "You may not have thought of it that way, but that is what you did. You came to seek help with your magic, with a power you can neither rid yourself of nor live without. It is an awesome, terrible burden, but no worse than the burden of the truth you hide. I can feel its weight from here, child. You wear it like chains wrapped about your body."

"You do know," she whispered insistently. Her dark eyes were huge and staring.

"Listen to me. Your burdens are inextricably bound together, the truth you hide and the magic you fear. I have learned that much in traveling with you, in watching you, in hearing of your concerns. If you would rid yourself of the magic's hold, you must first address the truth you have hidden in your heart. Of your parents. Of your birth. Of who and what you are. Tell me, Mareth."

She shook her head dully, her gaze falling away from his,

her arms coming about her small body as if to ward it from a chill.

"Tell me," he pressed.

She swallowed back the advent of her tears, fought down her sudden shaking, and lifted her face to the starlight.

Then slowly, tremulously, she began to speak.

22

"I AM NOT AFRAID OF YOU" was the first thing she said to him. The words came in a rush, as if by speaking them she might tap a hidden reservoir of strength. "You might think so after hearing what I have to say, but you would be wrong. I am not afraid of anyone."

Bremen was surprised by her declaration, but he did not let it show. "I make no assumptions about you, Mareth," he said.

"I might even be stronger than you," she added defiantly. "My magic might be more powerful than yours, so there is no reason for me to be afraid. If you were to test me, you might regret it."

He shook his head. "I have no reason to test you."

"When you hear what I have to say, you might think differently. You might decide you must. You might feel it necessary to protect yourself." She took a deep breath. "Don't you understand? Nothing between us is what it seems! We might be enemies of a sort that will demand that one of us hurt the other!"

He considered her words in silence for a moment, then said, "I don't think so. But say what you must to me. Hold nothing back."

She stared at him without speaking, as if trying to decide the depth of his sincerity, to uncover the truth behind his insistence. Her small body was coiled into itself, and her large, dark eyes were deep, liquid pools in which the reflection of her roiling emotions was clearly visible.

"My parents were always a mystery," she said finally. "My

mother died at my birth, and my father was gone even before that. I never knew them, never saw them, had no memory of them to carry with me. I knew of them because the people who raised me made it clear enough that I was not theirs. They did not do so in an unkind way, but they were hard, determined people, and they had worked all their lives for what was theirs and thought that it should be so for everyone. I was not theirs, not really, and so they laid no claim to me. They cared for me, but I did not belong to them. I belonged to people who were dead and gone.

"I knew when I was very little that my mother had died giving birth to me. The people who raised me made no secret of it. They spoke of her now and again, and when I was old enough to ask about her, they described her to me. She was small and dark like me. She was pretty. She liked to garden and ride horses. They seemed to think she was a good person. She lived in their village, but unlike them she had traveled to other parts of the Southland and seen something of the world. She was not born in the village, but had come there from somewhere else. I never knew where. I never knew why. I think she may have kept that to herself. If I had other relatives living somewhere in the Southland, I never learned of them. Perhaps the people who raised me never knew of them either."

She paused, but her gaze stayed fixed on the old man. "The people who raised me had two children, both older than me. They loved these children and made them feel a part of the family. They took them to visit other people and on picnics and gatherings. They did not do that with me. I understood from the beginning that I was not like these children. I was made to stay in the home, to look after things, to help with chores, to do what I was told. I was allowed to play, but I always understood that it was different for me than for my brother and sister. As I grew older, I came to see that my new parents were uneasy about me for reasons I did not understand. There was something about me that they did not like or trust. They preferred that I play by myself rather than with my brother and sister, and mostly that was what I did. I was given food and clothing and shelter, but I was a guest in the home and not a member of the family. Not like my brother and sister. I knew that."

"This must have made you bitter and discouraged even then," Bremen offered quietly.

Mareth shrugged. "I was a child. I did not understand enough of life to appreciate what was being done to me. I accepted my situation and did not complain. I was not treated badly. I think the people who raised me felt some sympathy for me, some compassion, or they would not have taken me in. They never said so, of course. They never explained their reasons, but I have to believe that they would not have cared for me—even in the way they did—if there was no love in their hearts for me."

She sighed. "I was apprenticed at twelve. I was told that this would happen, and like everything else, I accepted it as part of the natural course of my life, of growing up. That my brother and my sister were not apprenticed did not bother me. They had always been treated differently, and I accepted that their lives would be different from my own. After I was apprenticed, I saw the people who raised me only a few times. My foster mother came to see me once and brought me a basket of treats. It was an awkward visit, and she left quickly. One time I saw both of them on the street, passing by the potter's on their way to somewhere. They did not look at me. By then, I was aware of the potter's predilection for administering beatings at the least excuse. I already hated my new life, and I blamed the people who raised me for giving me up. I did not want to see them any more. After I fled the potter and the village of my birth, I never did."

"Nor your brother or sister?" Bremen asked.

She shook her head. "There was no need. Whatever ties we had formed while growing had long since been broken. Thinking of them now only makes me sad."

"You had a difficult childhood. You've come to understand that better now that you are grown, haven't you?"

The smile she gave him was cold and brittle. "I have come to understand many things that were hidden from me as a child. But let me finish my story and you can judge for yourself. What matters in all of this is that just before I left to apprentice to the potter, I began hearing things about my father. I was eleven by then and already knew that I would be apprenticed at twelve. I knew I would be leaving my home, and I suppose it made me consider seriously for the first time the scope and meaning of the wider world. Traders and trappers and tinkers passed through our village, so I knew there were other places to see, places far away. I wondered sometimes if my father was out there somewhere, waiting. I wondered if he knew of me. I had determined in my own childlike way that my parents had not married and so had not lived together as husband and wife. My mother bore me alone, my father already gone. What of him, then? No one would say. I thought to ask more than once, but there was something in the way my providers spoke of my mother and her life that made it clear I was not to ask. My mother had transgressed in some way, and she was forgiven her transgression only because she had died giving birth to me. I was a part of her transgression, but it was not clear to me how or why.

"When I was old enough to know that secrets were being kept from me, I began to want to uncover them. I was eleven—old enough to recognize deception and old enough to practice it. I began to ask questions about my mother, small and inconsequential questions that would not arouse anger or suspicion. I asked them mostly of my foster mother, because she was the less taciturn of the pair. I would ask the questions when we were alone, then listen at night at the door of my sleeping room to hear what she would say to her husband. Sometimes she would say nothing. Sometimes the words were obscured by the closed door. But once or twice I caught a sentence or two, a phrase, a word—some small mention of my father. It was not the words themselves that revealed so much, but the way in which they were spoken. My father was an outsider who passed through the village, stayed briefly, returned once or twice, and then disappeared. The people of the village shunned him, all save my mother. She was attracted to him. No reason for this was offered. Was she attracted to him for the way he looked or the words he spoke or the life he led? I could not learn. But it was clear they feared and disliked him, and some part of that fear and dislike had been transferred to me."

She went quiet for a moment, gathering her thoughts. She seemed small and vulnerable, but Bremen knew that impression was false. He waited, letting her eyes continue to hold his in the deep night silence.

"I knew even then that I was not like anyone else. I knew I had the magic, even though it was just beginning to manifest itself in me, not yet come to maturity, so that it was mostly vague stirrings and small mutterings in my child's body. It seemed logical to conclude that it was the magic that was feared and disliked, and it was this that I had inherited from my father. Magic was mistrusted in general in my village—it was the unwanted legacy of the First War of the Races, when Men had been subverted by the rebel Druid Brona and defeated in a war with the other Races and driven south into exile. Magic had caused all this, and it was a vast, dark unknown that lurked at the corners of the subconscious and threatened the unwary. The people of my village were superstitious and not well educated and were frightened of many things. Magic could be blamed for much of what they didn't understand. I think the people who raised me believed that I might grow into some manifestation of my father, the bearer of his magic's seed, and so they could never quite accept me as their child. In the eleventh year of my life, I began to understand why this was so.

"The potter knew my history as well, though he did not speak of it to me in the beginning when I went to work for him. He would not admit that he was afraid of a child, even one with my history, and he took pride in the fact that he took me in when no one else would. I did not realize that at first, but he told me later. 'No one would have you—that's why you're here. Be grateful to me.' He would say that when he had drunk too much and was thinking about beating me. His drinking loosened his tongue and gave him a boldness that was otherwise absent. The longer I was with him, the more he drank—but it was not because of me. He had been drinking too much for most of his life, and it was the aging and the incumbent failure to achieve success of any kind that encouraged him. As his drinking increased, his work time and output lessened. I took his place many times, taking on the tasks I could manage. I taught myself a great deal and acquired an early skill."

She shook her head sadly, a distance creeping into her voice. "I was fifteen when I left him. He tried once too often to

beat me for no reason, and I fought back. By then, I had matured. I had my magic to protect me. I did not understand the
extent of its power until the day I fought back. Then I knew. I
almost killed him. I ran from the village and its people and my
life, knowing I would never go back. I realized something on
that day that I had only suspected before. I realized that I was
indeed my father's child."

She paused, her face intense, a fierce resolve apparent in her
dark eyes. "I had discovered the truth about my father, you see.
The potter had gotten drunk one too many times and told me.
He would drink until he could barely stand, and then he would
taunt me. He would say it over and over. 'Don't you know who
you are? Don't you know *what* you are? Your father's child! A
black spot on the earth, birthed by a demon and his bitch! You
have the eyes, little girl! You have the stain of his blood and his
dark presence! Worthless to all but me, so better listen when I
tell you to do something! Better heed what I say! Else you'll
have no place in the world at all!'

"So it went, followed each time by a new beating. I didn't
feel the blows much by then. I knew how to cover myself and
how to say what he wished to hear so that he would stop. But
I grew tired of it. I grew angry at my degradation. On the day
I left him, I knew before he tried to strike me that I would resist. When he began to shout at me about my father, I laughed
in his face. I called him a liar and a drunk. I told him he didn't
know anything about my father. He lost control of himself
completely. He called me things I will not repeat. He told me
that my father had come down out of the north, out of the border country where his black order made its home. He told me
my father was a conjurer of magic and a stealer of souls. 'A demon disguised as a man! Him in his black robes! With his wolf's
eyes! Your father, girl! Oh, we knew what he was! We knew his
dark secret! And you, made in such a perfect image of him, secretive and sharp-eyed! You think we don't see, but we do! We
all do, the whole village! Why do you think you were given to
me? Why do you think those people who raised you were so
anxious to be rid of you? They knew what you were! They
knew you were a Druid's whelp!' "

She took a long, slow breath, looking at him, waiting for

him to speak. She wanted to hear his reaction, he could tell. She was hungry for it. But he did not answer.

"I knew he was right," she said finally, the words a low hiss of challenge unmistakably directed at him. "I think I had known for some time. There was talk now and again of the black-robed men who prowled the Four Lands, the ones who kept their order at the castle of Paranor. Conjurers of magic, all-powerful and all-seeing, creatures more spirit than human, the cause of so much pain and suffering among the people of the Southland. They spoke of how now and again one would pass close by. 'Once,' it was whispered when the speaker did not realize I could hear, 'one stayed. There was a woman seduced by him. There was a child!' Then hands would lift in a warding motion and the voice would go still. My father. That was who they were speaking of in their hushed, frightened voices. My father!"

She hunched forward, and Bremen could tell that in doing so she was bringing her formidable magic up from the center of her small body to the tips of her fingers, readying it. A twinge of doubt passed through him. He forced himself to remain calm, to stay perfectly still, to let her finish.

"I have come to believe," she said slowly, purposefully, "that they were speaking of you."

THE SHOPKEEPER was just closing up as Kinson Ravenlock stepped through the door from the darkness and stood looking at the sword. The hour was late, and the streets of Dechtera had begun to empty of everyone but the men passing to and from the ale houses. Kinson was weary of his search, and he had been on his way to find a room at one of the inns when he passed down a street lined with weapons shops and saw the sword. It was displayed in a window framed by crosshatched iron bars inset with small, grimy panes of glass. He had almost missed it in his need for sleep, but the brilliant glint of the metal blade had caught his eye.

He stared at the sword now, stunned. It was the most singular piece of workmanship he had ever encountered. Even the smeared glass and the poor light could not hide the high sheen of the blade's polished surface or the keenness of its edge. The

sword was huge, seemingly too large for an average man. Intricate scrollwork had been carved into the great hilt, a montage
of serpents and castles overlaid on a forest background. There
were other, smaller blades, equally cunning and fine, forged by
the same hands, if Kinson did not miss his guess, but it was the
sword that held him spellbound.

"Sorry, I'm closing up," the shopkeeper announced, beginning to extinguish the lamps at the rear of his worn but
surprisingly clean establishment. There were blades of every
kind—swords, daggers, dirks, axes, pikes, and others too numerous to count, mounted on every wall, on every available surface,
in cases and racks. Kinson took them all in at a glance, but his
eyes kept coming back to the sword.

"I won't take a minute," he said quickly. "I just wanted to ask
a question."

The shopkeeper sighed and walked over. He was lean and
wiry, with muscular arms and strong hands. He moved easily as
he approached Kinson, and it looked as if he could handle a
blade himself if the need arose. "You want to ask about the
sword, am I right?"

Kinson smiled. "I do. How did you know?"

The shopkeeper shrugged, running his hand through thinning dark hair. "I saw where your eyes traveled when you
walked through the door. Besides, everyone asks about the
sword. How can they not? As wondrous a piece of workmanship as you'll find in all the Four Lands. Very valuable."

"I'll grant you that," Kinson said. "I suppose that's why you
still have it for sale."

The shopkeeper laughed. "Oh, it's not for sale. It's just for
display. It belongs to me. I wouldn't sell it for all the gold in
Dechtera or any other city. Craftsmanship of that sort can't be
bought and only rarely can it be found."

Kinson nodded. "It is a fine blade. But it would take a strong
man to wield it."

"Such as yourself?" the shopkeeper asked, arching one
eyebrow.

Kinson pursed his lips thoughtfully. "I think it is too big
even for me. Look at its length."

"Ha!" The shopkeeper seemed amused. "Everyone thinks the

same! That is the wonder of the blade. Look, it has been a long day and I am tired. But I will show you a little secret. If you like what you see, maybe you will buy something and make the time I spend with you worth my while. Fair enough?"

Kinson nodded. The shopkeeper walked to the display window, reached down under the casing, and released something. There was a series of audible clicks. Then he took away a chain cleverly looped about the handle to secure the great sword to its mount. Carefully he lifted the blade down. He turned, grinning broadly, and held the weapon out before him, balancing it in his hands—easily, as if it had no weight at all.

Kinson stared in disbelief. The shopkeeper laughed in recognition, and then he passed the sword to the Borderman. Kinson took it from him, and his amazement grew. The sword was so light that he could hold it in one hand.

"How is this possible?" he breathed, bringing the shining blade up before his eyes, dazzled by its ease of handling as much as by its workmanship. He looked at the shopkeeper quickly. "It can have no strength if it is this light!"

"It is the strongest piece of metal you will ever encounter, my friend," the shopkeeper announced. "The mix of metals and the tempering of the alloy make it stronger than iron and as light as tin. There is no other like it. Here, let me show you something else."

He retrieved the sword from a wondering Kinson and restored it to its case, resecuring the locks and chain that held it in place. Then he reached farther in and brought out a knife, the blade alone fully twenty inches long, carved with the same intricate scrollwork, clearly crafted by the same skilled hands.

"This is the blade for you," the shopkeeper declared softly and passed it to Kinson with a smile. "This is what I would sell you."

It was as wondrous as the sword, if not so impressive in size. Kinson was immediately entranced. Light, perfectly balanced, finely wrought, sharp as a cat's claw, the knife was a weapon of impossible beauty and strength. Kinson smiled in recognition of the blade's worth, and the shopkeeper smiled back. Kinson asked the cost, and the shopkeeper told him. They bargained for a few minutes, and a deal was struck. It cost Kinson almost every coin he had, which was a considerable sum, but he did not once think to walk away.

Kinson stuck the knife and its sheath in his belt, where the blade rested comfortably against his hip. "My thanks," he offered. "It was a good choice."

"It is my business to know," the shopkeeper demurred.

"I still have my question to ask," Kinson said as the other moved to show him out.

"Ah, that's right. Your question. Haven't I answered it? I thought it was about the sword that you . . . ?"

"It is about the sword, indeed," Kinson interrupted, looking at the blade once more. "But another sword. I have a friend who is in need of such a weapon, but he would have it forged according to his own specifications. The task will require a master smith. The man who made your sword seems right for the job."

The shopkeeper stared at him as if he had lost his mind. "You wish to have a weapon forged by the maker of my sword?"

Kinson nodded, then added quickly, "Are you him?"

The shopkeeper smiled bleakly. "No. But you might as well ask me as ask the man who is, for all the good it will do you."

Kinson shook his head. "I don't understand."

"No, I don't guess you do." The shopkeeper sighed. "Listen close, and I'll explain."

BREMEN'S FIRST REACTION to Mareth's words was to want to tell her straight out that the charge was ridiculous. But the look on her face warned him to reconsider. She must have spent a long time arriving at her conclusion, and she had not done so lightly. She deserved to be taken seriously.

"Mareth, how did you decide I was your father?" he asked gently.

The night was fragrant with the smell of grasses and flowers, and the light of moon and stars lent a soft silver cast to the hills above the garish brightness of the distant city. Mareth glanced away for a moment, as if looking for her answer in the darkness.

"You think me a fool," she hissed.

"No, never that. Tell me your reasoning. Please."

She shook her head at something unseen. "From long before the time of my birth, the Druids kept to themselves at Paranor. They had withdrawn from the Races, abandoning their earlier practice of going out among the people. Now and again, one would return home to visit family and friends, but none of these were from my village. Few bothered to venture into the Southland at all.

"But there was one who did, one who visited regularly. You. You came into the Southland in spite of the suspicion directed at the Druids. You were even seen now and again. It was whispered among the people of my village that when my mother conceived me, you were the demon, the dark wraith, who seduced her, who made her fall in love with him!"

She went silent again. She was breathing hard. There was an unspoken challenge in her words that dared him to deny that it was so. She was all tension and hard edges, her magic a crackle of dark energy at the tips of her fingers.

Her eyes burned into him. "I have been looking for you for as long as I can remember. I have carried the burden of my magic like a weight around my neck, and not one day has passed when it has not reminded me of you. My mother could not tell me of you. The rumors were all I had. But in my travels I always looked. I knew that one day I would find you. I went to Storlock thinking to find you, thinking you might pass through. You didn't, but Cogline gave me entry into Paranor and that was better still, because I knew that eventually you would come there."

"And so you asked to come with me when I did." He considered. "Why did you not tell me then?"

She shook her head. "I wanted to know you better first. I wanted to see for myself what kind of man my father was."

He nodded slowly, thinking the matter through. Then he folded his hands in front of him, old bones and parchment skin feeling used and weathered beyond repair.

"You saved my life twice in that time." His smile was worn and his eyes curious. "Once at the Hadeshorn, once at Paranor."

She stared at him, thinking back on what she had done, having nothing to say.

"I am not your father, Mareth," he told her.

"Of course you would say that!"

"If I were your father," he said quietly, "I would be proud to admit it. But I am not. At the time of your conception, I was traveling the Four Lands and might even have come to the village of your mother. But I have no children. I lack even the possibility of children. I have been alive a long time, kept so by the Druid Sleep. But the Sleep has demanded much of me. It has given me time that I would not otherwise have, but it has exacted a price. Part of that price is an inability to sire children. Consequently, I have never entered into a relationship with a woman. I have never taken a lover. I was in love once, long ago, so long that I barely remember the face of the girl. It was before I became a Druid. It was before I began to live my present life. Since then, there has been no one."

"I do not believe you," she said at once.

He smiled sadly. "Yes, you do. You know that I am telling you the truth. You can sense it. I am not your father. But the truth of things may be harsher still. The superstitions of the people of your village probably helped make them believe that I was the man who conceived you. My name would be readily known to them, and perhaps they settled on it simply because your father was a black-cloaked stranger who possessed magic. But listen to me, Mareth. There is more to consider, and it will not be pleasant for you."

Her mouth tightened. "Why am I not surprised?"

"I have been giving thought to the nature of your magic, even before this. Innate magic, magic born to you, as indigenous to who and what you are as the flesh of your body. It happens seldom. It was a characteristic of the faerie people, but they have mostly been dead for centuries. Except for the Elves, and the Elves have lost their magic—all but a little. The Druids, myself included, lack any form of innate magic. So where did yours come from if your father was a Druid? Suppose for a moment that he was. Which of the Druids has that sort of power? Which of them, that magic would have been necessary for your conception?"

"Oh, Shades," she said softly, seeing now where he was going with this.

"Wait, say nothing yet," he urged. He reached forward and

took her hands in his. She let him do so, her dark eyes wide, her face stricken. "Be strong, Mareth. You must. Your father was described by the people of your village as a demon and a wraith, a dark creature who could take on different looks as needed. You used the words yourself. That sort of magic would not have been practiced by a Druid. For the most part, it *could* not have been. But there are others for whom the taking on of such magic would have been easy."

"Lies," she whispered, but there was no force behind the accusation.

"The Warlock Lord has creatures in his service who assume the appearance of humans. They do so for various reasons. They will try to subvert the ones they pretend to be. They will try to deceive them. They do so to win them over and to use them. Sometimes the subversion is done for no better purpose than to capture what was lost of their own humanity, to relive in some small way the life that was lost to them when they became the things they are. Sometimes they do so simply out of malice. The magic these creatures have embraced has become so much a part of who and what they are that they use it without thinking. They do not differentiate between two separate needs. They act on instinct and to sate whatever desire drives them at a given moment. Not out of reason or emotion, but out of instinct."

There were tears in Mareth's eyes. "My father?"

Bremen nodded slowly. "It would explain the magic born to you. Innate magic, the dark gift bequeathed you by your father. Not a Druid's gift, but the gift of a creature for whom magic has become lifeblood. It is so, Mareth. It is hard to accept, I know, but it is so."

"Yes," she whispered, speaking so low that he could barely hear her. "I was so sure."

Her head lowered, and she began to cry. Her hands clenched his, and the magic died away, fading with the anger and tension, curling into a hard knot deep within.

Bremen shifted closer, putting his thin arm around her shoulders. "One thing more, child," he told her softly. "I would be your father still, if you would have me. I would be as much a parent to you as if you were my own. I think much of you.

I would give you what advice I could in your struggle to comprehend the nature of your magic. The first thing I would tell
you is that you are not your father. You are nothing like him,
dark thing that he was, not even in your birthright. The magic
is your own. You have its power to bear, and that is a heavy
weight. But though the magic was given to you by your father,
it does not define your character or dictate the nature of your
heart. You are a good and strong person, Mareth. You are nothing of the dark creature who spawned you."

Mareth's head moved against his shoulder. "You cannot
know. I may be exactly that."

"No," he soothed. "No. You are nothing of him, child.
Nothing."

He stroked her dark hair and held her to him, letting her
cry, letting the pain of so many years leak away. She would be
empty and numb when it was gone, and she must be given
hope and purpose to fill her anew.

He thought now that he had a way to give her that.

Two FULL DAYS PASSED before Kinson Ravenlock returned. He
walked from the valley at sunset, striding out of the raw orange
light generated by the smoke and fire of Dechtera's great furnaces. He was eager to reach them, to give them his news, and
he tossed off his dusty cloak with a flourish and embraced them
both enthusiastically.

"I have found the man we want," he announced, dropping
down cross-legged in the grass and accepting the aleskin
Mareth passed him. "The very man, in my opinion." His smile
broadened, and he gave them both a quick shrug. "Unfortunately, he doesn't agree with me. Someone will have to persuade him I'm right. That's why I've come back for you."

Bremen nodded and motioned to the aleskin. "Drink, have
something to eat, and then tell us all about it."

Kinson put the aleskin to his mouth and tipped his head
back. West, the sun was sinking beneath the horizon, and the
quality and color of the light were changing rapidly as twilight
descended. In the wake of its quicksilver transition, Kinson
caught a glimmer of something dark and worrisome in the old

man's eyes. Without speaking, he glanced at Mareth. She met his gaze boldly.

The Borderman lowered the aleskin and regarded them solemnly. "Did something happen while I was gone?"

There was a moment of silence. "We told stories to each other," Bremen answered. His smile was melancholy. He looked at Mareth and then back again at Kinson. "Would you like to hear one of them?"

Kinson nodded thoughtfully. "If you think there is time."

Bremen reached for Mareth's hand, and the girl gave it to him. There were tears in her eyes. "I think we should make time for this one," the old man said.

And Kinson knew from the way he said it that he was right.

CHAPTER

23

URPROX SCREL SAT ALONE on the old wooden bench, hunched forward with his elbows resting on his knees, carving knife in one hand, block of wood in the other. His hands moved deftly as he worked, turning the wood this way and that, whittling with small flicks of his wrist, the shavings flying out in front of him. He was making something wonderful, although he wasn't sure yet what it was. The mystery was part of the pleasure. A block of wood always suggested certain possibilities before he ever took a knife to it. You just had to look carefully enough to see what they were. Once you had done that, the job was half-finished. The shaping always seemed to take care of itself.

It was evening in Dechtera, the light fading to hazy gray where the furnaces did not glare with their hot white eyes. The heat was oppressive, but Urprox Screl was used to heat, so it didn't bother him to sit there. He could have stayed home with Mina and the children, dinner complete, the day at its close, rocking on the long porch or sitting out under the shade of that old hickory. It was quiet there and cool, his home removed from the city's center. Unfortunately, that was the problem. He missed the noise and the heat and the stench of the furnaces. When he was working, he wanted them close by. They had been a part of his life for so long that it didn't seem right not to have them there.

Besides, this was his place of business, same as always, same as it had been for better than forty years. It had been his father's place of business before him. Maybe it would be his son's—one or the other of them. When he worked, this is where he liked to be. This is where he belonged, where his sweat and toil had shaped his life, where his inspiration and skill had shaped the lives of others.

It was a bold statement, he supposed, but he was a bold man. Or mad, depending on whom you asked.

Mina understood. She understood everything about her husband, and that was more than you could say for any other wife he knew. The thought of it made him smile. It gave him a special feeling for Mina. He began to whistle softly.

The people of the city passed down the street in front of Urprox Screl, hurrying this way and that, busy little beavers engaged in their tasks. He watched them surreptitiously from under the knit of his heavy dark brow without letting them know he was looking. Many of them were friends—or what passed for friends these days. Most had been shopkeepers, tradesmen, artisans, or laborers for the same amount of time as he had been a smith. Most had admired him—his skill, his accomplishments, his life. Some had believed that he embodied the heart and soul of this city.

He sighed, and the whistling died away. Yes, he knew them all, but they paid little attention to him now. If he caught someone's eye, he might get a solemn nod or a desultory wave. One or two might stop to speak to him. That was about the extent of it. Mostly, they avoided him. Whatever was wrong with him, they didn't want it rubbing off on them.

He wondered one more time why they couldn't just accept what he'd done and let it go at that.

He stared down momentarily at the carving. A dog running, swift and strong, legs extended, ears flattened, head up. He would give this one to his grandson Arken, his oldest girl's boy. He gave most of his carvings away, though he could have sold them had he chosen to do so. But money wasn't something he needed; he had plenty of that and could get more if it became necessary. What he needed was peace of mind and a sense of purpose. Sad to say, even two years later, he was having trouble finding both.

He glanced over his shoulder momentarily at the building

behind him, a dark, silent presence amid the cacophony of the city. In the growing twilight, it cast its squarish shadow over him. The great doors that led to its interior were closed tonight—he hadn't bothered to open them. Sometimes he did, just because it made him feel more at home, more a part of his work. But lately it had depressed him to sit there with the doors open and the interior dark and silent, nothing happening after all those years of constant heat and noise and activity. Besides, it only drew the curiosity seekers, suggesting to them the possibility of things that would never happen.

He stirred the wood shavings with the toe of his boot. Better to let the past stay closed away, where it belonged.

Darkness fell, and he rose to light the torches that bracketed the building's smaller side entry. These would cast the light he needed to continue his work. He should go home, he knew. Mina would be looking for him. But there was a restlessness about him that kept his hands moving and his thoughts adrift in the swell of the night sounds that rose with the coming of the dark. He could pick those sounds out, all of them, could separate them as surely as the shavings piled at his feet. He knew them all so well—as he knew this city and its people. His knowledge comforted him. Dechtera was not a city for everyone. It was special and unique and it spoke with a language of its own. Either you understood what it was saying or you didn't. Either you were intrigued by what you heard or you moved on.

Lately, for the first time in his life, he was thinking that perhaps he had heard about as much of the city's language as he cared to.

He was contemplating what that meant, his carving momentarily forgotten, when the three strangers approached. He didn't see them at first, cloaked and hooded in the darkness, just a part of the crowd that passed on the street before him. But then they separated themselves from its flow and came toward him, and there was no mistaking their intent. He was immediately curious—it was unusual for anyone to approach him these days. The hoods bothered him a little; it was awfully hot to be wrapped up so. Were they hiding from something?

He rose to meet them, a big, rawboned man with heavy arms, a deep chest, and wide, blocky hands. His face was surprisingly smooth for a man his age, brown from the sun and strong-featured, his broad chin thinly bearded, the black hair on his head rapidly receding from his crown toward his ears and neck. He set the knife and carving on the bench behind him and stood waiting with his hands on his hips. As the trio slowed before him, the tallest pulled back his hood to reveal himself. Urprox Screl nodded in recognition. It was the fellow who had visited with him yesterday, the Borderman, come down out of Varfleet, a quiet, intense man with a good deal more on his mind than he was giving out. He had purchased a blade from one of the shopkeepers and come to compliment Urprox on his workmanship. Ostensibly. It felt as if there might be something more to the visit than just that. The Borderman had said he would be back.

"Good as your word, I see," Urprox greeted, reminded now of the other's promise and wanting to take matters in hand early—his city, his home, his rules.

"Kinson Ravenlock," the Borderman reminded him.

Urprox Screl nodded. "I remember."

"These are friends who want to meet you." The hoods came back. A girl and an old man. They faced him squarely, but kept their backs to the crowd of passersby. "I wonder if we might speak with you for a few minutes."

They waited patiently as he studied them, making up his mind. It was nothing he could put his finger on, but something about them bothered him. An uneasiness stirred inside, vague and indefinable. There was an unmistakable sense of purpose about these three. They looked to have come a long way and to have endured some hardship. He felt certain the Borderman's question had been asked as a matter of courtesy and not to offer a choice.

He smiled affably. He was curious about them in spite of his misgivings. "What do you wish to speak to me about?"

Now the old man took charge, and the Borderman was quick to defer. "We have need of your skills as a smith."

Urprox kept his smile in place. "I am retired."

"Kinson says you are the best, that your work is the finest he has ever seen. He would not make that statement if it were not so. He knows a great deal about weapons and the artisans who craft them. Kinson has traveled to a good many places in the Four Lands."

The Borderman nodded. "I saw the shopkeeper's sword. I have never seen work like that, not anywhere. You have unique talent."

Urprox Screl sighed. "Let me save you the trouble of wasting any more of your time. I was good at what I did, but I don't do it anymore. I was a master smith, but those days are gone. I am retired. I don't do metalwork of any kind. I don't do specialty work, and I don't accept commissions. I do wood carving, and that is all I do."

The old man nodded, seemingly unfazed. He glanced past Urprox to the wooden bench and the carving that lay there, and asked, "Did you do that? May I have a look?"

Urprox shrugged and handed him the dog. The old man studied it for a long time, turning it over in his hands, tracing the shape of the wood. There was genuine interest in his eyes.

"This is very good," he said finally, handing it to the girl, who accepted it without comment. "But not as good as your weapons work. Your true skill lies there. In the shaping of metal. Have you been carving wood long?"

"Since I was a child." Urprox shifted his stance uneasily. "What do you want from me?"

"You must have had a very compelling reason to go back to wood carving after being so successful as a master smith," the old man pressed, ignoring him.

Urprox felt his temper slip a notch. "I did. I had a very good reason, and I don't want to talk about it with you."

"No, I don't suppose you do, but I am afraid that you must. We need your help, and my task in coming here is to persuade you of that."

Urprox stared at him, more than a little astonished at his candor. "Well, at least you are honest about your intentions. But now, of course, I am forewarned of them and am prepared to reject any argument you put forth. So you really are wasting your time."

The old man smiled. "You were already forewarned. You are astute enough to discern that we have traveled some distance to see you, and that we must therefore consider you quite important." The weathered face creased deeper. "Tell me, then. Why did you give it all up? Why did you quit being a smith? Why, when you had been one for so many years?"

Urprox Screl's brow darkened. "I got tired of it."

They waited for him to say more, but he refused to do so. The old man pursed his lips. "I think it was probably more than that."

He paused a moment, and in that moment it seemed to Urprox as if the old man's eyes turned white, as if they lost their color and their character and became as blank and unreadable as stone. It felt as if the old man was looking right through him.

"You lost heart," the other said softly. "You are a gentle man with a wife and children, and for all your physical strength you do not like pain. But the weapons you forged were causing pain, and you knew that was happening and you detested it. You grew weary of knowing, and you decided enough was enough. You had money and other talents, so you simply closed your shop and walked away. No one knows this but you and Mina. No one understands. They think you mad. They shun you as they would a disease."

The eyes cleared and fixed on him anew. "You are an outcast in your own city, and you do not understand why. But the truth is you are a man blessed with unique talent, and everyone who knows you or your work recognizes it and cannot accept that you would waste it so foolishly."

Urprox Screl felt something cold creep up his spine. "You are entitled to your opinion. But now that you've given it, I don't wish to talk to you anymore. I think you should leave."

The old man looked off into the darkness, but he did not move from where he stood. The crowds had thinned behind him, and the night had closed about. Urprox Screl suddenly felt very alone and vulnerable. Even this close to familiar surroundings, to people who knew him, and to help if he should need it, he felt completely isolated.

The girl handed back the carving of the dog. Urprox took it from her, looking deep into her great dark eyes, drawn to her in a way he could not explain. There was something in the look she gave him that suggested she understood what he had done.

He had not seen that look in anyone's eyes but Mina's. It surprised him to find it here, in the eyes of a girl who did not know him at all.

"Who are you?" he asked again, looking from one face to the other.

It was the old man who spoke. "We are the bearers of a charge that transcends all else. We have come a long way to fulfill that charge. Our journey has taken us to many places, and even though you are important to its success, it will not end here. You are but one piece in the puzzle we must assemble. We have need of a sword, Urprox Screl, a sword unlike any other ever forged. It requires the hands of a master smith to shape it. It will have special properties. It is intended not to destroy, but to save. It will be both the hardest and finest work you have ever done or will ever do."

The big man smiled nervously. "Bold words. But I don't think I believe them."

"Because you do not want to forge another weapon in your lifetime. Because you have left all that behind, and the pact you made with yourself will be compromised if you relent now."

"That states it nicely. I reached an end to that part of my life. I swore I would never go back again. I see no need to change my mind for you."

"What if I told you," the old man said thoughtfully, "that you have a chance to save thousands of lives by forging this sword we seek? What if you knew that this was so? Would that change your mind?"

"But it isn't so," Urprox insisted stubbornly. "No weapon could achieve that."

"Suppose that the lives of your wife and children were among those that you would save by forging this sword. Suppose that your refusal to help us would cost them their lives."

The muscles in the big man's shoulders bunched. "So my wife and children are in danger now—is that how you wish me to see it? You are indeed desperate if you are reduced to making threats!"

"Suppose I told you that all of this will come to pass within the next few years if you do not help us. All."

Urprox experienced a whisper of self-doubt. The old man seemed so certain. "Who are you?" he demanded a final time.

The other stepped forward then, coming very close. Urprox Screl could see every seam in his weathered face, every stray hair on his graying head and beard. "My name is Bremen," the old man answered, his eyes locking on the smith's. "Do you know of me?"

Urprox nodded slowly. It took every ounce of strength he possessed to hold his ground. "I have heard of you. You are one of the Druids."

Again, the smile. "Are you frightened by that?"

"No."

"Of me?"

The big man said nothing, his jaw clenched.

Bremen nodded slowly. "You needn't be. I would be your friend, though it might seem otherwise. It is not my intention to threaten you. I speak only the truth. There is need for your talent, and that need is real and desperate. It extends the length and breadth of the Four Lands. This is no game we play. We are fighting for the lives of many people, and your wife and children are among them. I do not exaggerate or dissemble when I say that we are all they have left to defend against what threatens."

Urprox felt his certainty waver anew. "And what exactly is that?"

The old man stepped back. "I will show you."

His hand rose and brushed at the air before Urprox Screl's bewildered eyes. The air shimmered and took life. He could see the ruins of a city, the buildings flattened into rubble, the ground steaming and smoking, the air thick with ash and grit. The city was Dechtera. Its people all lay dead in the streets and doorways. What moved through the shadows picking at the bodies was not human, but misshapen and perverse. Something imagined—yet real enough here. Real, and in the vision of Dechtera's destruction, all that would survive.

The vision vanished. Urprox shuddered as the old man materialized once more, standing before him, eyes hard and set. "Did you see?" he asked quietly. Urprox nodded. "That was the future of your city and its people. That was the future of your family. That was all that remained. But by the time that vision comes to pass, everything north will already be gone. The Elves and the Dwarves will be destroyed. The dark wave that inundated them will have reached here."

"These are lies!" Urprox spoke the words quickly, out of anger and fear. He did not stop to reason. He was incautious and headstrong in his denial. Mina and his children dead? Everyone he knew gone? It wasn't possible!

"Harsh truths," Bremen said quietly. "Not lies."

"I don't believe you! I don't believe any of this!"

"Look at me," the old man commanded softly. "Look into my eyes. Look deep."

Urprox Screl did so, unable to do otherwise, compelled to obey. He stared into Bremen's eyes and watched them turn white once more. He felt himself drawn into a liquid pool that embraced and swallowed him. He could feel himself join with the old man in some inexplicable way, become a part of him, become privy to what he knew. There were flashes of knowledge given in the moments of that joining, truths that he could neither challenge nor avoid. His life was suddenly revealed to him, all that had been and might be, the past and the future come together in a montage of images and glimpses that were so terrifying and so overwhelming that Urprox Screl clutched at himself in despair.

"Don't!" he whispered, shutting his eyes against what he was seeing. "Don't show me any more!"

Bremen broke the connection, and Urprox staggered back a step before straightening. The cold that had begun at the base of his spine had now seeped all the way through him. The old man nodded. Their eyes locked. "I am finished with you. You have seen enough to understand that I do not lie. Do not question me further. Accept that my need is genuine. Help me do what I must."

Urprox nodded, his big hands clenching into fists. The ache in his chest was palpable. "I will listen to what you have to say," he allowed grudgingly. "That much, at least, I can do."

But he knew, even as he spoke the words, that he was going to do much more.

* * *

SO BREMEN SAT HIM DOWN on the bench and then took a seat
next to him. They became two old friends discussing a business
proposition. The Borderman and the girl stood silently before
them, listening. On the street beyond, the people of the city
passed by unknowing. No one approached. No one even
glanced his way. Perhaps they could not even see him anymore,
Urprox thought. Perhaps he had been rendered invisible. For as
Bremen spoke, he began to recognize how much magic was at
work in this business.

Bremen told him first of the Warlock Lord and his invasion
of the other lands. The Northland was gone, the Eastland in-
vaded, the Westland at risk. The Southland would be last, and
by then, as the vision had shown, it would be too late for all of
them. The Warlock Lord was a creature of magic who had managed to survive beyond mortal life and had summoned creatures
of supernatural strength to aid his cause. No ordinary weapon
would destroy him. What was needed was the sword that
Urprox would forge, a thing of magic as well as iron, a blade
that combined the skills and knowledge of both master smith
and Druid, of science and magic alike.

"It must be strong in both ways," Bremen explained. "It must
be able to withstand the worst of what will be sent to destroy
it, whether iron or magic. The forging must make it as invulner-
able as possible, and that will be difficult. Science and magic.
You will provide the former, I the latter. But your work is paramount, because if the sword lacks the physical characteristics
needed to sustain it, the magic I supply cannot hold."

"What do you know of forging metals?" Urprox asked, interested now in spite of himself.

"That metals must be combined and tempered just so for the
alloy to gain the necessary strength." Bremen reached into his
robes and brought forth the formula that Cogline had supplied.
"This is what we will need to achieve the desired result."

Urprox took the sheet of paper and studied it carefully. He
nodded as he read, thinking, Yes, this is the right combination
of metals, the proper mix of firings. Then he stopped, smiling

broadly. "These temperatures! Have you looked closely at what this mix requires? No one has seen such temperatures in the firing of metal since the old world was destroyed! The furnaces and the formulas alike were lost forever! We haven't the means to achieve what is asked!"

Bremen nodded calmly. "What heat will your forge withstand? How strong a firing?"

The smith shook his head. "Any amount. Whatever heat we can generate. I built the furnace myself, and it has layered walls of stone and earth to insulate and preserve it. But that is not the problem. The problem is with the fuel. We lack a fuel strong enough to produce the amount of heat this formula requires! You must know that!"

Bremen took the formula from his hands and slipped it back inside his robes. "We need maintain the higher temperatures for only a short period of time. I can help with that. I possess the means that you lack. Do you understand?"

Urprox did. The old man would use magic to generate the necessary heat. But was that possible? Was his magic strong enough? The temperatures needed were enormous! He shook his head, staring at the other doubtfully.

"Will you do it?" Bremen asked quietly. "One last firing of the forge, one final molding of metals?"

The master smith hesitated, come back briefly to his old self in these past few moments, to the man he had been for so many years, intrigued by the challenge of forging this weapon, impelled by consideration for the safety of his family and his neighbors, of his city and his land. There were reasons to do what the old man asked, he admitted. But there were reasons to refuse as well.

"We need you, Urprox," the Borderman said suddenly, and the girl nodded silently in agreement. All of them waited for his response, expectant and determined.

Well, he thought, his wood carving was not of the same quality as his metalwork, that much was true. Never had been. It was an escape, though he might argue otherwise. Come right down to it, it was foolish to claim that it was of any real importance. So what would it mean for him to cast one last blade, a weapon that might have significance beyond any other he had ever forged, that might be used in a way that would save lives? Did the old man lie about this? He could not be absolutely sure, but he did not think so. He had been able to tell something of men, as he could of metal, all his life. He felt it was so here. This man, Druid or no, evinced honor and integrity. He believed in his cause, and it was clear that he was convinced that Urprox Screl should, too.

The big man shook his head, smiled, and shrugged. "Ah, well. If it will get you out of my life, I will make you your sword."

THEY TALKED until late into the night of what was needed to undertake the forging. Urprox would have to bring in fuel to fire the furnace and metals to mix the alloy. It would take several days to bring the temperature up to the level necessary to begin the process. The forging itself could be done fairly quickly if Bremen's magic was sufficient to raise the heat beyond that. The mold for the sword was already cast, and only small modifications were needed to give it the shape that Bremen required.

Bremen showed him the medallion he had hidden within his robes, showed him the strange, compelling image of the hand clenched about the burning torch. It was called the Eilt Druin, the Druid told him, and it must be embedded in the hilt of the sword when it was cast. Urprox shook his head. It would melt from the heat, he advised, the workmanship too fine to survive the tempering. But the old man shook his head and told him not to worry. The Eilt Druin was forged of magic, and the magic would protect it. The magic, he intoned, would give the sword the power necessary to destroy the Warlock Lord.

Urprox Screl didn't know if he believed this or not, but he accepted it at face value. It was not his problem, after all, to decide if the sword would do what the Druid intended. It was his job to forge it in accordance with the formula provided and the science he possessed, so that it would emerge from the firings as strong as possible. Three days, then, to prepare. But there were other considerations as well. Everyone knew that he was out of business. The moment materials began to arrive, there would be questions. The moment the furnace was fired, the questions would increase. And what of the attention that the forging of the sword itself would draw?

But the old man seemed unconcerned with this, telling Urprox Screl not to worry, simply to go about his business and to concentrate on readying himself and his forge for the task at hand. While preparations were under way, he and his companions would remain close at hand and deal with whatever interest the population of the city might evince.

So it began. They separated that night with a handshake to bind their agreement, the three outlanders more satisfied with the result than Urprox Screl, but the smith was excited and intrigued by the task set to him in spite of his misgivings. He went home to his family and in the slow hours of the early morning sat with Mina at the kitchen table and told her of his decision. As it always was between them, he held nothing back. She listened to him and questioned him, but she did not advise him to change his mind. It was for him to make the choice, she said, because he understood better than she what was being asked of him and how he would live with it afterward. For her part, it seemed as if he had been shown good reason to accept the work offered him, and judgment of the men and the girl should be based on his own evaluation of their character and not on the rumors and gossip of others.

Mina, as always, understood better than anyone.

Hard coal, mined in the Eastland borders and shipped west, filled the fire pit and the fuel bins of the forge by midday next. The doors to the building were thrown open, and the first firing began. The forge was lit and the heat brought up. Metals arrived, requisitioned in accordance with Cogline's formula. Molds were uncovered and brought out for cleaning. Disdaining help, Urprox worked alone in the shadowy, hot interior of the building. Help was not necessary. He had constructed his forge so that winches and pulleys guided by a single hand could move everything required from one corner to the other. As for the inevitable crowds that gathered to see what he was about, they did not intrude as much as he had feared. Instead, they contented themselves simply with watching. There was a rumor given out—from where, it was not certain—that Urprox Screl was firing the furnace not because he was back in business as a smith, but because he had a buyer for the forge who wanted to make certain that it would work as advertised before he laid down his money. The owner, it was whispered, was from the deep Southland, a man who was visiting with his young wife and aged father. They could be seen from time to time at Screl's side, or by the entry to the forge, or about the streets of the city, coming and going in pursuit of further information concerning their intended acquisition, trying to determine if the purchase they sought was a reasonable one.

For Urprox, the time passed swiftly. His doubts, so strong that first night, vanished with the unexpected exhilaration he experienced at preparing for the challenge of this unusual firing. No smith living had ever worked with magic in the Four Lands—at least not to anyone's knowledge—and it was impossible not to be excited by the prospect. He knew in his heart, just as Kinson Ravenlock had acknowledged, that he was the best at his trade, that he had mastered the skill of shaping metal into blades as no one else had. Now he was being asked to go beyond what he had ever attempted, to create a weapon that would be better than his best, and he was enough of a craftsman to appreciate the extent of the confidence being placed in his talent. He still did not know if the blade would accomplish the task that Bremen had set for it, if it would forestall in some way the invasion the old man had warned against, if it could in any way protect against the threat of the Warlock Lord. These were questions for others. For Urprox Screl, there was only the challenge of applying his skills in a way he had never dreamed possible.

So wrapped up was he in his preparations that he was two days into them before he remembered that there had been no mention at all of payment—and in the next instant realized that it made no difference, that payment in this case was not important.

He had forgotten nothing in the two years since he had closed down the forge, and it was rewarding to discover that he still knew exactly what to do. He went about his business with confidence and determination, building the heat in the fuel pit, measuring its potency with small tests that melted metals of varying hardness and consistency. Additional fuels and materials that he had requisitioned arrived and were stored. The Druid, the Borderman, and the girl stopped by to study his progress and disappeared again. He did not know where they went when they left him. He did not know how closely they monitored his progress. They spoke to him only occasionally, and then it was the old man who did most of the talking. Now and then he would question his commitment to this task, to his belief in the old man's tale of the destruction that threatened. But the questions were momentary and fleeting. By now he was like a runaway wagon, rolling ahead with such speed that nothing could slow him. The work itself was all that mattered. He was surprised at how much he had missed it. The acrid smell of fuel as it was consumed in the flames, the clanging of raw metals on their way to the crucible, the sear of the fire against his skin, the rise of ash and smoke from the furnace chimney—they were old friends come to greet him on his return. It frightened him to think how easily he had abandoned his vow not to go back into his trade. It frightened him even more to think that this time he might not be able to walk away.

On the third night, late into the evening, the three came to him for the last time—the Druid Bremen, the Borderman Kinson Ravenlock, and the girl whose name he never did learn. The forge was ready, and they seemed to know this without being told, arriving after sunset and greeting him in a manner that indicated they had come to witness the fulfillment of his promise. The metals they needed for the firing were laid out, the molds set open and ready for the pour, and the winches, pulleys, chains, and crucibles that would guide the raw material through the various stages of preparation carefully set in place. Urprox knew the old man's formula by heart. Everything was ready.

They sat together for a time in the shadows of the forge, waiting for the city to quiet and its people to sleep, letting the heat wash over them and the night draw on. They spoke little, listening to the sounds, lost in their separate thoughts. The populace of the city churned and bustled like waves washing against the rocks of some distant shore, always just out of sight.

Midnight approached, and the crowds drifted to the ale houses and pleasure dens, and the streets began to clear.

The old man rose then and took Urprox Screl's hand in his own and held it. "You must do your best work this night," he advised firmly. "You must, if we are to succeed."

The smith nodded. He was stripped to the waist and his muscles glistened with sweat. "I will do what is needed. Don't you forget to do the same."

Bremen smiled at the rejoinder, the seams of his aged face etched deep by the light that seeped from the furnace, back where the fires flared through cracks in the bin door. "You're not afraid of this at all, are you?"

"Afraid? Of fire and metal? Of shaping one more weapon after thousands, even if it's to be forged with magic?" Urprox Screl shook his head. "I should sooner be frightened of the air I breathe. What we do here tonight is no different than what I have done all my life. A variation perhaps, but no more. Besides, what is the worst that can befall me? That I fail? That won't happen."

"The magic is always unpredictable. Even if you are steady in the application of your smith's skill, the magic might not prove sufficient."

The smith studied the old man for a moment, then laughed slowly. "You don't believe that. You are as much a craftsman as I. You would die before you let the magic fail you."

There was a long silence as the two faced each other, the heat of the forge washing over them, its light flickering raggedly against their lined faces. "You are taking a final measure of me," the smith observed quietly. "Don't bother. It's not necessary. I am ready for this."

But the old man shook his head. "The measure I take is of what this will do to you. You cannot work with magic and come away unchanged. Your life will never be the same after tonight. You must sense that."

Urprox Screl gave the old man a slow, ironic smile. "I *depend* upon it. Let me confess something. Save for Mina and my children, I am sick of my life. I am tired of what I have become. I didn't understand that until you came. Now I understand it all too well. I would at this moment welcome any change."

He felt the other's eyes probe him for a moment, felt their weight settle somewhere deep within, and he wondered if he had spoken too rashly.

Then the old man nodded. "Very well. Let's begin."

THERE WOULD BE STORIES of what happened that night for years afterward, tales passed from mouth to mouth that would take on the trappings of legend. They would come from various sources, but all would have their genesis in the glimpses caught by passersby who paused for a momentary look at what was taking place within Urprox Screl's great forge. The doors stood open to the night so that fresh air could be drawn in and stale heat vented out, and those who forced themselves close enough were witnesses to visions they later declared to have been born out of madness.

A sword was forged by Urprox Screl that night, but the manner of its shaping would be forever in dispute.

It was agreed who was present. They passed through the smoky, ash-laden air like wraiths, bent down against the heat and glare of the forge, surging upward momentarily to carry out a task in response to the demands of the casting, then ducking away again. There was the smith, the acknowledged master of his trade, the man who had given up his work for two long years and then, for a single night, without a word to anyone, gone back to it. There was the old man cloaked in his black robes, the one who seemed at times almost ethereal, at times as hard and certain as stone. And there were the Borderman and the young woman. Each had a role to play. The smith and the old man worked shoulder to shoulder in the forging of the weapon. The younger man served as their helper, acting on command to fetch this or carry that, lending his strength and weight where it was needed. The girl stood by the door and made certain that no one tried to enter or linger too long to watch. Strangely enough, she was the one who made the strongest impression. Some said she changed shape to warn off those too curious, becoming for an instant a netherworld beast or a moor cat. Some said she danced naked before the great furnace in a rite that aided in the tempering. Some said that if she but looked at you, your mind was lost. All agreed that she was more than what she appeared.

That there was magic in use that night was unquestioned. The heat of the fire was too intense, its glare too strong, its explosions, when the molten ore spilled, too raw. Some said they saw green light lance from the old man's hands to feed the fires of the forge, saw it give aid to the winches and pulleys in lifting the casting away from the flames, watched it hone the blade after its molding to smooth and polish its rough surface. While the master smith sent the various metals into the furnace, while he mixed and then stirred the alloy, the old man muttered chants. The metals would go into the fire and come out again. The molten one would be poured into a mold, tempered, and hammered out again. And each time the old man's magic would flare brightly in support. Oh, yes, there was magic employed in the forging and make no mistake about it, the tale-tellers all agreed.

They spoke as well of an omnipresent image of a hand holding forth a burning torch. No one understood its significance, but it was a specter that seemed to appear everywhere. Some saw it on a medallion the old man took from beneath his robes. Some saw it reflected by the fires of the forge on the walls of the building. Some saw it rise out of the fires themselves, newly born in the pit's hottest core, a spirit risen from the dead. But those who saw it last saw it fixed to the handle of the great broadsword, fused with the metal cast in the forge, the image burnished and glowing, the hand clenched at the joinder of blade and pommel, the flame rising upward along the blade toward its tip.

The casting, tempering, shaping, and honing of the sword took the remainder of the night. There were strange noises beyond the clang of the smith's hammer and the whoosh of steam as the blade was cooled. There were colors in the firing that no one had ever seen before, a rainbow spectrum that transcended all experience of forging in a city of smiths. There were smells and tastes in the air that did not belong, dark and forbidding. The people who approached the forge that night took quick, anxious looks, wondered at the fury of what they witnessed, and then passed on.

By morning, the casting was complete and the three strangers were gone. No one saw them depart. No one knew where they went. The sword was gone as well, and it was assumed that the trio had taken it with them. The forge stood empty in the dawn light, its fires cooling as they would continue to cool for many days. Some few who ventured too close to the still open doors claimed that the earth sparked beneath their feet as they tried to peer inside. Magic, they whispered. You could tell.

Urprox Screl went home and did not come back. The forge, he announced, was closed once more. He spoke to his friends and neighbors in a normal way and assured them that nothing untoward had happened that night. He had cast a sword for potential buyers and they had gone back to consider the value of their purchase. He smiled when he said it. He seemed quite calm. But his eyes had a haunted, faraway look.

Within a month he had left the city. Mina and his children and grandchildren all went with him, the entire family. By then there were rumors that he had sold himself body and soul to the dark things that lived north. No one wanted much to do with him. It was just as well that he was gone, everyone agreed.

No one knew where he went. There were rumors, of course. There were always rumors.

Some said he went north into the Borderlands and settled his family there. Some said he changed his name so that no one would know who he was.

One man claimed, years later, to have seen him. A trader of jewelry, he traveled a broad stretch of the Four Lands in search of new markets. It was in a small village above the Rainbow Lake, he reported, that he had come upon Urprox Screl.

Only he wasn't using the name Screl anymore.

He was using the name Creel.

CHAPTER

24

IND AND RAIN TORE at the ramparts and walls of Stedden Keep, mirroring the fury of the battle being fought at the castle's broad gates. Twice the Northland army had come against the walls and twice the Dwarves had driven it back. Now it was nearing midnight, the skies black, the air thick with rain, the light so poor that it was impossible to see more than a few feet save when lightning scorched the whole of the Ravenshorn with its brilliant, momentary fire.

They were going to lose this one, too, Risca thought, striding down the stairway from the main wall to the central court in search of Raybur. Not that any of them had thought they wouldn't. That they had held this long was a minor miracle. That they were still alive after weeks of fighting and retreating was a bigger miracle still. But they were running out of time and chances. They had stalled for just about as long as they were able.

Where were the Elves? Why hadn't they come?

For weeks after their escape from the Wolfsktaag, the Dwarves had fought a holding action against the advancing Northlanders. The army of the Warlock Lord had smashed them at every turn, but still they had gone on fighting. They had been lucky in the Wolfsktaag; they had escaped with almost no loss of life. Their luck hadn't lasted. They had fought a dozen engagements since, and in several their pursuers had gotten the upper hand, through either perseverance or luck.

The Dwarves they had trapped, they had slaughtered on the spot. Though the Eastlanders had fought back savagely and inflicted heavy losses on their attackers, the losses seemed inconsequential. Outnumbered and overmatched, the Dwarves simply had no chance against an army of such strength and size. They were brave and they were determined, but they had been forced back steadily at every turn.

Now they were deep in the Ravenshorn and in danger of being dislodged from that protectorate as well. The Wolfsktaag and the Central Anar were lost. Culhaven had fallen early. The Silver River from the Rainbow Lake to the Cillidellan was in enemy hands. There was no way of knowing how much of the north was gone. All of it, in all probability. If the Ravenshorn was taken as well, the Dwarves would be forced to fall all the way back to the High Bens and the fortress at Dun Fee Aran. If that fell, too, they would have lost their last retreat. They would have no choice but to flee into the lands east, country into which they had barely ventured.

And that was what was going to happen, Risca supposed. Certainly they were not going to be able to hold here. Stedden Keep would fall by morning. The outlying moats and pit traps had already been crossed, and the Northlanders were building scaling ladders to throw up against the walls. The wind and the rain seemed to make no difference to their efforts. They were in the grip of something stronger than the elements—a fear, a madness, a horror of the creature commanding them. Magic drove them on, dark and terrible, and perhaps for them, in their present state, even death was preferable to facing the consequences of failure.

Risca reached the bottom of the stairs and crossed out of the tower into the courtyard. The sounds of battle washed over him, a cacophony that even the storm's fury could not surmount. A battering ram hammered at the gates, slamming into the portals with steady, mindless insistence. The gates shuddered, but held. Atop the battlements, the Dwarves sent arrows and spears flying into attackers massed so thick it was virtually impossible to miss. Oil fires climbed one wall, the remains of an earlier attack the Dwarves had repulsed. Defenders raced everywhere, trying to fill gaps in the line for which there simply weren't enough men.

Raybur appeared suddenly out of the chaos and seized his arm. "We'll only be able to hold until they complete the ladders!" he shouted into the teeth of the wind, bringing his face close to the younger man's. "We can't do more, Risca!"

Risca nodded. He felt worn and discouraged. He was tired of running, weary of being chased, and angry that it was about to happen all over again.

"The tunnels are readied," he replied, not bothering to raise his voice. He had just returned from making sure their escape route was safely in place. Geften had scouted the tunnels himself, making sure they were clear. The Dwarves would flee through the mountain corridors carved out of the rock at the rear of their fortress and emerge on the east side of the peaks. From there, they would descend into the densely forested valley beyond and melt away once more.

Raybur pulled him from the court into the lee of the tower entry from which he had emerged. There he braced him, his eyes hard.

"What's happened to the Elves?" the Dwarf King asked with tightly controlled fury.

Risca shook his head. "They would come if Tay Trefenwyd could find a way to bring them. Something's happened. Something we don't know anything about."

Raybur shook his bearded face in obvious distaste. "Makes things sort of one-sided in this war, doesn't it? Us and no one else against an army the size of that one out there?" Shouts broke from the walls, and defenders raced to fill a new breach. "How much longer are we supposed to hold on? We're losing more men with every new battle, and we don't have that many to lose!"

His anger was understandable. One of those lost already was his eldest son. Wyrik had fallen four days earlier, killed by a stray arrow. They had been in retreat across the Anar and into the Ravenshorn, intent on reaching the fortress at Stedden Keep. The arrow had gone through his throat and into his brain. He had died instantly, virtually before anyone had even noticed he was struck. Raybur had been next to him when it had happened, and had caught him in his arms as he fell.

The two men stood looking at each other in the damp shadows of the entry, both of them thinking of the boy's death, reading it in each other's eyes.

Raybur looked away, disgusted. "If we just had some word, some assurance that help is coming . . ." He shook his head once more.

"Bremen would never desert us," Risca declared quietly, firmly. "Whatever else happens, he will come."

Raybur's eyes narrowed. "If he's still alive."

The words hung there, blade-sharp in the silence, accusatory, bleak and despairing.

Then a terrible wrenching sound shattered their momentary consideration of the prospect of the old man's death, a horrifying groan of metal fastenings coming apart and wooden timbers giving way. Both men knew at once what it was, but Raybur said it first.

"The gates!"

They sprinted from the doorway into the rain-soaked night. A flash of lightning split the dark ceiling of the clouds. Ahead, the main gates had buckled under the onslaught of the battering ram. Already hinges were snapped and the crossbar splintered. The Dwarves were trying to shore up the sagging barrier with additional timbers, but it was only a matter of time now before everything collapsed. The pounding of the ram had intensified, and the cries of the attackers had risen in response. On the walls, the Dwarves drew back uncertainly from their defensive positions.

Fleer came running up to his father, his long hair flying. "We have to get everyone out!" he shouted, his face pale and stricken.

"Do so!" snapped Raybur in reply, his voice cold and harsh. "Withdraw from the walls, through the fortress corridors, and into the tunnels! I have had enough of this!"

Fleer raced away, and an enraged Raybur wheeled about and strode toward the gates, his rugged face flushed and set. Seeing what he intended, Risca went after him, grabbed his arm, and spun him about.

"No, Raybur," he declared. "I will stand against this rush, not you!"

"Alone?" the king snapped, shaking free of the other's hand.

"How many were you planning on asking to stand with you?" Risca's retort was sharp and brittle. "Now go! Lead the army out!"

Rain ran down into their eyes, forcing them to blink rapidly, two solitary figures locked in confrontation. "This is madness!" the king hissed.

Risca shook his head. "You are king, and you must keep yourself safe. What happens to the Dwarves if you fall? Besides, I have the Druid magic to protect me, which is more than you can say. Go, Raybur!"

The right gate collapsed, splintering, then crumbling into rubble. Dark forms surged toward the opening, weapons glinting. Risca brought up his hands, fingers crooked, the Druid magic summoned. Raybur hesitated, then darted away, calling his commanders to come to him, giving them their orders for a retreat. The Dwarves scrambled down from the battlements and raced for the tower doors and the safety of the corridors beyond. Already the men at the gates had fled. Risca stood alone in the rain, waiting calmly. It had been an easy enough decision. He was tired of running, of being chased. He was ready to stand and fight. He wanted this chance.

When the first wave of attackers was at the opening, he sent the Druid fire into them. He burned everything in sight. Flames climbed across the rubble and consumed the front ranks of Northlanders before they could even think to flee. In the darkness beyond, the others fell back, unable to withstand the heat. Risca held the fire in place, then let it die. The magic ran through him in an exhilarating rush that swept aside fear and doubt, weariness and pain. It became for him, as it always did in the fury of battle, the thing he lived for.

The battering ram resumed its pounding and the second gate collapsed, widening the entry further. But no one approached. Risca glanced upward through the curtain of rain.

The last of the Dwarves were coming down off the battlements and out of the watchtowers. In moments, he would be alone. He should flee now, he knew. He should run with the others, escape while he could. There was no point in remaining. Yet he could not make himself turn away. It was as if he held the outcome of this battle in his hands, as if by standing where he was, by holding firm, he could stop the onslaught that threatened to overwhelm them all.

Then something huge appeared in the charred, fire-scorched entry, a shadowy form that lumbered into the gap. Risca hesitated, waiting to see what it was. The dark shape hove into view, coming into the pale, uncertain light of the dying Druid fire. It was a creature out of Brona's netherworld, come out of hiding with the fall of night, a thing of ooze and slime, of spikes and armored plates, of heavy limbs and massive body. It stood upright, but it was scarcely human, bent down as if by the weight of its own ugliness, yellow eyes lit by its killing need. It caught sight of the Druid and slowed, turning to face him. It carried a huge club, both clawed hands wrapped around its grip.

"Well, now," Risca breathed out slowly.

The creature stood alone momentarily in the gap, then trudged slowly across the burning rubble. No one else appeared, although Risca could hear the Northlanders scrambling, bringing up what scaling ladders they had to place against the unmanned walls, massing in the darkness for the rush that would sweep them into Stedden Keep.

Meanwhile, this creature is sent to challenge me, Risca thought, knowing it could be for nothing less. Do they think I will not stand against it? Do they test me to see what sort of power I possess, what strength of will? What is the reason for this nonsense?

He could not answer any of these questions, of course. And now the monster was coming for him, pushing aside debris and bodies as it descended to the court out of the gap, lantern eyes fixed on the Druid.

They seek to trap me, the Druid thought suddenly. A diversion to distract me, a foil for my magic, and then they will come for me in force. The arrogance of it made him smile.

The netherworld creature lumbered toward him, picking up speed. The club lifted before it, both a shield and a weapon. There was still time to flee, but Risca held his ground. There were Northlanders watching. They knew who he was and they were waiting to see how he would react. He would give them something to remember.

When the creature was within two dozen feet, Risca brought up his battle-axe, gripped it in both hands, whirled about to gain momentum, and sent the gleaming blade flying at the monster. The beast was right on top of him by then, rushing to the attack, and had no chance to deflect the blow. The axe struck the heavy-browed forehead and split it apart with a grating of metal on bone. The force of the blow snapped the massive head back. Blood poured down the ruined face, a black ichor that filled the creature's gaping maw. The beast dropped to its knees, already dead, and began to topple forward.

Risca was already drawing back, racing for the safety of the door, when something moved in the shadows to either side and he threw up his magic instinctively. The sudden glare of the flames illuminated the handful of Skull Bearers that slunk from the shadows, dark-winged and red-eyed as they sought to close on him. Risca gritted his teeth in disgust. They had been quicker than he thought, coming over the wall while he obligingly waited on their decoy. He darted left at the closest of them, sending the Druid fire hammering into it. The winged hunter fell back, hissing in fury, and red fire exploded in front of Risca as he sought to gain the tower entry. Something slammed into him, knocking him sprawling—one of the Bearers, claws slashing. Risca rolled free and came back to his feet. Steam rose out of the places where the fire had burned, mingling with the rain and mist. Thunder rumbled and cracked with new fury. Cries of glee lifted as the Northlanders surged through the unprotected gap into the courtyard behind him.

Another of the Skull Bearers attacked, a sudden dark lunge that he only barely avoided. Spears and arrows flew all about him. He was so stupid, delaying like this! The thought came and went in a flash. He threw shards of Druid fire to either side and sprinted through weapons and teeth and claws for the doorway. He did not look back, knowing what he would find, afraid that it would freeze him where he stood. He threw back another of the Bearers, this one flinging itself in front of him in an effort to slow his escape. In desperation, he sent a wash of Druid fire in all directions, forcing back the enemies seeking to close, and he ran the last few yards to the entry as if on fire himself and catapulted through the open door.

Tumbling into the dark, he was back on his feet in an instant and racing ahead. It was pitch dark within the castle corridors, the torches all extinguished, but he knew Stedden Keep and did not require light to find his way. He heard the pursuit that came after him, and when he had gone the length of the first corridor, he turned long enough to fire the passageway from end to end. It was enough to slow them, no more. But that was all he needed.

Moments later, he was through a massive, iron-plated door that he slammed shut and barred against further pursuit. They would not catch him now. Not this night. But he had come too close to discount the possibility that next time he might not be so lucky.

He brushed away the blood that ran into his eyes, feeling the sting of the gash in his forehead. He was not badly hurt. Time enough to deal with it later. Raybur and the others would be waiting somewhere back in the tunnels. Risca knew the Dwarf King too well to think he would abandon him. Friends didn't do that.

He swallowed against the dryness in his throat.

What then, he wondered bleakly, of Tay Trefenwyd and the Elves?

NIGHT LAY OVER ARBORLON, a soft, warm blanket of darkness. No rain fell here as it did farther east. Jerle Shannara stood at a front window of the summerhouse and waited for dawn. He had not slept at all that night, beset by doubts whose roots he could trace to the loss of Tay Trefenwyd, haunted by the possibility of what might have been and what must now surely be. He was on the summit of a climb that had begun some weeks earlier and would culminate with the arrival of morning, and he could not shake the despair he felt at knowing that circumstance and fortune had determined his fate in ways he could never have foreseen and could not now change.

"Come to me, love," Preia Starle called to him from the darkened hall, standing with her arms wrapped protectively about her body.

"I was thinking," he replied distantly.

She walked over to him and put her arms about his waist, holding him against her. "You think too much lately."

It was true, he supposed. It hadn't been that way before, not when Tay had been alive, not before the coming of the Warlock Lord and the misery he had visited on the Elves. He had been freer then, unfettered by responsibilities or obligations of any real significance, his life and his future his own, all the possibilities in the world his to choose from. How quickly it had all changed.

He lifted one great hand and placed it over hers. "I still do not want to be king."

But king he would be at first light. He would be crowned at sunrise in the tradition of Elven Kings since the time of faerie. It was decided now, determined by the events that had begun with the assassination of Courtann Ballindarroch and culminated in the death of his last son. For weeks the Elves had held out hope that the king's heir would return from his ill-advised search for his father's murderers. But Alyten was a brash, foolish boy, and should never have gone looking for the trouble he found. The Northlanders were waiting for him, hoping he would seek them out. They let him stumble on them, drew him on, ambushed him, and killed him. Those with him who survived, a small number only, had brought him home. He was the last grown heir to the throne of the Ballindarroch family, and Jerle Shannara's last hope that the Elven people would not turn instead to him.

They did so immediately, of course. Many had never wanted Alyten as ruler in the first place. The Northlanders threatened anew, claiming the whole of the Streleheim, closing off all contact with other lands and their peoples. An invasion of the Westland would come soon—of that there was little doubt. It wanted only the return of the Warlock Lord, who had gone east to attack the Dwarves. Elven Hunters sent as scouts had been able to determine that much. Still the High Council would not act, awaiting Alyten's return, awaiting a formal declaration that he would be king. Now Alyten was gone, and there remained only the two grandchildren, too small to rule, too young even to appreciate the enormity of what they faced. Should a regent serve in their stead? Should they rule with the help of advisors? The feeling was immediate and strong that neither solution was sufficient to forestall the disaster that threatened, and that Jerle Shannara, as the king's first cousin and the most experienced fighter and strategist in the Westland, was the only hope.

Even so, the debate on this matter might have gone on indefinitely if not for the urgency of the circumstances and the determination of Preia Starle. She had come to Jerle almost at once after Alyten's body had been returned, when the debate was so fierce that it threatened to divide the Elven people irreparably.

"You cannot let that happen," she had told him. It was night, another slow, sleepy eve when the day's heat still lingered thick and pasty at the corners of the mouth and eyes. "You are the best hope of the Elven people, and you know it. We have to fight if we are to survive, Jerle. The Northlanders will give us no choice. When the time comes, who else but you will lead us? If you are to lead, then do so as king."

"My right to be king will be questioned forever!" he had snapped, tired of the discussion, sick at heart of the need for it.

"Do you love me?" she had asked suddenly.

"You know that I do."

"And I love you as well. So heed me now. Make me your wife. Make me your life's partner and helpmate, your closest confidante and forever friend. I am these things to you already, so the step that you must take is a small one. Bond with me in the eyes of the Elven people. Tell the High Council that you want to be king, that you and I will adopt those two small boys who have lost their family and make them our sons. They have no one else. Why should they not have us? It will stop the talk. It will end the objections. It will give the boys the chance to succeed you as king when they are grown. It will bind up the wounds caused by the deaths of all the other Ballindarrochs and let the Elven people get on with the business of surviving!"

So it had come to pass. The strength of her insistence had swayed him when nothing else could. He would wonder at it afterward, at the simplicity of the solution, at Preia Starle's remarkable resolve. He would have married her anyway, he told himself. He did love her and want her as his wife. She was his closest friend, his confidante, his lover. The Elves preferred a king with heirs and the Ballindarroch family had been well liked, so there was support for the adoption of the two boys. The acclaim for Jerle to be crowned king was overwhelming.

Wrapped in Preia's embrace, he looked out into the night, remembering. How far he had come in so little time.

"Do you want children of your own, Preia?" he asked her suddenly.

There was silence as she mulled the matter over—or at least her answer. He did not try to see her face.

"I want my life with you," she said finally. "For the moment, it is difficult to think of anything else. When the Elves are safe again, when the Warlock Lord is destroyed . . ." She paused, giving him a long, steady look. "Are you asking me if blood ties make a difference in my commitment to the boys we have agreed to take as our own? They do not. If we have no other children, the boys will do. They will be ours as if born to us. Are you satisfied?"

He nodded without speaking, thinking of how their relationship had evolved, how dramatically it had changed with Tay's death. He had pondered for a long time her admission that she might have loved his friend, that she might even have gone with him if he had asked. It did not bother him as much as perhaps it should. He had loved Tay himself, and now that he was dead it was hard to begrudge him anything.

"You will sit on the High Council," he told her quietly. "Vree Erreden will sit as well. When I am able to do so, I will make him First Minister. Do you approve?"

She nodded. "You have come a long way from your old opinion of the locat, haven't you?"

He shrugged. "I will ask that the Elven army be mobilized for a march east—no, I will insist on it." His shoulders bunched with his determination. "I will do what Tay would have done. I will see that the Dwarves are not abandoned. I will see that the Black Elfstone reaches Bremen. If I fail as king, then it will not be because I lacked courage or commitment."

It was a brash, uncompromising declaration, a buttress against the doubts and uncertainties that still lurked at the edges of his confidence. Preia would know. He could not afford hesitation. The line between success and failure, between life and death, would be a thin one.

Preia pressed herself against him. "You will do what you must, what you know is right. You will be king, and there will be no regrets. You will lead your people and keep them safe. It is your destiny, Jerle. It is your fate. Vree has seen it in his visions. You must see that it is true."

He took a long moment before answering. "I see mostly that I lack another choice and so must accept this one. And I think always of Tay."

They stood without speaking for a long time. Then Preia led him through the darkness of the summerhouse to their bed and held him until morning.

CHAPTER

25

ANXIOUS TO MAKE UP for the time they sensed they had already lost, the bearers of Urprox Screl's newly forged sword purchased horses and rode north through the Southland toward the border country and the Silver River. They traveled steadily, stopping only for food and rest, and they did not say much to one another. Memories of the forging of the sword dominated their thoughts, the images so vivid that days later it seemed as if the event had happened only moments ago. That the effects of the magic invoked had transcended the forging itself was undeniable. In some way, perhaps differently for each, the creation of the talisman had transformed them. They were newly born, the forging having reshaped them as surely as it had cast the blade itself, and they were left to puzzle out what form they had taken.

It was given to Kinson Ravenlock to bear the sword on their journey back. Bremen entrusted it to him as soon as they had departed the city, compelled to do so by a need that the Druid could not quite manage to hide from his friend. It was almost as if he could not bear the weight of the weapon, could not tolerate the feel of it. It was a strange, disturbing moment, but Kinson took the sword without a word and strapped it across his back. Its weight was nothing to him, though its importance to the future of the Races was impossible to ignore. But, not having witnessed for himself the visions at the Hadeshorn, Kinson was not burdened by a Druid's insight into what that future might be, and so the sword did not have the same power over him. He bore it as he would any weapon, and while his mind retraced endlessly the moments of its creation, it was not the past with which he was concerned, but the present.

At night, sometimes, he would take the blade out and examine it. He would not have done so if Mareth had not asked it of him on the first night out, her curiosity stronger than her trepidation, her own ruminations on what had transpired at the forge fueling her need to look closer at what they had made. Bremen had not objected, though he had risen and walked off into the dark, so Kinson had seen no reason not to accede to Mareth's request. Together, they had held the blade up to the firelight and examined it. It was a wondrous piece of work, perfectly balanced, smooth and sleek and gleaming, so light it could be wielded by a single hand in spite of its size and length. The Eilt Druin had been fused into the handle where the crossguard was set, the flame from the clenched hand rising along the blade as if to burn to its tip. No flaw appeared on the polished surface, a virtual impossibility in a normal forging, but facilitated in this instance by the nature of Cogline's formula and the use of Bremen's magic.

It occurred to Kinson after several days of bearing the sword that part of his lack of awe for the blade's worth lay in the fact that Bremen did not seem to know yet what the talisman was supposed to do. Certainly, it was meant to destroy the Warlock Lord—but how? The nature of the magic with which it was imbued remained a mystery, even to the Druid. It was intended for an Elven warrior—that much the vision of Galaphile had revealed. But what was the warrior to do with the blade? Was he to wield it as he would an ordinary weapon? Given the nature of the Warlock Lord's power, that did not seem likely. There must be a magic to it that Brona could not withstand, that could overcome all of the rebel Druid's defenses and destroy him. But what could that magic be? There was some magic in the Eilt Druin, it was said, but Bremen had never been able to discover what that magic was, and whatever it was, it did not appear to have been used even once in the long span of his lifetime.

Bremen admitted this to both the Borderman and the girl, and he did so not reluctantly but with a mix of puzzlement and curiosity. The mystery of the sword's magic was not an obstacle for the Druid, but a challenge that he confronted with the same determination he had evinced in his search for the blade's maker. After all, it was not reasonable to believe that the forging alone was sufficient to imbue the sword with the magic it required. Even the fusing of the Eilt Druin did not seem enough. Something further was needed, and he must discover what it was. He took reassurance, he confided to Kinson at one point, in the fact that they had come as far and accomplished as much as they had. Because of that, he believed everything they sought was within reach.

It was a dubious premise to Kinson's way of thinking, but Bremen had accomplished a good many things in their time together through sheer strength of belief, so there was no reason to start questioning him now. If the sword had magic that could destroy the Warlock Lord, Bremen would discover what that magic was. If a confrontation was fated, Bremen would find a way to make the result favor their cause.

So they traveled out of the deep Southland and back into the Battlemound, heading for the Silver River. Their destination, the old man advised his companions, was the Hadeshorn. There he would pay yet another visit to the spirits of the dead and attempt to ascertain what they must do next. Along the way, they would try to determine what had become of the Dwarves. The weather was hot and sultry as they rode, and they were forced to stop frequently to rest themselves and their mounts. Time crawled with weary reluctance. They saw nothing of the conflict they knew was taking place farther north, encountered no signs of a Northland presence, and heard no mention from those they passed of anything untoward. Yet there was a persistent, unsettling suspicion among the three that they had somehow strayed too far from where they had begun their journey and that on their return they would find too many chances irretrievably lost.

Late in the afternoon of their first day of travel through the Battlemound, Bremen called a halt while several hours of light yet remained and took them out of the flats and into the Black Oaks. Once again, they had been navigating a precarious passage between the two quagmires, keeping just clear of the dangers of each. Now he forsook caution and steered them directly into the forbidden forest. Kinson was alarmed, but held his tongue. Bremen would have a good reason for making this detour.

They rode just into the fringe, barely a hundred feet, the sunbleached lowlands still visible through breaks in the trees, the darker regions of the forest still ahead of them, then dismounted. Leaving Mareth to hold the horses, the Druid took Kinson into a stand of ironwood, examined the trees thoughtfully for a time, then found a branch that suited him and ordered Kinson to cut it. The Borderman obliged without comment, using his broadsword to hack through the toughened wood. Bremen had him lop off the ancillary branches and twigs, then took the rough-cut length of wood in his gnarled hands and nodded his approval. They retraced their steps to the horses, remounted, and rode out of the forest once more. Kinson and Mareth exchanged puzzled glances, but kept silent.

They camped a little farther on in a vale that was not much more than a depression amid the trees. There Bremen had Kinson further shave the ironwood branch to form a staff. Kinson worked at the task for the better part of two hours while the other two prepared dinner and saw to the animals. When he had done as much with the wood as he could, when he had smoothed down the bumps and knots where the smaller branches had been cut away, Bremen took it from him once again. The company of three was seated about a small fire, the day faded to a few faint streaks of brightness west, the night creeping in on the heels of lengthening shadows and darkening skies. They were settled close against the trees of the Black Oaks, well back from the flats. A stream ran out of the forest several yards away, churning determinedly across a series of rocks and twisting away again into the shadows. The night was still and empty-feeling, free of intrusive sounds, of movement, of the presence of watching eyes.

Bremen rose and stood before the fire with the ironwood staff held upright before him, one end butted firmly against the earth, the other pointed skyward, both hands fastened to the midsection. The staff was six feet in length, cut so at his instruction, still raw from the shaving Kinson had labored to complete.

"Stay seated until I am finished," he ordered mysteriously.

He closed his eyes and went very still. After a moment, his hands began to glow with white light. Slowly the light spread out along the length of the staff, traveling in both directions. When the staff was completely enveloped, the light began to pulse. Kinson and Mareth watched in silence, mindful of Bremen's admonition. The light infused itself into the wood, turning it oddly transparent. It snaked up and down in strange patterns, moving slowly at first, then more rapidly. All the while Bremen stayed as still as stone, eyes closed, brows knit in concentration.

Then the light died away, returning to the Druid's hands before fading. Bremen's eyes opened. He took a long, slow breath and held up the staff. The wood had turned as black as ink, and its surface was smooth and polished. Something of the light that had sealed it reflected in its deep sheen, just a spark that winked and disappeared before moving on to another spot, as elusive as the glint of a cat's eye.

Bremen smiled and handed the staff to Mareth. "This is for you."

She took it from him and held it, marveling at its feel. "It is warm yet."

"And will stay so." Bremen reseated himself, a hint of weariness creeping into his lined face. "The magic that infuses it will not be dislodged, but will reside within for as long as the staff is whole."

"And what is the purpose of this magic? Why are you giving the staff to me?"

The old man leaned forward slightly, the light changing the pattern in the wrinkles that etched his face. "The staff is meant to help you, Mareth. You have searched long and hard for a way to control your magic, to prevent it from running amok, perhaps even from consuming you. I have given much thought to what could be done. I think the staff is the answer. It is designed to act as a conduit. Plant one end firmly against the ground, and it will carry off the excess of any magic you wish to employ."

He paused, searching her dark eyes. "You understand what this means, don't you? It means that I believe you will have to use the magic again now that we are traveling north. Any other expectation would be unrealistic. The Warlock Lord will be looking for us, and there will come a time when you will have to protect yourself and perhaps others as well. I may not be there to help you. Your magic is too essential for you not to be able to rely on it. I am hopeful that the staff will allow you to employ it without fear."

She nodded slowly. "Even if the magic is innate?"

"Even so. It will take time for you to learn to use the staff properly. I wish I could promise you that time, but I cannot. You must remember the staff's purpose, and if you are required to defend yourself, order your thoughts with the staff in mind."

She cocked one eyebrow at him, then said, "Do not act recklessly. Do not call up the magic without first thinking of the staff. Do not employ the magic without setting the staff and opening a channel within to carry the excess out."

He smiled. "You are quick, Mareth. If I were your father, I would be proud indeed."

She smiled back. "I think of you as my father in any case. Not as I once did, but in a good way."

"I am flattered. Now, take the staff as your own and do not forget its use. Once to the Silver River, we are back in enemy country, and the battle with the Warlock Lord begins anew."

They slept well that night and set out again at dawn. They rode slowly, resting their horses often in the midsummer heat, working their way steadily north. To their right, the Battle-mound shimmered in the sun, barren and stark, empty of movement. To their left, the Black Oaks were a dark wall, as still as the flats, tall and forbidding. Again they rode mostly in silence, Kinson carrying the sword, Mareth the staff, and Bremen the weight of their future.

By nightfall, they had skirted the quagmire of the Mist Marsh and reached the Silver River. Anxious to gain the heights that lay just beyond so that he could view the Rabb Plains and the whole of the country north before the morrow, Bremen made the choice to cross. They found a shallows, the river low

from days of little rainfall and high heat, and with the sun setting wearily beyond the flat glimmer of the Rainbow Lake west,
they rode up through a series of hills and onto a bluff. There,
back within a thick band of trees, they dismounted, tethered
the horses, and proceeded on foot. By now the daylight had
faded to a silvery gray and the shadows of nightfall had begun
to lengthen. The air, still thick with heat, had taken on a smoky
quality and tasted of dust and parched grass. Night birds flew
through the darkness in search of food, flashes of movement
that appeared and were gone in an instant's time. All about
them, insects buzzed hungrily.

They reached the edge of the bluff, the sunlight streaking
the flats with red fire, and stopped.

Below them lay the whole of the Northland army. It was
camped several miles farther north, well out on the plains so
that the details of its battle pennants were obscured, but too
vast and dark to be mistaken for anything other than what it
was. Cooking fires were already lit, small flickers of light that
dotted the grasslands like fireflies. Horses and wagons circled
sluggishly, wheels and traces creaking, riders and drivers shouting roughly as they wrestled provisions and weapons into place.
Tents billowed in the hot breeze amid the army's protective
mass. One, an impenetrable black, its ribs all edges and spines,
stood alone at the exact center of the camp, a broad stretch of
open ground encircling it like a moat. The Druid, the Borderman, and the girl stared down at it in silence.

"What is the Northland army doing here?" Kinson asked
finally.

Bremen shook his head. "I'm not certain. It must have
come out of the Anar, where we saw it last, so perhaps now it
moves west . . ."

His voice died away, leaving the rest unsaid. If the army of
the Warlock Lord was withdrawing from the Eastland, then the
battle with the Dwarves was finished and would now in all likelihood be carried to the Elves. But what had become of Raybur
and his army? What had become of Risca?

Kinson Ravenlock shook his head despairingly. Weeks had
passed since the invasion of the Eastland. Much could have

happened in that time. Standing with Urprox Screl's sword strapped across his back, he wondered suddenly if they had come too late with the talisman to be of any use.

He reached down for the buckle to the strap that secured it, loosened the sword, and handed it to Bremen. "We have to find out what's going on. I'm the logical one to do that." He slipped off his own broadsword as well, leaving only a short sword and hunting knife. "I should be back by sunrise."

Bremen nodded, not bothering to argue the point. He understood what the Borderman was saying. Either of them could go down there, but it was Bremen they could least afford to lose at this point. Now that they had the sword, the talisman the visions of Galaphile had promised, they must discover its use and its wielder. Bremen was the only one who could do that.

"I will go with you," Mareth said suddenly, impulsively.

The Borderman smiled. It was an unexpected offer. He considered it a moment, then said to her, not unkindly, "Two make it twice as hard when you are sneaking about. Wait here with Bremen. Help keep watch for my return. Next time, you can go in my place."

Then he tightened the belt that sheathed the remainder of his blades, moved several dozen paces to his right, and started down the bluff slope into the fading light.

WHEN THE BORDERMAN HAD GONE, the old man and the girl moved back into the trees and set camp. They ate their meal cold, not wishing to chance a fire with the Northland army so close and Skull Bearers certain to be at hunt. Their journey and the heat of the day had drained them of energy, and they talked only briefly before Bremen assumed watch and Mareth slept.

The time passed slowly, the night darkening, the fires of the enemy camp growing brighter in the distance, the skies opening in a flood of stars. There was no moon this night; it was either new or so far south it could not be spied beyond the screen of trees that backed along the bluff. Bremen found his thoughts straying to other times and places, to his days at Paranor, now forever lost, to his introductions to Tay Trefenwyd and Risca, to his recruitment of Kinson Ravenlock, to his search for the truth about Brona. He thought of Paranor's long history, and he wondered if the Druid Council would ever convene again. From where, he asked himself, would new Druids come, now that the old were destroyed? The knowledge lost with their passing was irreplaceable. Some of it had been transferred to the Druid Histories, but not all. Though turned moribund and reclusive, those who had become Druids were the brightest of several generations of the people of the Four Lands. Who would take their place?

It was a pointless argument, given the fact that there was no reason to believe that anyone would be left alive to assemble a new Druid Council if he should fail in his effort to destroy the Warlock Lord. Worse, it made him consider anew the fact that he still lacked anyone to succeed him. He glanced at the sleeping Mareth and wondered momentarily if perhaps she might consider the position. She had grown close to him since leaving Paranor, and she was a genuine talent. The magic she possessed was incredibly powerful, and she had a deep appreciation for its possibilities. But there was nothing to guarantee that she would ever be able to master her lethal magic, and if she could not do so she was useless. Druids must have discipline and control before all things. Mareth was fighting to acquire both.

He looked back across the grasslands of the Rabb, then let his hand stray to his side, where it came to rest on the sword. Still such a mystery, he lamented. What was he required to do in order to discover the solution? He would travel to the Hadeshorn to ask help from the Druids, but there was no guarantee they would give it. On his last visit, they had refused even to appear to him. Why should it be any different now? Would the presence of the sword persuade them to rise from their netherworld confines? Would they be intrigued enough to show themselves? Would they choose to respond to his summons because they had been human once themselves and could appreciate humanity's need?

He closed his eyes and rubbed at them wearily. When he opened them again, one of the enemy watch fires was moving toward him. He blinked in disbelief, certain he must be imagining it. But the fire came on, a small, flickering brightness in the vast darkness of the plains, wending its way closer. It seemed to float. As it neared, he rose in spite of himself, trying to decide what he should do. Oddly, he did not feel threatened, only curious.

Then the light settled and took shape, and he could see that it was carried by a small boy. The boy was smooth-faced and his clear blue eyes were inquisitive. He smiled in greeting as he approached, holding the light aloft. Bremen blinked anew. The light was like nothing he had ever seen. It burned no flame, but shone out of a glass and metal casing, as if powered by a miniature star.

"Greetings, Bremen," the boy said softly.

"Greetings," Bremen replied.

"You look weary. Your journey has required much of you. But you have accomplished much, so perhaps the sacrifice was a fair trade." The blue eyes shone. "I am the King of the Silver River. Do you know of me?"

Bremen nodded. He had heard of this faerie creature, the last of his kind, a being said to reside close to the Rainbow Lake and along the near stretch of the river for which he was named. It was said he had survived for thousands of years, that he had been one of the first beings created by the Word. It was said that his vision and his magic were by equal measures ancient and far-reaching. He appeared on occasion to travelers in need, often as a boy, sometimes as an old man.

"You sit within the fringe of my gardens," the boy said. His hand gestured in a slow sweep. "If you look closely, you can see them."

Bremen did look, and suddenly the bluff and the plains faded away and he found himself seated in gardens thick with flowering trees and vines, the air fragrant with their smells, the whisper of boughs a soft singing against the silky black of the night.

The vision faded. "I have come to give you rest and reassurance," said the boy. "This night at least, you shall sleep in peace. No watch will be necessary. Your journey has taken you a long way from Paranor, and it is far from over. You will be challenged at every turn, but if you walk carefully and heed your instincts, you will survive to destroy the Warlock Lord."

"Do you know what I must do?" Bremen asked quickly. "Can you tell me?"

The boy smiled. "You must do what you think best. That is the nature of the future. It is not given to us already cast. It is given as a set of possibilities, and we must choose which of these we would make happen and then try to see it done. You go now to the Hadeshorn. You carry the sword to the spirits of the Druids dead and gone. Does that choice seem wrong to you?"

It did not. It seemed right. "But I am not certain," the old man confessed.

"Let me see the sword," the boy asked gently.

The Druid lifted it for the boy to inspect. The boy reached out as if he might take hold of it, then stayed his hand when it was almost touching, and instead passed his fingers down the length of the blade and drew his hand clear again.

"You will know what you must do when you are there," he said. "You will know what is required."

To his surprise, Bremen understood. "At the Hadeshorn."

"There, and afterward, at Arborlon, where all is changed and a new beginning is made. You will know."

"Can you tell me of my friends, of what has become . . . ?"

"The Ballindarrochs are destroyed and there is a new King of the Elves. Seek him for the answers to your questions."

"What of Tay Trefenwyd? What of the Black Elfstone?"

But the boy had risen, carrying with him the strange light. "Sleep, Bremen. Morning comes soon enough."

A great weariness settled over the old man. Though he wanted to do so, he could not make himself rise to follow. There were still questions he wished to ask, but he could not make himself speak the words. It was as if a weight were pulling at him, huge and insistent. He slid to the ground, wrapped in his cloak, his eyes heavy, his breathing slow.

The boy's hand wove through the air. "Sleep, that you may find the strength you need to go on."

The boy and the light receded into the dark, growing steadily smaller. Bremen tried to follow their progress, but could not stay awake. His breathing deepened and his eyes closed.

When the boy and the light disappeared, he slept.

* * *

AT DAWN, Kinson Ravenlock returned. He walked out of a blanket of morning fog that hung thick and damp across the Rabb, the air having cooled during the night. Behind him, the army of the Warlock Lord was stirring, a sluggish beast preparing to move on. He stretched wearily as he reached the old man and the girl, finding them awake and waiting for him, looking as if they had slept surprisingly well. He glanced at them in turn, wondering at the fresh resolve he found in their eyes, at the renewal of their determination. He dropped his weapons and accepted the cold breakfast and ale that he was offered, seating himself gratefully beneath the shady boughs of a small stand of oaks.

"The Northlanders march against the Elves," he advised, dispensing with any preliminaries. "They say that the Dwarves are destroyed."

"But you are not certain," Bremen offered quietly, seated across from him with Mareth at his side.

Kinson shook his head. "They drove the Dwarves back beyond the Ravenshorn, beat them at every turn. They say they smashed them at a place called Stedden Keep, but Raybur and Risca both appear to have escaped. Nor do they seem certain how many of the Dwarves they killed." He arched one eyebrow. "Doesn't sound like a resounding victory to me."

Bremen nodded, thinking. "But the Warlock Lord grows restless with the pursuit. He feels no threat from the Dwarves, but fears the Elves. So he turns west."

"How did you learn all this?" Mareth asked Kinson, obviously perplexed. "How could you have gotten so close. You couldn't have let them see you."

"Well, they saw me and they didn't." The Borderman smiled. "I was close enough to touch them, but they didn't get a look at my face. They thought me one of them, you see. In near darkness, cloaked and hooded, hunched down a bit, you can appear as they do because they don't expect you to be anything else. It's an old trick, best practiced before you actually try it." He gave her an appraising look. "You seem to have slept well in my absence."

"All night," she admitted ruefully. "Bremen let me do so. He didn't wake me for my watch."

"There was no need," the other said quickly, brushing the matter aside. "But now we have today to worry about. We have come to another crossroads, I'm afraid. We shall have to separate. Kinson, I want you to go into the Eastland and look for Risca. Find out the truth of things. If Raybur and the Dwarves are yet a fighting force, bring them west to stand with the Elves. Tell them we have a talisman that will destroy the Warlock Lord, but we will need their help in bringing him to bay."

Kinson thought the matter over a moment, frowning. "I will do what I can, Bremen. But the Dwarves were relying on the Elves, and it appears that the Elves never came. I wonder how willing the Dwarves will be now to go to the aid of the Elves."

Bremen gave him a steady look. "It is up to you to persuade them that they must. It is imperative, Kinson. Tell them that the Ballindarrochs were destroyed, and a new king was chosen. Tell them that is why the Elves were delayed. Remind them that the threat is to us all, not to any one." He glanced briefly at Mareth, seated next to him, then back to the Borderman. "I must go on to the Hadeshorn to speak with the spirits of the dead about the sword. From there, I will travel west to the Elves to find the sword's wielder. We will meet again there."

"Where am I to go?" Mareth asked at once.

The old man hesitated. "Kinson may have greater need of you."

"I don't need anyone," the Borderman objected at once. His dark eyes met the girl's and then quickly lowered.

Mareth looked questioningly at Bremen. "I have done all I can for you," he said quietly.

She seemed to understand what he was telling her. She smiled bravely and glanced at Kinson. "I would like to come with you, Kinson. Yours will be the longer journey, and maybe it will help if there are two of us to make it. You're not afraid to have me along, are you?"

Kinson snorted. "Hardly. Just remember what Bremen told you about the staff. Maybe you can keep from setting fire to my backside."

He regretted the words almost before he finished saying them. "I didn't mean that," he said ruefully. "I'm sorry."

She shook her head dismissively. "I know what you meant. There is nothing to apologize for. We are friends, Kinson. Friends understand each other."

She smiled reassuringly, her gaze lingering on him, and he thought in that moment that maybe she was right, that maybe they were friends. But he found himself wondering at the same time if she didn't mean something more.

C H A P T E R

26

LONE NOW, all those who had come with him from Paranor departed on journeys of their own, Bremen traveled north for the Hadeshorn. He went down onto the Plains of Rabb, easing his way through a mid-morning haze as the sun lifted into the cloudless blue sky. He walked his horse slowly, angling east away from the departing Northland army, wary of encountering the scouts they would be dispatching and the stragglers they were sure to leave behind. He could hear the army in the distance, a rumbling of wagons and machines, a creaking of traces and stays, a hum of activity that rose out of the brume, disembodied and direction-less. Bremen cloaked himself with his Druid magic so that he would not be seen even by chance, sorted through the maze of sounds to detect what threatened, and kept close watch over what moved in the blanket of mist.

Time slipped away, and the sun began to burn off the haze. The sounds of the departing army receded, moving west, away from where he rode, and Bremen relaxed his vigil. He could see the plains more clearly now, their parched, flat stretches of baked earth and burned-out grasses, their dusty sweep from the forests of the Anar to the Runne, trampled by the Northlanders, left littered and scarred. He rode through the army's discards and leavings, through the debris that marked its passing, and he pondered on the ugliness and futility of war. He wore Urprox Screl's sword strapped across his back, the weight of it his to bear now that Kinson was gone. He could feel it pressing against him as he rode, a constant reminder of the challenge he faced. He wondered at his insistence on assuming such responsibility. It would have been so much easier not to have done so. There was no particular reason why he should have taken on this burden. No one had forced him. No one had come to him and said that he must. The choice had been his, and he could not help but wonder this morning, as he rode toward the Dragon's Teeth and the confrontation that waited, what perverse need had driven him to make it.

He found no water on the plains as midday approached, and so he went on without stopping. He dismounted and walked the horse for a time, hooding himself against the noon heat, the sun a brilliant white orb that burned down with pitiless insistence. He pondered the enormity of the danger that the people of the Four Lands faced. Like the land beneath the sun, they seemed so helpless. So much depended on things unknown— the sword's magic, the sword's wielder, the varied quests of the individual members of their little company, and the coming together of all of these at the right time and place. The undertaking was ludicrous when dissected and examined in its separate parts, fraught with the possibility of failure. Yet when considered as a whole, when looked at in terms of need measured against determination, failure was unthinkable.

With night's fall, he camped on the open plains in a ravine where a small trickle of water and some sparse grass allowed the horse to gain nourishment. Bremen ate a little of the bread he still carried and drank from the aleskin. He watched the night sky offer up its display of stars and saw a quarter-moon on the rise crest the horizon south. He sat with the sword in his lap and pondered anew its use. He ran his fingers over the crest of the Eilt Druin, as if by doing so he might discover the secret of its magic. You will know what is required, the King of the Silver River had said. The hours slipped away as he sat thinking, the night about him still and at peace. The Northland army was too far away now to be heard, its fires too distant to be seen. The Rabb this night belonged to him, and it felt as if he were the only living person in all the world.

He rode on at dawn, making better time this day. The sky clouded across the sun, lessening the force of its heat. Dust rose from his horse's hooves, small explosions that drifted and scattered in a soft west wind. Ahead, the country began to change, to turn green again where the Mermidon flowed down out of the Runne. Trees lifted from the flats, small stands that warded springs and tributaries of the larger river. By late afternoon, he had crossed at a wide shallows and was moving toward the wall of the Dragon's Teeth. He could have stopped there and rested, but he chose to go on. Time was a harsh taskmaster and did not allow for personal indulgence.

By nightfall, he had reached the foothills that led up into the Valley of Shale. He dismounted and tethered his horse close by a spring. He watched the sun sink behind the Runne and ate his dinner, thinking of what lay ahead. A long night, for one thing. Success or failure, for another. He could break it down quite simply, but the uncertainty was still enormous. His mind drifted for a time, and he found himself picking out bits and pieces of his life to reexamine, as if by doing so he might find some measure of reassurance in his capabilities. He had enjoyed some small measure of success in his efforts to thwart the Warlock Lord, and he could take heart from that. But he knew that in this dangerous game a single misstep could prove fatal and all that had been accomplished could be undone. He wondered at the unfairness of it, but knew that never in the history of the world had fairness determined anything that mattered.

When midnight came, he rose and walked up into the mountains. He wore the black robes of his office, the insignia of the Eilt Druin emblazoned on his breast, and he carried Urprox Screl's wondrous sword. He smiled. Urprox Screl's sword. He should call it something else, for it belonged to the smith no longer. But there was no other name for it as yet, and no way to give it one until its real owner was discovered or its purpose determined. So he put the matter of the sword's name aside, breathing in the night air, so cool and clean in these foothills, so clear that it seemed as if he could see forever.

He passed through the draws and defiles that led to the Valley of Shale, and it was still several hours before dawn when he reached his destination. He stood for a time at the rim of the valley and looked down at the Hadeshorn, the lake as still and flat as glass, reflecting an image of a night sky bright with stars.

He looked into the mirror of the silent waters, and he found himself wondering at the secrets that it hid. Could he unlock just a handful of those? Could he find a way to discover just one or two, those that would give him a chance of successfully carrying on his struggle? There, in the depths of that lake, the answers waited, treasures hoarded and protected by the spirits of the dead, maybe because it was all that remained to them of the life they had departed, maybe because in death you had so little you could call your own.

He sat then amid the jumbled rock and continued to stare at the lake and to ponder its mysteries. What was it like when your life was gone and you assumed spirit form? What was it like to live within the waters of the Hadeshorn? Did you feel in death anything of what you felt in life? Did you carry all your memories with you? Did you have the same longings and needs? Was there purpose in being when your corporeal body was gone?

So many unknowns, he thought. But he was old, and the secrets would be revealed to him soon enough.

An hour before dawn he picked up the sword and went down into the valley. He worked his way carefully across the loose obsidian, cautious of a misstep, trying hard not to think of what lay ahead. He calmed himself, retreating deep inside as he walked, collecting his thoughts and shaping his needs. The night was peaceful and silent, but he could already sense something stirring within the earth. He came down off the valley slope and walked to the edge of the Hadeshorn and stopped. He stood there for a moment without moving, a sense of uncertainty creeping through him. So much depended on what happened next, and he knew so little of what he should do.

He placed the sword before him at the water's edge and straightened. There was nothing he could do about it now. Time was slipping away.

He began the incantations and hand motions that would summon the spirits of the dead. He worked his way through them with grim determination, blocking out what he could of the doubts and uncertainties, casting off what he could of the fear. He felt the earth rumble and the lake stir in response to his efforts. The sky darkened as if clouds had appeared to cloak it, and the stars disappeared. Water hissed and boiled before him, and the voices of the dead began to rise in whispers that turned quickly to moans and cries. Bremen felt his own resolve toughen as if to shield him in some way from what the dead might do to him. He went hard and taut inside, so that the only movement came from the quicksilver flight of his thoughts. He was finished now with the summoning, and he picked up the sword again and stepped back. The lake was churning wildly, spray flying in all directions, and the voices were a maddening cacophony. The Druid stood rooted in place and waited for what must come. He was shut away in the valley now, isolated from the living, alone with the dead. If something went wrong, there was no one to help him. If he failed, there was no one to come for him. Whatever transpired this day, it was on his shoulders.

Then the lake exploded at its center in a volcanic surge, and a geyser rose straight into the air, a vast, black column of water. Bremen's eyes went wide. He had never seen that happen before. The column lifted skyward, and its waters did not falter or dissipate. All about it fluttered the ghostly, shimmering forms of the spirits of the dead. They appeared in swarms, emerging not from the lake itself, but from the column, disgorged from its churning mass. They swam through the air as if still in water, their small forms a brilliant kaleidoscope against the black of the night. As they whirled, they cried out, their voices sharp and poignant, as if all that they had ever wanted was to be found in this single moment in time.

Booming coughs rose suddenly from the column's center, and now Bremen fell back in spite of himself, the earth beneath his feet heaving with the force of the sound. He had overstepped himself in some way, he thought in horror. He had done something wrong. But it was too late to change things, even if he had known what to do, and it was too late to flee.

In his hands, the embossed surface of the Eilt Druin, embedded in the pommel of the sword, began to glow.

Bremen flinched as if he had been burned. *Shades!*

Then the column of water split asunder, cracked down the middle as surely as if struck by lightning. Light blazed from within, so brilliant that Bremen was forced to shield his eyes.

He brought his arms up protectively, the sword held before him as if to ward off what threatened. The light flared, and as it did a line of dark forms began to emerge. One by one, they materialized, cloaked and hooded, as black as the night around them, steaming with an inner heat.

Bremen dropped to one knee, unable to stand longer in the face of what was happening, still trying to shield his eyes and at the same time watch. One by one, the robed figures began to approach, and now Bremen recognized who they were. They were the ghosts of Druids past, the shades of those who had gone before, of all who had lived once in this world, larger in death than in life, apparitions that lacked substance, yet still radiated a terrible presence. The old man shrank from them in spite of himself, so many come at once, more coming still, a seemingly endless line floating in the air before him, approaching across the roiling waters of the lake, inexorable and dark.

He heard them speak now, heard them call to him. Their voices lifted above those of the smaller forms accompanying them, speaking his name over and over again. *Bremen, Bremen.* Foremost was Galaphile, and his voice was strongest. *Bremen, Bremen.* The old man wanted desperately to flee, would have given anything to be able to do so. His courage failed and his resolve turned to water. These apparitions were coming for him, and he could already feel the touch of their ghostly hands on his body. Madness buzzed inside his head, threatening to overwhelm him. On they came, huge forms wending their way through the darkness, faceless apparitions, ghosts out of time and history. He found he could not stop himself from shaking, could not make himself think. He wanted to shriek his despair.

Then they were before him, Galaphile first, and Bremen lowered his head into the crook of his arm helplessly.

—Hold forth the sword—

He did so without question, thrusting it before him as he would a talisman. Galaphile's hand reached out, and his fingers brushed the Eilt Druin. Instantly, the emblem flared with white light. Galaphile turned away, and another Druid approached, touched the emblem, and departed. So it went, as one by one the spirits paraded before the old man and touched the sword he held, their fingers brushing the image of the Eilt Druin before they passed on. Over and over again the emblem flared brightly in response. From within the shelter of his raised arm, Bremen watched it happen. It might have been a blessing that they bestowed, an approval that they gave. But the old man knew it was something more, something darker and harsher. There was a transference being wrought upon the sword by the touch of the dead. He could feel it happening. He could sense it taking hold.

It was what he had come for. It could not be mistaken for anything else. It was what he had been seeking. Yet even now, at the moment of its happening, he could not decipher its meaning.

So he knelt there at the edge of the Hadeshorn in the gloom and the spray, dismayed and confused, listening to the sounds of the dead, a witness to their passing, and wondered at what was taking place. At last the Druids had all come before him, touched the Eilt Druin, and gone on. At last he was alone, hunched down in the night. The sounds of the spirit voices faded, and in the ensuing silence he could hear the rasp of his own labored breathing. Sweat drenched his body and glistened on his face. His arm was cramped from holding forth the sword, yet he could not make himself withdraw it. He waited, knowing there was more, that it was not yet finished.

—Bremen—

His name, spoken by a voice he now knew. He lifted his head cautiously. The Druid shades were gone. The column of water was gone. All that remained was the lake and the blackness of the night and, directly before him, the shade of Galaphile. It waited on him patiently as he rose and drew the sword against his body as if to find strength there. There were tears on his face, and he did not know how they had gotten there. Were they his own? He tried to speak and could not.

The shade spoke instead.

—Heed me. The sword has been given its power. Carry it now to the one who will wield it. Find him west. You will know. It belongs now to him—

Bremen's voice groped for words that would not come. The spirit's arm lifted to him.

—Ask—

The old man's mind cleared, and his words were harsh and filled with awe. "What have you done?"

—Given what part of us we can. Our lives have passed away. Our teachings have been lost. Our magic has dissipated in the wane of time. Only our truth remains, all that belonged to us in our lives, in our teachings, in our magic, stark and hard-edged and killing strong—

Truth? Bremen stared, uncomprehending. Where did the sword's power lie in this? What form of magic came from truth? All those Druids passing before him, touching the blade, making it flare so brightly—for this?

The shade of Galaphile pointed once more, a gesture so compelling that Bremen's queries died in his throat and his attention was immediately commanded. The dark figure before him swept away all but its own presence as its arm lifted, and the silence surrounding it was complete.

—Listen, Bremen, last of Paranor, and I will tell you what you would know. Listen—

And Bremen, captured heart and soul by the power of the shade's words, did so.

WHEN IT WAS FINISHED and the shade of Galaphile was gone, when the waters of the Hadeshorn had become still and flat once more and the dawn was creeping silver and gold out of the east, the old man walked to the rim of the Valley of Shale and slept for a time amid the littered black rock. The sun rose and the day brightened, but the Druid did not wake. He slept a deep, dream-filled sleep, and the voices of the dead whispered to him in words he could not comprehend. He woke at sunset, haunted by the dreams, by his inability to decipher their meaning and his fear that they hid from him secrets that he must reveal if the Races were to survive. He sat amid the heat and shadows in the darkening twilight, pulled the remainder of his bread from his pack, and ate half of it in silence, staring out at the mountains, at the high, strange formations of the Dragon's Teeth where the clouds scraped against the jagged tips on their way east to the plains. He drank from the aleskin, now almost empty, and thought on what he had learned.

Of the secret of the sword.

Of the nature of its magic.

Then he rose and went back down out of the foothills to where he had left his horse the night before. He found the horse gone. Someone had taken it, the thief's footprints plain in the dust, one set only, approaching, then departing, the horse in tow. He gave the matter almost no thought, but instead began to walk west, unwilling to delay the start of his journey longer. It would take him at least four days afoot, longer if he had to avoid the Northland army, which he almost certainly would. But there was no help for it. Perhaps he could find another horse on the way.

The night deepened and the moon rose, filling out again, brightening the sky, the clouds brief shadows against its widening crescent as they sailed past in silent procession. He walked steadily, following the silver thread of the Mermidon as it snaked its way west, keeping in the shadow of the Dragon's Teeth, where the moonlight would not reveal him. He considered his choices as he walked, turning them over and over in his mind. Galaphile came to him, spoke to him, and revealed to him anew. The spirits of the Druids filed past him once more, solemn and voiceless wraiths, their hands reaching for the pommel of the sword, lowering to the image of the Eilt Druin, touching it momentarily and lifting away.

Passing on the truths they had discovered in life. Imbuing it with the power such truths could provide.

Empowering it.

He breathed deeply the night air. Did he understand fully now the power of this talisman? He thought so, and yet it seemed so small a magic to trust in battle against so powerful an enemy. How was he to convince the man who bore it that it was sufficient to prevail? How much should he reveal of what he knew? Too little, and he risked losing the bearer to ignorance. Too much, and he risked losing him to fear. On which side should he err?

Would he know when he met the man?

He felt adrift with his uncertainty. So much depended on this weapon, and yet it had been left to him alone to decide on the manner of its use.

To him alone, because that was the burden he had assumed and the pact he had made.

The night wore on, and he reached the juncture of the river where it branched south through the Runne. The wind blew out of the southwest and carried on its back the smell of death. Bremen drew up short as the stench filled his nostrils. There was killing below the Mermidon, and it was massive. He debated his course of action, then walked on to a narrows in the river's bend and crossed. Below lay Varfleet, the Southland settlement from which Kinson had been recruited five years earlier. The stench rose from there.

He reached the town while morning was still several hours away, the night a silent, dark shroud. The smell sharpened as he neared, and he knew at once what had happened. Smoke rose, lazy swirls of gray ribbon in the moonlight. Red embers glowed. Timbers jutted from the earth like spears. Varfleet had been burned to the ground, and all of its people killed or driven off. Thousands of them. The old man shook his head hopelessly as he entered the silent, empty streets. Buildings were razed and looted. People and animals lay dead at every turn, sprawled in grotesque, careless heaps amid the rubble. He walked through the devastation and wondered at its savagery. He stepped over the body of an old man, eyes open and staring sightlessly. A rat eased from beneath the corpse and scurried away.

He reached the center of the village and stopped. It did not appear as if there had been much of a battle; there were few spent weapons to be found. Many of the dead looked as if they had been caught sleeping. How many of Kinson's family and friends lay among them? He shook his head sadly. The attack was two days old, he guessed. The Northland army had come out of the Eastland and moved west above the Rainbow Lake on its way to do battle with the Elves. It was Varfleet's misfortune that it lay in the invaders' path.

All of the Southland villages between here and the Streleheim would suffer a similar fate, he thought in despair. A great emptiness welled up inside him. The words that would describe what he was feeling seemed so inadequate.

He gathered his dark robes about him, hitched the sword higher on his back, and walked from the village, trying not to look at the carnage. He was almost clear when he sensed movement. Another man would have missed it completely, but he was a Druid. He did not see with his eyes, but with his mind.

Someone was alive in the debris, hiding.

He veered left, proceeding carefully, his magic already summoned in a protective web. He did not feel threatened, but he knew enough to be careful in any event. He worked his way through a series of ruined homes to a collapsed shed. There, just within a sagging entry, a figure crouched.

Bremen drew to a halt. It was a boy of no more than twelve, his clothing torn and soiled, his face and hands covered in ash and grime. He pressed back into the shadows as if wishing the earth itself might cover him up. There was a knife in one hand, held protectively before him. His hair was lank and dark, cut shoulder-length and hanging loose about his narrow face.

"Come out, boy," the old man said softly. "It's all right."

The boy did not move an inch.

"There is no one here but you and me. Whoever did this is gone. Come out, now."

The boy stayed where he was.

Bremen looked off into the distance, distracted by the sudden flash of a falling star. He took a deep breath. He could not afford to linger and could do nothing for the boy in any event. He was wasting his time.

"I'm leaving now," he said wearily. "You should do the same. These people are all dead. Travel to one of the villages farther south and ask for help there. Good luck to you."

He turned and walked away. So many would be left homeless and shattered before this was over. It was depressing to consider. He shook his head. He walked for a hundred yards and then suddenly stopped. When he turned, there was the boy, his back against a wall, the knife in his hand, watching.

Bremen hesitated. "Are you hungry?"

He reached into his pack and pulled out the last of his bread. The boy's head craned forward, and his face came into the light. His eyes glittered when he saw the bread.

His eyes . . .

Bremen felt his throat tighten sharply. He knew this boy! It was the boy he had seen in Galaphile's fourth vision! The eyes betrayed him, eyes so intense, so penetrating that they seemed to strip away the skin. Just a boy, an orphan of this carnage, yet there was something so profound, so riveting about him . . .

"What is your name?" Bremen asked the boy softly.

The boy did not answer. He did not move. Bremen hesitated, then started toward him. Instantly the boy drew back into the shadows. The old man stopped, set down the bread, turned, and walked away.

Fifty yards farther on, he stopped again. The boy was following, watching him closely, gnawing on the confiscated bread as he advanced.

Bremen asked him a dozen questions, but the boy would not talk to him. When Bremen tried to approach, the boy quickly backed away. When the Druid tried to persuade the boy to come closer, he was ignored.

Finally the old man turned and walked on. He did not know what to do about the boy. He did not want the boy to come with him, but Galaphile's vision suggested there was a link of some sort between the two. Perhaps if he was patient he would discover what it was. As the sun rose, he turned north again and recrossed the Mermidon. Following the line of the Dragon's Teeth, he walked on until sunset. When he made camp, there was the boy, sitting just beyond the clearing in which he had chosen to settle, back in the shadow of the trees, watching. Bremen had no food, but he put out a cup of ale. He slept until midnight, then woke to continue his journey. The boy was waiting. When he began walking, the boy followed.

So it continued for three days. At the end of the third day, the boy came into the camp to sit with him and share a meal of roots and berries. When he woke the next morning, the boy was sleeping next to him. Together, they rose and walked west.

That night, as they reached the edge of the Plains of Streleheim and prepared to cross, the boy spoke his first words.

His name, he told the old man, was Allanon.

THE

FOR THE

CHAPTER

27

I̵T WAS LATE AFTERNOON, and the light was gray and misty in the study of the Ballindarroch summerhouse, where Jerle Shannara stood looking down at the maps spread out on the table before him. Outside, the rain continued to fall. It felt as if it had been raining for weeks, although the Elven King knew well enough that it hadn't and that the feeling was generated mostly by his present state of mind. It just seemed as if every time he took a moment to consider the weather, it was raining again. And today's rain was stronger than usual, driven by a west wind that whipped the branches of the trees and scattered leaves like scraps of old paper.

He looked up from his perusal of the maps and sighed. He could take some consolation in the fact that the weather was making it more difficult for the Warlock Lord to maneuver his army than it was for Jerle to maneuver his. Of the two, the Warlock Lord's was the more unwieldy—a vast, sprawling, sluggish beast burdened by baggage and siege machines. It could advance a distance of maybe twenty miles a day in the best of weather. It had reached the Streleheim three days earlier and had only just completed its crossing of the Mermidon. That meant that it was at least another two days from the Rhenn. The Elves, on the other hand, were already in place. Alerted by their scouts, they had known of the Northland army's advance for more than a week so they had been given plenty of time to prepare. Once the presence of the Northlanders was detected, it was easy enough to guess which approach they would choose

in attacking Arborlon and the Elves. The Rhenn was the easiest
and most direct route into the Westland. A large army would
have difficulty proceeding any other way and then would have
to attack the Elven home city at its most strongly defended positions. North, south, or west, the city was warded—by mountains, cliffs, and the Rill Song. Only from the east was she
vulnerable, unprotected by natural defenses. The sole strategic
defensive position available to her defenders was the Valley of
Rhenn. If the passes there should fall, the way to Arborlon
would lie open.

The maps showed as much, for all the good that did. Jerle
had been staring at them for over an hour and hadn't learned
anything new. The Elves must hold the Rhenn against the
Northland army's eventual assault or they were lost. There was
no middle ground. There was no secondary defensive position
worth considering. It made the choices available to him as commander of the Elven forces quite clear. All that was left to determine was tactics. The Elves would defend the Rhenn, but *how*
would they defend? How far should they extend their lines to
slow the initial attack? How many times could they afford to
fall back? What protective measures should they take against an
encircling strike launched by a smaller force that could penetrate the forests? What formations should they employ against
an army that outnumbered them five to one and would make
use of the siege machinery it had been assembling during its
march west?

The maps didn't provide specific answers to any of this, but
studying them helped him reason out what was needed.

He looked out the windows again into the rain. Preia would
be back soon, and they would have dinner—their last before
leaving for the Rhenn. Much of the army was encamped already
in the valley. The High Council had declared a state of emer-
gency, and the newly crowned king had taken charge. His
power was absolute now, fixed and unchallenged. He had been
crowned two weeks earlier, taken Preia as his wife, and adopted
the two Ballindarroch orphans as his sons. With the matter of
the succession to the Elven throne settled, he had turned his attention to the High Council. Vree Erreden had been named
First Minister and Preia a full council member. There had been

some grumbling, but no opposition. He had requested permission to mobilize the Elven army and march east in support of the Dwarves. There had been more grumbling and a threat of opposition, but before the matter could be brought to a head it had been learned that the Northland army was approaching the Streleheim and there would be no need for the Elves to march anywhere.

Reflecting back on the matter, Jerle shook his head. He did not know what had become of the Dwarves. No one did. He had dispatched riders east to discover if the Dwarf army had been destroyed, which was what the rumors all reported, but no definitive word had been brought back. He was left to conclude that the Dwarves were in no position to help and the Elves must stand alone.

He shook his head wearily. The Elves had been left with no allies, no magic, no Druids, and no real chance of winning this war—visions and prophecies and high hopes notwithstanding.

He looked down at the maps again, carefully configured topographies of the Rhenn and the land surrounding, as if the answer to the problem might lie there and perhaps he might have missed it. There was a time not so long ago when he would not have allowed himself to make so honest an assessment of the situation. There was a time when he would never have admitted that he could lose a battle to a stronger enemy. He had changed much since then. Losing Tay Trefenwyd and the Ballindarrochs, nearly losing Preia, becoming King of the Elves in less than ideal circumstances, and discovering that his view of himself was more than a little flawed had given him a different perspective. It was not a debilitating experience, but it was sobering. It was what happened when you grew up, he supposed. It was the rite of passage you endured when you left your boyhood behind for good.

He found himself studying the scars on the backs of his hands. Little maps of their own, they traced the progress of his life. Warrior since birth, now King of the Elves, he had come a long way in a short time, and the scars provided a more accurate accounting of the cost of his journey than mere words. How many more scars would he incur in his battle with the Warlock Lord? Was he strong enough for this confrontation?

Was he strong enough to survive? He carried not only his own destiny into battle, but that of his people as well. How strong did he have to be for that?

The doors leading out onto the terrace flew open with a crash, blown back against the walls by the force of the wind, their curtains whipping wildly. Jerle Shannara reached for his broadsword as two black-cloaked figures surged into the room, rain-soaked and bent. Maps scattered from the table onto the floor, and lamps flickered and went out.

"Stay your hand, Elven King," commanded the foremost of the intruders, while the second, smaller figure turned to close the doors behind them, shutting out the wind and rain once more.

It went quiet again in the room. Water dripped from the two onto the stone floor, puddling and staining. The king crouched guardedly, his sword halfway out of its sheath, his tall form coiled and ready. "Who are you?" he demanded.

The taller of the two pulled back his hood and revealed himself in the gray, uncertain light. Jerle Shannara took a long, deep breath. It was the Druid Bremen.

"I had given up on you," he declared in a whisper, his emotions betraying him. "We all had."

The old man's smile was bitter. "You had reason. It has taken a long time to reach you, almost as long as it took to discover that it was you I sought." He reached beneath his sodden cloak and withdrew a long, slim bundle wrapped in dark canvas. "I have brought you something."

Jerle Shannara nodded. "I know." He shoved his half-drawn sword back into its scabbard.

There was surprise in the Druid's sharp eyes. He looked at his companion. "Allanon." The boy pulled back the hood of his cloak, revealing himself. Dark eyes burned into the Elven King's, but the smooth, sharply angled face revealed nothing. "Remove your cloak. Wait outside the door. Ask that no one enter until this discussion is finished. Tell them the king commands it."

The boy nodded, slid the cloak from his shoulders, carried it to a hanging rack, then slipped through the door and was gone.

Bremen and Jerle Shannara stood alone in the study, the maps still scattered on the floor about them, their eyes locked. "It has been a long time, Jerle."

The king sighed. "I suppose it has. Five years? Longer, perhaps?"

"Long enough that I had forgotten the lines on your face. Or perhaps you have simply grown older like the rest of us." The smile came and went in the encroaching twilight. "Tell me what you know of my coming."

Jerle shifted his feet to a less threatening stance, watching as the other removed his cloak and tossed it aside wearily. "I am told that you bring me a sword, one forged with magic, one that I must carry into battle against the Warlock Lord." He hesitated. "Is this true? Have you brought such a weapon?"

The old man nodded. "I have." He took the canvas-wrapped bundle and laid it carefully on the table. "But I wasn't certain it was meant for you until I saw you standing crouched to strike me down, your weapon coming out of its sheath. In that moment, seeing you that way, I knew you were the one for whom the sword was intended. A vision of you holding the sword was shown to me at the Hadeshorn weeks ago, but I failed to recognize you. Did Tay Trefenwyd tell you of the vision?"

"He did. But he did not know that the sword was meant for me either. It was the locat Vree Erreden who advised me. He saw it in a vision of his own, saw me holding the sword, a sword with an emblem emblazoned on the pommel, an emblem of a hand holding forth a burning torch. He told me it was the insignia of the Druids."

"A locat?" Bremen shook his head. "I would have thought it would be Tay who . . ."

"No. Tay Trefenwyd is dead, killed in the Breakline weeks ago." The Elven King's voice was quick and hard, and the words tumbled out. "I was with him. We had gone to recover the Black Elfstone, as you had charged us. We found the Stone, but the creatures of the Warlock Lord found us. There were but five of us and a hundred of them. There were Skull Bearers. Tay knew we were doomed. His own magic was gone, used up in his struggle to gain possession of the Elfstone, so he . . ."

Words failed the king, and he could feel the tears spring to his eyes. His throat tightened, and he could not speak.

"He used the Black Elfstone, and it destroyed him," the old man finished, his voice so soft it could barely be heard. "Even though I warned him. Even though he knew what would happen." The worn, aged hands clasped tightly. "Because he had to. Because he could do no less."

They stood mute before each other, eyes averted. Then Jerle bent to retrieve the scattered maps, picking them up and stacking them back on the table next to the canvas bundle. The old man watched him for a moment, then bent to help. When the maps were all in place again, the old man took the king's hands in his own.

"I am sorry he is gone, more sorry than I can possibly tell you. He was a good friend to us both."

"He saved my life," Jerle said quietly, not knowing what else to say, deciding after a moment that this was enough.

Bremen nodded. "I was afraid for him," he murmured, releasing the big man's hands once more and moving over to a chair. "Can we sit while we talk? I have walked all night and through the day to reach you. The boy accompanied me. He is a survivor of an attack on Varfleet. The Northland army is ravaging the land and its people as it goes, destroying everything, killing everyone. The Warlock Lord grows impatient."

Jerle Shannara sat across from him. The old man's hands, when they clasped his own, had felt like dried leaves. Like death. The memory of their touch lingered. "What has become of the Dwarves?" he said, in an effort to direct his thoughts elsewhere. "We have not been able to learn anything of them."

"The Dwarves withstood the Northland invasion for as long as they were able. The reports vary as to what happened afterward. I know the rumors, but I have reason to believe they are wrong. I have sent friends to discover the truth and to bring the Dwarves to our aid if they are able to come."

The king shook his head, a discouraged look in his eyes. "Why should they come to our aid when we did not come to theirs? We failed them, Bremen."

"You had reason."

"Perhaps. I am no longer certain. You know of Courtann Ballindarroch's death? And of his family's destruction?"

"I was told."

"We did what we could, Tay and I. But the High Council would not act without a king to lead them. There was no help for it. So we abandoned our efforts to help the Dwarves and went instead in search of the Black Elfstone." He paused. "I question now the wisdom of our choice."

The Druid leaned forward, his dark eyes intense. "Do you have the Elfstone in your possession?"

The king nodded. "Hidden safely away, awaiting your arrival. I want nothing more to do with it. I have seen what it can do. I have seen how dangerous it is. The only comfort I take from this whole business is that the Stone will be used to aid in the destruction of the Warlock Lord and his creatures."

But Bremen shook his head. "No, Jerle. The Black Elfstone is not intended for that purpose."

The words were sharp and stunning. The king's face went hot, and his throat tightened with rage. "Are you telling me Tay died for nothing? Is that what you are saying?"

"Do not be angry with me. I do not make the rules in this game. I am subject to fate's dictates as well. The Black Elfstone is not a weapon that can destroy the Warlock Lord. I know you find this difficult to believe, but it is so. The Elfstone is a powerful weapon, but it subverts those who use it. It infects them with the same power they seek to overcome. The Warlock Lord is so pervasive an evil that any attempt to turn the Elfstone against him would result in the user's own destruction."

"Then why did we risk so much to recover it?" The king was livid, his anger undisguised.

The old man's words were soft and compelling. "Because it could not be allowed to fall into Brona's hands. Because in his hands it would become a weapon against which we could not stand. And because, Elven King, it is needed for something more important still. When this is over and the Warlock Lord is no more, it will allow the Druids to give aid to the Lands even after I am gone. It will allow their magic and their lore to survive."

The king stared wordlessly at the Druid, uncomprehending. A soft knock on the door distracted them both. The king blinked, then demanded irritably, "Who is it?"

The door opened, and Preia Starle stepped through. She seemed unruffled by his abrupt manner. She glanced at Bremen, then back to Jerle. "I would like to take the boy to the Home Guard barracks for food and rest. He is exhausted. He is not needed to keep further watch. I have seen to it that no one will disturb you while you talk." She returned her gaze to Bremen. "Welcome to Arborlon."

The old man rose and made a short bow. "My Lady Preia."

She smiled in response. "Never that to you. Just Preia." The smile faded. "You know what has happened, then?"

"That Jerle is king and you are queen? I discovered that before anything else on arriving in the city. Everyone speaks of it. You are both blessed, Preia. You will be strong for each other and for your people. I am pleased by the news."

Her eyes shone. "You are very gracious. I hope that you can be strong for us as well in what lies ahead. Excuse me now. I will take the boy with me. Don't be worried for him. We are already becoming fast friends."

She went back through the door and closed it behind her. Bremen looked at the king once more. "You are fortunate to have her," he said quietly. "I expect you know that."

Jerle Shannara was thinking of another time, not so far in the past, when he had been confronted with the possibility of losing Preia. It haunted him still, the thought that his assumptions about her had been so wrong. Tay and Preia, the two people closest to him in all the world: he had misread them both, had failed to know them as well as he should, and had been taught a lesson in the process that he would never forget.

The room was silent again, twilight filling the corners with shadows, the rain a soft patter without. The king rose and lit anew the lamps that the wind had blown out. The gloom receded. The old man watched him without speaking, waiting him out.

The king sat down again, uneasy still. His brow furrowed as he met Bremen's sharp gaze. "I was just thinking how important it is not to take anything for granted. I should have kept that in mind where the Black Elfstone was concerned. But losing Tay was impossible to bear without thinking he had died for good cause. I assumed wrongly that it was to assure the Warlock Lord's destruction. It is difficult to accept that he died for anything else."

"It is difficult to accept that he died at all," Bremen said quietly. "But the reason for his death is nevertheless tied to the destruction of the Warlock Lord and no less valid or important because the Elfstone has a different use than you believed. Tay would understand that, if he were here. As king, you must do the same."

Jerle Shannara's smile was sardonic and filled with pain. "I am new to this still, this business of being king. It is not something I sought."

"That is not a bad thing," the Druid replied, shrugging. "Ambition is not a character trait that will help you in your confrontation with the Warlock Lord."

"What will help me, then? Tell me of the sword, Bremen." The king's impatience broke past his anger and discouragement. "The Northland army marches against us. They will reach the Rhenn in two days' time. We must hold them there or we are lost. But if we are to have any real chance, I must have a weapon that the Warlock Lord cannot stand against. You say you have brought one. Tell me its secret. Tell me what it can do."

He waited then, flushed and anxious, staring at the Druid. Bremen did not move, holding his gaze, saying nothing. Then he rose, walked to the map table, picked up the canvas-wrapped bundle, and handed it to the king. "This belongs now to you. Open it."

Jerle Shannara did so, untying the cords that bound the canvas, stripping the wrapping carefully away. When he was finished, he held in his hands a sword and sheath. The sword was of unusual length and size, but light and perfectly formed. The hilt was engraved at the guard with the image of a hand holding forth a burning torch. The king slid free the sword from its sheath, marveling at the smooth, flawless surface of the blade, at the feel of it in his hand—as if it belonged there, as if it really was meant for him. He studied it for a moment in silence.

The flame from the torch climbed toward the tip of the blade, and in the dimness of the study he could almost imagine that it flickered with a light of its own. He held the sword out before him, testing its heft and balance. The metal glittered in the lamplight, alive and seeking.

The king looked at Bremen and nodded slowly. "This is a wondrous blade," he said softly.

"There is more to it than what you perceive, Jerle Shannara—and less," replied the old man quickly. "So listen carefully to what I tell you. This information is for you alone. Only Preia is to know otherwise, and only if you deem it essential. Much could depend on this. I must have your word."

The king hesitated, glanced at the sword, and then nodded. "You have it."

The Druid came to him. He stood very close and kept his voice low. "By accepting this sword, you make it your own. But you must know its history and its purpose if it is to serve you well. Its history first, then."

He paused, choosing his words carefully. "The sword was forged by the finest smith in the Southland from a formula come out of the old world. It was tempered by heat and magic. It was constructed of an alloy that renders it both light and strong. It will not shatter in battle, whether struck by iron or magic. It will survive any test to which it is put. It is imbued with Druid magic. It holds within its metal span the power of all the Druids who ever were, those who came together at Paranor over the years and then passed from this world to the next. After it was forged, I carried it to the Hadeshorn and summoned their spirits from the netherworld. All appeared, and one by one they passed before me and touched this blade. When the blade was forged, the Eilt Druin, the medallion of office of the High Druids, the symbol of their power, was set within the pommel. You have seen it for yourself. A hand holding forth a burning torch. It was this that the spirits of the dead came to witness and to imbue with the last of their earthly power, all that they could carry with them beyond this life.

"All of which brings us to the sword's purpose. It is a finely crafted blade, a weapon of great strength and durability—but that alone is not enough to render it capable of destroying the

Warlock Lord. The sword is not meant to be used as other weapons. It can be; most certainly it shall. But it was not forged for the sharpness of its blade or the toughness of its metal, but for the power of the magic which resides within it. That magic, Elven King, is what will give you victory when you face the creature Brona."

He took a deep breath, as if talking of this exhausted him. His seamed face was weary and pale in the failing light. "The power of this sword, Jerle Shannara, is truth. Truth, plain and simple. Truth, whole and unblemished. Truth, with all deceptions and lies and façades stripped away so that the one against whom the magic of the sword is directed stands fully revealed. It is a powerful weapon, one which Brona cannot stand against, for he is cloaked by these same deceptions and lies and façades, by shadings and concealments, and these are the trappings of his power. He survives by keeping the truth about himself at bay. Force him to confront that truth, and he is doomed.

"I did not understand the secret of the sword's power when it was made known to me at the Hadeshorn. How can truth be strong enough to destroy a creature as monstrous as the Warlock Lord? Where is the Druid magic in this? But after a time, I began to see. The words 'Eilt Druin' mean literally 'Through Truth, Power.' It was the credo of the Druids at their inception, the goal they set for themselves when they assembled at Paranor, and their purpose among the Races from the time of the First Council forward. To provide Mankind with truth. Truth to give knowledge and understanding. Truth to facilitate progress. Truth to offer hope. By doing so, the Druids could help the Races rebuild."

The dark eyes blinked, distant and worn. "What they were in life is embodied now in the blade you bear, and you must find a way to make their legacy serve your needs. It will not be easy. It is not as simple as it first appears. You will carry the blade in battle against the Warlock Lord. You will bring him to bay. You will touch him with the sword, and its magic will destroy him. All that is promised. But only if you are stronger in your determination, in your spirit, and in your heart than he is."

The Elven King was shaking his head. "How can I be all this? Even if I accept what you have told me, and I do not know yet that I can—it is difficult to think so—how can I be stronger than a creature who can destroy even you?"

The old man reached down for the hand that gripped the sword and lifted it so that the blade was poised between them. "By first turning the sword's power upon yourself!"

Fear came into the Elven King's eyes and glittered sharply in the light. "Upon myself? The Druid magic?"

"Listen to me, Jerle," the other soothed, tightening his grip so that the arm that held the sword could not fall away, so that the sword was a silver thread that bound them, bright and shining. "What is required of you will not be easy—I have told you that. But it is possible. You must turn the power of the sword upon yourself. You must let the magic fill you and reveal to you the truths in your own life. You must let them be laid bare, exposed for what they are, and confronted. They will be harsh, some of them. They will be difficult to face. We are creatures who constantly reinvent ourselves and our lives in order to survive the mistakes we have made and the failings we have exposed. In many ways, it is this that makes us vulnerable to a creature like Brona. But if you withstand the self-scrutiny that the sword demands, you will emerge from the experience stronger than your adversary and you will destroy him. Because, Elven King, he cannot permit such scrutiny of his life, for beyond the lies and half truths and deceptions he is nothing!"

There was a long silence as the two men faced each other, eyes locked, a measure of each being taken by the other. "Truth," said the Elven King finally, his voice so soft the Druid could barely hear him. "Such a frail weapon."

"No," said the other at once. "Truth is never frail. It is the most powerful weapon of all."

"Is it? I am a warrior, a fighter. Weapons are all I know— weapons of iron wielded by men of strength. You are saying that none of this will serve me, that I must abandon all of it. You are saying that I must become something I have never been." He shook his head slowly. "I don't know if I can do that."

The old man released him, and the sword dropped away between them. The dried parchment hands settled on the king's powerful shoulders, gripping them. There was unexpected strength in that aging body. There was fierce determination in those eyes.

"You must remember who you are," the Druid whispered. "You must remember how you got to be that way. You have never failed to confront a challenge. You have never shunned a responsibility. You have never been afraid. You have survived what would have killed almost anyone else. That is your history. That is who and what you are."

The hands tightened. "You have great courage, Jerle. You have a brave heart. But you give too much importance to Tay Trefenwyd's death and not enough to your own life. No, do not be angry. This is not a criticism of Tay, not a belittling of what his loss means to us. It is a comment on the need for you to remember that it is always the living who matter. Always. Give your life the due it deserves, Elven King. Be strong in the ways you must. Do not dismiss your chances against the Warlock Lord simply because the weapon with which you are given to do battle is unfamiliar. It is unfamiliar to him as well. He knows of man-made blades. He will suspect yours to be just another. Surprise him. Give him a taste of another kind of metal."

Jerle Shannara moved away then, shaking his head, looking down at the sword doubtfully. "I know better than to disbelieve what I find difficult to accept," he said, stopping before the window and looking out into the rain. "But this is hard. This asks so much." His mouth tightened in a hard line. "Why was I chosen for this? It doesn't make sense to me. So many others would be better suited to a weapon of this sort. I understand iron and brute strength. This . . . this clever artifice is too obscure for me. Truth as a weapon makes sense only in terms of councils or politics. It seems useless on a battlefield."

He turned toward the Druid. "I would face the Warlock Lord without hesitation if I could wield this sword as a simple blade forged of metal and a master smith's skill. I could accept it as a weapon without question if I could bear it just as it appears." Anguish pulsed in his blue eyes. "But this? I am wrong for this, Bremen."

The Druid nodded slowly, not in agreement so much as in understanding. "But you are all we have, Jerle. We cannot know why you were selected. It may be because you were fated to become King of the Elves. It may be for reasons beyond what we can see. The dead know things we cannot. Perhaps they could tell us, but they have not chosen to do so. We must accept this and go on. You are to be the bearer of the sword. You are to carry it into battle. It is predestined. There is no other choice. You must do the best you can."

His voice trailed off in a whisper. Outside, the rain continued to fall in a soft, steady patter, cloaking the forestland in a silver shimmer. Twilight had fallen, and the day had gone west with the sun. Arborlon was silent and damp within her forest shelter, a city slowly pulling on her nighttime wrappings. It was silent in the study, silent in the summerhouse, and there might have been no one alive in all the world but the two men who stood facing each other in the candlelit gloom.

"Why must no one know of the sword's secret but me?" Jerle Shannara asked quietly.

The old man smiled sadly. "You could answer your own question if you chose, Elven King. No one must know because no one would believe. If your doubts of the sword's capabilities are so great, think of what the doubts of your people will be. Even Preia, perhaps. The power of the sword is truth. Who will believe that such a simple thing can prevail against the power of the Warlock Lord?"

Who, indeed? thought the king.

"You have said it yourself. A sword is a weapon of battle." The smile turned to a weary sigh. "Let the Elves be content with that. Show them the sword you carry, the weapon that has been bequeathed to you, and say only that it will serve them well. They require no more."

Jerle Shannara nodded wordlessly. No, he thought, they do not. Belief is best when uncomplicated by reason.

He wished, in that sad, desperate moment of self-doubt and fear, of silent acquiescence to a pact that he could neither embrace nor forsake, that belief could be made so simple for him.

CHAPTER

28

Y MIDAFTERNOON of the following day, Jerle Shannara was nearing the Valley of Rhenn and the confrontation that fate had ordained for him. He had ridden out shortly after sunrise in the company of Preia, Bremen, and a handful of advisors and his army commanders, taking with him three companies of Elven Hunters, two afoot and one on horse. Four companies were already in place at the mouth of the valley, and two more would follow on the morrow. Left behind were the remaining members of the Elven High Council under the leadership of First Minister Vree Erreden, three companies of reserves, and the citizens of the city and the refugees come off the land in fear of the impending invasion. Left behind as well were the arguments and the debates over courses of action and political wisdom. Few choices and little time remained, and the use put to both would be determined in large part by the army that approached.

The Elven King said nothing to anyone of his conversation with the Druid. He chose to make no public announcement concerning the sword he had been given. He spoke of it to Preia alone, saying only that it was a weapon the Warlock Lord could not stand against. His stomach churned and his face heated as he spoke the words, for his own belief was fragile. He worried as a dog would its bone the concept of truth as a weapon of battle. He replayed his conversation with the old man over and over again as he rode east, lost in his own thoughts, so distanced by them that several times when Preia, riding next to him, spoke, he did not respond. He rode armored and battle-ready. The sword, strapped to his back, was so light in comparison with the chain mail and plate that it might have been forged of paper. He thought often on the feel of it as he traveled, its weight as ephemeral as the use to which it was intended to be put. He could not grasp it as possibility, could not settle on it as fact. He needed to be shown how it worked. He needed to know from experience its use. It was how his mind worked. He could not help himself. What he could see and feel—that was real. All else was little more than words.

He did not reveal his doubts to Bremen. He kept a smile on his face when the old man approached. He kept his confidence about him. He did it for himself, but also for his people. The army would draw its confidence from him. If the king seemed certain of himself, then they would be as well. He had always known that battles were won on as little as that, and he had always responded. This army, as this nation, was his to command—to use well or badly. What waited would test them all in ways they had never been tested before. Since this was so, he intended to do his part.

"You have said nothing for hours," Preia observed at one point, waiting until he was looking at her before she spoke to make certain he heard.

"Haven't I?" he replied. He was almost surprised to find her there, so wrapped up was he in his internal debate. She rode a wiry white-flecked gray called Ashes, weapons strapped all about her. There had never been any question about her coming, of course. Their newly adopted sons had been left in the care of others. Like Jerle, Preia Starle was born for battle.

"Something is bothering you," she declared, holding his gaze. "Why don't you tell me what it is?"

Why, indeed? He smiled in spite of himself. She knew him too well for him to pretend something different. Yet he could not speak of his doubt. He could not, because it was something he must resolve for himself. No one could help him with it. Not now, at least—not when he had not found solid ground himself on which to stand.

"I lack the words to explain," he said finally. "I am still working it through. Be patient."

"It might help if you tried the words on me."

He nodded, looking past the beauty of her face and the intelligence mirrored in her clear ginger eyes to the warmth and caring that resided in her heart. He felt different about her these days. The distance he had always kept between them was gone. They were bound together so inextricably that he felt certain that whatever happened to one, happened to the other even though it were death itself.

"Give me a little time," he told her gently. "Then we will talk."

She reached for his hand and held it momentarily. "I love you," she said.

So it was that the afternoon found them coming up on the Rhenn, and still he did not speak of what was troubling him and still she waited for him to do so. The day was bright and warm, the air sweet with the smell of still damp grasses and leaves, the forest about them lush with the infusion of the rains of the past few weeks. The clouds had moved on finally, but the ground remained soft, and the rutted trail swampy where the Elves had traveled east over its worn track. Reports had been coming in all day from where the bulk of the army had settled its defense at the head of the valley. The Northland army continued to approach, coming slowly across the Streleheim from both north and south, units arriving at varying rates of speed depending on size and mobility, foot and horse and pack. The army of the Warlock Lord was huge and growing. Already it filled the plains at the mouth of the valley for as far as the eye could see. The Elves were outnumbered by at least four to one and the odds would increase as more units arrived. The reports were delivered by messengers in flat, even tones, carefully kept devoid of emotion, but Jerle Shannara was trained to decipher what was hidden in the small nuances of pause and inflection, and he could detect the beginnings of fear.

He would have to do something to put a stop to it, he knew. He would have to do something quickly.

The realities of the situation were grim. Riders had been sent east to the Dwarves to beg their assistance, but the paths out were closed off by Northland patrols, and it would be days before a rider could work his way around them. In the meantime, the Elves were on their own. There was no one who would come to their aid. The Trolls were a subjugated people, their armies in thrall to the Warlock Lord. The Gnomes were disorganized in the best of times and had no love of the Elves in any event. Men had withdrawn into their separate city-states and lacked any sort of cohesive fighting force. The Dwarves were all that remained, if they survived. There was still no word on whether Raybur and his army had escaped the Northland invasion.

So there was good reason to be afraid, Jerle Shannara thought as they rode up from the forests at the west entrance to the Rhenn—Elven King, companions and advisors, and three companies of fighting men. There was good reason—but in this case reason must not be allowed to prevail.

What, he pondered, could he do to overcome it?

BREMEN, riding some yards back with the boy Allanon amid the king's advisors and the commanders of the Elven army, was pondering the same question. But it was not the Elves' fear that troubled him—it was the king's. For even though Jerle Shannara would not admit to it, or even be cognizant of it for that matter, he was frightened. His fear was not obvious, even to him, but it was there nevertheless. It was a subtle, insidious stalker, lurking at the corners of his mind, awaiting its chance. Bremen had sensed it the day before, at the moment he had revealed the power of the sword—there, lodged just behind the king's eyes, back in the depths of his confusion and uncertainty, back where it would fester and grow and in the end prove his undoing. Despite the old man's efforts and the strength of his own conviction concerning the power of the talisman, the king did not believe. He wanted to, but he did not. He would try to find a way, of course, but there was no guarantee he would ever do so. It was something that Bremen had not considered in the course of all that had happened. Now he must do so. He must put the matter right.

He rode all that day watching the king, observing the silence in which he had wrapped himself, studying the hard set of his jaw and neck, unpersuaded by the smiles and the outward

confidence displayed to others. The war taking place inside
Jerle Shannara was unmistakable. He was struggling to accept
what he had been told, but he was failing in his effort. He was
brave and he was determined, so he would carry the sword into
battle and face the Warlock Lord as he had been told he must.
But when he did so his lack of belief would surface, his doubt
would betray him, and he would die. The inevitability of it was
appalling. Another, stronger voice than his own was needed.
The old man found himself wishing that Tay Trefenwyd were
still alive. Tay had been close enough to Jerle Shannara that he
might have found a way to reach him, to convince him, to
break down his misgivings and his doubts. Tay would have
stood with the king against the Warlock Lord, just as Bremen
intended to do, but it would have meant more with Tay. It
might even have proved to be the difference.

But Tay was gone, so the voice and the strength that were
needed must come from someone else.

There was Allanon to think about, too. From time to time
the old man glanced at the boy. His young companion was still
reticent, but he was no longer refusing to speak. Preia Starle
was in part responsible for this. The boy was taken with her
and listened to her advice. After a time, he began to open up.
All of his family had been killed in the Northland raid, he had
revealed. He had escaped because he had been elsewhere when
the attack had commenced, and he had hidden as it swept by
him. He had seen a great many atrocities committed, but he
would not speak of the particulars. Bremen did not press him.
It was enough that the boy had survived.

But there was still Galaphile's vision to consider, and that
was a matter less easily dismissed. What did it mean—himself,
standing with the boy at the edge of the Hadeshorn in the
presence of Galaphile's shade, the bright, effervescent forms of
the spirits of the dead swirling above the roiling waters, the air
dark and filled with cries, and the boy's strange eyes fixed on
him, staring? Staring at what? The Druid could not decide. And
what was the boy doing there in the first place—there, in the
Valley of Shale, at the waters of the Hadeshorn, at a summoning of the dead, where no human was allowed, where only
he dared walk?

The vision haunted him. Oddly, he was afraid for Allanon. He was protective of him. He found himself drawn to the boy in a way he could not quite explain. Perhaps it had something to do with the fact of their aloneness. Neither had a family, a people, or a home. Neither really belonged anywhere. In each there was a separateness that was undeniable, and it was as much a state of mind as it was a fact of life and just as unalterable. That Bremen was a Druid set him apart in ways he could not change, even if he wished. But the boy was just as distanced—in part by the insight he clearly possessed into other people's thinking, a gift that few appreciated—and in part by an extraordinary perception that bordered on prescience. Those strange eyes mirrored his keen mind and intellect, but they hid his other gifts. He looked at you as if he could see right through you, and the look was not deceiving. Allanon's ability to reveal you was frightening.

What was Bremen to do with this boy? What was he to make of him? It was a day for dilemmas and unanswered questions, and the old man bore the burden of their nagging weight in stoic silence as he rode east. The resolution of both, he supposed, would come soon enough.

WHEN THEY ARRIVED at the Valley of Rhenn, Jerle Shannara left the others and with Preia rode out to survey the defenses and to let the Elven Hunters know that he had arrived. He was greeted warmly everywhere, and he smiled and waved and told his men that everything was going well and that they would have a surprise or two for the Northlanders before long.

Then he rode down through the valley to have a look at the enemy camp. He took a guide this time, for the valley floor was already dotted with traps, many of them new, and he did not want to stumble into one by mistake. Preia stayed with him, the queen as familiar a sight to the soldiers by now as the king. Neither of them spoke as they followed the guide's lead over grassy hillocks, down broad rises, across a stretch of burned-out flats, and up onto a promontory in the cliffs that warded the right flank to where he could see out across the whole of the valley. A small encampment of scouts and runners was in place, keeping watch. He greeted them, then walked to the bluff edge for a look.

Before him stretched the seething mass of the Northland army, a huge and sluggish morass of men, animals, wagons, and war machines cloaked in dust and heat. There was movement everywhere as stores and weapons were brought up and sorted and units jockeyed for position along the army's front. Siege machines were being assembled and hauled to one side. The army had settled itself about a mile from the valley's east end, out where it could see any attack being mounted against it, out where it had room to spread and grow. Jerle could feel the uneasiness of the men standing with him. He could sense in Preia's silence her cold appraisal of their chances. This army that had come to invade their homeland was a juggernaut that would not be turned away easily.

He took a long time to study it after that first glance. He looked at where the supplies and equipment and weapons were being placed. He counted the siege machines and the catapults. He sought out the standards of the companies assembled to fight him and made a rough count of cavalry and foot, both light and heavy. He watched the approach of several supply trains from out of both the north and south Streleheim. He considered his options carefully.

Then he remounted and rode back to the far end of the valley and called together his commanders and advisors for a council of war.

They gathered in a tent set well back from the front lines of the Elven defense, Home Guard set all about to insure privacy. Preia was there, of course, along with Bremen. Kier Joplin commanded the horse, and Rustin Apt and Cormorant Etrurian the foot soldiers. There were captains Prekkian and Trewithen, of the Black Watch and Home Guard respectively. There was one-eyed Arn Banda, who commanded the archers. These were the heart of his command, the men on whom he most relied, the men he must convince if they were to have any chance against the army that would come against them.

"Well met, my friends," he greeted, standing before them, loose and easy, his armor removed now. They were seated in chairs arranged in a wide circle so that he could see or ap-

proach any or all if the need arose. "I have been to the head of
the valley and seen the army that threatens us. I think our
course is clear. We must attack."

There was a gasp of surprise and dismay, of course—he had
expected as much. "At night!" he shouted amid the sudden
din. "Now!"

Rustin Apt, aging and powerful, so broad and compact it
seemed nothing could move him once he set his feet, surged
from his chair. "My lord, no! Attack? You can't be . . ."

"Careful, Rustin." The king cut him short with a sharp motion. "I can be or do anything in the right situation. You know
me well enough. Now, listen a moment. This Northland army
languishes before us, fat and bold, thinking itself too big to be
trifled with, thinking us safely settled in the protection of our
defenses. But it grows and it grows, and our Elven Hunters see
this and despair. We cannot sit by and do nothing until it grows
so big it will swallow us in one gulp. We cannot sit by and wait
for the inevitable attack. We must carry the battle to them,
now, on our terms, in a time of our choosing, when we are
ready and they are not."

"All well and good," said Kier Joplin quietly. He was small
and compact with quick, dark eyes. "But what part of the army
will you use to conduct this assault? Darkness will help, but
horsemen will be heard from a long way off and foot soldiers
will be cut to pieces before they can retreat to safety."

There was a muttered assent. Jerle nodded. "Your reasoning
follows my own. But suppose the enemy can't find us? Suppose
we become invisible just when they think they have us? Suppose that we attack in sequence, a strike here, a strike there, but
give them nothing more than shadows to spar with?"

Now there was silence. "How would you do that?" Joplin
asked finally.

"I will tell you. But first I want you in agreement with my
thinking. I am convinced we must do something if we are to
bolster the army's confidence in itself. I see it flagging. Am I
right in my assessment?"

Silence once more. "You are," Joplin said finally.

"Kier, you have put your finger on the danger an attack
faces. Now I want you to consider the possible gains. If we can

throw them off balance, disrupt them, unnerve them, even hurt them a little, we gain time and confidence both. Sitting here waiting gains us neither."

"Agreed," said Cormorant Etrurian quickly. He was a thin-faced, rawboned fellow, well seasoned in the border wars, a former aide to old Apt. "On the other hand, a defeat would be disastrous at this juncture. It might even spur an earlier attack on our defenses."

"You might be wrong about them not expecting us as well," voiced his aged mentor, huffing back to his feet. "We don't know what might have happened with the Dwarves. This is a battle-tested army we face, and they may know more tricks than we do."

"We are badly outnumbered as it is," Etrurian added with a scowl. "My lord, this is just too dangerous a tactic."

Jerle nodded at each new comment, biding his time, waiting to speak until they had vented all their objections. He glanced at Preia, who was watching him carefully, then at Bremen, whose expressionless face revealed nothing of what he was thinking. He looked from one face to the next, trying to decide how many of those gathered he could count firmly in his camp. Preia, of course. But the others, his commanders and Bremen alike, were still making up their minds or had already decided against him. He didn't want to force the matter on them if they would not support it, king or no, but he was firmly decided. How to persuade them, then?

The voices of opposition died away. Jerle Shannara straightened. "We are friends here, all of us," he began. "We are working for the same end. I know the enormity of the task before us. We are all that stands between the Warlock Lord and the devastation of the Four Lands. Perhaps we are the only fighting force left with the strength to face him. So caution is necessary. But so is risk. There can be no victory without risk—certainly none here, in this place and time, against this enemy. There is an element of risk in any battle, an element of chance. We cannot ignore that. What we must do is minimize it."

He walked close to Rustin Apt and knelt before him. The seasoned commander's hard eyes grew startled. "What if I could show you a way to attack this enemy by night—a way that has a strong chance of succeeding, that risks only a few of us, and that if successful will disrupt him sufficiently that we will gain both confidence and time?"

The old man looked uncertain. "Can you do that?" he growled.

"Will you stand with me if I can?" the king pressed, ignoring the question. He glanced left and right. "Will you all?"

There were murmurs of approval. He looked at them in turn, made them meet his gaze, made them give him their assent. He nodded to each, drawing them to him with his eyes and smile, binding them to him with their unspoken promise, making them a part of the plan he had formed.

"Listen closely, then," he whispered, and he told them what he would do.

THE ATTACK DID NOT TAKE PLACE that night, but on the night following. It took another day to complete preparations, to choose the men who would participate, and then to send Kier Joplin and his riders north and Cormorant Etrurian and his Hunters south, both commands departing at sunrise and staying within the concealment provided by the forests and bluffs so that they could make their way to their respective destinations unseen. Their commands were necessarily small, for stealth and swiftness would serve their cause far better than size. Each had specific instructions on what to do and when to do it. Coordinating the various elements of the assault called for precise timing. If the strikes did not take place in their proper sequence, the assault would fail.

Jerle Shannara led the center group, a company composed of archers and Home Guard. The fighting would be most fierce where they went, and he would not allow anyone else to stand in his place. Bremen was furious. He approved of the plan. He applauded the king's innovation and daring. But it was madness for the king to lead the attack himself.

"Think, Elven King! If you fall here, all is lost no matter what is gained!" He had made his argument to Jerle and Preia Starle after the others had departed. The wispy hair and beard had flown in all directions with the old man's angry gestures.

"You cannot risk your own life in this! You must stay alive for your confrontation with Brona!"

They had stood close to one another amid the shadows, the day gone to dusk. Outside, preparations were already under way for the morrow's strike. Jerle Shannara had convinced his commanders, the force of his arguments and reason too strong for any to stand against, too persuasive for any to ignore. One by one, they had capitulated—Joplin first, then the others. In the end, they had been as enthusiastic about the plan as he was.

"He is right," Preia Starle had agreed. "Listen to him."

"He is wrong," Jerle had replied, his voice quiet, his manner calm, holding them both speechless with the force of his conviction. "A king must lead by example. Here, particularly, in this situation, where so much is at risk. I cannot ask another to do what I would not do myself. The army looks to me. These men know I lead, that I do not stay behind. They will expect no less of me here, and I will not disappoint them."

He would not give in on this. He would not compromise. So he was leading as he said he would, the misgivings of the Druid notwithstanding, and Preia, as always, was with him. They crept out of the dark at midnight, slipped from the valley, and crossed the plains toward the enemy camp. They were only several hundred strong, with twice as many archers as Home Guard. A handful crept ahead, as silent as ghosts, and dispatched the Northland sentries that patrolled the camp perimeter. Soon the main body of the attack force was less than fifty yards out. There they crouched, weapons in hand, waiting.

When the attack came, it was sharp and unrelenting. It began north, with Kier Joplin. The Elven Commander had bound with heavy fabric the hooves of his men's horses and then walked two hundred riders down out of the north Streleheim after sunset. When the Elves were less than a hundred yards from the north perimeter of the camp they removed the baffles, waited until an hour past midnight, then mounted their horses and charged. They were on top of the Northlanders before the alarm could be given. They struck at the flanks of the latest supply train, newly arrived and not yet unloaded, its handlers waiting for the morning light. The Elves snatched brands from the smoldering watch fires as they rode in and set the wagons ablaze. Then they wheeled across the staging area for the siege machines and fired the nearest of those as well. Flames soared skyward as the riders raced through the camp and disappeared again into the night. They were gone so fast that a response was still forming when the second strike commenced.

This one came from Cormorant Etrurian to the southwest. He waited until he saw the flames of the first strike and then attacked. With five hundred foot soldiers already in place, he drove a wedge deep into the enemy horse camp, killing handlers and setting free their animals, chasing them into the night. Hand-to-hand fighting was fierce for a few moments, but then the Elves swung west, raking the camp perimeter as they retreated, breaking quickly for the darkness of the plains.

The Northland response was swifter this time, but confused, for the attack seemed to be coming from everywhere. Massive Rock Trolls, only half-armored, but gripping huge battle-axes and pikes, swept aside everything that stood in their path as they sought to engage their attackers. But siege machines and supply wagons were burning north, and the horses were scattered south, and no one seemed certain where the enemy could be found. Bremen, hidden in the flats with Jerle Shannara's command, had used his magic to cloak the Elves and to create the illusion of attackers at points where none were present. The old man could sustain that for only a short time, but long enough to confuse even the deadly Skull Bearers.

By then, Jerle Shannara's force had joined the attack. Flanked and protected by the Home Guard, the archers set themselves in rows facing the Northland perimeter, drew back their longbows, and sent a hail of arrows into the enemy. Screams rose as the arrows found their mark. Volley after volley showered down on the Northlanders as they sought to rise and arm themselves. The king held his men in place for as long as he dared and then held them longer still. A rush of Gnomes charged out of the camp in a maddened frenzy, trying to reach the bowmen, but the archers simply lowered their fire and raked the disorganized counterattack until it broke apart.

Finally Jerle Shannara began to disengage his men, the ranks withdrawing in turn, one always covering the retreat of the others. The men under Cormorant Etrurian had already gone past, trotting swiftly through the night, vague shadows on plains swept by clouds of smoke and ash from the fires. Rock Trolls appeared, huge, cumbersome behemoths marching out of the garish firelight, their pikes and battle-axes held ready. Arrows were of no use against them. The bowmen fell back, running through the thin line of Home Guard that yet held fast. Jerle withdrew his men quickly, having no wish to do battle with Rock Trolls this night. No enemy cavalry would pursue, for the Northland horses were captured or scattered. The Trolls were all they must avoid.

But the Trolls came on more quickly than the king had expected. The Home Guard stood virtually alone on the plains now, the bowmen and Elven Hunters fled back to the safety of the Rhenn, the horsemen under Kier Joplin returned north. Gnome arrows flew out of the glare of the Northland camp, sent by archers rushed to the fore. Several of the Home Guard went down and did not move. Bremen, who had come onto the plains with the attackers to lend his protection to the king, brushed past them, black robes flying, and threw Druid fire into the teeth of the advancing Trolls. The grasslands exploded in flames, and for a moment the pursuit broke apart. The Home Guard began to fall back anew, the old man and the king in their midst, besieged on all sides as they hastened toward the shelter of the valley. Smoke rolled across the flats, carried on the back of a sudden wind, filled with heat and ash. Preia Starle darted ahead, trying to find a path through the haze. But the confusion brought on by the smoke and the howls of their pursuers was too great. The small band of Home Guard broke apart, some going one way with Bremen, some another with the king. Jerle Shannara called out, heard his name called in response, and suddenly everything disappeared in the smoke.

Then something huge crashed into those who fled with the king, sending the Home Guard spinning away into the night, flinging aside those closest as if they were stuffed with straw. A massive form materialized, a brutish monster in service to the Dark Lord, called from the netherworld and abroad with the night, all teeth and claws and scales. It came at Jerle Shannara with a howl, and the king barely had time to draw free his sword. Up flashed the magical blade, its bright surface fiery in the near dark. *Now!* thought the king, wheeling to strike. *Now, we shall see!* He willed the sword's magic forth, calling on it to protect him as the creature closed, summoning its great power. But nothing happened. The beast reached for him, fully twice as tall and again as broad, and in desperation the king struck at it as he would at any enemy. The sword hammered into the beast, the force of the blow slowing the attack. But still no magic appeared. Jerle Shannara felt his stomach knot with sudden fear. The beast was cut at from either side by Home Guard come back into the fray, but it smashed the life out of the closest, brushed aside the rest, and came on.

In that moment Jerle Shannara realized that he could not compel the sword's magic and that any hope he might have had that it would protect him was lost. He had thought, despite what Bremen had admonished, that there was magic of a sort that would strike down an enemy—something of fire, something with an otherworldly edge. But truth was what the sword revealed, the old man had insisted, and it seemed plain now that truth was all the sword could offer. Fear threatened to paralyze the King, but with a fierce cry he launched himself at the attacking beast. With both hands wrapped about the pommel of the broadsword, he defended himself in the only way left to him. The sword's bright blade flashed downward and cut deep into the massive creature, dark blood spurting at the juncture of the blow. But the beast broke past the king's guard, knocked aside his weapon, and threw him to the ground.

Then Bremen appeared, come out of the dark like an avenging wraith, hands thrust forward, bathed in Druid fire. The fire lanced from his fingertips in a frantic burst and slammed into the monster as it reached for the king, enveloping it, consuming it, turning it into a writhing torch. The beast reared back, shrieked in fury, turned, and raced away into the night, flames trailing after. Bremen did not wait to see what became of it. He reached down for the king, Elves of the Home Guard reappearing to assist him, and hauled Jerle Shannara to his feet.

"The sword . . ." the king began brokenly, shaking his head in despair.

But Bremen stopped him with a hard look, saying, "Later, when there is time and privacy, Elven King. You are alive, you fought well, and the attack succeeded. That is enough for one night's work. Now come, hurry away, before other creatures find us."

They fled once more into the night, the king, the Druid, and a handful of Home Guard. Smoke and ash chased after them, and farther off, lighting the whole of the horizon like beacons, the fires from the supply wagons and the siege machines burned on. Preia Starle returned out of the dark, breathless, harried, eyes revealing both anger and fear. She shouldered her way under Jerle Shannara's left arm and bolstered him as he walked. The king did not resist. His eyes met her own and looked away. His mouth was set.

The fear that smoldered in the dark corners of his consciousness had burst forth in flames this night—fear that somehow the sword with which he had been entrusted was not right for him and would not respond when needed. It had emerged to challenge him, and he had failed to meet that challenge. If not for Bremen, he would be dead. A thing of lesser magic would have finished him, a thing of far less power than the Warlock Lord. Doubt riddled his resolve. All he had believed possible just hours earlier was lost. The magic of the sword was wrong for him. The magic would not answer to his call. It needed someone else, someone more attuned to its use. He was not that man. He was not.

He could hear the words echo in the pounding of his heart, cold and certain. He tried to close his mind and his ears to the sound, but found he could not. In hopeless despair, he ran on.

CHAPTER

29

ITH BREMEN GONE WEST to bear the Druid sword to the Elves, Kinson Ravenlock and Mareth turned east along the Silver River in search of the Dwarves. They traveled that first day through the hill country that buttressed the river's north bank, winding their way steadily closer to the forests of the Anar. Mist clung to the hills with dogged persistence, then began to burn away as the sun rose higher in the midday sky. By early afternoon, the travelers had reached the Anar and started in. Here the land flattened and smoothed. Sunlight pierced the leafy canopy and dappled the earthen carpet. They had enough food and water for that day only, and they divided it carefully when they paused for their lunch, reserving enough for dinner in the event that no better choice presented itself.

The Anar was bright with the green of the trees and the blue of the river, with shafts of sunlight from the mostly cloudless sky, and with birdsong and the chittering of small creatures darting through the undergrowth. But the trail was trampled and strewn with the leavings of the Northland army, and no human life revealed itself anywhere. Now and again the faint scent of charred wood and old ashes wafted on the wind, and moments of silence would descend—a quiet so intense it caused the man and the woman to look about guardedly. They passed small cottages and outbuildings, some still standing, some burned out, but all vacant. No Dwarves appeared. No one passed them on the trail.

"We shouldn't be surprised," Mareth observed at one point when Kinson had remarked on the subject. "The Warlock Lord has only just withdrawn from the Eastland. The Dwarves must still be in hiding."

It seemed a logical conclusion, but it bothered Kinson nevertheless to pass through country so improbably deserted. The absence of even the most transient peddler was disturbing to him. It suggested that there was no reason for anyone to be here anymore, as if life no longer had a purpose in these forests. It gave him pause to think that an entire people could vanish as if they had never been. He had no frame of reference for an eradication of this magnitude. What if the Dwarves had been annihilated? What if they had simply ceased to exist? The Four Lands would never recover from such a loss. They would never be the same.

As they walked, content to stay silent, mulling over their separate thoughts, the Borderman and the Druid apprentice did not speak to each other much. Mareth walked with her head up and her eyes forward, and her gaze seemed directed to something beyond what either of them could see. Kinson found himself wondering if she was pondering the possibility of her heritage in light of what she had learned from Bremen. That she was not his daughter, after thinking for so long that she must be, would be shock enough for anyone. That she was perhaps the daughter of one of the dark things that served the Warlock Lord was worse. Kinson did not know how *he* would react to such a revelation. He did not think he would accept it easily. It did not matter, he thought, that Bremen insisted it could have no bearing on the sort of person Mareth was. There was more than logic at issue here. Mareth was well-reasoned and intelligent, but the vicissitudes of her childhood and the complexities of her adult life had rendered her vulnerable to an undermining of the few beliefs she had managed to hold on to.

From time to time he considered speaking to her of this. He considered telling her she was the person she had always believed herself to be, he could see the goodness in her, he had witnessed the force of it firsthand, and she could never be betrayed by so tenuous a heritage as her blood. But he could not think of a way to frame the words so as not to make them appear condescending, and he was afraid to risk that happening. She seemed content simply to have him there, and in spite of his rude remarks when Bremen had suggested she come with him, he was secretly happy that she had. He had grown comfortable with her, with the history they shared, with their talks, with the way in which each knew what the other was thinking, and in the closeness he felt toward her in dozens of small ways he could not easily define. The latter came from such small things as the sound of her voice, the way she looked at him, and the sense of companionship that transcended simply the sharing of the journey. It was enough, he decided in the end, that he was there if she should decide she needed to talk. She knew that her father's identity and origins made no difference to him. She knew that none of it mattered.

They reached Culhaven at sunset, the light fading, the air cooling, the smell of death harsh and pungent amid the shadows. The home city of the Dwarves had been burned to the ground, and the land ravaged. Nothing remained but scorched earth, rubble, a few burned timbers, and scattered bones. Many of the dead had been left to lie where they had fallen. They were indistinguishable from one another by now, but the smallness of the bones revealed that some had been children. The Borderman and the apprentice Druid came out of the trees into the clearing where the city had stood, paused in sad appraisal, and then began to walk slowly through the carnage. The attack was weeks old, the fires long burned away, the land already regenerating from beneath the ruins, small green shoots poking up out of the ash. But Culhaven was empty of human life, and across the whole of its blackened sprawl the silence hung in curtains of indifference.

At the center of the city they found a vast pit into which hundreds of Dwarves had been thrown and their bodies burned.

"Why didn't they run?" Mareth asked softly. "Why did they stay? They must have known. They must have been warned."

Kinson stayed silent. She knew the answer as well as he did. Hope could play you false. He looked off into the distance, across the broad expanse of the ruins. Where were the Dwarves who were still alive? That was the question that needed answering now.

They moved on through the destruction, their pace quickening, for there was nothing left to see that they had not already seen in abundance. The light was fading, and they wanted to be well beyond the ruins when they set their camp for the night. They would find no food or water here. They would find no shelter. There was nothing to keep them. They walked on, following the river to where it wound sluggishly out of the deep woods east. Perhaps things would be better farther on, Kinson thought hopefully. Perhaps farther on there would be life.

Something scurried through the rubble to one side, causing the Borderman to start. Rats. He had not seen them before, but of course they were there. Other scavengers as well, he supposed. He felt a chill pass through him, triggered by a memory of a time in his boyhood when he had fallen asleep in a cavern he was exploring and had awakened to find rats crawling over him. Death had seemed oddly close in those brief, horrifying moments.

"Kinson!" hissed Mareth suddenly and stopped.

A cloaked figure was standing before them, unmoving. A man, it appeared—there was enough of him revealed to determine this much at least. Where he had come from was a mystery. He had simply materialized, as if conjured from the air itself, but he must have been in hiding, waiting for them. He stood close to the riverbank on which they walked, shadowed by the night and the remains of a stone wall. He did not threaten them; he simply stood there, waiting for them to approach.

Kinson and Mareth exchanged a quick glance. The man's face was concealed in the shadows of his hood and his arms and legs in the folds of his cloak. They could tell nothing of who he was, nothing of his identity.

"Hello," Mareth ventured softly. She held the staff Bremen had given her like a shield before her.

There was no reply, no movement.

"Who are you?" she pressed.

"Mareth," the other called to her in a slow, whispery voice.

Kinson stiffened. The voice had the feel of rat's feet and the presence of death. He was back in that cave again, a boy once more. The voice scraped against his nerve endings like metal on stone.

"Do you know me?" Mareth asked in surprise. The voice did not seem to trouble her.

"I do," said the other. "We all do, those of us who are your family. We have waited for you, Mareth. We have waited a long time."

Kinson could hear the catch in her voice. "What are you talking about?" she asked quickly. "Who are you?"

"Perhaps I am the one you have been searching for. Perhaps I am he. Would you think harshly of me if I were? Would you be angry if I told you I was . . ."

"No!" she cried out sharply.

"Your father?"

The hood tilted back, and the face within revealed itself. It was a hard, strong face, and the similarities to Bremen's were more than token, though the man before them was younger. But the resemblance to Mareth was unmistakable. He let the young woman look on him momentarily, let her study him well. He seemed oblivious of Kinson.

He smiled faintly. "You see yourself in me, don't you, child? You see how alike we are? Is it so hard to accept? Am I so repulsive to you?"

"Something is wrong here," Kinson warned softly.

But Mareth didn't seem to hear him. Her eyes were fixed on the man who said he was her father, on the dark-cloaked stranger who had appeared so unexpectedly before them. How? How had he known where to look?

"You are one of them!" Mareth snapped coldly at the stranger. "One of those who serve the Warlock Lord!"

The strong features did not recoil. "I serve who I choose, just as you do. But your service to the Druids was prompted by your search for me, was it not? I can read it in your eyes, child. You have no real ties to the Druids. Who are they to you? I am your father. I am your flesh and blood, and your ties to me are clear. Oh, I understand your misgivings. I am not a Druid. I am pledged to another cause, one that you have opposed. All your life, you have heard that I am evil. But how bad am I, do you think? Are the stories all true? Or are they perhaps shaded by those who tell them to serve a purpose of their own? How much of what you know can you believe?"

Mareth shook her head slowly. "Enough, I think."

The stranger smiled. "Then perhaps I should not be your father."

Kinson watched her hesitate. "Are you?"

"I don't know. I don't know if I want to be. I would not wish your hatred if I were. I would wish your understanding and your tolerance. I would wish for you to listen to all that I would tell you of my life and of how it affects you. I would wish for an opportunity to explain why the cause I serve is neither evil nor destructive, but premised on truths that would liberate us all." The stranger paused. "Remember that your mother loved me. Could her love have been so misguided? Could her trust in me have been so badly misplaced?"

Kinson felt something shift imperceptibly—a current of air, a hint of smoke, a ripple in the river's flow—something he could not see, but could only feel. The short hairs on the back of his neck stiffened. Who was this stranger? Where had he come from? If he was Mareth's father, how had he found them here? How did he know who she was?

"Mareth!" he warned again.

"What if the Druids have been wrong in all that they have done?" the stranger asked suddenly. "What if everything you have believed is premised on lies and half truths and misrepresentations that go all the way back to the beginning of time?"

"That isn't possible," Mareth answered at once.

"What if you are betrayed by those you have trusted?" the stranger pressed.

"Mareth, no!" hissed Kinson in fury. But instantly the stranger's eyes settled on him, and suddenly Kinson Ravenlock could neither move nor speak. He was frozen in place, as much so as if he had been turned to stone.

The stranger's eyes shifted back to Mareth. "Look at me, child. Look closely." To Kinson's horror, Mareth did. Her face had assumed a vacant, faraway look, as if she were seeing something entirely different from what was before her. "You are one of us," the stranger intoned gently, the words soft and coaxing. "You belong with us. You have our power. You have our passion.

You have all that is ours save one thing only. You lack our cause. You must embrace it, Mareth. You must accept that we are right in what we seek. Strength and long life through use of the magic. You have felt it flowing through you. You have wondered how it can be made your own. I will show you how. I will teach you. You need not shun what is part of you. You need not be afraid. The secret is in giving heed to what it asks of you, of not trying to restrain it, of not fleeing from its need. Do you understand me?"

Mareth nodded vaguely. Kinson saw an imperceptible change in the features of the stranger before them. No longer was he quite so human. No longer did he resemble either Bremen or Mareth. He was, instead, becoming something else.

Slowly, painfully, the Borderman strained against the invisible chains that bound his muscles. Carefully, he eased his hand along his thigh to where his long knife was sheathed.

"Father?" Mareth called out suddenly. "Father, why did you abandon me?"

There was a long silence in the deepening night. Kinson's hand closed about the handle of his knife. His muscles screamed with pain, and his mind felt drugged. This was a trap of the same sort as the one the Warlock Lord had set for them at Paranor! Had the stranger been waiting for them, or just for whoever happened through? Had he known that Mareth, in particular, would come? Had he hoped it might be Bremen? His fingers tightened on the knife.

The stranger's hand lifted free of the cloak and beckoned to the young woman. The hand was gnarled, and the fingers were clawed. But Mareth did not seem to see. She took a small step forward.

"Yes, child, come to me," the stranger urged, his eyes gone as red as blood, fangs showing behind a smile as wicked as a snake's strike. "Let me explain everything to you. Take my hands, your father's hands, and I will tell you what you are meant to know. Then you will understand. You will see that I am right in what I tell you. You will know the truth."

Mareth took another step forward. The hand that held the Druid staff lowered slightly.

In the next instant Kinson Ravenlock wrenched free of the magic that ensnared him, threw off its shackles, and unsheathed his long knife. In a single fluid motion, he flung the knife at the stranger. Mareth cried out in fear—for herself or her father or even Kinson, the Borderman could not tell. But the stranger transformed in the blink of an eye, changing from something human to something that was definitely not. One arm swept up, and a sheet of wicked green fire burst forth, incinerating the long knife in midair.

What stood before them now in a haze of smoke and flickering light was a Skull Bearer.

A second burst of fire exploded from the creature's clawed fingers, but Kinson was already moving, flinging himself into Mareth and carrying her from the trail and into a pocket of ash-coated rubble. He was back on his feet instantly, not waiting to see if she had recovered, dodging around a wall and toward the Skull Bearer. He would have to be quick now if he wanted to live. The creature was slouching toward them, fire sparking from the tips of its fingers, red eyes burning out of the shadows beneath its hood. Kinson darted across an open space, the fire just missing him as he threw himself down and rolled behind the skeleton of a small tree. The Skull Bearer swung toward him, whispering words insidious and hateful, words filled with dark promise.

Kinson drew out his broadsword. He had lost his bow, which might have made a better weapon—though in truth he possessed no weapon that could make a difference. Stealth and guile had protected him in the past, and neither was of any use now.

"Mareth!" he cried out in desperation.

Then he launched himself from his hiding place and charged toward the Skull Bearer.

The winged hunter shifted to meet the attack, hands lifting, claws sparking. Kinson could tell already that he was too far away to close with the monster before the fire struck. He dodged to his left, looking for cover. There was none to be found. The Skull Bearer rose before him, dark and forbidding. Kinson tried to cover his head.

Then Mareth cried out sharply, "Father!"

The Skull Bearer whirled at the sound of the young woman's voice, but already the Druid fire was lancing from the raised tip of Mareth's staff. It slammed into the winged hunter's body and flung it backward against a wall. Kinson stumbled and fell trying to shield his eyes. Mareth's face was harsh in the killing light, and her eyes were cast of stone. She sent the fire into the Skull Bearer in a steady stream, burning through its defenses, through its toughened skin, and into its heart. The creature screamed in hatred and pain, flinging up its arms as if to fly away. Then the Druid fire consumed it completely, and it was turned to ash.

Mareth threw down the staff in fury, and the Druid fire died away.

"There, Father," she hissed at the remains, "I have given you my hands to hold in yours. Now explain to me about truth and lies. Go on, Father, speak to me!"

Tears began to stream down her small, dark face. The night closed about once more, and the silence returned. Kinson climbed slowly to his feet, walked to her, and carefully drew her against him. "I don't think he has much to say on the subject, do you?"

She shook her head wordlessly against his chest. "I was such a fool. I couldn't seem to help myself. I couldn't stop myself from listening to him. I almost believed him! All those lies! But he was so persuasive. How did he know about my father? How did he know what to say?"

Kinson stroked her hair. "I don't know. The dark things of this world sometimes know the secrets we keep hidden. They discover our fears and doubts and use them against us. Bremen told me that once." He lowered his chin to her hair. "I think this creature was waiting for any of us to come—for you, me, Bremen, Tay, or Risca—any of those who threaten his Master. This was a trap of the same sort set by the Warlock Lord at Paranor, designed to snare whoever walked into it. But Brona used a Skull Bearer this time, so he must be very afraid of what we might do."

"I almost killed us," she whispered. "You were right about me."

"I was wrong," he replied at once. "Had I come alone, had you not been with me, I would be dead. You saved my life. And you did so with your magic. Look at the ground on which you are standing, Mareth. Then look at yourself."

She did as he asked. The ground was blackened and scorched, but she was untouched. "Don't you see?" he asked softly. "The staff channeled your magic, just as Bremen said it would. It carried off the part that would threaten you and kept only what was needed. You have gained control of the magic at last."

She looked at him steadily, and the sadness in her eyes was palpable. "It doesn't matter anymore, Kinson. I don't want control of the magic. I don't want anything to do with it. I am sick of it. I am sick of myself—of who I am, of where I came from, of who my parents were, of everything about me."

"No," he said quietly, holding her gaze.

"Yes. I wanted to believe that creature or I would not have been so mesmerized. If you hadn't broken his hold on me, we would both be dead. I was useless. I am so caught up in this search to discover the truth about myself that I endanger everyone around me." Her mouth tightened. "My *father*, he called himself. A Skull Bearer. Lies this time, but maybe not the next. Perhaps it is true. Perhaps my father is a Skull Bearer. I don't want to know. I don't want anything more to do with magic and Druids and winged hunters and talismans." The tears had started again, and her voice was shaking. "I am finished with this business. Let someone else go on with you. I quit."

Kinson looked off into the darkness. "You can't do that, Mareth," he told her finally. "No, don't say anything, just listen to me. You can't because you are a better person than that. You have to go on. You are needed to help those who cannot help themselves. It isn't a responsibility you went looking for, I realize. But there it is, your burden to bear, given to you because you are one of only a few who can shoulder it. You, Bremen, Risca, and Tay Trefenwyd—the last of the Druids. Just the four of you, because there is no one else, and perhaps there never will be."

"I don't care," she murmured dully. "I don't."

"Yes, you do," he insisted. "You all do. If you didn't, the struggle with the Warlock Lord would have been finished long ago, and we would all be dead."

They stood looking at each other in the ensuing silence, like statues left standing amid the ruins of the city.

"You are right," she said finally, her voice so soft he could barely hear her. "I do care."

She moved against him, lifted her face to his, and kissed him on the mouth. Her arms slipped around his waist and held him to her. Her kiss lasted a long time, and it was more than a kiss of friendship or gratitude. Kinson Ravenlock felt something grow warm deep inside that he hadn't even known was there. He kissed Mareth back, his own arms coming about her.

When the kiss was finished, she stayed pressed against him for a moment, her head lowered into his chest. He could feel her heart beat. He could hear her breathing. She stepped back and looked at him without speaking, her huge, dark eyes filled with wonder.

She bent down to pick up the fallen staff and began walking toward the woods again, following the Silver River east. Kinson stared after her until she was only a shadow, trying to make sense of things. Then he gave it up and hurried to catch her.

THEY WALKED FOR TWO DAYS afterward and encountered no one. All of the villages, farms, cottages, and trading centers that they passed were burned out and deserted. There were signs of the Northland army's passage and of the Dwarves' flight, but there were no people to be found. Birds flew across the skies, small animals darted through the undergrowth, insects hummed in the brambles, and fish swam in the waters of the Silver River, but no humans appeared. The man and the woman kept careful watch for any more of the Skull Bearers or any of the other myriad netherworld creatures that served the Warlock Lord, but none came. They found food and water, but never in abundance and always in the wild. The days were slow and hot, the sticky swelter of the Anar cooled infrequently by passing rains. The nights were clear and deep, filled with stars and bright with moonlight. The world was peaceful and still and empty. It began to feel as if everyone, friend and foe alike, had vanished into the firmament.

Mareth did not speak again of her origins or of abandoning her quest. She did not mention her loathing of the magic or her fear of those who wielded it. She traveled mostly in silence, and when she did have something to say it concerned the country through which they passed and the creatures living there. She seemed to have put the events of Culhaven behind her. She seemed to have settled on staying with Kinson, though she gave her decision no voice. She smiled often in his direction. She sat close to him sometimes before sleeping. He found himself wishing more than once that she would kiss him again.

"I am not angry anymore," she said at one point, her eyes directed ahead, carefully avoiding his. They were walking side by side across a meadow filled with yellow wildflowers. "I was angry for so long," she continued after a moment. "At my mother, at my father, at Bremen, at the Druids, at everyone. Anger gave me strength, but now it only drains me. Now I'm simply tired."

"I understand," he replied. "I have been traveling for more than ten years—for as long as I can remember—always in search of something. Now I just want to stop and look around a little. I want to have a home somewhere. Do you think that's foolish?"

She smiled at his words, but she didn't answer.

Late on their third day out of Culhaven, they reached the Ravenshorn. They were within its shadow and climbing into the foothills when the sun began to sink beneath the western horizon. The sky was a wondrous rainbow of orange, crimson, and purple, the colors spilling everywhere, staining the earth below, reaching out to the darkening corners of the land. Kinson and Mareth had paused to look back at the spectacle when a solitary Dwarf appeared on the trail before them.

"Who are you?" he asked bluntly.

He was alone and bore only a heavy cudgel, but Kinson knew at once there would be others close at hand. He told the Dwarf their names. "We are searching for Risca," he advised. "The Druid Bremen has sent us to find him."

The Dwarf said nothing, but instead turned and beckoned for them to follow. They walked for several hours, the trail climbing through the foothills to the lower slopes of the mountains. Daylight faded, and the moon and stars came out to light their way. The air cooled, and their breath puffed before them in small clouds. Kinson searched for signs of other Dwarves as they traveled, but he never saw more than the one.

At last they crossed into a valley where several dozen watch fires burned and ten times as many Dwarves huddled close about them. The Dwarves looked up as the Southlanders came into view, and some rose from where they had been sitting. Their stares were hard and suspicious, and their words to each other were kept purposefully low. They carried few possessions, but every last one of them wore weapons strapped to his waist and back.

Kinson wondered suddenly if he and Mareth were in danger. He moved closer to her, his eyes darting left and right. It did not feel safe. It felt ugly and threatening. He wondered if these Dwarves were renegades fled from the main army. He wondered if the army even existed anymore.

Then abruptly Risca was there, waiting for them as they approached, unchanged from the time they had left him at the Hadeshorn save for the new lacing of cuts that marked his face and hands. And when a smile appeared on his weathered face and his hand stretched out in greeting, Kinson Ravenlock knew that everything was going to be all right.

CHAPTER

30

TEN DAYS FOLLOWING Jerle Shannara's midnight assault, the army of the Warlock Lord attacked the Elves at the Valley of Rhenn.

The Elves were not caught unprepared. All that night the level of activity in the enemy camp had been unusually high. Watch fires were built up until it seemed as if the entire grassland were ablaze. The siege machines that had been salvaged from the raid were hauled forward, massive giants looming out of the night, the squarish, bulky towers swaying and creaking, the long, bent arms of the catapults and throwers casting their shadows like broken limbs. Long before daybreak the various units of the army began to assemble, and from as far away as the head of the pass the Elves could hear the sounds of armor and weapons being strapped in place. The heavy tromp of booted feet signaled the forming up of battle units. Horses were saddled and brought around, and the cavalry mounted and rode off to assume positions on the army's flanks, warding the archers and foot soldiers. There was no mistaking what was happening, and Jerle Shannara was quick to respond.

The king had used well the time that his raid had gained him. It had taken the Northlanders even longer to recover than he had hoped. The damage his raid had inflicted on the siege machines and supply wagons was extensive, requiring that new machines be built, old ones be repaired, and more supplies be brought down from the north. Some of the scattered horses were recovered, but a large number had to be replaced. The

Northland army swelled anew as further reinforcements arrived, but the Elves were encouraged by the fact that they had damaged this superior force so easily. It had given them renewed hope, and the king was quick to take advantage of it.

The first thing Jerle did was to relocate the greater part of his army from the west end of the valley to the east, from the narrow pass to the broad mouth opening onto the flats. His reasoning was simple. While it was easier to defend the deeper pass, he preferred to engage the enemy farther out and make it fight for every foot of ground as it advanced through the valley. The danger, of course, lay in spreading his lesser force too thinly before a superior army. But to offset that risk, the king employed his engineering corps to construct a series of deadly traps in the wide gap opening out onto the plains through which the Northlanders must pass. He met as well with his commanders to discuss strategy, working out a complex but comprehensive set of alternatives he believed would offset the magnitude of the Northland strike. The larger army would win if it could bring its superior size and strength to bear. The trick was to prevent this from happening.

So when dawn arrived on that tenth day and the Northland army stood revealed, the Elves were waiting. Four companies of foot soldiers and archers stood arrayed across the wide mouth of the valley's east entrance, arms at the ready. Cavalry under Kier Joplin had already fanned out to either side along the fringe of the Westland forests that screened the cliffs and hills. On the high ground, three more companies of Elven Hunters had set themselves in place, warded by earthworks and barricades, with bows, slings, and spears in hand.

But the army assembled before them was truly daunting. It numbered well over ten thousand, spread out all across the plains for as far as the eye could see. The huge Rock Trolls stood centermost, their great pikes lifted in a forest of wood and iron. Lesser Trolls and Gnomes flanked and fronted them. Heavy cavalry ranged behind, lances set in stirrup rests. Twin siege towers bracketed the army, and catapults and throwers were scattered through its midst. In the blaze of new sunlight and old shadows, the Northland army looked to be large enough to crush any obstacle it encountered.

There was an expectant silence as the sun lifted out of the horizon and the new day began. The two armies faced each other across the grassland, armor and weapons glinting, pennants flying in a soft breeze, the sky a strange mix of brightening blue and fading gray. Clouds sailed overhead in vast, thick masses that threatened rain before the day was through. The acrid smell of scorched earth wafted on the air, a residue from the watch fires doused. Horses stamped nervously and shifted in their traces. Men took deep breaths and closed off thoughts of home and family and better times.

When the Northland army began its advance toward the valley, the earth shook with the sound. Drums thudded in steady cadence to mark time for the foot soldiers marching in step. The wheels of the catapults and siege towers rumbled. Boots and hooves thudded so heavily that the trembling of the ground could be felt all the way back to where the Elves stood waiting. Dust began to rise from the parched plains, the wind stirring it in wild clouds, and the size of the army seemed to swell even more, to rise on the dust as if fed by it. The silence shattered, and the light changed. In the roil of the dust and the thunder of the army's coming, Death lifted its head in expectation and looked about.

Jerle Shannara sat atop his charger, a white-faced bay called Risk, and watched in silence as the enemy advanced. He did not like the effect that it was having on his men. The sheer number of the enemy was disheartening, and the sound of its coming was immense and heart-stopping. The king could feel the fear it generated in his soldiers. His impatience with what was happening began to grate on him. It began to work against his own resolve.

Finally, he could abide it no longer. Impulsively he spurred forward to the head of his army, leaving Preia, Bremen, and his personal guard staring after him in shock. Charging to the fore, exposed to all, he reined in and began to walk Risk up and down the front ranks, speaking boldly to the Elven Hunters who stood there looking up at him in delighted surprise.

"Steady now," he called out calmly, smiling, nodding in greeting, meeting every pair of eyes. "Size alone won't make the difference. This is our ground, our home, our birthright, our nation. We cannot be driven from it by an invader who lacks heart. We cannot be defeated while we believe in ourselves. Stay strong. Remember what we have planned for them. Remember what we must do. They will break first, I promise you. Keep steady. Keep your wits."

So he went, up and down the lines, pausing now and again to ask a man he recognized some small question, demonstrating to them the confidence he felt, reminding them of the courage he knew they possessed. He did not bother to glance at the juggernaut that approached. He pointedly ignored it. They are nothing to us, he was saying. They are already beaten.

When the behemoth was two hundred yards away, the thunder of its approach so pervasive that there was room for no other sound, he raised his arm in salute to his Elven Hunters, wheeled Risk into their front ranks, and took his place among them. Dust gusted across the plains, shrouding the marching army and the rolling machines. Drums hammered out the cadence. The siege weapons lurched closer, hauled forward by massive ropes and trains of pack animals. Swords and pikes glittered in the dusky light.

Then, when the advancing army was a hundred and fifty yards away, Jerle Shannara signaled for the plains to be fired.

Forward raced a long line of archers, dropping to one knee to light their arrows. Six-foot-long bows were lifted and tilted skyward, and bowstrings were drawn taut and released. The arrows flew into the midst of the Northland army, landing in grasses that the Elves had soaked with oil under cover of darkness the night before, when they knew the attack was at hand. Flames sprang to life all about, rising into the dust-clogged air, blazing skyward amid the close-set enemy ranks. Down the long lines the fire raced, and the Northland march slowed and broke apart as the screams of frightened men and animals rose into the morning air.

But the army did not retreat or try to flee. Instead it charged, its forward ranks breaking free of the deadly flames. Gnome archers loosed their arrows in wild bursts, but they lacked Elven longbows and the arrows fell short. The soldiers with their hand weapons came on, howling in rage, anxious to close with the enemy that had surprised them. Fully a thousand in number, most of them Gnomes and lesser Trolls, ill-disciplined and impulsive, they surged forward into the trap that waited.

Jerle Shannara held his soldiers in place, the bowmen drawn back again into the ranks of Elven Hunters. When the enemy was close enough to smell, he brought up his sword in signal to the haulers set in lines amid the swordsmen. Back they pulled on the heavy, greased ropes concealed in the grasses, and dozens of barricades buttressed with sharpened stakes lifted to meet the rush. The attackers were too close to slow, pressed on by those who pushed from behind, and were driven onto the deadly spikes. Some tried to cut at the ropes, but the blades slid harmlessly along the greased cords. The cries of attack changed to screams of pain and horror, and Northlanders died in agony as they fell on the barricades or were trampled underfoot.

Now the Elven bowmen loosed their arrows a second time in long, steady waves. The Northlanders, slowed by the barricades blocking their path of attack, were easy targets. Unable to protect themselves, with nowhere to hide, they were felled by the dozens. The flames of the grass fires closing in from behind gave them no chance to retreat. The rest of the Northland army had split apart in an effort to skirt the center of the inferno and lend support to those trapped in front. But the positioning of the siege machines and the trains of animals hauling them forward hampered their progress, and now Elven cavalry rode at them from both sides, sweeping across their flanks with javelins and short swords. One of the towers caught fire, and in an effort to douse the flames, the occupants frantically splashed down buckets of water drawn from containers stored within the wooden shell. Catapults loosed their deadly hail of stones and jagged metal, but their aim was obscured by the smoke and dust.

Then Jerle Shannara had the ropes to the spiked barricades released, and the barricades dropped away. The Elves marched forward, lancers and swordsmen set in staggered lines, their ranks tight, the shield of the man on the right protecting the man on the left. Straight into the ravaged Northland front they marched, a steady, relentless advance. Dismayed at their predicament, the Northlanders who were trapped between the Elves and the fire threw down their weapons and tried to flee. But there was no escape. They were hemmed in on all sides now, and with no place to go they were quickly cut to pieces.

But the grass fires began to die, and a company of the Rock Trolls that formed the core of the Northland army's strength marched into view, their great pikes lowered. They held their ranks and maintained their pace without slowing as they trampled over their own dead and dying, making no distinction between friend and enemy. Anything caught in their path was killed. Jerle Shannara saw them coming and gave the order to retreat. He pulled back his front lines to their original position and set them in place again. On his right, Cormorant Etrurian commanded. On his left, Rustin Apt. Arn Banda set the bowmen amid both companies, staggering their lines, and had them loose their arrows at the advancing Trolls. But the Trolls were too well armored for the arrows to do much damage, and the king signaled the archers to fall back.

Out of the fire and smoke the Rock Trolls marched, the finest fighters in the Four Lands, massive of shoulder and thigh, heavily muscled, armored and steady. Jerle Shannara signaled anew, and up came a new set of spikes to block their path. But the Rock Trolls were more disciplined and less easily confused than the Gnomes and lesser Trolls, and they set themselves in place to push back the spiked barricades. Behind them swarmed the balance of the Northland army, appearing out of the haze in seemingly endless numbers, hauling with them their siege towers and catapults. Cavalry rode their flanks, engaging Kier Joplin's command, keeping it at bay.

Jerle Shannara withdrew his army another hundred yards, well into the broad eastern mouth of the Rhenn. Line by line, the Elves fell back, a disciplined, orderly retreat, but a retreat nevertheless. Some among the Northland army cheered, believing the Elves had panicked. Surely the Elves would break and flee, they thought. None among them noticed the lines of small flags through which the elves carefully withdrew and which they surreptitiously removed in their passing. Advancing implacably, relentlessly into the valley, the Rock Trolls were oblivious of the ordered form of the Elven retreat. Behind them smoke and fire gusted and died as the wind faded with the approach of midmorning. Kier Joplin's command rode back into the valley ahead of the Northland assault, anxious to avoid being cut off. They galloped past the foot soldiers and wheeled about on their flanks, forming up anew. The entire Westland army was in place now, stretched across the mouth of the valley, waiting. There was no sign of panic and no hint of uncertainty. They had set a second trap, and the unsuspecting enemy was marching directly into it.

So it was that when the front ranks of the Rock Trolls reached the entrance to the valley, the ground beneath their feet began to give way. The heavily armored Trolls tumbled helplessly into pits the Elves had dug and concealed several days earlier and themselves carefully avoided during their retreat. The ranks parted and moved ahead, avoiding the exposed drops, but there were pits staggered over a span of fifty yards at irregular intervals, and the ground continued to collapse no matter which way the Trolls turned. Confusion slowed their advance, and the attack began to falter.

Immediately, the Elves counterattacked. The king signaled the men concealed on the cliffs to either side, the casks of the flammable oil were rolled down hidden ramps onto the grasslands to smash apart on exposed rocks and spill into the pits. Once more fire arrows arced skyward and fell into the spreading oil, and the entire eastern end of the valley was abruptly engulfed in flames. The Rock Trolls in the pits were burned alive. The balance of the assault came on, but the solidarity of the Troll ranks was shattered. Worse, the Trolls were being overrun by the unwitting Northlanders who had followed in their wake. Confusion began to overtake the army. The fire chased them, the arrows from the Elven longbows fell among them, and now the Elven army was marching into their midst, bearing massive, spiked rams before them. The rams tore into their already decimated ranks and scattered the Trolls further. On came the Elven Hunters, who fell upon the rest with their swords. Those trapped between the Elves and the fire stood their ground and fought bravely, but died anyway.

In desperation the remaining Northlanders charged the cliffs to either side of the pass, trying to gain a foothold there. But the Elves were waiting once more. Boulders tumbled from the heights and crushed the climbers. Arrows decimated their ranks. From their superior defensive positions, the Elves repelled the assault almost effortlessly. Below, in the inferno of the pass, the front quarter of the Northland army milled about helplessly. The attack stalled and then fell apart. Choking on dust and smoke, burned by the grass fires, and bloodied by the weapons of the Elves, the army of the Warlock Lord began to withdraw once more onto the Streleheim.

Impulsively Jerle Shannara unsheathed the sword entrusted to him by Bremen, the sword whose magic he could not command or even yet believe in, and he thrust it aloft. All about him the Elves lifted their own weapons in response and cheered.

Almost instantly the king recognized the irony of his gesture. Quickly he lowered the sword once more, a fool's stick in his hands, a simpleton's charm. As he wheeled Risk about angrily, his euphoria drained from him and was replaced by shame.

"IT IS THE SWORD OF SHANNARA NOW, Elven King," Bremen had told him when he had revealed to the old man after the midnight raid how the talisman's magic had failed him. "It is no longer a sword of the Druids' or of mine."

The words recalled themselves now as he rode back and forth across his lines, resetting them in preparation for the next attack, the one he knew would probably come just before sunset. The Sword was back in its sheath, strapped to his waist, an uncertain, enigmatic presence. For while Bremen had been quick enough to name the Sword, he had been slow to provide reassurance that its magic could be mastered, and even now, even with all he knew, Jerle Shannara still did not feel as if it was truly his.

"It is possible for you to command the magic, Elven King," the old man had whispered to him that night. "But the strength to do so is born out of belief, and the belief necessarily must come from within you."

They had huddled together in the dark those ten days earlier, dawn still an hour or more away, their faces smeared with soot and dirt and streaked with sweat. Jerle Shannara had come close to dying that night. The Warlock Lord's nether-world monster had almost killed him, and even though Bremen had arrived in time to save him, the memory of how near death had come was yet vivid and raw. Preia was somewhere close, but Jerle had chosen to talk with the Druid alone, to confess his failure in private to exorcise the demons that raged within. He could not live with what had befallen him if he did not think he could prevent it from happening again. Too much depended on the Sword's use. What had he done wrong in calling on the power of the talisman that night? How could he make certain it did not happen again?

Alone in the darkness, huddled so that the pounding of their hearts and the heated rush of their breathing was all they could hear, they had confronted the question.

"This sword is a talisman meant for a single purpose, Jerle Shannara!" the old man had snapped almost angrily, his voice rough and impatient. "It has a single use and no other! You can-not call on the magic to defend you against all creatures that threaten! The blade may save your life, but the magic will not!"

The king stiffened at the rebuke. "But you said . . ."

"Do not tell me what I said!" Bremen's words were sharp and stinging as they cut apart his objection and silenced him. "You were not listening to what I said, Elven King! You heard what you wanted to hear and no more! Do not deny it! I saw; I watched! This time, pay me better heed! Are you doing so?"

Jerle Shannara managed a furious, tight-lipped nod, his tongue held in check only by the knowledge that if he failed to do as he was bidden, he was lost.

"Against the Warlock Lord, the magic will respond when you call on it! But only against the Warlock Lord, and only if you believe strongly enough!" The gray head shook reprovingly. "Truth comes from belief—remember that. Truth comes with recognition that it is universal and all-encompassing and plays no favorites. If you cannot accept it into your own life, you cannot force it into the lives of others. You must em-brace it first, before you can employ it! You must make it your armor!"

"But it should have served so against that creature!" the king insisted, unwilling to admit that his judgment had been wrong. "Why did it not respond?"

"Because there is no deception about such a monster!" the Druid replied, his jaw clenched. "It does not do battle with lies and half truths. It does not armor itself in falsehoods. It does not deceive itself into thinking it is something it is not! That— *that*, Elven King, is the sole province of the Warlock Lord! And that is why the magic of the Sword of Shannara can be used only against him!"

So they had debated, the argument raging back and forth, on until dawn, when they had rested at last. Afterward, the king had been left to think on what he had been told, to try to reconcile the words with his expectations. Gradually he had come to accept that what Bremen believed must be true. The magic of the Sword was limited to a single use, and though he might wish it otherwise, there was no help for it. The magic of the Sword was meant for Brona alone and no other. He must embrace this knowledge, and somehow he must find a way to make the magic, however foreign and confusing, his own.

He had gone to Preia finally, having known all along that he would do so eventually, just as he did with all things that troubled him. His counselors were there to advise him at every turn, and some—especially Vree Erreden—were worth listening to. But no one knew him as Preia did, and in truth none among them was apt to be as honest. So he had made himself confide the truth in her, though it was difficult to admit that he had failed and was fearful he might fail again.

It was later that same day, his conversation with Bremen still fresh in his mind, his memories of the previous night still vivid. The Valley of Rhenn was hushed beneath a clouded sky, and the Elves were watchful, wary of a Northland response to the previous night's attack. The afternoon was gray and slow, the summer heat settled deep within the parched earth of the Streleheim, the air thick with dampness from an approaching rain.

"You will find a way to master this magic," she said at once when he had finished speaking. Her voice was firm and insistent, and her gaze was steady. "I believe that, Jerle. I know you.

You have never given up on a challenge, and you will not give up on this one."

"Sometimes," he replied quietly, "I think it would be better if Tay were here in my place. He might make a better king. Certainly, he would be better suited to wield this sword and its magic."

But she shook her head at once. "Do not ever say that again. Not ever." Her clear, ginger eyes were bright and sharp. "You were meant to live and be King of the Elves. Fate decreed that long ago. Tay was a good friend and meant much to both of us, but he was not destined for this. Listen to me, Jerle. The Sword's magic will work for you. Truth is no stranger. We have begun our lives as husband and wife by revealing truths that we would not have admitted a month before. We have opened ourselves to each other. It was difficult and painful, but now you know it can be done. You know this. You do."

"Yes," he admitted softly. "But the magic still seems . . ." He faltered.

"Unfamiliar," she finished for him. "But it can be made your own. You have accepted that magic is a part of your Elven history. Tay's magic was real. You have discovered for yourself that it could perform miracles. You watched him give his life in its service. All things are possible with magic. And truth is one of them, Jerle. It is a weapon of great power. It can strengthen and it can destroy. Bremen is no fool. If he says that truth is the weapon you require, then it must be so."

But still it nagged at him, whispered of his doubts, and caused him to waver. Truth seemed so small a weapon. What truth could be powerful enough to destroy a being that could summon monsters from the netherworld? What truth was sufficient to counter magic powerful enough to keep a creature alive for a thousand years? It seemed ludicrous to think that truth alone was sufficient for anything. Fire was needed. Iron, sharp-edged and poison-tipped. Strength that could split rocks asunder. Nothing less would do, he kept thinking—even as he sought to embrace the magic Bremen offered. Nothing less.

Now, riding the battlefield with the Sword of Shannara strapped to his side, his Elven Hunters buoyed by the euphoria of their victory, he wondered anew at the enormity of the responsibility he had been given to fulfill. Sooner or later he would have to face the Warlock Lord. But that would not happen until he forced a confrontation, and that in turn would not happen until the Northland army itself was threatened. How could he hope to bring such a thing about? For while the Elves had held against one assault, there was nothing to say that they would be able to hold against another, and another, and another after that—the Northland army coming on relentlessly. And if they did somehow manage to hold, how could he turn the tide of battle so that the Elves could take the offensive? There were so many of the enemy, he kept thinking. So many lives to expend and no thought being given to the waste of it. It was not so for him—and not so for the Elves who fought for him. This was a war of attrition, and that was exactly the kind of war he could not hope to win.

Yet somehow he must. For that was all that was left to him. That was the only choice he had been given.

He must, or the Elves would be destroyed.

THE NORTHLAND ARMY came again an hour before sunset, appearing out of the scorched, dusty, smoke-shrouded grasslands like disembodied wraiths. Foot soldiers marched in behind massive shields constructed of wood so green it would not burn. Cavalry rode their flanks to ward against attacks from the cliffs north and south. They advanced slowly and steadily out of the haze, the grass fires having burned themselves out earlier, though the air was still acrid and raw. They skirted the charred pits and their crumpled dead, and once inside the valley they began to probe for new traps. Five thousand strong, they were packed close behind their shields, and their weapons bristled at every turn. The drums beat in steady cadence and they chanted as they marched, boots thudding, iron blades and wooden hafts rapping in time. They brought up their siege towers and catapults and set them in place at the valley entrance. A vast, dark mass, they rose up against the coming night until it seemed as if there were enough of them to overrun the entire world.

Jerle Shannara had drawn his army deeper into the valley,

bringing them back to a midway point before setting their lines. He had chosen a position where the valley began to rise toward the Rhenn's narrow western pass, giving his Hunters the high ground on which to position themselves. His tactics necessarily changed now, for the wind had shifted within the valley, blowing back against the defenders, and fire would only aid the enemy here. Nor had he ordered pits dug this deep within the valley; there would not be enough room to maneuver his own army if he did, and besides, the enemy would be looking for them now.

Instead, he had ordered dozens of spiked barricades built, ties sharpened at both ends and lashed crosswise to a central axle so that they resembled cylindrical pinwheels. Each was twenty feet in length and light enough to haul forward and set in place so that the downward-pointing spikes were jammed into the earth. These he had positioned at staggered intervals in a narrow ribbon all across the width of the Rhenn just below his forward lines.

When the army of the Warlock Lord spilled into the valley and began its determined march forward, the first resistance it encountered was the maze of spiked barricades. As the front ranks of the enemy reached them, Jerle Shannara ordered his bowmen, set in lines of three behind cover along the slopes, to loose their arrows. The Northlanders, slowed by the barricades and unable to push them aside, could not escape. Caught in a withering crossfire, they were killed by the dozens as they sought to crawl over, under, or past the spikes. The cavalry tried to mount a sustained charge against the Elves positioned on the heights, but the slopes were too steep for horses and the Northland riders were swept down again.

Screams rose from the dying, and the attack stalled. The Northlanders hid behind their shields, but they could not advance their cover beyond the Elven barricades. Axes were brought up to hew through the barricades, but those who rushed out to chop apart the spiked pinwheels lasted only moments. Worse, to break past even one of the barricades required cutting it through in a dozen places. The light failed, dusk descended, and the world turned shadowy and uncertain. The Northlanders brought fire to the barricades and set some ablaze, but the Elves had purposely made them of green wood. The grasses caught fire, but the Elves had dug trenches to separate themselves from the barricades, and the fires burned themselves out east of the defensive lines.

The Elves waited until darkness began to mask everything, then counterattacked from the slopes in a series of controlled strikes. Because the Elves had the Northlanders bottled up on the valley floor, their target was certain even in the deepening gloom. One company after another came down off the heights, forcing the Northlanders to turn first one way and then another to defend themselves. Fierce hand-to-hand fighting ensued, and the valley became a charnel house.

Still the enemy would not fall back. Northlanders died by the hundreds, but there were always more waiting to be brought up, a huge, massive force crushing relentlessly inward. Even as the Elves fought to hold their positions against those already in place, reinforcements were advancing. Slowly, inexorably, the enemy pushed forward. The barricades held the Northland army in check at the valley's center, but the slopes were being overrun. The Elves under Cormorant Etrurian who held the cliffs were slowly driven from their defensive positions and compelled to fall back. Foot by foot, yard by yard, the Northlanders advanced, seizing the heights and breaking free of the vise that Jerle Shannara had clamped about them.

Word of what was happening reached the king. The skies were clouded and rain was beginning to fall, turning the ground slick and treacherous. The sounds of battle echoed off the slopes of the valley, creating a maelstrom of confusion. The darkness made it virtually impossible to see anything beyond a few yards. Jerle Shannara took only a moment to consider. Quickly he sent runners to withdraw Etrurian's men to the barricades established as a redoubt high on the slopes parallel to his own lines. There they were to stand and hold. He sent runners to pull back Arn Banda and the longbows. Then he marshaled two companies of Elven Hunters under Rustin Apt and formed them up to attack. When Etrurian's fighters and the bowmen were safely withdrawn, he ordered pikes brought to the fore, and he marched his command directly into the heart of the enemy advance. He engaged the Northlanders just as they were breaking through on the right flank and pinned their front ranks against the barricades. He ordered torches lit to identify their position to the reentrenched bowmen, then had them rake the enemy from the slopes.

Caught in an enfilading fire, the Northlanders rallied under a massive clutch of Rock Trolls and counterattacked. They shoved and twisted their way past the barricades and hammered into the Elven Hunters. Huge, winged shapes appeared out of the smoky haze as Skull Bearers took to the skies to lend their support. The line of defense buckled. Grizzled Rustin Apt went down and was carried from the field. Trewithen and the Home Guard hurried forward to reinforce the sagging defense, but the enemy were too many and the entire Elven front began to collapse.

In desperation, Jerle Shannara put his spurs to Risk and charged into the battle himself. Surrounded by Home Guard, he cut his way into the enemy front, rallying his Elven Hunters to him. Northlanders came at him from all sides. They tried to drag him from his horse, to knock him from the saddle, to do anything to slow him. Behind him, the Elven army, battered and worn, surged to its collective feet and followed in his wake. Battle cries rose out of the shrieks and moans of the injured and dying, and the Elves thrust into the Northlanders yet again. Jerle fought as if he might drive the enemy all the way back to the Northland by himself, his gleaming sword catching light from the torches, ringing out as it hammered down against enemy weapons and armor. Massive Trolls appeared in his path, great faceless monsters with battle-axes. But the king cut his way through them as if they were made of paper, refusing to be stopped, seemingly invincible. He outdistanced even his personal guard, and his soldiers threw themselves at the enemy in an effort to reach him.

Then lightning struck an outcropping on the slope closest to where the battle was being fought, and fiery clots of earth and shards of broken rock exploded skyward and showered across the valley floor. Men covered their heads and cowered at the fury of the explosion, and for just an instant time froze. As the Northlanders hesitated, turned momentarily to statues, Jerle Shannara stood tall in his stirrups and thrust the Sword of

Shannara skyward in defiance of everything. Battle cries rose from the throats of his men, and they charged into the enemy with such ferocity that they overran them completely. Those farthest away and yet able to escape retreated behind the shattered barricades, the fight gone out of them. For a moment they held their ground in the forest of jagged wooden bones and scorched earth. Then sullenly, wearily they withdrew to the Rhenn's east pass.

Massed against the barricades, streaked by rain, dirt, sweat, and blood, Jerle Shannara and the Elves watched them go.

The victory for this day, at least, belonged to them.

CHAPTER

31

AWN BROKE THROUGH skies turned gloomy and gray from the night's heavy rain, and the scorched and rutted floor of the Valley of Rhenn was blackened and steaming in the half-light. Drawn up in their ranks, weapons held ready, eyes peering expectantly through the gloom, the Elves stood waiting for the attack they knew would come. But no sound came from the heavy mist that cloaked the camp of the army of the Warlock Lord within the valley's eastern pass, and nothing moved in the empty, blasted landscape before them. The light brightened with the sun's rise, but the mist refused to thin and still there was no sign of an attack. That the massive army had withdrawn was unthinkable. All that night it had scratched and worried at itself like a stricken animal, the sounds of pain and anguish rising up out of the mist and rain, transcending the fading thunder of the receding storm. All that night the army had tended to its needs and regrouped its forces. It held the eastern pass entire, the floor and the heights alike. It brought forward all of its siege machines, supplies, and equipment, and settled them within the lines of its encampment across the broad mouth of the pass. Its progress might be slow and lumbering, but it remained an inexorable, unstoppable juggernaut.

"They're out there," muttered one-eyed Arn Banda, standing just to Bremen's left, his face twisted in a worrisome scowl.

Jerle Shannara nodded, his tall form fixed and unmoving. "But what are they up to?"

Indeed. Bremen pulled his dark robes closer to his lean body to ward off the dawn chill. They could not see the far end of the valley, their eyes unable to penetrate the gloom, but they could feel the enemy's presence even so. The night had been filled with sound and fury as the Northlanders prepared anew for battle, and it was only in the last hour that they had gone ominously still. The attack this day would take a new form, the old man suspected. The Warlock Lord had been repulsed the previous day with heavy losses and would not be inclined to repeat the experience. Even his power had limits, and sooner or later his hold on those who fought for him would weaken if no gains were made. The Elves must be driven back or defeated soon or the Northlanders would begin to question the Master's invincibility. Once that house of cards began to topple, there would be no stopping it.

There was movement to his right, small and furtive. It was the boy, Allanon. He glanced over surreptitiously. The boy was staring straight ahead, his lean face taut, his eyes fixed on nothing. He was seeing something, though—that much was clear from his expression. He was looking through the mist and gloom to something beyond, those strange eyes penetrating to what was hidden from the rest of them.

The old man followed the direction of the boy's gaze. Mist swirled, a shifting cloak across the whole of the valley's eastern end. "What is it?" he asked softly.

But the boy only shook his head. He could sense it, but not yet identify it. His eyes remained fixed on the haze, his concentration complete. He was good at concentrating, Bremen had learned. In fact, he was better than good. His intensity was frightening. It was not something he had learned while growing or been imbued with as a result of the shock he had suffered in the destruction of Varfleet. It was something he had been born with—like the strange eyes and the razor-sharp mind. The boy was as hard and fixed of purpose as stone, but he possessed an intelligence and a thirst for knowledge that were boundless. Just a week earlier, following the night raid on the Northland camp, he had come to Bremen and asked the old man to teach him to use the Druid magic. Just like that. Teach me how to use it, he had demanded—as if anyone could learn, as if the skill could be taught easily.

"It takes years to master even the smallest part," Bremen had replied, too stunned by the request to refuse it outright.

"Let me try," the boy had insisted.

"But why would you even want to?" The Druid was genuinely perplexed. "Is it revenge you seek? Do you think the magic will gain you that? Why not spend your time learning to use conventional weapons? Or learning to ride? Or studying warfare?"

"No," the boy had replied at once, quick and firm. "I don't want any of that. I don't care about revenge. What I want is to be like you."

And there it was, the whole of it laid bare in a single sentence. The boy wanted to be a Druid. He was drawn to Bremen and Bremen to him because they were more kindred than the old man had suspected. Galaphile's fourth vision was another glimpse of the future, a warning that there were ties that bound the boy to the Druid, a promise of their common destiny. Bremen knew that now. The boy had been sent to him by a fate he did not yet understand. Here, perhaps, was the successor he had looked so long to find. It was strange that he should find him in this way, but not entirely unexpected. There were no laws for the choosing of Druids, and Bremen knew better than to try to start making them now.

So he had given Allanon a few small tricks to master—little things that required mostly concentration and practice. He had thought it would keep the boy occupied for a week or so. But Allanon had mastered all of them in a single day and come back for more. So for each of the ten days leading up to now, Bremen had given him some new bit of Druid lore with which to work, letting him decide for himself which way to take his learning, which use to employ. Caught up in the preparations for the Northland attack, he had barely had time to consider what the boy had accomplished. Yet watching him now, studying him in the faint dawn light as he gazed out across the valley, the old man was struck anew by the obvious depth and immutability of the boy's determination.

"There!" cried Allanon suddenly, his eyes widening in surprise. "They are above us!"

Bremen was so shocked that for a moment he was rendered speechless. A few heads lifted in response to the boy's words, but no one moved. Then Bremen swept his arm skyward, showering the gloom with Druid light in a wide, rainbow arc, and the dark shapes that circled overhead were suddenly revealed. Skull Bearers wheeled sharply away as they were exposed, their wings spread wide as they disappeared back into the haze.

Jerle Shannara was beside the Druid in a moment. "What are they doing?" he demanded.

Bremen's eyes remained fixed on the empty skies, watching the Druid light as it faded away. The gloom returned, fixed and pervasive. There was something wrong with the light, he realized suddenly. The look of it was all wrong.

"They are scouting," he whispered. Then, turning quickly to Allanon, he said, "Look out across the valley again. Carefully this time. Don't try to see anything in particular. Look into the haze and the gray. Watch the shifting of the mists."

The boy did, his face screwed up with the effort. He stared at nothing, his gaze hard and intense. He quit breathing and went still. Then his mouth dropped open, and he gasped in shock.

"Good boy." Bremen put his arm about the youngster's shoulders. "I see them now, too. But your eyes are the sharper." He turned to face the king. "We are under attack by the dark things that serve the Warlock Lord, the creatures he has summoned from the netherworld. He has chosen to use them this day rather than his army. They come at us from across the valley floor. The Skull Bearers spy out the way for them. The Warlock Lord uses his magic to conceal their approach, changing the light, thickening the mists. We do not have much time. Deploy your commanders and have your men stand firm. I will do what I can to counter this."

Jerle Shannara gave the order and his Elven commanders scattered to their units, Cormorant Etrurian to the left flank and an injured, but still mobile, Rustin Apt to the right. Kier Joplin was already in place, the cavalry drawn up behind the foot soldiers in relief. Arn Banda raced away to the south slope to alert the archers positioned there. Prekkian and the Black Watch and Trewithen and most of the Home Guard were being held in reserve.

"Come with me," Bremen said to the king.

They set off for the far right of the front lines, the king, the Druid, Allanon, and Preia Starle. They walked quickly through the startled Elven Hunters to the foremost ranks of the army, and there the Druid wheeled back again.

"Have those closest raise their weapons and hold them steady," the Druid ordered. "Tell them not to be afraid."

The king did so, not bothering to ask why, trusting to the Druid's judgment. He gave the order, and spears, swords, and pikes lifted overhead in response. Bremen narrowed his gaze, clasped his hands before him, and summoned the Druid fire. When it was gathered in a bright blue ball in the cup of his hands, he sent bits and pieces of it spinning away to bounce from weapon to weapon, from iron tip to iron tip, until all had been touched. The bewildered soldiers flinched at the fire's coming, but the king ordered them to stand firm and they did so. When all the weapons of one unit were thus treated, they moved on to the next and repeated the process, passing down the ranks of uneasy soldiers, the Druid imbuing the iron of their weapons with his magic while the king reassured them of the need, warning them at the same time to be ready, advising them that an attack was at hand.

When it came, the Druid magic was in place and the core of the Elven army warded. Dark shapes hurtled out of the gloom, launching themselves at the Elven ranks, howling and screaming like maddened animals, things of jagged tooth and sharpened claw, of bristling dark hair and rough scales. They were creatures of other worlds, of darkness and madness, and no law but that of survival had meaning for them. They fought with ferocity and raw power. Some came on two legs, some on four, and all seemed born of foul nightmares and twisted images.

The Elves were thrown back, giving ground mostly out of fear, terrified by these beasts that sought to rend them limb from limb. Some of the Elves died at once, the fear clogged so deeply in their throats and hearts that they could not move to defend themselves. Some died fighting, ridden down before they could strike a telling blow. But others rallied and were astonished to find that their magic-enhanced weapons would cut through the bodies and limbs of these monstrous attackers, drawing blood and cries of pain. The army reeled in shock from the initial strike, then braced itself to make a stand.

But the monsters broke through on the right flank, following in the wake of a thing so huge that it towered over even the tallest of its fellows. It was armored in leathery skin and pieces of metal fastened about its vital parts, and its massive claws tore apart the men who stood in its path. The grizzled Rustin Apt led a counterattack to drive it back, but he was brushed aside.

Bremen, seeing the danger, rushed to intercept the beast.

In the Druid's absence, Jerle Shannara held the center, watching the crush of monsters push inward. Calling encouragement to his men, casting aside his promise to stay back, he drew forth his sword and moved through the ranks to join the battle, Preia at his side, his guard warding them both. At the forefront of the Elven center, huge wolves crouched before the iron tips of the Elven pikes and swords confronting them, feinting and withdrawing, waiting for an opening. As Jerle Shannara arrived, a dark shadow swooped down out of the haze and shattered the front rank of Elven Hunters. A Skull Bearer lifted away, claws red with blood. Instantly the wolves launched themselves into the line, biting and tearing. But the weapons of the defenders slashed and cut at the attackers, and the Druid magic penetrated their toughened hide. The foremost died in a flurry of blows, and the remainder withdrew, growling and snapping defiantly.

On the right flank, Bremen reached the crush of monsters that had broken through. On seeing the old man, they came at him in a crush. These were two-legged creatures with massive chests and heavily muscled limbs capable of tearing a man in two, heads set deep between neckless shoulders wrapped in folds of skin so tight that only their feral eyes showed. They rushed the Druid with howls of glee, but Bremen sent the Druid fire into them and threw them back. All about, Elven Hunters rallied to the old man's defense, falling on the flanks of the attackers. The monsters whirled and struck back, but the Elven blades and the Druid fire tore into them.

Then the huge creature that had first breached the Elven lines rose before Bremen in challenge, eyes gleaming, leathery body slick with blood. "Old man!" the creature hissed, and fell on him.

Druid fire exploded from Bremen's hands, but the creature was close enough that it fought past the killing flame and seized the old man's wrists. Bremen sheathed his forearms in the fire in an effort to break free, his own strength no match for the other's, but the creature hung on grimly. The clawed hands tightened and the great arms began to force the Druid back. Slowly, Bremen gave ground. All about, the monsters that had broken through surged forward with new confidence. The end was near.

Then Allanon appeared, sprinting out of the gloom, leaping upon the creature's unprotected back, and fastening his hands over the yellow eyes. Howling in fury, he found some reservoir of strength within himself and coupled it with some small part of the magic he had mastered. Uncontrolled, unmanageable, as wild as a storm wind, fire exploded out of his hands in every direction. It erupted with such force that it threw the boy backward to the ground, where he lay stunned. But it also exploded into the attacker's face, tearing into it and leaving it ruined.

The monster released Bremen instantly, flung up its hands in rage and pain, and reeled away. Bremen scrambled to his feet, ignoring the weakness that flooded through him, ignoring his injuries, and sent the Druid fire into the creature once more. This time the fire traveled down the monster's throat to its heart and burned it to ash.

Jerle Shannara, in the meantime, had moved to the army's left flank. Cormorant Etrurian was down, sprawled on the earth, surrounded by his men as they fought to protect him. The king charged into their midst and led a quick, decisive counterattack against the humped creatures that bounded across the Elven front wielding two-edged axes and wickedly serrated knives. Banda had turned his archers' fire directly down the slope, and the longbows raked the mists and the creatures hiding in them.

The Elves recovered Etrurian and carried him away, and Kier Joplin spurred his horsemen forward to help fill the gap. Leaving Joplin in command, the king returned swiftly to the center of his lines, where the fighting had grown fierce once more. Twice he was struck blows that staggered him, but he shrugged them off, scorning both shock and pain, and fought on. Preia was beside him, quick and agile as she slashed and parried with her short sword, protecting his left. Home Guard fought beside them, some dying where they stood as they kept the king and queen safe. The netherworld creatures had penetrated the Elven ranks at every turn, and the Elves were fighting attacks that seemed to come from every direction.

Finally Bremen rallied the left flank of defenders sufficiently that the attackers who had broken through were repelled. Beaten decisively, the survivors turned and ran, their misshapen forms fading back into the mists as if they had never been. The army surged forward against those who battled still at the center, and they, too, gave way. Slowly, steadily, the Elves regained the offensive. The army surged forward, and the netherworld beasts fell back and disappeared.

In the gray, hazy emptiness that remained, the army of the West stared after them in exhausted silence.

THE NORTHLANDERS ATTACKED AGAIN late that afternoon, sending in their regular army once more. By now the mists had burned away, the skies had begun to clear, and the light was strong and pure. The Elves watched the enemy come down the ruined length of the Rhenn from their new defensive position, one still deeper back in the valley, close to its western pass, warded by both high ground and recently constructed stone walls that bristled with sharpened spikes. They were a ragged and bloodied command, close to exhaustion but unafraid. They had survived too much to be frightened anymore. They held their positions calmly, packed close together, for the valley narrowed sharply where they waited. The slopes were so steep at this point that only a small contingent of bowmen and Elven Hunters were required to defend the high ground against an assault. The larger part of the army was arrayed on the valley floor, their compact lines ranging from slope to slope. Cormorant Etrurian had returned, his shoulder and head bandaged, his lean face grim. Together with an even more debilitated Rustin Apt, he commanded the divisions that would confront the heart of the Northland attack. Arn Banda was on the north slope with the bulk of his bowmen. Kier Joplin and the cavalry had been withdrawn to the head of the pass, because there was no longer any room for them to maneuver. The Home Guard and the Black Watch were still being held in reserve.

Just behind the Elven lines, on a promontory that allowed them to overlook the battle, stood Bremen and the boy Allanon.

The king and Preia Starle were astride Risk and Ashes at the center of the Elven defense, Home Guard surrounded them.

Across the plains and down the corridor of the valley, the Northland drums boomed and the thud of hooves and booted feet echoed. Masses of foot soldiers marched to the attack, their numbers so great that they blanketed the entire valley floor with their approach. Behind them came the war machines— siege towers and catapults, hauled forward by teams of horses and sweating men. Cavalry formed a rear guard, lines of horsemen bearing lances and pikes, pennants flying. Massive Rock Trolls bore the Warlock Lord and his minions in carriages and litters draped in black silk and decorated with whitened bones.

It is the end of us, Bremen realized suddenly, the thought coming to him unbidden as he watched the enemy advance. They are too many, we are too weary, the battle has raged too hotly and for too long. It is the end.

He was chilled at the certainty of his premonition, but there was no denying its force. He could feel it pressing down on him, an inexorable certainty, a terrifying truth. He watched the masses of Northlanders roll on, dragging their war machines, filling the scarred, blackened bowl of the Rhenn with their bodies, and they became in his mind's eye a tidal wave that would roll over the Elves and leave them drowned. Two days of battle only had they fought, but already the outcome was inevitable. If the Dwarves had joined them, it might have been different. If any of the Southland cities had mounted an army, it might have changed things. But the Elves stood alone, and there was no one to help them. They were reduced by a third already, and even though the damage inflicted on the enemy was ten times worse, it did not matter. The enemy had the lives to give up; they had the numbers to prevail.

The old man blinked wearily and rubbed at his chin. That it should end like this was almost more than he could bear. Jerle Shannara would not be given a chance to test his sword against the Warlock Lord. He would not even have a chance to confront him. He would die here, in this valley, with the rest of his men. Bremen knew the king well; he knew he would give up his own life before he would save himself. And if Jerle Shannara died, there was no hope for any of them.

Beside him, the boy Allanon shifted uneasily. He could sense the impending disaster as well, the old man thought. The boy had courage; he had shown that much this morning when he had saved Bremen's life. He had used the magic without concern for his own safety, with no thought but one—to save the old man. Bremen shook his ragged gray head. The boy had been left battered and stunned, but he was no less willing now than he had been before. He would do whatever he could in this battle, just like the king. Bremen could tell—the boy was already choosing a place to make his stand.

The Northland army was within two hundred yards when it rumbled to a halt. With a flurry of activity, the sappers and haulers began to bring up the catapults and siege towers. Bremen's throat tightened. The Warlock Lord would not launch a direct attack. Why waste lives when it was not necessary? Instead, he would use the catapults and the bowmen hidden within the towers to rake the Westland defenses with deadly missiles, to thin their numbers further, to wear them down until they were too few to provide any resistance.

The war machines spread out across the width of the valley floor, lined up axle to axle, the slings of the catapults loaded with rocks and chunks of iron, the bays of the towers filled with bowmen at every slit. Within the Elven ranks, no one moved. There was nowhere to go, no place to hide, no better defense to which to withdraw. For if the valley was lost, the Westland was lost as well. The drums throbbed on, beating out their ceaseless cadence, matching the thunder of the wheels on the war machines, reverberating in the old man's chest. He glanced at the darkening sky, but sunset was still an hour away and darkness would come too late to help.

"We have to stop this," he whispered, not meaning to speak, the words just slipping out.

Allanon looked up at him wordlessly and waited. Those strange eyes fixed on him and would not move away. Bremen held his gaze. "How?" asked the boy softly.

And suddenly Bremen knew. He knew it from the eyes, from the words the boy spoke, and from the whisper of inspiration that rose suddenly within. It came to him in a moment of terrifying insight, born of his own despair and fading hope.

"There is a way," he said quickly, anxiously. The creases in his aging face deepened. "But I need your help. I lack the strength alone." He paused. "It will be dangerous for you."

The boy nodded. "I am not afraid."

"You may die. We may both die."

"Tell me what to do."

Bremen turned toward the line of siege machines and placed the boy in front of him. "Listen carefully, then. You must give yourself over to me, Allanon. Do not fight against anything you feel. You will become a conduit for me, for my magic, the magic I possess but lack sufficient strength to wield. I shall wield it through you. I shall draw my strength from you."

The boy did not look at him. "You will let your magic feed on me?" he asked softly, almost reverently.

"Yes." Bremen bent close. "I will ward you with every protection I have. If you die, I will die with you. It is all I can offer."

"It is enough," the boy replied, his eyes still turned away. "Do what you must, Bremen. But do it now, quickly, while there is still time."

The Northland army was massed before them, fronted by the huge war machines, bristling with weapons at every turn. Dust lifted from the burned, parched valley floor, filling the air with grit that curtained off the world beyond so thoroughly that it might have ceased to exist. Light reflected from metal blades and points, pennants flew in bright colors, and the sounds that rose from the throats of the attackers were thick with the expectation of victory.

Together, the Druid and the boy faced into them, into the men and animals, the machines, the sound and movement, standing still and alone on the promontory. No one saw them, or if they did, paid them any attention. Even the Elves took no notice, their eyes on the army before them.

Bremen took a deep breath and placed his hands on Allanon's slender shoulders. "Clasp your hands and point them at the towers and the catapults." His throat tightened. "Be strong, Allanon."

The boy's hands clasped together, the fingers laced, and the thin arms lifted and pointed toward the Northland army. Bremen stood just behind him, his hands still, his eyes closed. Within, he summoned the Druid fire. It sparked and came to life. He must be careful of its use, he reminded himself. The balance of what was needed and what he could afford to give was a delicate one, and he must be careful not to upset it. An error either way, and there would be no help for either of them.

On the battlefield, the arms of the catapults were being drawn back and the archers in the towers were readying their bows.

Bremen's eyes opened anew, and they were as white as snow.

Below, as if warned by a premonition, Jerle Shannara turned suddenly to look back at him.

Abruptly the Druid fire raced down Bremen's arms and into Allanon's body, then lanced from the boy's clenched fists over the heads of the waiting Elven army, over the torn, rutted, scorched grasslands, and into the midst of the enemy war machines two hundred yards away. It struck the towers first, engulfing them so completely that they were ablaze before anyone could do much more than blink. It jumped from there to the catapults, incinerating their handlers, snapping their ropes, and warping their metal parts. It moved as if a living thing, choosing first one target and then the next, the fire bright blue and so brilliant that the men of both armies were forced to shield their eyes from its glare. Up and down the front ranks of the Northland army it raced, swallowing everything and everyone. In moments, the flames were rising hundreds of feet into the air, soaring skyward in monstrous leaps, clouds of smoke billowing after.

Shrieks and cries rose from the Northland juggernaut as the fire tore through it. But within the ranks of the watching Elven army there was only stunned silence.

Bremen felt an ebbing of his magic, a wilting of his fire, but within the boy Allanon there was power still. Allanon seemed to grow even stronger, his thin arms stretched forth, his hands lifting. Bremen could feel the slender body shake with the force of the boy's determination. Still the fire arced from his hands, leaping beyond the war machines into the midst of the astonished Northland army, carving a deadly, fiery path. *Enough!* thought Bremen, sensing a dangerous tilt in the balance of things. But he could not break the joining between the boy and himself; he could not slow the torrent of his magic. The boy was stronger than he was now, and it was the old man who was being drained.

Back fell the Northlanders in the face of this new onslaught, not merely in retreat, but routed completely, their courage shattered. Even the Rock Trolls backed away, moving swiftly from the conflagration that consumed their fellows for the cover of the valley slopes and the pass beyond. Even for them, this day's battle was finished.

Then finally Allanon's strength failed, and the Druid fire that spurted from his clenched hands died away. He gasped audibly and sagged against Bremen, who was himself barely able to stand. But the old man caught and held the boy close, waiting patiently for the pulse of their bodies to steady and their heartbeats to slow. Like scarecrows, they clung to each other, whispering words of reassurance, staring out across the raging inferno that consumed the Northland war machines and lit the backs of the retreating enemy with fingers the color of blood.

West, the sun sank below the horizon, and night crept cautiously from hiding to cloak the dead.

IN THE AFTERMATH of the destruction of the Northland war machines, and with darkness spreading across the whole of the Four Lands and the fires at the center of the Rhenn beginning to burn down, Jerle Shannara approached Bremen. The old man was sitting on the promontory with Allanon, eating his dinner.

It was quiet now, the Northland army withdrawn into the gap at the eastern flat, the Elves still maintaining their lines across the western narrows. Meals were being consumed throughout the ranks of the defenders, the Elven Hunters eating in shifts to guard against any surprise assault. Cook fires burned at the rear of the encampment, and the smell of food wafted on the evening air.

The old man stood as the king came up to him, seeing in the other's eyes a look he did not recognize. The king greeted them both, then asked Bremen to walk alone with him. The boy went back to his meal without comment. Together, the Druid and the king moved off into the shadows.

When they were far enough away from everyone that they could not be heard, the king turned to the old man. "I need you to do something," he said quietly. "I need you to use your magic to mark the Elves in a way that will allow them to recognize each other in the dark in a battle with the Northlanders, so that they will not kill each other by mistake. Can you do that?"

Bremen considered the question for a moment, then nodded slowly. "What are you going to do?"

The king was worn and haggard, but there was a cold determination in his eyes and a harshness to his features. "I intend to attack—now, tonight, before they can regroup."

The old man stared at him speechlessly.

The king's mouth tightened. "This morning my Trackers brought word of a Northland flanking movement. They have sent separate armies—smaller than the one we face, but still sizeable—both north and south of the Rhenn to get behind us. They must have sent them at least a week ago, given their present positions. Their progress is slow, but they are closing in on us. In another few days, they will cut us off from Arborlon. If that happens, we are finished."

He looked off into the dark, as if searching for what to say next. "They are too many, Bremen. We knew that from the start. Our only advantage is our defensive position. If that is taken from us, we have nothing left." His eyes shifted back to the old man. "I have sent Prekkian and the Black Watch to give warning to Vree Erreden and the Council and to prepare a defense of the city. But our only real hope is if I do what you have told me I must—confront the Warlock Lord and destroy him. To do that, I must first scatter the Northland army. I will never have a better chance to do so than now. The Northlanders are disorganized and weary. The destruction of their war machines has unnerved them. The Druid magic has left them frightened. This is the time to strike."

Bremen took a long time to consider his reply. Then at last he nodded slowly. "Perhaps you are right."

"If we attack them now, we will catch them unprepared. If we strike hard enough, we might be able to break through to where the Warlock Lord hides himself. The confusion of a nighttime attack will aid us, but only if we can distinguish ourselves from our enemy."

The Druid sighed. "If I mark the Elves to make them recognizable to each other, I provide the enemy with a way to recognize them as well."

"We cannot help that." The king's voice was steady. "It will take the Northlanders a while before they realize what the marks mean. By then, we will have won or lost the battle in any case."

Bremen nodded without speaking. It was a bold tactic, one that might doom the Elves, that might result in their complete destruction. But the need for such a tactic was at once apparent, and the Druid saw in this king the one man who might be able to employ it successfully. For the Elves would follow Jerle Shannara anywhere, and faith in their leader was what would sustain them best.

"But I am afraid," the king whispered suddenly, bending close, "that I will not be able to invoke the power of the Sword when it is needed." He paused, his eyes fixed and staring. "What if it will not respond to me? What will I do?"

The Druid reached out, took the king's hands in his own, and clasped them tightly. "The magic will not fail you, Jerle Shannara," he replied softly. "You are too strong of heart for that, too fixed of purpose, too much the king your people need. The magic will appear when you summon it, for that is your destiny." His smile was bleak. "You must believe that."

The king took a deep breath. "Come with me," he asked.

The old man nodded. "I will come."

* * *

NORTH FROM THE RHENN, where clouds layered the open grasslands with shadows and the plains stretched away empty and silent, Kinson Ravenlock slipped noiselessly from the clamor and
sprawl of the Northland camp and worked his way back the
way he had come. It took him the better part of an hour, keeping to the ravines and dry riverbeds, staying off the high, open
flats. He went swiftly, anxious to reach those who waited,
thinking that perhaps they had not come too late after all.

More than ten days had passed since Mareth and he had set
out from the Eastland with what remained of the Dwarf army.
The Dwarves were still almost four thousand strong, and they
had made good time. They had chosen an unusual route, however. Their passage had taken them north across the Plains of
Rabb, through the Jannisson, and onto the Streleheim, where
they had crossed in the shadow of the old growth that
shrouded doomed Paranor. The decision to come this way had
been debated long and hard by Raybur and the Dwarf Elders,
though no longer than the decision on whether the Dwarves
should come at all. As to the latter, Kinson had been forceful
in presenting Bremen's arguments, and Risca was firmly on his
side. Once Raybur was persuaded, the matter was settled.
Choosing their route of travel was less soul-wrenching, but
equally troubling. Risca was convinced they would have a better
chance of approaching unseen if they came down from the
north through enemy country—the Northland army having
moved into the Westland by now to besiege the Elves at the
Rhenn, so that their scouts would be looking for intervention to
come from the east or south if it was to come at all. In the end,
his argument had prevailed.

The bulk of the Dwarf army had taken up a position north
half a day at the edge of the Dragon's Teeth. Risca, Kinson,
Mareth, and two hundred more had come on ahead to take
measure of the situation. With the approach of sunset, Kinson
Ravenlock had gone on alone for a closer look.

Now, barely three hours after leaving, the Borderman
emerged from the shadows to rejoin his companions.

"There was an attack earlier this day," he advised breathlessly. He had run much of the way back, anxious to impart his news. "It failed. The Northland war machines all lie burned in the Valley of Rhenn. But more are being built. The enemy encamps at the valley's eastern mouth. It is a huge force, but it looks disorganized. Everyone is milling about, and there is no sign of the dark things. Even the Skull Bearers do not fly this night."

"Did you get through to the Elves?" Risca asked quickly. "Did you see Bremen or Tay?"

The Borderman took a long drink from the aleskin Mareth offered him and wiped at his mouth. "No. The valley is blocked. I could have gotten through, but I decided not to chance it. I decided to come back for you instead."

The two men looked at each other, then out across the plains. "There are a lot of men dead back there," the Borderman said softly. "Too many, if even a tenth of them are Elves."

Risca nodded. "I'll send word to Raybur to bring the army forward at first light. He can choose his own ground from which to attack." His bluff face was taut, and his eyes shone. "In the meantime, we are supposed to wait here for his arrival."

The Borderman and the girl looked at each other and shook their heads slowly.

"I'm not waiting," Kinson Ravenlock declared.

"Nor I," said Mareth.

The Dwarf hefted his battle-axe. "I didn't think so. Looks like Raybur will just have to catch up with us, won't he? Let's get going."

CHAPTER

32

I T WAS THREE HOURS after sunset and nearing midnight
when Jerle Shannara led the Elves into their final battle. He left behind the sick and wounded and a token
force to act as protectors and rear guard and took with
him only those who were whole. Elven Hunters, Home Guard,
bowmen, and others afoot numbered just over two thousand.
Cavalry numbered about four hundred. He assembled them on
the flat at the head of the valley, close to where the wreckage
of the Northland war machines still smoldered, and unit by unit
walked among them and explained what he intended.

As he did so, Bremen passed through their ranks as well,
carrying with him a small pot of glowing light. The light was
bluish in color, giving off a phosphorescent glow that shone
most brightly in darkness. It seemed to be neither paste nor liquid, but simply glowing air. It was formed mostly of Druid
magic, but of other substances as well, though nothing anyone
could identify. Bremen's voice was low and reassuring as he approached each man with the pot. One by one, he marked their
shoulders with the light, using a frayed stick to dip into the
glow, carrying just a little of the mysterious substance to streak
each soldier's clothing.

When they started forward into the darkness, into the heart
of the Rhenn, each man wore strips of cloth tied over the bright
markings to hide his coming from the enemy. Select members
of the Home Guard went first, fanning out in front of the attack
force, some climbing the slopes to the valley's ridges and then

slipping forward to secure the heights that warded the east pass. When they had been given sufficient lead time, Jerle Shannara took the main body of the army forward. Commanding from the center with Preia Starle and Bremen at his side, he placed Cormorant Etrurian on his left flank and Rustin Apt on his right. Arrayed across the width of the advance, just back of the front rank of Elven Hunters, were Arn Banda's bowmen. Behind them came more Elven Hunters, and much farther back, held in reserve for when the foot soldiers were fully engaged, walked the Elven horse under Kier Joplin.

The king's strategy was simple. The Elves were to advance as close to the Northland lines as possible without being seen and then strike out of the darkness, taking advantage of surprise and confusion to overrun the perimeter, hoping their momentum would carry them into the heart of the enemy camp and the sanctuary of the Warlock Lord. There Jerle Shannara would bring the rebel Druid to bay and destroy him. That was the whole of it. There were so many things that could go wrong with this plan that it wasn't worth trying to consider them all. Timing and surprise were everything. Determination and heart would make the difference. If the Elves were to lose control of the former or not muster enough of the latter, they would be destroyed.

But on this night, warded by Druid magic and armored by stubborn faith, the Elves gave themselves over to their king and to fate. Their doubts and fears dissipated with the first step taken, with the realization that the attack was under way and there was no turning back, and with an overwhelming rush of expectation that supplanted all else. They went swiftly down the valley corridor, noiseless in the way that only Elves could be, sharp eyes picking out the obstacles that lay in their path so that they could avoid them, ears pricked to the warning sounds of danger. There was no light to guide them, the skies clouded once more, the air thick with lingering smoke from the afternoon's conflagration. Ahead, the watch fires of the enemy provided a series of lonely beacons, small pinpricks of yellow that flickered in the gloom.

Jerle Shannara gave no thought to failure as he led the way, the Sword of Shannara strapped across his back. He did not think of anything but the task at hand, closing off all distractions, shelving for another time considerations that did not bear on this night's work. Preia walked at one elbow and Bremen at the other, and in their presence the King of the Elves felt oddly invincible. It was not that he couldn't die; he would never presume immortality. But it seemed to him in those desperate moments that failure was unthinkable. There was strength surrounding him, yet dependency as well. An odd mix, but familiar to a king. The Elves would give their lives for him, but he must be ready to give up his for them as well. Only in the setting and maintaining of that balance could any of them hope to survive, to persevere, to achieve the victory they sought.

The king's eyes shifted to the shadows on the heights, searching for sentries who might give the alarm. None appeared. The Home Guard had dispatched them without being discovered, it seemed. Behind, far back in the valley's cradle, he could hear the faint jingle of traces and the creak of leather as the cavalry followed them in. Ahead, the flames of the watch fires grew distinguishable, and beyond their perimeter, the camp of the Northland army. The size of the camp seemed immense, a sprawling maze of tents and stores and men, a jumble of life, like a small city. There were so many of them still, the king thought. The Elven attack would have to be certain and quick.

The Westlanders were within fifty yards of the camp when he brought them to a halt, there to crouch just beyond the revealing light of the watch fires. Sentries stood staring off into the night, some glancing idly over their shoulders at what was taking place in the camp. They showed no concern for what might lie within the darkness; they evidenced no expectation of an attack. Jerle Shannara felt a hot surge of satisfaction in his chest. He had guessed right, it seemed. He thought suddenly of all he had endured to reach this point, and he found himself wishing that Tay Trefenwyd were there with him. Together, they could have overcome anything. It would never be the same for him again without Tay, he thought. Never.

With a gesture, he sent word through the Elven ranks to stand ready. Then Banda brought his bowmen to their feet, arrows notched in the strings of longbows. The king lifted his sword, and the arrows flew skyward in a deadly hail. By the time the arrows fell, finding their unsuspecting targets, the Elves were hurtling forward in attack.

They were swift and deadly in their coming. In seconds, they had crossed the open ground and were through the camp perimeter. The sentries all lay dead, felled by arrows or spears. Northlanders who were crouched about the cooking fires leaped to their feet as the Elves swept into them, reaching for their weapons, crying out in warning. But the Elves were among them so quickly that most were killed before they could defend themselves. Jerle Shannara led the way, cutting a path through the outer lines almost at will, his Home Guard flocking to his side. Preia went with him, a steady presence at his shoulder. Bremen fell behind, too old and slow to keep up, calling after the king to go on, not to wait. On the heights, the enemy not already dispatched were engaged in hand-to-hand combat with the Home Guard who had slipped among them while they slept. In the smoky darkness, only the Elves could recognize each other, the Druid markings agleam on their shoulders. Everywhere, the enemy camp was in turmoil.

Then abruptly the king found himself in the midst of a company of newly awakened Rock Trolls, the huge creatures surging upward from their blankets in response to the alarm, their armor scattered about them, but their weapons already in hand. Jerle Shannara broke for the center of the camp, trying to avoid being slowed, but several of the Trolls managed to get in front of him, and he was forced to stand and fight. He closed with the nearest, swinging the Sword of Shannara in a bright arc, and the Troll went down. Others fought to reach the king, recognizing him now, calling out in their guttural voices to their fellows. But Home Guard threw themselves into the path of the counterattack, swarming over the Trolls from every direction to bear them to the earth and certain death.

From out of the darkness behind him, the king heard Kier Joplin's horns sound the charge, and the Elven cavalry thundered into battle. An explosion rocked the encampment, and a pillar of fire lifted skyward. In its ragged glare, the king caught sight of Bremen, standing in the midst of fleeing Gnomes and lesser Trolls, a thin, ragged figure with his skinny arms stretched wide before him and the boy Allanon at his side.

Ahead, the dark, skull-draped tents of the Warlock Lord and his minions came into view. A surge of excitement rushed through Jerle Shannara, and he redoubled his efforts to break through the enemy soldiers confronting him. Then something monstrous rose out of the night to one side, and he was forced to turn and face it. It had the look of a wolf, but its head was vaguely human behind jaws lined with rows of jagged teeth. It tore at the Elves that sought to reach it, flinging them away. It reached for Preia Starle, but she sidestepped its lunge and left her sword buried in its neck. The beast came on, wounded, but unslowed, jaws snapping. Jerle Shannara was bowled over, unable to avoid its rush, and he fought in vain to escape from between its legs as his Elven Hunters hacked desperately at it. Then, when the creature rose on its hind legs to tear at him, he jammed the Sword of Shannara deep into its chest and through to its heart, and the beast collapsed in a lifeless heap.

The king scrambled to his feet. "The tents!" he cried to every Elf within hearing distance, and with Preia at his side he charged ahead.

BEYOND THE MOUTH of the Rhenn, on the camp's northern perimeter, Kinson, Mareth, and Risca and the Dwarves were working their way toward the eastern heights in an effort to find an opening through the Northland lines. When the Elven attack began, they froze, uncertain what was happening. Shouts and screams rose out of the Northland camp, and everything quickly turned to chaos. Instantly, the battle-tested Dwarves formed a defensive wedge fronting the stricken camp and watched as the Northlanders closest to the perimeter rose swiftly from their sleep, snatched up their weapons, and began to look about wildly.

"What's happening?" Mareth hissed in Kinson Ravenlock's ear.

Then they heard the Elven battle cry ring out, lifting above the clamor, one voice after another taking it up.

"The Elves are attacking!" exclaimed Risca in wonder.

Arrows flew into the camp from the heights, raking the startled soldiers clustered there. Within the mouth of the valley, at the forefront of the Northland perimeter, weapons clashed sharply. The Dwarves stood transfixed as the battle was joined, listening as the sounds heightened and then drew closer. The Elves had penetrated the Northland defenses and were plunging directly into the heart of the enemy camp.

"What should we do?" Kinson asked of no one in particular, staring through the darkness to where knots of enemy soldiers appeared and faded in the smoky haze of the watch fires.

Directly in front of them, a Skull Bearer took flight, rising like a specter, wings spread wide, claws flexing. Banking away from the Dwarves, the winged hunter streaked east onto the plains. An instant later, another followed.

"They're fleeing!" Mareth burst out in disbelief.

Then something at the camp's very center exploded skyward in a pillar of flame, rising into the darkness like a fiery spear thrust at the clouds by some unseen hand. It hung against the black for long moments, then disappeared into smoke.

Risca hefted his great battle-axe and looked at the others. "I've seen enough. The Elves need us. Let's not keep them waiting."

The command moved forward, Risca in the lead, Kinson and Mareth to either side. The Dwarves spread out in attack formation. Risca took them slightly east of the heights, wary of the bowmen hiding there, anxious to avoid being mistaken for Northlanders. They veered left, angling toward the rear of the encampment where the Gnome horsemen were already struggling to mount and ride. When they were just below the picket lines, Risca gave the Dwarf battle cry and led his Hunters in.

Almost at once, they were set upon. Whether it was by chance or as a result of the defenders' quick reaction, the Dwarves found themselves instantly surrounded by an entire company of Rock Trolls, all fully armored and bearing pikes. Two dozen Dwarves died in the first minute of fighting, unable to stand against the more powerful Trolls. Risca rallied those closest, called up the Druid fire, and burned a path through the

Northlanders, forcing them to fall back. A counterattack ensued, spearheaded by a handful of the huge wolves that Brona
had summoned from the Black Oaks. Again the Dwarves were
forced back, and this time their charge broke apart at its center.

In the confusion, Kinson and Mareth were separated from
Risca. The Druid went left toward the rear of the Northland
camp, while the Borderman and the girl turned right, following
in the wake of a knot of Dwarves who were intent on linking
up with the Elves already fighting at the camp's center. Risca,
caught up in the fury of the battle, did not immediately miss
them, his mind on something else entirely. The intensity of the
Northland defense here, at the rear of the encampment, when
the main thrust of the Elven attack was coming from the front,
convinced him that the Warlock Lord was close at hand. Having seen two of the Skull Bearers take flight already, he suspected that the attack was proving to be more devastating than
the Elves realized and that Brona was preparing an escape. With
Rock Trolls and netherworld creatures to defend him, he would
slip from the camp with his winged hunters and retreat north
once more. Northlanders were already racing away into the
night, fleeing the camp like snakes driven from their nest.
Gnomes and lesser Trolls were abandoning the struggle, leaving
others to fight in their place. The cavalry was scattering in every direction, leaderless and panicked. The back of the Northland army was broken, and it did not require much insight to
deduce that its leaders—for whom the passing of time meant
nothing—intended to take refuge once more in their safehold
beyond the Knife Edge, there to regroup and plan a new
invasion.

But Risca had lived through too much to let that happen.
The Druid was determined to stop them here.

With a dozen of his Dwarves in tow, he fought his way
toward the twenty or so Gnome horsemen still held in check by
one of the Skull Bearers. Raging among them, a savage wraith
with glowing eyes and billowing cloak, the Skull Bearer was
forming the terrified Gnome riders into lines clearly intended to
act as a flanking guard. Beyond, where the night was blackest
and the camp unlit, there was movement amid the black silk

tents. Horses shrilled as they were whipped into place, and huge darkened carriages rolled through the gloom and smoke on their way to the plains.

Risca, his battle-axe in hand and the Druid fire hot within his breast, moved to intercept them.

JERLE SHANNARA FOUGHT his way forward with unrelenting ferocity. He was at the forefront of the Elven attack still, deep now within the Northland camp, leading everyone as they closed on the dark, whispery canopy of the Warlock Lord's tent. He had entered a black pool of ground, a place where no light penetrated. The watch fires he had left behind at the perimeter of the camp cast strange shadows in the deepening gloom, but there was little to see by and less to trust. The creatures that sought to stop him grew quickly indistinguishable, some of them Trolls and Gnomes, some of them other beings entirely. He drove into them without regard for their identity, with no concern for anything but breaking past. Preia fought at his side, as hard and ferocious as he was. The Home Guard came after, trying vainly to keep up. All about, the Northland camp was chaotic with sound and movement.

Ahead, somewhere in the darkness, close by the darkened tents, there was the sound of carriages and wagons rolling, of traces creaking, of whips snapping, of horses crying out in response to the demands of their handlers.

Then Preia went down, knocked from her feet by a dark shape that bounded out of the blackness on all fours. Jaws widened and teeth gleamed as a huge, bristling body fell upon the queen. Jerle whirled to defend her, but he was struck at the same time by another of the shapes, caught off guard and sent sprawling. Others appeared, wolves who charged out of the gloom, tearing into the Elves who sought to penetrate this forbidden ground. They came in such numbers that for a moment it seemed they would prove unstoppable. Preia had disappeared in a tangle of bodies. Jerle Shannara was fighting from his back and knees, swinging the Sword at everything that came close, struggling to regain his feet.

"Shannara! Shannara!" came the rallying cry, as Elven Hunters and Home Guard raced to give aid.

Druid fire erupted then, scorching the nearest of the wolves in midleap, and Bremen entered the fray, his robes in tatters, his eyes gleaming like those of the creatures he sought to dispatch. The wolves drew back in fear, teeth bared. Another disappeared in blue flame, and the rest scattered, howling with rage and terror. The king scrambled to his feet, wheeling in search of Preia. But she was already standing beside him, her face streaked with sweat and twisted with pain, blood all across one arm where the tough leather clothing and soft flesh had been ripped to the bone. She was binding up the wound, but her face was pale and stricken.

"Go on!" she screamed at him. "Don't wait! I'm coming!"

He hesitated only a moment, then raced ahead once more, a handful of the Home Guard following. The wolves having been the last of creatures set at guard over the Warlock Lord, the way lay open. Ahead the ground was a black hole, but Jerle Shannara did not slow. Only one thing mattered—that he find the enemy leader and bring him to bay. He crossed the unlit ground in a dead run, heedless of what he might be rushing into, no longer caring what waited, so caught up in his determination to bring this battle to an end that he would have faced anything.

From somewhere behind, he heard Bremen shout in warning, calling after him futilely, the old man so worn from the battle, so drained of strength by his use of the magic, that he could not follow.

Jerle Shannara reached the tent of the Warlock Lord on the fly, his sword sweeping down, tearing through the dark fabric, sending the necklace of skulls and bones that draped the stanchions clattering away into the night. The tent wall shredded beneath his blade, and a cold, dry wind brushed at his face as he charged through the opening.

The interior was so black he couldn't see. Blind to what might be waiting, fighting to protect himself, he swung the Sword of Shannara in a wide arc, cutting out at everything within reach. But his blade whistled uselessly through the air. He launched himself across the darkness to the tent's far side and sliced the concealing fabric apart, opening it to the night. Smoke and sound rushed in, and the coldness gave way to summer's warmth and the feel of sweat against his skin.

Hurriedly he wheeled back, dropping into a protective crouch.

But the tent was empty.

AT THAT SAME MOMENT, Risca and his Dwarves attacked what remained of the Gnome riders. The Skull Bearer who was holding the last few in check fell back before the onslaught of Risca's Druid fire, and the terrified Gnomes bolted into the night. For an instant no one opposed the Dwarves. Then the heavy rumble of ironbound wheels sounded, and a caravan of dark-cloaked riders and shuttered carriages approached from out of the besieged camp. Risca threw himself into the caravan's path and launched the Druid fire at the lead animals, causing them to shy and rear and bring the carriages to a sudden, uncertain halt.

Almost immediately a crush of beasts swarmed out from behind the lurching transports and screaming horses, charging from where they had been trailing after, a vicious, enraged collection of netherworld monsters. The attack was ferocious, and it bore back Risca and the Dwarves in spite of their efforts to contain it. Teeth and claws tore and great muscled limbs hammered at the Eastlanders. The Dwarves fought with grim determination, rallying about their leader. Risca sent wave after wave of Druid fire into the attackers, fighting simply for space in which to stand.

By now the cloaked drivers were turning their carriages aside and moving off in another direction, lashing their horses, screaming with frustration. Risca fought to reach them, to bring the caravan to a stop once more. But the netherworld creatures were everywhere, and he could not bring the Druid fire to bear. Their superior numbers were beginning to tell. One by one, Risca's companions were dropping away, dying where they stood.

Then suddenly the attackers scattered, and waves of panic-stricken Northlanders surged out of the killing ground, streaming past the Dwarves on their way to the darkened plains. The whole of the Northland army seemed to be in flight, as if each soldier had decided at the same moment that he had endured enough and that all that was left to him was to try to escape. Gnomes and Trolls swarmed out of the fiery battlefield and raced into the night. The tide was massive and unstoppable, and for a few long moments Risca and his companions disappeared in its wake.

When the rush slowed, Risca looked about. He was alone on the eastern perimeter of the disintegrating camp. The Dwarves who had fought at his side were all dead. The netherworld beasts had disappeared, fleeing with the Northlanders. The fighting in the camp continued unabated as the Elves pressed ahead against those of the enemy who had not broken, the two sides engaged in a desperate, furious struggle.

North, where the Streleheim stretched away under leaden skies, the Warlock Lord's caravan was beginning to draw away.

A red haze clouded the Druid's vision, and a feeling of helplessness washed through him. He wheeled about in search of a horse, but there were none at hand. The fleeing Northlanders gave him a wide berth, catching sight of the flicker of Druid fire at the tips of his right hand and the gleam of his battle-axe in his left. Blood streaked his face, and his eyes glittered with cold rage.

In the distance, the caravan faded into the night.

CHAPTER

33

BY DAWN the Northland army had been routed, and the Elves were riding in pursuit of the Warlock Lord. The battle had raged on through most of the night, evolving from a single engagement into dozens of small, hard-fought clashes. While some of the Northlanders had fled early, many had remained. The more tightly knit and better-disciplined units had held their ground to the end. The fighting had been bitter and desperate, and no quarter had been given.

When it was finished, the Northland army was scattered in all directions. The number of dead on both sides was staggering. The Elves had lost almost half of those who had gone into battle that night with Jerle Shannara. Rustin Apt was dead at the mouth of the pass and his command decimated. One-eyed Arn Banda was dead on the heights. Cormorant Etrurian had sustained so severe a wound that he would lose his arm. Only Kier Joplin of the Elven horse and Trewithen of the Home Guard remained whole, and between them they could muster only eight hundred men who were fit enough to go on.

It was a chill, crisp day, a clear marker for the end of summer and the beginning of autumn. The sun rose hazy and pale against the ragged peaks of the Dragon's Teeth just east of where Jerle Shannara's command rode, and the grasslands were patchy with low banks of fog. There was frost on the ground, silver and damp in the growing light, and the breath of the men and horses clouded the air. Hawks wheeled through the sky, rising and falling on the wind, silent spectators to the hunt taking place below.

Jerle Shannara never hesitated in taking up the pursuit of Brona. He could not do otherwise, he believed. He was beyond trepidation or lack of resolve now, beyond fatigue and hunger, beyond quitting. He was bloodied and cut from the night's fighting, but he felt no pain. He wore the Sword of Shannara strapped to his back and no longer gave thought to whether the magic would respond to his summons. The time for deliberation was long since past, and all that remained was a shouldering of the responsibility given to him. Doubts and fears lingered at the back of his mind, but the steady passing of the miles swept them further from his consciousness. He could feel only the rush of his blood, the pounding of his heart, and the strength of his determination.

Preia Starle went with him, although she was so badly hurt that she needed to be helped into the saddle. Her arm was wrapped and bound and the bleeding had slowed, but her face was pale and drawn and her breathing ragged. Yet she would not stay behind when Jerle asked her to do so. She was strong enough to ride, she insisted, and she would. She would see the end of this business as she had seen the beginning—at his side.

Bremen and the boy Allanon came, too, though Bremen was as weakened now as Preia, his extended use of the Druid magic having left him so spent that he had little left to give. He had not said this, but it was apparent to anyone with eyes and common sense. Yet he had promised he would be there for the king when it came time to use the Sword, and he would not forsake his promise now.

Mareth, Kinson Ravenlock, and Risca accompanied them as well, better rested and stronger. For them, the battle lay ahead, and conscious of the exhaustion that threatened the others they had quietly vowed among themselves to give what protection they could. Behind them rode Kier Joplin with his cavalry and Trewithen with his Home Guard, together with a handful of the Dwarves who had come south with Risca. In all, they numbered less than nine hundred. Whether they were enough to bring the Warlock Lord to bay was not something they cared to consider too closely. No one knew how many had fled with the rebel Druid or how many more had rejoined him since. Certainly there would be Skull Bearers and netherworld beasts and wolves from the Black Oaks and Rock Trolls and others from the lands north and east. If even a small part of the army that had besieged the Rhenn had been reassembled, the Elves would be in trouble.

Yet somewhere farther north, at the edge of the high plains, Raybur was advancing with four thousand Dwarves. If the Elves could just manage to drive the Warlock Lord that way, they would have a chance.

The sun rose higher in a sky that was a strange mix of gray and silver, and the light chased back the nighttime shadows and the chill. But the mist refused to give way, clinging tenaciously to the flats, folding in on itself about the broad swales and shallow ravines that crisscrossed the plains. Pools of it collected between stretches of high ground, leaving the grasslands looking vaguely swamplike. Nothing moved in the distance, the horizon empty and still. Overhead, the hawks had disappeared. Jerle Shannara's command traveled in tight-lipped silence, maintaining a steady, even pace, keeping close watch over the land about.

It was nearing midafternoon when they finally caught up with the Warlock Lord. There had been reason to believe they were closing the gap since midday, when they had begun to find abandoned carriages and wagons that had broken down during the enemy flight. An hour earlier they had cut across their quarry's trail, a rutted mass of tracks from wheels, animals, and men that made it difficult even for the Trackers to determine how many traveled with the Warlock Lord. Preia had climbed down to look—against the king's wishes—and reported in her quiet, assured way that there were less than a thousand.

Now, as the Elven command drew to a halt on a rise several hundred yards south from where the remnant of the Northland army had been forced to make its stand, they were able to see for themselves that the queen's guess had been right. The dark carriages and wagons were drawn up in the shadow of a series of hills that rose east in stepping-stone fashion toward the Dragon's Teeth. The creatures of the Warlock Lord were backed against them—Rock Trolls and other things human; nether-world creatures cloaked and hooded; gray wolves that crouched and circled at the edges of the mist; and Skull Bearers, some soaring like great dark birds above the assemblage.

Beyond, arrayed across the high ground in battle formation, blocking any path north, were the Dwarves under Raybur. The Warlock Lord had been stopped in his flight.

Yet the mist was deceiving, its shadowy images illusory. Many of the creatures, hunkered down atop the flat, their bod-ies wrapped in shrouds of swirling gray, were dead. They lay at peculiar angles, crumpled against rocks and impaled on weap-ons. Arms and legs crooked skyward like broken sticks. Dark outlines shimmered in the haze, the burnt, scorched leavings of those dead who had come from the netherworld. A battle had been fought already this day. The rebel Druid and his fol-lowers had come upon the Eastlanders and attempted to break through their lines. But the attempt had failed. The Dwarves had repelled them. So the Warlock Lord had collected what was left of his army and withdrawn to his present position. The Dwarves were poised for another strike. Both sides were waiting.

Jerle Shannara stared. Waiting for what?

Recognition came swiftly. For me, he thought. For the Sword of Shannara.

He realized then that it would all end here, on this lonely stretch of the Streleheim, on this already bloodied ground. He would face the Warlock Lord in combat, and one or the other of them would be killed. It had been prophesied by a distant, perverse fate that had long ago laid the matter to rest.

He looked at the others, surprised at how calm he felt. "We have him trapped. He cannot escape. The Dwarves have denied him flight into the deep Northland, and now he must face us."

Risca hefted his battle-axe. "Let's not keep him waiting."

"One moment." It was Bremen, old and battered almost be-yond recognition in the failing afternoon light, a worn-out stick man with nothing left to lean on but ragged determination. "He is waiting for us, indeed. He wants us to come. That should give us pause."

The Dwarf's face was hard, his eyes set. "He has no choice but to wait. What troubles you, Bremen?"

"Think, Risca. He seeks to do battle with us because if he wins he might yet escape." The old man's eyes traveled from face to face. "If he destroys us all, all those who remain of the Druids, and the King of the Elves in the bargain, he would eliminate the greatest of the dangers that threaten him and perhaps facilitate a means for avoiding his own death. He could hide then and recover. He could wait for a chance to return."

"He will not escape me," Risca muttered darkly.

"Do not underestimate him, Risca," the old man cautioned. "Do not underestimate the power of the magic he wields."

There was a long silence. Risca remembered how close he had come to dying the last time he had sought to engage the Warlock Lord. His gaze leveled on the old man, then shifted toward the hazy flats. "What are you suggesting? That we do nothing?"

"Only that we be cautious."

"Why would we be anything else?" Risca's voice was filled with impatience. "We are wasting time! How long are we going to stand here?"

"He waits for me," Jerle Shannara said suddenly. "He knows I come for him." The others looked at him. "He will do battle with me now because he believes it is the easiest course for him to follow. He has no fear of me. He believes that I will be destroyed."

"You won't face him alone," said Preia Starle quickly. "We will be with you."

"All of us!" snapped Risca, daring anyone to challenge him.

"But there is danger in this," Bremen cautioned again. "All of us grouped together. We are tired and spent. We are not as strong as we should be."

Mareth stepped forward now, her dark face intense. "We are strong enough, Bremen." She gripped the Druid staff tightly in both hands. "You cannot expect us simply to stand and watch."

"We came a long way to see an end to this," echoed Kinson Ravenlock. "This is our fight as well."

They stared at the old man, all of them, waiting for him to

speak. He looked at them without seeing, his eyes distant and lost. He seemed to be considering something more than what they could comprehend, something far beyond the here and now, beyond the immediate danger.

"Bremen," the king said softly, waiting until the aged eyes found him. "I am ready for this. Do not doubt me."

The Druid studied him for a long moment, then nodded in weary resignation. "We shall do as you wish, Elven King."

Risca ordered signal flags raised on lances to advise Raybur of what they intended. A return signal quickly appeared. The Dwarves would advance on the Elves' command. The way north would be blocked against any who tried to flee. It was up to Jerle Shannara and the Elves to hammer shut the jaws of the trap.

The king called forward Trewithen and a dozen Home Guard to stand with him. Risca called for six of his Dwarves. While they assembled, Jerle Shannara pulled Preia Starle aside and spoke quickly. "I want you to wait here for me," he told her.

She shook her head. "I cannot do that and you know it."

"You are injured. You lack the speed and strength you could call upon if you were whole. How do you expect to make up for that?"

"Do not ask this of me."

"It will distract me if I have to worry about you!" His face was flushed and his eyes angry. His voice dropped to a whisper. "I love you, Preia."

"Would you ask Tay Trefenwyd to stay behind if he were here?" she replied softly. She gave him a moment to consider, her eyes searching his. A small, fragile smile followed. "I love you, too. So don't expect less of me than I do of myself."

At the same moment, Kinson Ravenlock was speaking with Mareth. "Will you be all right when this begins?" he asked her quietly.

She looked at him in surprise. "Of course. Why wouldn't I be?"

"You will have to use your magic. It will not be easy. You have spoken yourself of your distaste for it."

"I have," she agreed, moving close, touching him lightly on the shoulder. "But I will do what I must, Kinson."

Bremen moved to the forefront of the company and turned to face them. "I will ward us with enough magic to deflect a first strike, but I can do no more. My strength is at an end. Risca and Mareth must stand for us all. Look out for each other, but mostly look out for the king. He must be given a chance to use the Sword against Brona. Everything depends on it."

"He will have his chance," Risca promised, standing directly before the old man. "We owe Tay Trefenwyd that much."

They started forward then, Jerle Shannara leading, Preia Starle at his side, the king and queen flanked on the right by Risca and on the left by Bremen. The boy Allanon and Kinson Ravenlock and Mareth walked several paces back. Home Guard and Dwarf Hunters spread out to either side. Behind, the rest of the army followed. North, the Dwarves started down off the heights. The light was beginning to fail now as sunset approached, the shadows lengthening, the chill of early evening creeping into the air. Before them on the flats, the things in the mist shifted to attack.

The gray wolves struck first, hurtling forward in dark knots, tearing at the front ranks of Elves and Dwarves, slashing with their teeth before darting away. Risca threw out sheets of the Druid fire to scatter the closest, and instantly he was set upon by others. Huge netherworld creatures lumbered into view, brushing back the fire, knocking aside the blades. Rock Trolls marched to the fight in tight formations, their great pikes lowered in a line of gleaming metal tips. Smoke from the Druid fire mingled with the mist, and the whole of the battleground was enveloped in a gray haze.

Jerle Shannara walked ahead untouched. Nothing approached him as he advanced, all would-be attackers veering to the side and away. The Warlock Lord is waiting for you, a voice whispered deep inside. The Warlock Lord wants you for his own.

Rock Trolls closed with Kinson Ravenlock and bore him back, and the Borderman went down in a tangle of massive limbs. Mareth's staff sparked with blue flame, but she could not use the fire without risking harm to Kinson. Elven Hunters rushed to the Borderman's aid, striking at the Trolls; then other creatures joined the fray, and everyone was swallowed in the melee.

A Skull Bearer appeared to confront Jerle Shannara, then stepped to one side to challenge Bremen instead. "Old man," it hissed with sullen anticipation.

Allanon stepped in front of Bremen protectively, knowing the Druid was spent, that his magic was all but gone. But then Risca intervened, his fire hammering into the Skull Bearer with such force that it threw the monster backward and left it a smoking ruin. The Dwarf shouldered his way to the forefront of the attack, his clothing ripped from his battle with the gray wolves, his face streaked with blood. "Come ahead!" he roared, and lifted his battle-axe in challenge.

Kinson was back on his feet, battered and shaken, his broadsword striking at the Rock Trolls that sought to close with him. Home Guard and Dwarf Hunters stood shoulder to shoulder with the Borderman and forced back the Northlanders. Ahead, the dark, silken coverings of the carriages and wagons rippled in the swirl of the mist like death shrouds.

Jerle Shannara walked on. He was alone now, save for Preia. Bremen and Allanon had fallen back, and Risca had disappeared in the fighting. Elven Hunters and Home Guard darted through the haze, but the king occupied a space into which it seemed no one dared to step. The haze opened down a corridor before him, and he could see a dark cloaked figure standing at the end of the shifting passageway. The hood lifted and within the shadows red eyes burned with rage and defiance. It was the Warlock Lord. A robed arm lifted and beckoned to the king.

Come to me, Elf King. Come to me.

Farther back, Bremen was struggling to reach the king. Allanon was supporting him now, providing him with a strong shoulder on which to lean. The old man had summoned the Druid fire anew, using the boy for added strength, but his weakness was profound. He watched the Warlock Lord materialize out of the mist, watched him beckon Jerle Shannara forward, and felt his throat tighten. Was the king ready for this confrontation, or would his resolve fail him? The Druid did not know— could not know. The king understood so little of the Sword's demanding magic, and when faced with its power he might falter. There was great strength in Jerle Shannara, but uncertainty, too. When the Warlock Lord was before him, which would prevail?

Mareth had reached Kinson and was pulling him clear of the fighting, driving back the Rock Trolls with Druid fire as she did so. She swept the ground before them, and the Northlanders retreated before her fury. Kinson staggered as he tried to keep up with her, deep slashes to his side and legs leaking bright red blood, one arm hanging limp. "Go on!" he told her. "Protect the king!"

The fighting was ferocious now, the Elves and Dwarves having closed with the Northlanders from both sides. Screams and cries rose in the fading afternoon light, mingling with the clash of weapons and the grunts of men struggling and dying. Blood soaked the earth in dark stains, and bodies lay broken and twisted in death.

One of the wagons was pulled over, and creatures that looked to be made of sticks and metal poured out of the shattered bed, hissing like snakes stirred from a den. They came at Raybur with wicked intent, but the Dwarves protecting the king drove them back.

Frustrated in their efforts, they turned instead toward Bremen and Allanon.

In a rush, they closed about the old man and the boy. They were wiry and gnarled and lacking human features, their faces blunt and broken, as if shaped by some monstrous birthing. They broke past the Home Guard that sought to stop them and flung themselves forward recklessly. Allanon tried to summon the Druid fire, but this time his efforts failed him. Bremen was down on one knee, his head lowered, his concentration focused on Jerle Shannara, seeking him out in his mind as he walked deeper into the mist.

It would have been the end for them both but for Kinson Ravenlock. Trailing after Mareth, weakened from his wounds, he caught sight of the attack as it converged on the old man and the boy. Reacting on instinct, he drew on what fragile reserves of strength remained to him and rushed to their defense. He reached them just as the horde of wiry creatures broke past the Home Guard. His broadsword swung in a wide arc, and three of the creatures went down. Then he charged into the rest, flinging them back, hammering at them with his weapon. Teeth and claws slashed at him, and he could feel new wounds open. There were too many for him to contain, and he called to Bremen and the boy to run. A moment later the creatures overwhelmed him and bore him to the ground.

But Mareth saved him once more, appearing in a blaze of Druid fire, her staff flaring wildly. The netherworld creatures turned to strike at her, but the fire cast them away as if they were old and brittle. A counterattack ensued as other beings descended on the young woman, trying to break past her shield of flame. Kinson tried to get to his feet, but he was borne back again in the struggle. Home Guard, Dwarves, Rock Trolls, and monsters appeared in droves, and for a moment it seemed as if all the remaining soldiers of both armies had converged at this single point on the battlefield.

Ahead, walled away by the mist, Jerle Shannara advanced toward the Warlock Lord. Brona had grown in size with each step the Elf King had taken until now he seemed enormous. His dark form blocked the light at the tunnel's far end, and his eyes were bright with fiery disdain. Creatures faded in and out of the haze about him protectively. Jerle felt his confidence begin to waver. Something surged out of the mist and snatched Preia from his side. He wheeled to save her, but she was already gone, disappeared into the gloom. The king cried out in fear and anger, then heard her voice whisper hurriedly in his ear, felt her hand clutch his arm, and realized she had never left him at all and what he had seen was only an illusion.

The Warlock Lord's laughter was wicked and sly.

Come to me, Elf King! Come to me!

Then Preia stumbled and went down. Jerle reached for her without taking his eyes from the dark figure ahead, but she pulled away from him.

"Leave me," she said.

"No," he replied at once, refusing to listen.

"I am hindering you, Jerle. I am slowing you down."

"I won't leave you!"

She reached for his face, and he could feel the blood on her hands, slippery and warm. "I cannot stay on my feet. I am bleeding too badly to go on. I have to stop now, Jerle. I have to wait here for you. Please. Leave me."

She looked at him unflinchingly, her ginger eyes fixed on his, her face white and twisted with pain. Slowly he straightened, drawing away from her, fighting to keep the tears from his eyes. "I will be back for you," he promised.

He left her stretched out on her side, propped up on one elbow, her short sword in her free hand. He took only a few steps before looking back to make certain she was all right. She nodded for him to go on. When he looked back for her a second time, she was gone.

Kinson Ravenlock had climbed back to his feet once more and was trying to bring his broadsword to bear against the crush of enemies that threatened to engulf Mareth when he was struck such a terrible blow that he was knocked to the ground and left gasping for breath. Mareth turned toward him, and as she did so she was set upon by a huge wolf. It was on her before she could bring the Druid fire to bear, slamming into her with such force that she lost her grip on the Druid staff. She went down in a heap, the wolf tearing at her. Kinson heard her scream and tried desperately to go to her, but his legs would not respond. He lay there spitting blood, his breathing harsh and shallow, his consciousness fading away.

Then the Druid fire exploded out of Mareth, flying her in all directions. The attacking wolf was incinerated. Everyone standing for a dozen yards around was consumed. Kinson covered his head instinctively, but the fire singed his face and hands and sucked away the air he tried to breathe. The Borderman cried out helplessly, and everything disappeared in a huge rush of flame.

In the tunnel of mist that led to the Warlock Lord, Preia Starle watched as one of the Skull Bearers materialized out of the gloom and started toward her. Jerle was no longer visible, too far ahead now to be seen. She could have called out to him, but she chose not to. Painfully, she pulled herself to her knees, but could get no farther. Frustration tore at her. Yet it had been her choice to come. She watched as the creature approached, her sword held protectively before her. She would have only one chance to strike, and that might not be enough in any case. She took a deep breath, wishing she had strength enough to stand.

The Skull Bearer hissed at her, and its great, leathery wings flapped softly against its humped back.

"Little Elf," it whispered in pleasure, and its red eyes gleamed.

It reached for her, and she drew back her sword to strike.

Jerle Shannara had closed the distance between himself and the Warlock Lord to less than a dozen yards. He watched the dark cloaked form shift and change before him as if part of the mist that swirled about them both. Within the hooded shadows the twin fires of its eyes burned with fierce intent. No part of what was left of Brona revealed itself. The Warlock Lord floated above the earth as if weightless—an empty shell. The strange, compelling voice continued to call to the Elf King.

Come to me. Come to me.

Jerle Shannara did. He brought up his sword, the talisman he had carried to this confrontation, the magic he did not know how to use, and he advanced to do battle. As he did so, a flash of light danced off the surface of the blade, ran its polished length, and disappeared into his body. He faltered as the light entered him, feeling it pulse with energy. A warm flush enveloped him, spreading outward from his chest to his limbs. He felt the warmth return to the Sword, carrying with it some part of himself, joining the two so that he became one with the blade. It happened so fast that it was done before he could think to stop it. He stared at the Sword in wonder, now an extension of himself, then at the dark figure before him, and then at the world of mist and shadows as it slowly began to recede.

Down he went then, deep inside himself, drawn by a force he could not resist. He grew tiny as the world about grew large, and soon he was reduced to an insignificant speck of life in a vast, teeming universe of lives. He saw himself as he was, almost without presence, little more than dust. He was borne on the back of a wind over all the world that was and all that would ever be, the whole of it revealed in a vast tapestry that spread much farther than he could hope to see or even to travel. This was what he was, he realized. This was his worth in the larger scheme of things.

Then the world he flew above seemed to shed its skin in layers, and what had been bright and perfect turned dark and flawed. All the horrors and betrayals of all the creatures throughout time flared to life in tiny segments of revelation. Jerle Shannara recoiled from the pain and dismay he felt at each, but there was no turning away. This was the truth of things—the truth that he had been told the Sword would reveal to him. He shuddered at the vastness of it, at the depth and breadth of its permutations. He was horrified and ashamed, stripped of his illusions, forced to see his world and its people for what they were.

He felt in that instant as if he might fail in his resolve. But the images withdrew, the world darkened, and for a moment he was back in the mist, standing frozen before the towering form of the Warlock Lord, the Sword of Shannara gleaming with white light.

Help me, he prayed to no one, for he was all alone.

The light filled him anew, and again the world of mist and shadows receded. He went back down inside himself, and this time he was brought face-to-face with the truth of his own life. With inexorable purpose it unfolded before him, image by image, a vast collage of experiences and events. But the images were not of the things he wished to see; they were of those he wished forgotten, of those he had buried in his past. There was nothing of himself of which he was proud, with which he had ever hoped to be confronted. Lies, half truths, and deceptions rose like ghosts at haunt. Here was the real Jerle Shannara, the creature who was flawed and imperfect, weak and insecure, insensitive and filled with false pride. He saw the worst of what he had done in his life. He saw the ways in which he had disappointed others, had ignored their needs, had left them in pain. So many times he had failed to do what was needed. So many times he had misjudged.

He tried to look away. He tried to make the images stop. He would have run from what he was being shown if he could have freed himself from the Sword's magic to do so. These were truths that he could not face, their harshness so intense that they threatened his sanity. He might have cried out in despair—he could not tell. He realized in that moment the terrible power of truth, and he saw why Bremen had been so concerned for him. He did not have the strength for this; he did not have the resolve. The Druid had been wrong to come to him. The Sword of Shannara was not meant for him. Choosing him to bear it had been wrong.

Yet he did not give way entirely before what he was shown, even when it touched on Tay Trefenwyd and Preia Starle, even when it revealed the depth of their friendship. He forced himself to watch it, to accept it, and to forgive himself for the jealousy it aroused in him, and he felt himself grow stronger by doing so. He found himself thinking that perhaps this was indeed a weapon that could be used against the Warlock Lord, a creature whose entire being was founded on illusion. What price would the magic exact from Brona when he was forced to discover that he was composed of little more than men's fears, a mirage that could vanish with a simple change in the light? Perhaps this creature was so badly formed that nothing of its humanity, of its flesh and blood, of its emotion and reason remained. Perhaps truth was anathema to it.

The images faded and the light died. Jerle Shannara watched the air before him clear and the dark form of the Warlock Lord materialize once more. How long had the magic taken to reveal itself to him? How long had he stood there, transfixed? The cloaked form advanced now, a steady, relentless closing of the space between them. The Warlock Lord's voice hissed with anticipation. Wave upon wave of nausea struck at the Elf King, hammering at the firmness of his purpose, breaking past his physical strength to drain the courage from his heart.

Come to me. Come to me.

Jerle Shannara saw himself as nothing, as helpless before the monster he confronted. So vast and terrible was the Warlock Lord's power that no man could prevail against it. So immutable was that power that no magic could overcome it. The voice whispered the words insistently.

Put down the sword. Come to me. You are nothing. Come to me.

But the Elf King had already seen himself reduced to his essence, had witnessed the worst of what he was, and even the terrible despair that ripped through him as the Warlock Lord approached was not enough to turn him aside. Truth did not frighten him now. He lifted the Sword before him, a bright silver thread within the gloom, and cried out, "Shannara! Shannara!"

Down came the Sword, smashing through the Warlock Lord's defenses, shattering his magic, and penetrating to the cloaked form beyond. The Warlock Lord shuddered, desperately trying to hold back the blow. But now the Sword's light was pulsing from the blade into the cloaked shadows, and the images of his own life were ripping through him. The Warlock Lord fell back a step, then another. Jerle Shannara pressed forward, repulsed by the rage and hatred that emanated from his adversary, but relentless in his determination. The struggle between them would end here. The Warlock Lord would die this day.

The robed arms flung toward him, and a skeletal hand pointed with cold purpose.

How can you judge me? You left her to die! You abandoned her for this! You killed her!

He flinched from the words, and he saw in harsh images Preia Starle's helpless form sprawled on the ground, bleeding and broken, a Skull Bearer reaching for her with claws extended. Dying because of me, he thought in horror. Because I failed her.

The Warlock Lord's voice pressed in upon his thoughts.

And your friend, Elf King. At the Chew Magna. He died for you! You let him die for you!

Jerle Shannara screamed in dismay and rage, and wielding the Sword as he would an ordinary weapon, he slashed at the Warlock Lord with all the power he could muster. The Sword cut downward through the dark robes, but the light that shone from the blade flickered as if stricken. The Warlock Lord crumpled, his hateful voice fading in a whisper of despair, his dark robes collapsing in a heap.

Left behind was a shadowy presence that fled instantly into the mist.

The Elf King went rigid in the ensuing silence, staring at the air before him, then at the empty robes, his eyes filled with uncertainty and questions that refused all answers.

MARETH STOOD ALONE on a stretch of ground scorched black by her magic. The Druid fire had expended itself finally, and her power was contained once more. Bodies lay everywhere, and an eerie silence hung across the battleground like a pall. She squinted through the haze and watched it begin to clear. There was a long, low wail of anguish, a cacophony of voices lifting in despair. Out from the mist rose wraiths as substanceless as smoke, dark images against the failing daylight, shapeless and adrift. Were they the spirits of the dead? They rose into the red of the sunset and disappeared, gone as if they had never been. Below, the bodies of the Skull Bearers turned to ash, the netherworld creatures faded away, and the wolves ran howling across the empty plains.

It is finished, she thought in stunned disbelief.

The mist churned and brightened and then disappeared. The battleground lay revealed, a charnel house, strewn with dead and wounded, bloodied and scorched and ruined. At its center stood the Elf King with his sword lowered and his eyes fixed on nothing.

Mareth reached for the Druid staff she had lost in her struggle. She saw Risca then, sprawled amid a cluster of enemy dead. He had sustained so many wounds that his clothing was soaked through with his blood. There was a startled look in his open, staring eyes, as if he were surprised that the fate he had challenged so often had claimed him at last. When had he fallen? She hadn't even seen. Her gaze shifted. Kinson Ravenlock lay a few feet behind her, his chest rising and falling weakly against the bloodied ground. Beyond, a little farther back on the flats, crouched Bremen and the boy. Her eyes locked on the Druid's, and for a moment they stared fixedly at each other. She thought of how long and hard she had looked for him, of how much she had given of herself to become a Druid, and of the price that had been exacted from her. Bremen and she. They were the past and present of things, the Druid in twilight and the Druid to be. Tay Trefenwyd was gone. Risca lay dead. Bremen was an old man. Soon, she would be all that remained of their order, the last of the Druids.

Her eyes left Bremen's, and she picked up the staff. She held it in her hands as if it were weighted with the responsibility of being who and what she was, and she gazed out across the battleground in despair.

Tears came to her eyes.

Let it end here, she thought.

Then she cast the staff away from her and bent to cradle Kinson.

CHAPTER

34

ERLE SHANNARA SAVED THE LIFE of his queen that day, for by banishing the Warlock Lord he banished the Skull Bearers as well, including the one that threatened Preia. Without the power of the Warlock Lord to draw upon, Preia's assailant simply faded away. Preia recovered from her injuries and returned with Jerle to the Westland. Together, they ruled the Elven nation for many years. They never fought in another battle; the need for them to do so never arose again. Instead, they gave their energies over to learning how to govern in an increasingly complex and demanding world. With Vree Erreden to advise them, they were able to master the craft of statesmanship. They had three children of their own, all daughters, and when Jerle Shannara died, many years later, the eldest of the sons they had adopted from the last of the Ballindarrochs succeeded him. The Shannara line would subsequently multiply and continue afterward for more than two hundred years.

The Sword of Shannara was carried by the king until his death. His son, on succeeding him, carried it afterward for a time, then had it set in a block of Tre-Stone, taken to Paranor, and placed in the Druid's Keep.

Kinson Ravenlock did not die from his wounds, but recovered after weeks of convalescence in the fledgling outpost of Tyrsis. Mareth stayed at his side and cared for him, and when he was well enough they traveled west along the Mermidon to a wooded island in the shadow of the Dragon's Teeth, where they made their home. They lived together afterward and eventually married. They farmed, then built a trading center and opened a supply route along the river. Others from the Borderlands moved up to join them, and soon they were in the midst of a thriving community. In time the trading settlement would become the city of Kern.

Mareth never again used her magic in the Druid cause. She turned her skills instead to healing and was widely sought after throughout the Four Lands. She took Kinson's name when she married him, and there was never afterward any mention of her own. Kinson worried after her for a long time, thinking her magic would break free again, that it would undermine her resolve, but it never did. They had several children, and long after they were gone a child born of their lineage would figure prominently in another battle with the Warlock Lord.

Raybur survived and returned home with the Dwarves to begin the arduous task of rebuilding Culhaven and the other cities the Northland army had destroyed. He took Risca with him and buried the Druid in the newly replanted Gardens of Life, high on a promontory where it was possible to watch the Silver River flow for miles through the forests of the Anar.

The Northland army was virtually annihilated that day on the Streleheim. Those Trolls and Gnomes who had fled earlier from the Valley of Rhenn eventually found their way home. The power of the Warlock Lord was broken, and the Races north and east began the painful process of rebuilding their shattered lives. Both Gnome and Troll nations, tribal by nature, distanced themselves from the other Races, and for a time there was little contact. It would be more than a hundred years before a form of parity returned between victors and vanquished and commerce could be resumed on an equal footing.

Bremen disappeared soon after the final battle. No one saw him go. No one knew where he went. He said goodbye to Mareth, and through her to a still unconscious Kinson. He told the young woman that he would not see either one of them again. There were rumors afterward that he had returned to Paranor to live out the last years of his life. Kinson thought sometimes to go in search of him, to find out the truth of things. But he never did.

Jerle Shannara saw him once more, less than a month after

the battle at the Rhenn, late at night for only a few minutes when the old man came to Arborlon to spirit away the Black Elfstone. They spoke of the talisman in whispers, as if the words themselves were too painful to bear, as if even mention of the dark magic might scar their souls.

That was the last time anyone saw him.

The boy Allanon disappeared as well.

Slowly the world returned to the way it had been, and memories of the Warlock Lord began to fade.

THREE YEARS PASSED. On a late summer's day warm and bright with sunshine, an old man and a boy climbed through the foot-hills of the Dragon's Teeth toward the Valley of Shale. Bremen was wizened and bent with age now, and the gray of his hair and beard had gone white. He no longer moved easily, and his eyes were beginning to fail. Allanon was fifteen, taller and much stronger, his shoulders broad, his arms and legs rangy and pow-erful. Already he was approaching manhood, his face beginning to reveal the dark shadow of a beard, his voice deep and rough. By now he was nearly Bremen's equal in use of the Druid magic. But it was the old man who led and the boy who followed on their last journey together.

For three years Allanon had trained with Bremen. The old man had accepted that the boy would succeed him when he was gone, that Allanon would be the last of the Druids. Tay and Risca were dead, and Mareth had chosen another path. The boy was young, but he was eager to learn and it was clear from the first that he possessed the determination and strength necessary to become what he must. Bremen worked with him every day for those three years, teaching him what he knew of the magic of the Druids and the secrets of their power, giving him the chance to experiment and to discover. Allanon was fierce in this as in all things, single-minded almost to a fault, driven to suc-ceed. He was smart and intuitive, and his prescience did not di-minish with his growth. Frequently Allanon saw what was hidden from the old man, his sharp mind grasping possibilities that even the Druid had not recognized. He stayed with Bre-men at Paranor, the two of them closeted away from the world, studying the Druid Histories, practicing the lessons that the ancient tomes taught. Bremen used his magic to conceal their presence in the empty fortress from others. No one came to disturb them. No one sought to intrude.

Bremen thought often on the Warlock Lord and the events that had led to his banishing. He spoke of it with the boy, relating to him all of what had transpired—of the destruction of the Druids, of the search for the Black Elfstone, of the forging of the Sword of Shannara, and of the battle for the Rhenn. He imparted the particulars orally to Allanon and then inscribed them on the pages of the Druid Histories. In private he worried for the future. His own strength was failing. His life was coming to an end. He would not see his work completed. That would be left to Allanon and those who succeeded him. But how insufficient that seemed! It was not enough to hope that the boy and his successors would carry on without him. His was the responsibility and his the hand that was needed to carry it out.

So four days earlier he had called the boy to him and told him that his lessons were finished. They would be leaving Paranor for the Hadeshorn to make one last visit to the spirits of the dead. They packed provisions and departed the Keep at sunrise. Before doing so the old man summoned the magic that warded Paranor's walls and closed the ancient fortress away. Out from the depths of the Druid Well rose the ancient magic that lived there, swirling upward in a wicked green light. By the time the boy and the old man were safely clear, Paranor had begun to shimmer with the damp translucence of a mirage, melting slowly into the sunlight, disappearing into the air. It would appear and fade again at regular intervals thereafter, sometimes at brightest noon, sometimes at darkest night, but it would never stay. The boy said nothing as they turned away and walked into the trees, but the old man could see from his eyes that he understood what was happening.

Thus they approached at sunset the entrance to the Valley of Shale and made camp in the shadow of the Dragon's Teeth. They ate their dinner in silence, watching the darkness deepen and the stars brighten. With the coming of midnight, they rose and walked to the edge of the valley and looked down into its obsidian bowl. The Hadeshorn glimmered with starlight, placid and undisturbed. No sound came from the valley. Nothing stirred on its broken surface.

"I will be leaving you this night," the old man said finally.

The boy nodded, but said nothing.

"I will be here when you have need of me again." He paused. "That will not happen for a while, I expect. But when it does, this is where you will come."

The boy looked at him uncertainly.

Bremen sighed, noting the confusion in his eyes. "I must tell you something now that I have never told to anyone, not even Jerle Shannara himself. Sit with me and listen."

They seated themselves on the carpet of broken rock, solitary figures silhouetted against the backdrop of the stars. The old man was silent for a moment as he worked to arrange the words he needed to speak, the lines of his face deepening.

"Jerle Shannara failed in his attempt to destroy the Warlock Lord," he said finally. "When he faltered in his use of the Sword, when he allowed himself to be distracted by self-doubt and recrimination, he let Brona escape. I knew of this failure because, although too weakened by my own use of the Druid magic to go on, I followed the king in my mind's eye and thereby witnessed the confrontation. I watched him hesitate at the last moment, then attempt to use the talisman as an ordinary weapon, forgetting my repeated warnings to rely on the magic alone. I saw the dark shadows rise out of the mist as the Warlock Lord's robes collapsed beneath the Sword's final blow, and I knew what that meant. The Warlock Lord and his Skull Bearers had been driven from their substantive forms by the magic, had been compelled to become dark spirits once more, and had fled back into the ether—but they had not been destroyed."

He shook his head. "There is no reason to tell any of this to the king. Telling him would accomplish nothing. Jerle Shannara was a brave and resourceful champion. He overcame his own misgivings and fear to employ the Druid magic against the most formidable enemy in the history of the Four Lands. He did so under the most adverse of conditions and cruelest of circumstances, and in all ways but one he succeeded in accomplishing what was expected of him. It is enough that he defeated the Warlock Lord and drove him from the Four Lands. It is enough that the magic of the Sword of Shannara has diminished the rebel Druid's power so utterly that it will be centuries before he can regain form. There is sufficient time in the scheme of things to prepare for when that happens. Jerle Shannara did the best he could, and I think you should leave it at that."

His aging eyes fixed on Allanon. "But you must know of his failure, because you are the one who must guard against its consequences. Brona lives and will one day return. I will not be there to face him. You must do so in my place—or if not you, another like you, one you will choose as I have chosen you."

There was a long silence as they stared at each other in the soft, enveloping darkness.

Bremen shook his head helplessly. "If there were another way to do this, I would choose that way." He felt uncomfortable speaking of it, as if by doing so he was looking for an excuse to change his mind when he knew he could not. "I wish I could stay longer with you, Allanon. But I am old, and I can feel myself weakening almost daily. I have kept myself whole for as long as I can. The Druid Sleep is no longer enough. I must take another form if I am to be of service to you in the battle you face. Do you understand what I am saying?"

The boy looked at him, his dark eyes intense. "I understand." He paused, the light changing in his eyes. "I will miss you, Father."

The old man nodded. The boy called him that now. Father. The boy had adopted him, and it felt right that he had done so. "I will miss you, too," he replied softly.

They talked more of what it was that would happen then, of the past and the future and the inextricable link that bound the one to the other. They shared the memories they had forged in their time together, repeated the vows they had made, and recounted the lessons that would matter in the years ahead.

Then, as the night lengthened and dawn approached, they walked together into the Valley of Shale. A mist had formed as the air cooled, and now it hung like a shroud above the valley, cloaking it in shimmering darkness, screening away the stars and their silver light. Their boots crunched on the loose rock, and their hearts beat with rough anticipation. They felt the heat rise off their bodies as they worked their way downward along the valley slopes, then across the floor toward the lake. The Hadeshorn gleamed like black ice, smooth and still. Not even the faintest ripple scratched its mirrored surface.

When they were a dozen feet from the lake's dark edge, Bremen withdrew the Black Elfstone from his robes and passed it to the boy.

"Keep it safe for when you would return to the Keep," he reminded him. "Remember what it is for. Remember what I have told you of its power. Be wary."

"I will," Allanon assured him.

He is just a boy, the old man thought suddenly. I am asking him to take on so much, and he is just a boy. He stared at Allanon in spite of himself, as if by doing so he might discover something he had missed, some particular of his character that would further reassure him. Then he turned away. He had done what he could to prepare the boy. It would have to be enough.

He walked alone to the shore's edge and stared out over the dark waters. He closed his eyes, gathered himself for what was needed, then used the Druid magic to summon the spirits of the dead. They came swiftly, almost as if expecting his call, as if waiting for it. Their cries rose out of the silence, the earth rumbled, and the waters of the Hadeshorn rolled like a cauldron set upon a fire. Steam hissed, and voices whispered and moaned within the shadowy depths. Slowly the spirits began to lift out of the mist and spray, out of the whirlpool of darkness, out of the tortured cries. One by one they appeared, the tiny, silver shapes of the lesser spirits first, then the larger, darker form of Galaphile.

Bremen turned then and looked back to where Allanon stood waiting. He saw in that instant the particulars of Galaphile's fourth vision, the one he had failed to understand for so long—himself, standing before the waters of the Hadeshorn; Galaphile's shade, approaching through the mist and the swirl of lost spirits; and Allanon, his eyes so sad, watching it happen.

The shade came steadily on, an implacable presence, a shadow drawn blacker than the night through which he passed. He walked upon the waters of the Hadeshorn as if upon solid ground, advancing to where Bremen waited. The old man stretched out one hand to greet the spirit, his thin body rigid and worn.

"I am ready," he said softly.

The shade gathered him in his arms and bore him away across the waters of the Hadeshorn and down into their depths.

Allanon stood alone on the shore, staring silently. He did not move as the waters went still again. He stayed motionless as the darkness faded and the sun crested the Dragon's Teeth. One hand clutched the Black Elfstone tightly within his dark robes. His eyes were hard and steady.

When the sun had risen completely into the morning sky and the last of the shadows had been chased from the valley, he turned and walked away.

About the Author

A writer since high school, Terry Brooks published his first novel, *The Sword of Shannara*, in 1977. It became the first work of fiction ever to appear on *The New York Times* Trade Paperback Bestseller List, where it remained for five months. He has published twelve consecutive bestselling novels since.

The author was a practicing attorney for many years, but now writes full-time. He lives with his wife, Judine, in the Pacific Northwest and Hawaii.